Praise for C. Hope Clark

Lowcountry Bribe is a fast-paced roller coaster ride of a mystery, full of intriguing characters and a heroine as feisty as she is vulnerable. A rare glimpse into a rural part of the Lowcountry most coastal residents and visitors didn't know existed. From an author who knows her stuff.
—Katherine R. Wall, author *JERICHO CAY,* the 11th Bay Tanner mystery, St. Martin's Minotaur

Terrific. Smart, knowing, clever . . . and completely original. A taut, high-tension page-turner—in a unique and fascinating setting. An absolute winner!
—Hank Phillippi Ryan, Agatha, Anthony and Macavity winning author

In C. Hope Clark's novel, *TIDEWATER MURDER,* Carolina Slade establishes herself as a new genre superstar, taking her place beside Dave Robicheux and Harry Bosch. Well-written and informative about a little-known arm of law enforcement, Clark has written a story that carries the reader along as surely as the tides of the lowcountry. Don't miss this one!
—Carl T. Smith, author of *A Season for Killing* and *Lowcountry Boil*

Riveting. A first-rate mystery and a real education. C. Hope Clark continues her series following Carolina Slade, an agriculture investigator, in *TIDEWATER MURDER.* All I can say is if all government employees had Slade's get-the-job-done tenacity, I wouldn't mind paying taxes.
—Donnell Ann Bell, author of *The Past Came Hunting* and *Deadly Recall.*

High tension in the Lowcountry. Feds, farmers and foreigners collide in this coastal crime novel with as many twists and turns as a tidal estuary.
—Janna McMahan, National Bestselling author of *Anonymity* and *Calling Home*

I want Carolina Slade to be my new best friend. Smart, loyal, tough but compassionate, she's the kind of person I want on my side if I'm in trouble. In her second outing, a missing tomato crop, dead bodies, and Gullah voodoo lead Slade into the dark heart of the new south, where the 21st century collides with the past and the outcome can be deadly. As a native South Carolinian, I thoroughly enjoyed revisiting my home state in this engrossing and unusual mystery, and I look forward to seeing more of Hope Clark's refreshing heroine.

—Sandra Parshall, award-winning author of the *Rachel Goddard* mysteries
sandraparshall.com

This story sweeps you up in an instant and carries you far, far away. Clark's intensely lush and conversational writing will keep you wanting more, turning the pages almost faster than you can read them.

—Rachel Gladstone, *Dish Magazine*

Carolina Slade is the real deal—Southern charm, a steely determination, and a vulnerability she'll never admit to. Slade is at her absolute best in C. Hope Clark's *Palmetto Poison* so hold on for the ride!

—Lynn Chandler-Willis, Bestselling author and winner of the 2013 Minotaur Books/PWA Best First Private Eye Novel Competition

Other Titles by C. Hope Clark from Bell Bridge Books

Carolina Slade Mystery series

Lowcountry Bribe
Book One

Tidewater Murder
Book Two

Palmetto Poison
Book Three

The Edisto Island Mysteries

Murder on Edisto

Edisto Jinx

Echoes of Edisto

Murder on Edisto

Book One: The Edisto Island Mysteries

by

C. Hope Clark

Bell Bridge Books

Bell Bridge Books
PO BOX 300921
Memphis, TN 38130
Print ISBN: 978-1-61194-541-6

Bell Bridge Books is an Imprint of BelleBooks, Inc.

Copyright © 2014 by Hope Clark writing as C. Hope Clark

Printed and bound in the United States of America.

We at BelleBooks enjoy hearing from readers.
Visit our websites
BelleBooks.com
BellBridgeBooks.com
ImaJinnBooks.com

10 9 8 7 6 5 4 3 2 1

Cover design: Debra Dixon
Interior design: Hank Smith
Photo/Art credits:
Beach (manipulated) © Ben Goode | Dreamstime.com
Tree (manipulated © Mark Vandyke | Dreamstime.com

:Lemj:01:

Dedication

To Deni, the spirit of Edisto Beach and the energy behind this tale.

Chapter 1

Boston, October

SERGEANT DETECTIVE Callista Jean Morgan leaned stiffly against a display beside the drug store pharmacy, hands stuffed in her size six jeans, waiting for a prescription. She moved further away as a woman seated herself nearby, hacking, a tissue wadded up one nostril. Callie had to stay healthy for the Leo Zubov prosecution. Her mind played with future testimony against the man and envisioned her upcoming day in court with the pernicious ass. Thrill shivered up her spine.

The speedier the trial the better. The Russian drug czar deserved nothing but the best the legal system could dole out to the *bratchnie*. Whatever locked him away the quickest and the longest suited her. Since reaching detective, Callie had spent most of her five years running the mazes Zubov incessantly built through Boston's criminal underground. She'd pursued one trail after another down a hundred dead ends . . . until last week.

The bastard had threatened her and her family, as well as every cop, clerk, and janitor in the Boston Police Department. This time, however, he'd be dried-up and ancient by the time he got out of jail. Hallelujah and amen!

Her fifteen-year-old son Jeb loitered a few feet away, reading the ingredients on a bag of candy for diabetics. "Oxymoron," he said, tossing the item back on the shelf. "Why eat candy if there's no sugar in it?"

"I'm impressed you know the meaning of that word," she said.

"So you *are* listening." Jeb stepped in front of her and stared deep into her eyes with his familiar please-let-me-have-something squint. "Can I drive home?"

She gazed up at her six-foot, dashing young sophomore. Too short to reach the second shelf of her kitchen cabinets, Callie often wore boots with heels. She restrained herself from tousling his blond curls, a contrast to her auburn bob. Instead, she glanced out the store's plate glass window. Seven p.m. The sun was about gone for the day. "I'm not sure, Jeb. It's getting dark."

He acted forlorn. "But the permit says I can drive at night with an adult in the car."

Callie's recurring nightmare involved an out of control truck rushing toward her Explorer, with Jeb at the wheel. Sometimes he was seven with pinchable cheeks, sometimes a tall, lanky fifteen. She would throw a protective arm across his chest, her foot stomping a nonexistent brake. She'd wake in a sea of sweat, her pulse thundering.

She never told her husband John. He dreamed nightmares of his own.

Jeb struck a silly pose, eying her, waiting for her answer. "Oh, come on, Mom."

"Hush, I'm considering it."

She figured eighteen about the proper age to get his license. Maybe when he went to college. She grinned at the exaggeration, then let the grin slide away as she realized how soon that time would come.

For the sake of their careers, she and John had chosen not to have more children after Jeb. But after a glorious drunken celebratory anniversary weekend, nine months later God gave them Bonnie. Even at thirty-eight, Callie delivered a perfect child . . . then lost her bright-eyed gift one horrific night when Bonnie simply stopped breathing.

Today would have been the baby's first birthday.

John hadn't mentioned the occasion. Neither had she. They were both at a loss what to do other than privately, silently relive the hurt.

"Callie Morgan?" called the pharmacist.

"That's me."

A young tech read the order. "Two prescriptions, right?"

"Do you need instructions how to use this medication?" he asked.

Birth control and an antidepressant. What was there to know other than she feared to relinquish either one since Bonnie's death.

Callie's phone rang, playing "Dixie." A waiting gentleman scowled.

"Great, Mom," Jeb whispered. "The South lost, remember?"

After studying caller ID, she wedged the phone on her shoulder as she paid the white-coated man. "Sorry," she said, with her best South Carolina Lowcountry drawl three degrees thicker than usual. "My apologies, sir."

Red-faced, Jeb walked in the opposite direction toward the vitamins.

Phone to her ear, she answered, "Callie Morgan."

"It's Waltham. You sitting down?"

She frowned at her boss's gravelly, no-nonsense tone. "No, why?" Captain Detective Stan Waltham rarely led with gratuitous niceties. Callie's Southern gentility usually drew at least one pleasantry out of the man. Not this time.

"The Feds stepped in on your case."

"Why?" She closed her eyes. No! "Don't tell me Zubov walks. We have him, Stan. He was at the buy, for God's sake." She walked away from the waiting herd of sick people. "What happened?"

"Officially they've told me jack shit, but a Homeland Security buddy I served with in the Gulf dropped me a whisper. Apparently Zubov has intel on some terrorist business, so they—"

"Damn it, he's *not* walking."

Drugs, guns, human slavery—the local Russian criminal element did it all, but narcotics were Leo's specialty. The bastard's white-powdered tentacles reached into and beyond the city, across the state, into New York and who-knows-where else. Far-reaching, but old school. No history of terrorist activity.

"Not sure about the details, Callie, but you and I are done with him."

She spun around only to meet a tall, blue-haired woman. Callie glared as they maneuvered to pass each other. "Who the hell do I have to talk to?"

"Nobody, we're—"

Her phone beeped. John calling.

"You need to take that?" Stan asked.

"Not now." Callie let the call go to voice mail. "So, whose office door are we knocking on tomorrow?"

John rang again.

She'd left her husband at home with his head immersed in a work file strewn across the coffee table. His distraction from the day's significance. Hers was to run the drug store errand, taking Jeb for comfort.

"I better take this call, Stan, but this thing with Leo isn't over."

"Yes, it is, Callie."

"We'll talk in the morning."

She answered the waiting call, visualizing John running an impatient hand through his thick blond hair. "Everything okay?" she asked. "John?"

"Don't come home." His fast, blunt message held an unfamiliar concern, his order so eerily strict.

Callie stiffened. Was he so entrenched in his misery that he couldn't face her tonight? Dammit, Bonnie's death wasn't her fault.

"Talk to me, John."

"Intruders—"

The phone died.

Her heart seemed encased in ice. They'd always feared one of their arrests would seek revenge, finding his way to their doorstep. Adrenaline crashed through the chill and pumped madly into her system. She tried to call back. Shit. She tried again. The call routed to voice mail.

"Jeb!" She ran down the aisle where he leaned on the wall reading magazines and grasped his arm.

"Geez, Mom. What—"

She dragged him toward the door, his long legs stumbling. Outside she key-fobbed the locks, jumped into the driver's seat, and fired the engine. As soon as Jeb shut his door, she slammed her portable blue light on the dash and sped into traffic.

Jeb's palms slapped the dash and center console as he stared wide-eyed. "Mom, you're scaring me. What's wrong?" His voice had reverted to adolescence, breaking between words.

"Buckle your seatbelt." Callie glanced both ways before she ran a red light.

She dialed dispatch. "This is Detective Callista Morgan. All available units to 475-C Dorchester Avenue. Suspected intruder. Be advised this is the residence of a Boston PD detective and a deputy US marshal."

She disconnected and dropped the phone in a cup holder.

A horn blared as she gripped the steering wheel with both hands, zipping the car around an Escalade and a minivan.

"Mom!" Jeb shouted as he slammed into the door. "What—"

"That was your dad," Callie said, channeling all her faculties into driving. She sped around an SUV through an amber light. "Something's wrong. I need you to hold it together."

He pushed himself back into his seat, fear etched in his face.

Callie's heart hammered her ribs as she bridled the gas and brake pedals to ride a razor edge between arriving quickly and not arriving at all, streetlights passing like a carnival ride.

A city bus and a utility van blocked both lanes as she took another corner. Foot hard on and then off the brake, and onto the accelerator, she veered around them via the oncoming lane.

She didn't want Jeb seeing this side of her. But she damn sure didn't want him seeing the worst case scenario playing out in her head.

She swallowed once, then again as the first wouldn't go down. Panic almost overwhelmed her. This could be any of his cases. Any of hers. Names and file numbers raced in her head as fast as the blocks she whizzed past. But it was the Russian's name that stuck.

She glanced at Jeb. Was the fear in his eyes mirroring hers? She wouldn't glance again.

Three blocks ahead, in spite of the city lights, an angry glow shone in the dusk, setting fire to the October sky.

The stench of burning wire, insulation, and wood wafted into the car vents as she turned onto her street, tires squealing. Three Boston PD units sat several doors down from her address. Flames licked out the bottom floor windows of her two-story white-clapboard home, getting lost in clouds of gray smoke choking the air. Flickering shadows confirmed advancement to the second floor.

Oh my God, John!

She jammed the car into park and leaped out. An officer turned and caught her in mid-stride. She struggled to get free, but he tightened his hold.

"You can't go in there, Detective Morgan."

She stared helplessly at the blaze, the wall of heat searing her face.

"Did anyone . . . did my husband get out?" Craning her neck, she scoured the gawking faces. Sleeve over her nose, she shouted, "He's blond, six-feet—" then she gagged on thick fumes.

"We don't know yet if anyone—"

An explosion shot flames out of the roof. She pulled against the officer. "John!"

Fire fighters labored to unravel more hoses. In the background, she heard Jeb screaming for his father above all the sirens and people hollering.

A deafening blast. The force hurled her and the cop backward across the lawn. Air whooshed from her lungs as her back slammed into the grass. She lay half-dazed, but pain still tore through her left forearm.

Two fire fighters lifted her and smothered her burning sleeve, careful not to hit the jagged piece of half-embedded shrapnel that had ripped open her arm.

She stared numb at the burning wreckage of her home as someone fussed over her. No one could have survived that explosion. Then, as if to confirm the terrible finality, she caught the reality of John's death in the sorrow of a fire fighter's eyes, the slow shake of his head to his partner. Their glances back at her.

Jeb beat his way through the throng and threw himself into her arms. At first she didn't hear his sobs, then her son's deep wrenching cries reverberated against her collarbone. She dug her fingers into his hair, her injured arm around his trembling body.

"Shhh," she said against Jeb's shoulder. She couldn't bring herself to say everything would be all right. Nothing would ever be right again. As she stroked his head, she squeezed her eyes shut, and her tears leaked into his shirt. She could pray John was kidnapped, but her heart told her it just wasn't so.

Chapter 2

Middleton, South Carolina, June, Thirty-Two Months Later

CALLIE CRUMPLED the legal envelope into her purse. *Damn!* Gift or nightmare, she wasn't yet certain, but the surprise offer from her parents wasn't in her plans. Not that she had plans.

Eighteen-year-old Jeb drove them away from the Middleton subdivision with her folks, Lawton and Beverly Cantrell, three car-lengths behind. The Ford's dash clock read noon. The June temp had already reached ninety-six degrees.

Jeb turned the five-year-old Escape onto Highway 61. "What's in the envelope?"

"A deed." Tension twisted her stomach. "Don't follow so close behind that truck."

He stared wide-eyed. "A deed to what?"

"Watch the road, Jeb." Callie chewed the inside of her cheek and practiced slow breathing as she reconnoitered the road ahead. Kids eighteen and under comprised a large proportion of traffic accidents. "The beach house."

"The beach house," he mimicked in droll fashion. "Like wow. Who gets handed a freakin' house? Come on! Act excited!" He flicked her arm. "Now you're stuck with me on the weekends, unless you want me to commute the forty-five miles each day between Edisto and college in downtown Charleston."

"Not when you're driving like this, no."

He winked. "Dang, we own a piece of the beach!"

"It's not on the sand."

"I know where it is. You can still hear the waves, for Pete's sake."

She sighed. "This was supposed to be a reflective summer, Jeb. You and I enjoying the ocean. Me deciding where to live and work." Callie recognized her mother's *coup*, anchoring them close, as permanent as she could.

Callie grinned weakly at her son, loving him so much, wanting desperately to take him up on his offer to stay home when college started in August. But he deserved a new start, a new normal.

Not that living on Edisto Beach was horrible confinement. Her childhood there held beautiful memories, and until classes started, Jeb could create some of his own. The soft breezes, pelicans, and rattling fronds of the trees supplied backdrop to shell collecting, kayaking, and making new friends while seated, kicking in tidal pools. Who couldn't like that?

She hoped he would develop his own close relationship with her old white-headed neighbor Papa Beach, too. The man was a pure Godsend.

Papa had first called her three months ago from his place, asking her to visit Edisto. Her father might've prompted that first call, but the request beckoned her like cotton candy at the fair. She eagerly escaped the social rigidity of the Cantrells' political lives to the healing voice of her childhood mentor. She'd spent hours chatting, sometimes sitting with him on the sand watching the orange and purple watercolor horizon. She went back three more times.

Now eighty years old, Henry Beechum, Papa Beach only to Callie, had once soothed her little girl fears, no matter how silly. And now he'd convinced her to stay at Edisto to heal amidst the Lowcountry nature and low-key lifestyle. He said her life decisions could be better made in a peaceful environment. Papa never dictated. He suggested. He listened. And he let her cry.

Callie tugged her sleeve down over the left forearm scar out of habit, then back up due to the heat. The surprise real estate gift from her father was noble, but panic seized Callie when he'd said the word *deed*. A deed made things complicated. Why couldn't her parents let life evolve instead of forcing its hand? Why did they think she left home to start with?

She hadn't even thanked her daddy, because that represented gratitude, not the manic fear that crawled inside her.

Callie massaged her neck. Electricity, insurance, taxes . . . in her name only.

She'd tried to remain in Boston after John's murder, working long, exhausting hours before rushing home to stand guard over Jeb, to soothe his grief while fighting to ignore her own. Jeb's grades had faltered, and he avoided going out at night, harboring a phobia about coming home to his mother being gone, too. They ate dinners in front of the television, watching anything but police dramas that brought reality into their living room.

Her daddy had coaxed her back to South Carolina after that long painful year in Boston. Seven times mayor of Middleton, he'd been elected under the delicate yet crafty oversight of his wife with a poli-sci major from Columbia College—in South Carolina, not New York. What Beverly didn't have in sheepskin prestige she made up for in a dynamic crusade to keep Lawton Cantrell in power. The woman held a master's degree in manipulation.

One month turned into two as Jeb acclimated and regained his fun-loving self after Callie's extended leave of absence. At that point, Callie hadn't the heart to drag him back to Massachusetts, so she enrolled him in high school. After six months of watching him thrive, she resigned from the Boston PD. Jeb was healing.

She was not.

Callie's head slumped against her palm. She wanted to remain untethered. Scholarships and a childhood college fund established by her parents covered Jeb's tuition. John's insurance money and pension investment would cover them for a few years, but eventually she had to consider a job. But not yet. Just not yet.

She ought to feel lucky with a house dropped in her lap. So why didn't she?

An hour later, Jeb pulled the SUV off Jungle Road, the Cantrells easing up in the BMW behind him. He parked in the drive and opened the car door. "How awesome is this?"

Callie stared at the house that hadn't changed a nail in the thirty years she'd known it. Raised fourteen feet off the ground by pilings embedded ten feet deep to protect against hundred-year floods and hurricanes, the three-bedroom house welcomed visitors with teal shutters and beige-painted stairs set against creamy siding. Not huge, but tasteful, with simple class.

Her fingernails bit into the seat, as she conceded that the house was probably the best logical choice for her at the moment. *Damn you, Mother.*

"Mom?"

She feigned a smile at Jeb and whispered, "Give me a minute."

He studied her like a textbook. "You need something?"

Callie shook her head. Then she quit rubbing the scar on her forearm and gripped the door handle as she looked up at the porch. The wind caught the teal and peach sign hanging atop the entrance's twenty steps. It swung on tiny chains without a care in the world, like the beach child she used to be.

Her mother had named the cottage Chelsea Morning, after the Neil Diamond song. Callie knew every word to every one of the singer's tunes, songs that had served as her lullabies and the background music to her adolescence. Slow, cleansing breaths. She played *Holly Holy* in her head.

Then she heard it: the gentle call of the surf, a distant rush and draw as rollers churned against the shore only to be sucked back into an immense ocean that never slept. A rogue seagull hovered over her head, calling once, then as he flew away on the salty current, she inhaled.

Three blocks from the water, the place held just enough privacy to deter heavy seasonal car traffic, but sat close enough for salt to devour the paintwork. The view out back, however, would later see a tired sun sink all haze-hot and liquid orange into the marsh, setting the tips of the reeds on fire before darkness swallowed the day.

Fire.

Sunsets, dusk . . . fire. The time of day John died. The sun's last rays dancing with licks of flame that shot her husband's ashes into the New England air.

Callie shut down the thought before the nightmare of Boston surged back.

Jeb knocked on her window, his brows raised. He cut a glance over his shoulder at his grandmother, who waited with a suitcase in one hand and a blue orchid in the other.

Callie exhaled and exited the car.

Her father appeared with a box in one arm, offered the support of his other, and escorted her up the steps. Jeb bounded inside. Beverly strutted behind him as if waltzing into the Ritz Carlton in a white mink wrap, a poodle with its snout high at the end of a jewel-studded leash. "Let's get you two settled in," she said.

The woman disappeared into the master bedroom, still talking. "You haven't met the neighbor to the left. She's into yoga, and not just the exercises. Incense, bells, candles, mindless stuff. She'll try to convert you into a meditating New Age fanatic."

Callie stopped outside her childhood room, tuning out her mother. Her favorite quilt rested on her old double bed. She lowered the packing box onto it and sank into the mattress. She ran her palms gently across the stitched image of a gold starfish, her favorite sea creature. Beverly had remembered. This was the comforter pulled out of the closet each time they shifted Chelsea Morning from a rental to their short-term retreat. Bless her mother's rare journey into sentimentality. Maybe there was hope for her—for them—yet.

Bending until her cheek touched the ruffled cotton pillow sham, Callie inhaled, taking in the aroma of lilac fabric softener. She ached to crawl under the quilt's protection—to escape to a time when her life was one amazing ride after another, and her heart wasn't so bruised.

Over two years later, and she still couldn't call herself a *widow*.

Beverly labeled Callie's emotional concerns as *spells*. Jeb babied her, when it should be the other way around. But deep in the recesses of her soul, her panic attacks and fear-ridden dreams stemmed from the fact she'd always consider the Zubov family a threat to her family's well-being. Leo had died, but there were dozens of them still breathing. She didn't know how to get over that.

Leo had given the order to kill everyone in her house that night. She was as sure of it as the barnacles clinging to the beach piers. John just happened to be the only one there. Zubov meant to send a strong message.

She'd gotten the point then, and every day and night since.

Then the bastard had died before witness protection could whisk him away. Stroke. The Russian mafia martyred him as they did all their dead. The fact that Leo's obese body and lavish lifestyle exacerbated his demise meant nothing. To his family, the people who cuffed him became the focus for revenge.

Her mother's voice lifted in singsong fashion from the other room, her Carolina drawl thick. "Callie? Would you like me to sort your hanging clothes in any order? I have my closet color coordinated, but—"

"No." Callie cleared her throat, regretting her harsh reply. "Just hang them. I'll sort everything later."

This room had so many little girl memories. What she'd be when she grew up. How to kiss a boy. When to wear make-up. Crying herself to sleep over acne ruining her life. She smiled.

Callie dragged herself up and left the bedroom, hefting a box containing framed pictures and her small jewelry collection onto the dresser in the other bedroom. Her parents' dresser. Hers was in the room with seahorses and starfish, and she bet she'd still find grains of sand in the recesses of the white rattan. After her folks left, she might switch rooms.

"I'm sorry, dear, but I went ahead and sorted your clothes." Beverly's muffled announcement radiated from the closet. "I think you'll like what I've done."

Callie shook her head at the woman's remarkable gift to turn a deaf ear. Yeah. She would definitely switch rooms.

Callie lifted a family picture of Jeb, John, and herself on Jeb's four-teenth birthday, spent on a Boston shore, tiny Bonnie in her arms. Callie brushed her finger across the glass. "I only intended to visit Edisto for the summer, you know."

Beverly ventured out of the closet. "Did I hear you right, dear?" She spread her arms wide. "We just gave you all this, so I—"

"Don't get it." Callie set down the picture and faced her mother. "You've never gotten it." A tear threatened, not what she intended, but she held her composure. Who got mad over a new house?

Her lithe, prim mother with a magazine-perfect bob of white waves and celery capris shifted her feet, but left her gaze on her daughter.

An overwhelming year of biting her tongue, stifled under the same roof with her parents' overbearance, spilled over. "Where I went to school, my choice of husband." She mimicked her mother's voice. "*Massachusetts is a long way from good people, dear.*" Callie inhaled, regretted the overreaction, and waited for her mother's next blow.

Instead, her mother sighed. "I know you feel you must lash out, dear, but it's been over two years since John left."

"And Bonnie."

"Yes," her mother said. "But they left some time ago, don't you think—"

Callie's jaw tightened. "For God's sake, Mother, they're dead, not on vacation." *And buried in Boston, a thousand miles away.*

"I understand that," Beverly replied, seating herself on an ottoman.

"Like it or not, the house is yours. Sell it if you wish, but we wanted to give you a place of your own." She cocked her head like a petulant headmistress. "It's time for Jeb to have a home, too."

"Jeb's home is *my* decision to make! Where I live is *my* choice." Callie tucked trembling hands in her jeans, unable to mark that one point in time that caused the chasm between her and her mother. To identify what to fix—and fix it.

"I hurt, too, you know," Beverly said, slipping easily into her feel-sorry-for-me voice. "I never got to see my granddaughter."

There it was. Callie clenched her teeth at Beverly's well-worn trump card.

"*Your* daughter lived," Callie replied. "Anyway, you never came to Boston to visit."

"My dear, you never asked me to."

Callie moved the box of photographs to the floor with a thud. She'd decided years ago that to become a self-assured police officer, she couldn't afford the emotional bombardment of her mother's judgment. "Don't you see *why* I moved so far away? To get away from your control. John, Jeb, and the Boston PD completed me, and Bonnie . . ." She drew in sharply. "Bonnie became the cherry on top."

Her mother folded her hands slowly, which she always did when she wanted to cement a point. "Law enforcement changed you, dear."

Callie's eyes narrowed. "Law enforcement *defined* me, Mother." Her clenched fist struck her chest. "It led me to John and gave you grandchildren. All achieved without your input."

"That's enough," said her father from the doorway.

Jeb peered uneasily over Lawton's shoulder.

Callie's heart sank at her father's mask of disappointment. These thrusts of iron will dug under Callie's skin. Here she stood, caught between the guilt of being an ingrate and her need to be a grown woman with a mind of her own.

"Wish you wouldn't fight," Jeb said softly, the pain clear in his eyes.

Beverly wouldn't think such a comment was directed at her, so Callie stopped arguing. Just like she always did.

"We're fine, dear," Beverly said, the timbre of her voice now oh-so-damn level.

If Callie heard *dear* one more friggin' time.

She approached her father, the parent who could display affection, and employed the nickname that melted his bones—given to him the first time he let her drive the boat when she was only eight. "Captain?"

Lawton yanked an initialed handkerchief from his pocket, the cloth a traditional stocking stuffer from Beverly each Christmas. "What, Callie Scallywag?" Her father's cheeks and neck flushed red from the heat as he wiped his forehead with the handkerchief.

"Jeb and I don't need help unpacking," she said, rubbing his sweaty sleeve. "We'd like to enjoy the peace. Walk the beach maybe."

"The beach sounds great," Jeb said, a huge smile returning to his face.

Lawton studied his daughter.

"Nonsense." Beverly strode past toward the kitchen, drawing them behind her into the living room. "I can throw together a snack for us to eat on the porch."

Lawton winked at Callie and pushed his handkerchief back into his pocket. "Bev, sweetheart, don't I have some sort of breakfast meeting tomorrow morning?"

"Yes," Beverly said, peeking around the refrigerator door. "You're due at the Rotarians' breakfast at seven."

Lawton ran an arm around Jeb's shoulders. Both men were six foot, the long noses and chins obviously alike. He squeezed Jeb once then faked a punch to the boy's gut, raising a flinch then a grin from Jeb. "I haven't even thought about preparing what to say," Lawton said.

Beverly appeared with cheese and condiments. "You don't ever prepare."

Lawton walked to the kitchen, lifted the items from his wife, and returned them to the refrigerator. "Let's go."

"But—"

He took her arm gently. "They need time to themselves."

As her mother walked off to get her purse, Callie ran to her father and threw her arms around his neck. "Thanks for the house, Daddy," she whispered.

"You're welcome," he whispered back. "I'll tell your mother."

TENSION DRAINED away as Callie's gaze followed her parents' white BMW on its way toward Highway 174, back to their Middleton kingdom. From his duffel bag in the hallway, Jeb dug out swimming shorts, flip-flops, and sunglasses before bolting toward the door.

"Got your phone?" Callie hollered.

He frowned. "It'll get messed up or stolen."

Her concern escalated as he touched the doorknob. She had to adjust to him being out of reach. The ocean was just down the street. She walked over and caressed his warm cheek. "Okay, but try not to stay too long. You'll burn."

His mouth twisted into a familiar half-grin that made her heart leap at the memory of John. She nudged a blond lock back from his face. "Go. Have fun."

As the latch caught behind him, Callie inhaled, then glanced around, absorbing what was now hers. Her fingers rubbed a knotted piece of driftwood on the bookcase. The cliché coastal decorations had to go. She would repaint the canary yellow walls to a neutral and turn the place into a real residence.

She returned to the bedroom to unpack. The nearest box stood out from all the others with no label. After ripping the tape free, the flaps sprung up. Bonnie's white blanket ballooned out, the one from her car seat, the only item of hers unclaimed by fire and smoke.

As her hands entwined in the cotton, sobs crept up, then unable to fight them back, she let them engulf her. Her body shook as she hugged the blanket, rocking, rocking. That tiny, sweet-smelling baby girl. How often did she have to relive the morning she'd found Bonnie cold and oh so blue?

Her heart hit her chest and scared her. The first sign. Spinning around, she fumbled for her water bottle on the nightstand, missing it twice before she snared it and darted to the front porch. She rested elbows on the railing, head drooped, forehead almost touching the wood, breathing deep as she surveyed the crushed-shell drive. A renter's golf cart puttered alongside Jungle Road fifty feet away.

Don't panic. Don't panic.

She forced in deep breaths again and again to lower her racing pulse.

The house had turned claustrophobic without warning. *Damn it.* Sucking in, she closed her eyes and counted to ten. She listened to her breathing and her pulse, controlling them both by sheer act of will. A sip of water helped. She opened her eyes, assimilating the surf noise, the gulls overhead. She eased back into the world.

And now she was tired.

A gull squawked and landed on the step ten feet away, dropped a sticky white present for her and lifted off again. She smiled. That sort of crap was doable. Lifting elbows, she brushed off the grains of sand.

She had tossed the antidepressants back in Boston, not wanting a crutch. Then during one particularly needy night, she'd learned alcohol provided a decent substitute. Running held off the escalating urge to drink herself into oblivion, so she'd bought two hundred dollar sneakers to guilt herself into keeping the habit. Pouring herself into sport instead of a glass, she had dropped a scary fifteen pounds off her petite frame, but earned it back in muscle within two months. Twice she'd run so long she almost collapsed . . . back in Boston. Middleton had been another story. Anyway, time to sweat out this day and burn off the melancholy.

A local patrol car in white and navy crawled by, the sandy-haired officer's elbow draped out the open window, his tanned hand holding the roof. He raised a couple fingers off the steering wheel as their eyes met.

The uniform; the love of seeing a man wear it. A deep sense of longing stirred. She waved a reply in kind, a benign hello she still used when she saw another badge. She missed the work and being married to a man who also loved it.

The warm gust of brine-laden breeze whipped a lock into her eyes. She tucked overgrown bangs behind her ears and filled her lungs again with the salt air. Jeb would come in near dark, his hair sticky, cheeks sun-kissed, and she'd have to remind him to leave his gritty shoes at the door. He'd earned the right to enjoy his life, and she was determined to ensure that happened.

She straightened to go inside for her sneakers when a rebellious gust of wind raised the clackety echoes of a bamboo chime from the gray-sided house next door.

Where *was* Papa Beach today? Her favorite neighbor had yet to make an appearance. Surely her father had called to let him know they were coming.

She'd make him her first house guest to celebrate their arrival, even ask him to bring his Korean War photos that Jeb enjoyed. She went inside to get her new keys, unable to leave a door unlatched like the natives. Shoes on and house locked, she clomped down the stairs.

Making her way across the twenty yards between them, she headed up the neat, well-tended steps to Papa Beach's residence next door. Her mood lifted as she forecasted the hug, the joke about how big she'd grown—though she'd seen him only three weeks ago—and a piece of grape saltwater taffy.

Which hand holds the surprise, Callie?

Um, that one, Papa B, she'd say, only for it to always be the other.

She reached the top landing of his tiny home, half the size of most on this end of the island. Her smile vanished.

The doorknob hung by its guts, the doorframe splintered. She tensed and instinctively reached for her Glock only to grab an empty waistband.

Chapter 3

CALLIE NUDGED PAPA Beach's door open with her toe. The familiar smell of old leather and cough medicine struck her nose.

"Papa, you there?" She stilled, listening. "It's Callie." Only the mantle clock ticked in response from the fake fireplace in the far corner.

A floor lamp had fallen, busted on the rug beside the bottomed-out corduroy recliner. She eased past them. Pictures of Papa's wife and adult son hung askew on the paneled wall, and a photograph of an old naval ship lay on the floor, the glass shattered. Blood pounded in Callie's ears at the thought of what she might find.

Papa's framed silver dollar collection display was missing from over the sofa. She used to read aloud the years on the coins in order. Twenty-five of them.

His cozy, dated living room had served as her playhouse, reading room, and occasional naptime in her youth—a place to escape from parents who didn't understand, and to fall into Papa's sparkling blue eyes with their rascally tease. His place endured time in her mind as a bastion against change, a haven for comfort, and a getaway from a life that wasn't fair.

She approached the kitchen. The back door gaped open, and the warm breeze wafted in, pushing a faint wisp of gunpowder through the room.

No, no, please don't let it be.

She rounded the entryway and stiffened. Papa Beach sprawled across the linoleum, a leg caught in the rung of a chair beside his dinette table, a neat bullet hole in his temple.

Scanning the room and its exits warily, she stooped and checked the body for a pulse—nothing. She touched the man's sleeve as her grief crept in.

Slowly rising, she took in her surroundings, so comfortable in this kitchen. Her breath caught. Two cups on the counter. One with a dry tea bag awaiting its hot water, the other next to a box of instant hot chocolate. Spoons set out. Napkins. A sleeve of cookies. He'd been expecting her.

The back porch screen slammed. Jerking around, weaponless, she snatched a knife out of a kitchen drawer and bolted in pursuit.

The porch was positioned twelve feet off the ground. Someone ran underneath, their feet crunching shells before they crashed the line of oleander bushes.

Adrenaline surged as it had in chases along Boston streets. After she scurried down the steps, she flattened against the house then waded into the tall bushes, checking low for waiting legs. She stopped beneath overhanging palmetto fronds to listen. Nothing. *Damn it!* She gazed up and down the deserted road running behind the string of houses, secluded from tourist traffic. Whoever it was moved fast and was armed. A knife was a poor defense against a gun. She could be just as dead as Papa Beach if she dared to follow.

What the hell was she even doing? She wasn't a cop anymore. The locals should handle it now. Jeb didn't need to lose another parent.

She returned to her place, dialing 9-1-1 as she ran up the stairs to retrieve her Glock 32. The son-of-a-bitch just might double back, thinking she identified him.

"9-1-1. What's your emergency?" said the operator as Callie dropped the knife on her coffee table and peered out her back door.

"My name is Callie Morgan, former Boston homicide detective. I'm at 18A Jungle Road with a GSW victim, deceased male approximately eighty years old. No perpetrator on site."

A jogger approached up the secluded back road in shorts and microfiber shirt, panting, an iPod strapped to his deeply tanned arm. "Hey," she called from her doorway, waving him toward her.

The man slowed then jogged in place as Callie trotted down her steps.

"I'll be outside the crime scene address," Callie told the protesting operator and then hung up. She turned her attention to the jogger and pointed up the road. "Did anyone run past you?"

The guy removed his ear buds, pushing dark hair from his eyes. "Pardon?"

"Did you see anybody running, acting oddly?"

The jogger stopped and raised a brow, devouring her with a long, lazy leer. "Why?"

Darn tourists. Callie rested her fist on a hip. "Did you or didn't you see anyone?"

He reared back. "No, no. I didn't see anyone, but I wasn't really looking."

"What's your name?"

His snicker irritated her as he pointed south. "Mason Howard. I rent Water Spout, the house about ten blocks over. What's your name, Miss Spitfire?"

Scowling, she didn't dare turn, or he'd see the gun tucked behind her. "Callie Morgan. Just moved in."

"So, is there some sort of problem?" he asked with no identifying accent. "You're flustered as hell."

"No, no, it's okay," she lied and motioned toward the empty boxes piled near the trash can. "Some kid going through my stuff, I think."

"Oh, well, I'll be moving on then. Got another couple miles to go.

Nice to meet you, Callie Morgan. Hope to see you again." He replaced his ear buds and took off.

Rich, bubble-headed tourist, she thought. Assuming he really rented the prestigious Water Spout.

She returned to the base of Papa Beach's front stairs to wait.

And the world seemed to freeze. Standing alone in that vacuum where time had stopped, she fought to hold her despair at bay. Papa had been the sweetest person ever, a gentle soul who would've given a robber whatever he demanded. He was to be her foundation here, the person who'd let her cry in his arms against one of his favorite Hawaiian shirts. Papa never judged her. He always understood.

She hit the railing with the butt of her hand. There was no need to shoot an old man in cold blood.

The same Edisto PD unit she'd seen earlier braked to an abrupt stop in the sandy roadside. Rubbing her bruised hand, she walked toward the navy blue and gray uniformed officer as he exited. This was the beginning of the circus performance that comprised a murder investigation, and the man better give Papa's death the proper respect.

"Callie Morgan?" he asked.

"Yes," she said, reading M. Seabrook on his nametag. "I'm carrying, just to let you know." She kept palms up in view and slightly turned to reveal her weapon. "Hasn't been fired. I used to be a detective. I live right here." She motioned to Chelsea Morning.

His blue eyes studied her face. "I've seen you from a distance a time or two. You resemble your father." He paid special attention to the gun. "May I?"

She placed the Glock in his huge, long-fingered hands. "Naturally I went and got my personal weapon."

He smelled it, gave it a once over, to include the magazine, and gave it back. "Is the victim Henry Beechum?"

Papa'd hate being called a victim. "Yes," she replied, breaking eye contact to study the wood grain on the stairs, picking it once with her fingernail.

"Damn," he said, glancing up at the house. "See how he was killed?"

"Single shot to the head." She glanced toward the rear of the house. "I started to give chase but lost the perp."

His frame filled out as he reached his full height of six foot plus, his right hand resting on the grip of his gun, his vest giving him an intimidating girth. "You gave chase? See anyone?"

Callie shook her head, frustrated she couldn't add more.

"Stay right here, if you don't mind." Seabrook entered the home and exited barely a minute later. He took out a memo book as he clomped down the steps. "Appears he was killed by a .22."

"Yeah, that's what I thought, too."

"Run through it for me, Ms. Morgan."

She related the events. "I was unarmed, so I retreated and called y'all."

"But you took the time to take care of the unarmed issue," he said without glancing up from his pad.

A cop shouldn't say something so stupid. If someone murdered once, they'd murder again more easily, especially if he sensed eyes on him. "The only other person was a jogger, tanned real dark who said he currently rented Water Spout." She gave his name and description.

"Mason, yeah, he's harmless," he said with a hint of disapproval.

Of course, a uniform would know the important vacationers. Water Spout was one of the most affluent homes on the water. However, Callie couldn't care less where the attitude came from if the man did his job right and gave Papa his due attention.

"Do you have a current carry permit for that Glock?" Seabrook asked.

"Yes, I do."

"I'll need to see it at some point."

"No problem."

He tucked the memo book in his pocket. "You know we need you to stay right here, ma'am."

"Of course." Cops always spoke in the collective. She used to say *we*, too, even if she was the only badge on site.

He returned up the stairs, his black leather duty belt squeaking. Two more Edisto units arrived. One officer posed outside on guard; the other joined Seabrook. Probably the entire on-duty force.

She slumped on the bottom step, covering her mouth as men walked around her, pretending she wasn't there. Someone needed to call his son . . . who'd post a For Sale sign in the yard by week's end.

Pauley Beechum saw his father no more than once a year, at Christmas, to collect a check and drop his annual guilt trip on Papa for not moving down to Florida to save him the trip to South Carolina. Papa always feared his son would eventually force him to move out of his cherished beach home. But Papa had died here, like he planned. Not exactly like he planned, but . . . shit. None of that mattered.

A couple in their late-twenties watched from their screened porch across the street. Nobody she knew. In the house on the other side of Chelsea Morning, a petite woman in black yoga pants and a lime green gauze shirt peered over. Wouldn't take long for a dozen more to emerge and gawk. How many of these people even knew this jewel of a man? He'd resided on the island longer than most of them had lived.

If she were still a detective, she'd be all over them, asking what they heard, saw, leaning on them when they claimed to know nothing. She despised it when people played ignorant after hearing a gunshot or an abused wife's screams in the apartment next door.

But she wasn't a detective. Elbows resting on her knees, palms covering her eyes, she blocked out the sunshine as melancholy slipped over her like a sleeve. Papa B would be the last person to drag her back into police work after all she'd endured. She had planned long chats with the old man to redefine her direction of a life torn asunder by the law enforcement environment.

Papa had been murdered for a few coins . . . with a .22 in the temple.

Like John.

On Bonnie's birthday.

Her old horrors burst vividly in her mind, laced with Zubov's sarcastic scowl and threat to take her down. She and the rest of the Boston PD believed his family had made good on that threat killing John, miscalculating their arrival such that they missed Callie. All Jeb knew about was the fire, and Callie's resignation and relocation removed her and Jeb from the Russian family's purview. However, the mafia had a long reach and longer memory. They were never totally out of her thoughts.

Her eyes shot wide. *Jeb. Alone on the beach.*

Callie jumped up as a Colleton County Sheriff's Department cruiser stopped with its nose against a copse of palmetto trees to the right of Papa's place. Two deputies exited the vehicle and approached. She, however, took off running toward the beach.

"Ma'am?" yelled one of them. "Hey! We need to talk to you."

"I have to find my son!" Callie sprinted toward the ocean, panic driving every muscle. No time to explain about explosions, Russians, and a vendetta she couldn't afford to forget.

Jeb would freak having his mother search for him, but he'd get over it. At Palmetto Boulevard, she dodged traffic like a soccer player, finally reaching the sand on the other side of the four-lane.

Fear brought her breaths fast and shallow. If anything happened to Jeb . . .

The tide was out, and sun worshipers *en masse* sprawled across the wide span of sand. She yelled Jeb's name, then held a hand above her eyes to cut the sun's glare.

Teens everywhere. Left toward the Pavilion Restaurant. Right toward the south. Dozens in the water.

She ran close to the dunes to avoid climbing and jumping across the piers, and she called every few strides. Her legs pumped, feet pushing deep in the loose sand. Sweat soaked her shirt and stung her eyes. Jeb would be near girls, closer to the gift shop, a game room.

She paused, scanning the surf as she reached a group of young people fifty feet out in the water. The wind was strong, and it blew under her shirt, lifting its hem.

"She's got a gun!" someone yelled.

Families scattered, snatching up children.

Shit! She spun and ran, frustrated by the attention. But there was no tactful, methodical way to search. Time was too precious. And she might need the gun.

"Jeb!" *Where the hell was he?*

Tourists darted away as she zigzagged, the balls of her feet digging deeper. She halted here and there, double-checking every tall blond-headed boy.

She must've sprinted a half mile before she stopped to scream his name again. "Jeb!"

Her heart thundered against her ribs. Losing Jeb would finish her. The pain would be too much. She snatched a glance behind her, the beach now deserted, except for towels and shoes left by the chaos she'd caused. Before her, crowds watched warily, pondering which way to run.

A police officer ran from around a dune, his boots kicking up sand. "Wait up, Ms. Morgan."

Damn it! She considered running on, more anxious to hunt than waste time talking.

"Ms. Morgan!"

He reached her and took a firm hold of her arm. "Give me the weapon."

She stared into Seabrook's sunglasses; the calming techniques the doctor taught her in Boston vanished from her mind. "Jeb," she said between ragged breaths as she removed the gun from her waistband. "Help me find my son."

"Right now you need to settle down." He took the gun. "You can't just bolt from a crime scene. You especially ought to know that. And you've put the fear of God into all these people." He released her. "Besides, you don't seem like you're in any condition to find your son. Get in front of your panic. Inhale deep. There you go. Now exhale."

She gulped another lungful of air. She didn't need another full blown anxiety attack. She eased down onto the sand and ran hot grains of sand through her fingers. Once, twice.

"I've got . . . to find my son."

Seabrook hunched within inches of her face. "We'll find your boy. You're doing nobody any good like this. Let's get back. Can you get up?"

He helped her rise and escorted her to his cruiser. Sunbathers who'd returned parted to let them pass. "Nothing here to see, folks. Go back to your business."

People wandered away, peering over their shoulders.

He assisted her into the rear seat of the cruiser as if she were his prisoner, hand on her head, and shut the door. Bending at the waist, clutching her middle, she fought a surge of anxiety. Rocking, rocking, rocking. *Get a grip, Callie. Get a goddamn grip!*

Seabrook settled into his seat. "Now, what's going on?" He turned on the air conditioning, and a chill rippled her shoulders as the cold hit her damp shirt.

"A murderer's out there and so is my son."

"Okay." His mouth moved like he sorted which words to use. "Don't take this wrong, because I don't know you, or your boy, but why would Henry Beechum's murderer want to hurt your son?"

"Who cares? What parent takes a chance like that?"

Seabrook obviously sought a logical answer for irrational behavior. "You're a former detective, right?" He swiveled to face her and removed his hat. "You've seen plenty of robberies ending with bodies." He locked eyes on her. "What's really got you on edge?"

Her jaw tightened. "I have a history that justifies my behavior," she said. "And we don't have time to tell it. I must find Jeb. He's without his cell phone."

"Give me the abridged version," he said. "Then we'll hustle back. We'll find Jeb before the day's out. Promise."

Her heartbeat began to slow to a more manageable pace at the man's sympathetic tone. "You're good at this," she said and swallowed again.

His boyish grin accented warm blue eyes with a spark of rebelliousness, though he had to be forty-five. "Have to admit I had to wing this one. We don't get many beachcombers running around here armed."

She wanly smiled. "I married a guy from Boston, a deputy US marshal. My husband died two years ago in a fire, but the autopsy proved he'd been shot. I believe the man responsible was a Russian drug dealer I arrested, or his family. Russians hold grudges. I've earned the right to overreact."

Seabrook whistled through his teeth. "Sorry. Had no idea."

"We didn't exactly post a press release. And I don't have time to fill you in." Callie caught herself rubbing the scar again and redirected her attention. "So, radio someone and find Jeb before I think too much about that guy still running loose and go all ballistic on you again."

He cut her a glance. "We sure don't want that." The radio crackled as he keyed the mic.

"Thanks." She sank into the seat. "Oh," she said, sitting back up. "Where'd you put my Glock?"

"You can pick it up from the station tomorrow."

Her eyes narrowed. "Why not when we get to the house?"

"Your go-all-ballistic comment sort of shot that option."

Fine. She had another weapon at the house. She'd decided long ago that one gun was far from enough to protect a single mom and her child, who'd once had a price on their heads.

Chapter 4

WITH THE AIR-conditioner blowing full blast to cool Seabrook's cruiser, Callie spouted Jeb's description: eighteen, six foot one, wavy blond hair, slim build, a hundred fifty pounds. He wore sky blue swim shorts, black flip-flops, navy beach towel.

The cop radioed the boy's description to dispatch then cranked the engine. "We'll find him," he said, as if he hadn't a doubt.

But they'd be hunting for a generic kid. She knew his walk, his voice. "On second thought, let me out. I can identify him quicker. He'll come to my voice. Let me out. Now."

"Not after the mayhem you just caused. I said we'll find him."

"There's more to this than—"

"I heard you about the Russians." Seabrook glanced in his rearview mirror before he pulled into the spotty beach traffic.

She flopped her head against the seat. Papa's murderer had stripped her of social graces. Nothing she could say now would be trusted.

Seabrook drove toward the crime scene, soon turning the cruiser onto Jungle Road. He maneuvered the car and accompanying silence with smooth ease, no edges to the man like one might expect from an officer full of machismo. "You're an experienced cop," he said. "You gave chase when most would have frozen. Nobody's beating you up, so don't do it to yourself. I know it sounds like too much to ask, but relax."

She stared out the window, trying to ignore the polite lecture. If the killer had been after her, why'd he kill Papa? And what hit man would hang around a crowded beach hunting for a boy with so many witnesses? Maybe she was overthinking this.

Actually, Jeb could be on his way home by now. The waning sun slipped behind palms, the shadows of houses lengthening.

The memory of the fire erupted in her mind's eye again, the orange and yellow flickers painting the night with an obscene beauty as it consumed her husband. She never came home at dusk, and Jeb understood why. She hadn't realized the time of day until now. No wonder she'd panicked.

Uniforms littered the frontage to hers and Papa's homes. Neighbors and onlookers crowded the drive. This was too damn close to déjà vu.

She gripped the partition between them as she scoured the crowd. "Stop, Seabrook."

"Hold on. I'm trying to find a spot that doesn't block the road."

The drum in her chest returned. She craned to see. "Open the damn door."

"Settle down, Ms. Morgan, or I'll leave you back there." He was tame, steady, which only aggravated her more. Did he not hear a word she said?

Seabrook parked next to three squad cars, exited, and opened the rear door to release Callie. She leaped out and darted toward Chelsea Morning, the first place Jeb might be.

"Mom!" Jeb yelled, breaking loose from a group of youngsters. "Someone killed Papa Beach."

She bolted to him, hugging him hard, relishing his skinny arms around her. "I know, baby. We're okay." Fighting her panic, hoping Jeb couldn't tell, she squeezed him again. "I was worried sick," she said, drawing back to gaze at him. "Where've you been?"

He stared quizzically. "I was at the beach. You knew that. A cop said you ran off when they showed up. I was afraid—I mean, when I came home and you were gone." He drew her back to him and whispered in her ear, "You sure you're okay?"

"I'm good," she whispered back. "Especially now." Jeb hugged tighter, and for a moment she let his embrace feel like John's.

Her husband could always settle her like this, and Papa B used to know when she needed to talk just by seeing her across the yard. John had loved talking to Papa B during their vacations. Neither could help her now.

"Ma'am." The ruddy-faced, red-headed Colleton deputy got in her face. "We might've shot you running from a murder scene like that."

Cops raining lead on the streets of Edisto Beach, at the peak of tourist season. *Right.* She sidestepped the man and his coffee odor.

"Hold it right there," he started.

"It's okay, Don," Seabrook said. "I spoke with her already."

The deputy threw him a disgruntled look, thrusting his belly out more, stretching the bottom button on his gray uniform. "I'll take care of this, Seabrook."

"With due respect, it's my jurisdiction," Seabrook gently reminded the older cop.

The deputy arched a bushy red eyebrow. "Assigned to you because you can't deal with the load."

"I'm sorry, Deputy Raysor," Callie said, glancing at his nametag. She didn't want anyone to lose face over her actions, and this blowhard seemed intent on making a stand. "I'm a former Boston detective. A dozen scenarios played out in my mind. Jeb's my son, and he's all I have."

Raysor removed his hat, wiped his brow with the sleeve of his shirt, and lowered his voice. "A former detective, huh? Peculiar behavior, if you ask me."

"I know, I know, and again, my apologies."

"Call me Don, but that don't mean we're drinking buddies." He squinted. "You hear me?"

She nodded, then caught Seabrook's narrow smile from the corner of her eye. Seabrook might be all right. The jury was still out on Raysor.

Raysor adjusted his hat back in place, rocking it forward then slightly back as he turned away. "Get these rubberneckers out of here, and somebody take a statement from this lady before she bolts again."

"Officer Raysor?" Callie said. "Don?"

He made a half turn. "Ma'am?"

Callie moved closer and away from the ears of eager onlookers. "If this were my case, I'd consider the missing coin collection as a possible ruse."

"Well, it's not your case," Raysor grumbled and crossed his arms across his barrel chest. "But let's hear it, *ex*-detective."

Seabrook sidled up to hear.

"An opportune thief might take the antique coins, but why kill the old man?" she said. "He could've gone down with a slap."

Raysor stared skeptically. "The old man probably interrupted the guy who then overreacted. Panic, nerves. If you've got a gun, you tend to use it. But then I'm a lowly deputy, so what do I know?"

Her experience had to amount to something, though, even to this yahoo, and her cop senses were screaming this crime wasn't a happenstance murder. "The killer turned the place upside down, yet he took nothing of real value," she said. "Not even the victim's wallet, I bet."

"You disturbed the robber." Raysor tipped his hat. "But go on. I'm listening."

"I think he took the coins to make it appear like a robbery."

"She has a point," Seabrook said. "The body shows signs of torture."

Callie's eyes widened. "What?" She glanced back to ensure Jeb remained out of earshot.

"Everybody's a sleuth," Raysor said, groaning. "So what in particular was the guy searching for?"

"Maybe he was after information." Even as she said the words, she felt the suggestion weak. Still, what if they wanted info on her? But then, why not just come get her at Chelsea Morning? She was alone.

Raysor leaned in and glared. "Let us get on with our job. I know in your eyes we appear to be a herd of Barney Fifes, but I assure you we know what we're doing, *ex*-detective. Besides, state law enforcement's coming from Columbia. I'm sure they know their jobs as well as you *used to* know yours."

He tipped his hat and strolled away, shaking his head.

Seabrook gave Callie an apologetic wink and followed the deputy.

The only other homicide in this community she was aware of had been a domestic issue three years earlier when an outraged husband from New Jersey sliced open his wayward wife. Callie's mother had called her about *that* event after not speaking to Callie for two months.

The atmosphere of Edisto Beach wasn't conducive to serious crime. The occasional robbery, yes. Alcohol-induced brawls, marijuana trippers here and there. All expected. But murder?

"Ms. Morgan." Seabrook waved her over after Raysor drove off. "Can we go in your house to take your statement, please?"

"Sure." She turned to Jeb. "You okay?"

He nodded. "What about you? I mean, you knew Papa—"

"Shush," she replied, laying fingers across his lips. "Go be with your new friends. I'm good."

Jeb returned to a young crowd gathered under a palmetto that immediately swarmed him for info.

Pride swelled in Callie at the maturity of her son, his effort to fill his dad's shoes, and his ability to realize that his mother was anything but fine.

She'd been a complete fool on the beach. She saw that now. But kicking into overdrive had helped her catch criminals. Fast, intense, focused. Now, however, she couldn't exactly control the speed, or the steering.

THE NEXT MORNING, Jeb hung around the house, chattering like a hyper chickadee about the previous day's events. Events she preferred to ponder alone. Maybe she'd revisit the crime scene and scout for what others might have missed. But not with Jeb around. She'd always done her damnedest to not let her job cross Jeb's path.

In Boston, she'd fallen apart after a year of hunting John's killer and pretending all was fine to Jeb. The obsession had eroded her ability to compartmentalize, organize, and dissect a crime. She couldn't end the day without devising new strategy against the Zubovs. Vengeance muddled clarity.

She moved from room to room, her son on her heels as she dusted, washed clothes, and settled her belongings amongst those already in place. Occasionally she glanced out the window at the yellow crime scene tape fluttering in the breeze.

"The kids I met said Papa Beach got shot with his own gun," he said.

She snapped towels, fresh from the dryer. "Jeb, how would they know? Quit with the amateur investigating. And get out from under my feet. I know what you're doing, and I'm fine. I used to work in the middle of this kind of crap."

"Yeah, but . . . you know."

Lifting a stack of linens, she shoved them into his arms. "Are you spying for your grandparents? I'll skin you for that. I don't need a sitter."

He hesitated enough for her to see the *yes* in his eyes. She filled the dryer again and switched it on. "Go to the beach before I put you in the corner." She waved at him dismissively, internally not wanting him to leave the house. "Meet somebody," she said. "Maybe even a hot girl in some knock-out bikini."

He scowled. "My mom isn't supposed to talk about hot girls. And since when do you want me out from under your own bodyguard protection?"

Her son was too sharp. Finding a dead body next door, minutes after overcoming an anxiety attack, was ample reason for her overreaction yesterday. Today, however, she liked to think she controlled herself better. "If you take your phone and call me periodically, and stay around friends, I won't worry so much." She sighed. "I'm trying to give you space. College is only two months away, and I'm struggling with it." She put the fabric softener and soap up on the shelf over the washer. "Stick around, however, and I'll educate you on my dating secrets."

"You win." His smile shone from a deeper place. "Don't need a lesson on prehistoric social skills." Bare feet slapping the oak floor, he disappeared into his bedroom to change. Shortly thereafter, he exited the house, locking the door as John had taught him.

Callie poured herself an ice water and fought not to mark time with constant peeks at the clock. Fought not to glance out the window at yellow crime scene tape.

She needed something to do. After lifting her .38 from the credenza drawer, she pulled out the gun cleaning kit. Then she dialed a familiar number and rested the phone on her shoulder as she took the weapon apart. "Stan Waltham, please. Tell him it's Callie Morgan."

Stan shot straight with her, respected her, and when she'd left the police department, she swore she saw moisture in his brown eyes. His gruff exterior enveloped a marshmallow core. Ten years older, he played the handsome father-figure one minute and a stand-up buddy the next. She still remembered the musk of his cologne when he hugged her goodbye that long moment outside the bar. She missed him more than anything else about Boston.

"Morgan! How're you doing?"

"Making it, Stan." Her shoulders relaxed hearing his thick Massachusetts accent and gravelly voice. Her last call had been two months ago, which meant he'd cut that curly black and gray hair at least three times. "Wanted to let you know where I am. And check on life back in Beantown."

"Missing you around here, Chicklet." He chuckled as he used her old nickname derived from her small size when compared to his six-foot five. Stan's square jaws usually chomped on gum, cinnamon-flavored, a habit cultivated when he quit smoking. "What'll it take to get you to come back? Boston's overrun with crime now. They're thinking about shutting us down, moving us to New York, and letting the clans and mobs have it."

She smiled and envisioned his tilted, box-like head and mouth stuck in a tight grin as she put a drop of cleaning oil on a patch. "I had them all under my thumb. What did you expect?"

"You still in Summerton?" he asked.

"Middleton," she corrected, "and the answer is no. I'm at Edisto Beach now. Expected to just visit, but I sort of got stuck here for a while." She changed ears on the phone. "I need to ask you something."

He grunted. "You sort of got stuck living on the shore? Sucks, Morgan. How do you stand all that sun and sand—the balmy breezes and shit?"

"You sound like my son, except for the shit part."

"Always liked that kid."

"Listen, Stan, we had a murder down here, and that just doesn't happen," she said. "My next door neighbor was killed. A lovely old man who wouldn't harm a soul."

"And you're wondering about Zubov," he said. "I'm sorry about your friend, Chicklet. You've suffered enough."

"Thanks." She inhaled deep, taking in the gun's odor. "What's the word from the family?"

"I'd have called if I heard anything."

She knew that, but still. "What are the chances my friend takes a bullet to the head while I'm moving in next door?"

"They bag the perp?"

"No."

"Anybody see the guy?"

"No. I started to chase him, but he vanished. Plus I wasn't armed."

"Damn, Morgan." Stan smacked his gum a few times. "Anything stolen?"

"A coin collection, maybe more. I'm not allowed in. You know small town cops. They've even got a deputy on loan who thinks he's mayor." She tucked her chin-length hair behind her ears, but it swung back as soon as she pulled away. She continued on, enjoying the unbiased ear of someone who recognized her abilities.

The line fell silent for a few moments. Then Stan's office chair creaked. "You're doing it again."

Callie lined up the weapon's pieces on a cloth, each parallel and neat. "What's to say they didn't come down—"

"Stop it."

Scrunching an oily rag, Callie kneaded it as Stan went down a familiar path. "The Russians have a long reach."

"It's been two years," he said, concern underpinning his wisdom.

She wrung the cloth. "They left hints on the street."

"They were bragging, and you were still here. You left, so let them feel they won this one. I'm telling you, there hasn't been as much as a whiff of your name in twelve months." He sucked on the gum. "You still seeing someone about the episodes, or are you over them?"

"I'm better now," she lied, suddenly feeling the need to don her sneakers, hit the flat sand, and let eight-minute miles push the paranoia out of her system. She'd left her doctors in Boston. Why pay them two hundred dollars an hour when she could call someone for free who actually understood?

"What can I do?" he finally asked.

She outlined her scar with a finger, knowing the raised eight-inch length and half-inch width from memory. Her constant reminder of when her life fell off its axis. What *could* he do? Heaven help her, but she almost wished he'd come down and be that rock-steady assurance that a phone call couldn't offer. "Can you run a check on Henry Beechum? And do another on his son, Pauley. He's maybe five years older than me, lives in Kissimmee, Florida. I vaguely recall him having a history of trouble. He used Papa for little more than a bank."

"Sure. What else can I do?"

"You're doing it," Callie said low. "Just being there and not brushing me off as a dimwit."

"Just a friend doing friend-stuff," he said.

She heard a knock and a man speak in the background. "You probably need to take that."

"No, I don't." With a half-muted voice, he told somebody he'd be with them in a moment. "Call me any time you like. How'd you end things with the local cops?"

"Like I said, the county mounty's all bluster. But Officer Seabrook's nice."

"Really?"

"Not like that, you oaf."

"Okay, okay, but it might be time you were wined and dined, sweetheart."

Callie blushed, and she was glad he couldn't see her. "You'll call me if you hear anything on the street, right?"

"Of course." He coughed. "Let me know when you're up for company down there. Never been to a Southern shore."

"It's called a beach, Stan, and I will."

"Take care, Chicklet."

She didn't know what she'd do without these calls. He didn't call her crazy. He didn't talk as if she were afflicted. He'd known John and felt her pain.

She hung up, missing the attentiveness of a man so damn much, even if he was married.

Then she reassembled her weapon.

Chapter 5

CALLIE JUMPED AT the rapid-fire knock on her front door, as if the visitor had read her crossing-the-line thoughts about Stan.

"Hey, neighbor!" A female voice shouted as the handle was tested. "Anybody in there? Why's the door locked?"

Who the hell . . . Callie walked over and peered past the clear decorative rolling wave etched in the door's beveled window.

The antsy visitor on the porch stood no taller than Callie's diminutive five-foot two. She appeared to be in her late forties but animated enough to pass for less. She continued to tap with a fingernail in staccato fashion on the glass. "Yoo-hoo!"

Callie tucked the cleaned .38 in her back jean pocket. "May I help you?"

"Hey," the woman said in a mild drawl, pointing next door to the yellow home with sky blue shutters. "I'm Sophie Bianchi, your neighbor."

Callie recalled the curious onlooker with the gauzy green top and leotards from yesterday. The basket in her arm contained an assortment of jars and candles. Before Callie could offer a welcome, the visitor tried to push the door open. It stopped at Callie's well-placed foot.

Sophie feigned a hurt expression. "You're not gonna let me in?" She flipped her hand once as if casting a spell. "Look at me. I'm not a rapist. Nor a burglaring murderer." She flattened her fingertips on her collarbone. "I'm just your neighbor, honey. Probably the best friend you'll ever make on this island."

Callie moved her foot. The welcome gesture seemed nice. "Um, come on—"

With a dip to one side, wrist bangles jingling, Sophie entered, sweeping her skirt around the door.

Callie secured the house and followed her guest. *Interesting.* "Make yourself at home."

Strolling into the kitchen, Sophie set the basket on the table and moved items around inside it. She extracted a bundle of dried plant and waved the bouquet triumphantly.

"This first, hon." She flicked her lighter and lit the end of the muted green bunch until smoke rolled into the air, then Sophie danced on the balls of her sandaled feet around the kitchen table.

Callie wet a dish towel. "What're you doing?" With her luck, stray sparks would put holes in her furniture or light the curtains.

Sophie giggled and wafted the smoke into the corners of the room. "Saging your home, silly."

Gliding into the living room as if detached from the ground, she hummed, repeating her motions, light catching some of her skirt's gold lamé ribbons. The woman's arms were toned and tanned, her figure a tiny hourglass. Short curls kicked up in pixie-esque style, jet-black with streaked red highlights. And those aqua eyes. Had to be contacts.

"What's saging?" Callie asked, uncertain about the flamboyance.

"Smudging. Clearing your new home." She dipped and dove smoothly, as if controlled by music playing in her head. "One more room and I'm done."

Back in the kitchen, Sophie pushed smoke up and over Callie's head as she held her ground. Then Sophie rested the spent sage sticks in the sink. "There. Cleansed of all negative energy. Both you and the house." She held out her hand. "Nice to meet you."

Callie accepted. "Didn't know I needed cleansing."

Snickering, Sophie fell into a chair as if she'd lived in the house for years. "When you move in, you sage to dispel the ugly influence of cosmic junk left behind by the previous owners. You were around that murder yesterday," she said with a finger pointed, "so saging *you* couldn't hurt."

"The previous owners were my parents." The thought that Beverly's presence needed a purge from these walls amused Callie. "Appreciate it, though, because I'm sure there was a *serious* accumulation of negative cosmic junk left behind."

"See?" Sophie beamed, then threw a glance toward the hallway, to the front door. "No more need to keep your doors locked, either." Her gaze darted to Callie's backside as the gun hit the chair. "Oh, my goodness. No need for that gun, either."

Callie removed the weapon, placing it atop the fridge. Her mother had no right to tell her what to do anymore, so a neighbor most assuredly didn't. "Sorry," Callie said, "but doors stay locked around here."

"No, no, no." Sophie shook her shag. "When you think about negative events, you attract them to you. Don't ponder such incidents, and they won't occur. Therefore, no need for locks or guns."

Now all they needed was a crystal ball. "I can't live in an unlocked house. We'll have to agree to disagree on that one. I'm Callie Jean Morgan, by the way."

Sophie jumped up and ran around the table. Her tiny arms reached around and hugged the life out of a stunned and stiffened Callie. "Everyone says you're here to stay. We need more natives." She brushed Callie's arm with fingers bedecked with three rings, and seemed to not notice the scar. "You're the right age; we could have fun together." She sat back down. "So who's the striking blond young man who left here a while ago?"

"My son Jeb." Callie tugged her shirtsleeve back over the scar. "He heads to college in the fall."

Sophie squealed like an eighth grader abuzz with her BFF about the prom. "I have a son at the College of Charleston and a daughter who's a high school senior. Zeus and Sprite."

Callie sucked her lip to avoid breaking out in laughter.

Sophie wriggled. "Please tell me your son's going to the same school. I have a sixth sense about such things."

Then she ought to know, shouldn't she? "Yes, he is. How old is your son . . . er, Zeus?" Entertained at the names, Callie tried to envision these kids.

"Twenty. Let's take them out for seafood. When are you free?" She scrunched her nose. "You don't actually work or anything, do you?"

"I'm taking a sabbatical . . . of sorts. You?"

Sophie blew out a smug, fat gust of air. "Alimony and child support." Her thin lips shifted to the side. "I'm not rich, but I can't complain. My ex played pro football for a few years. When he hooked up with a groupie, I found a new home at the beach. Best move I ever made." She waved her bejeweled fingers. "Trust me, he can afford it. Plus, I teach yoga in the bar at the Pavilion."

"Yoga at a bar," Callie repeated, remembering Beverly's warning about the yoga neighbor, unable to envision her mother contorted on a mat in a bar.

"Come to my next lesson," Sophie said. "My schedule's on a magnet in your basket. First visit's free." She leaned back as she analyzed Callie's body. "You're a runner."

Callie crossed her legs, not surprised that her mother found Sophie too ethnic. "I do run. I'd intended to map out a five-mile route before you showed up."

Sophie nodded, knowingly. "That basket will do you good, girl. I've included a blue quartz crystal for healing your mind and body, along with a CD of music made by crystal bowls to unlock the Chakras, your energy centers. A lavender and flaxseed face mask. And a black candle to light on each New Moon for good luck."

Holy hippie. "Thanks," Callie replied. "I'm fresh out of lavender and flax."

Sophie cocked her head, all cute and understanding. "Go ahead and laugh. I can tell you need my class. You're strung like piano wire. Not enough fluidity in your life." She pointed up to Callie's head, then down to the floor. "I see it all over you. Bet you can't put your hands flat on the floor."

"Yes, I can."

Sophie scowled. "Show me. Feet together, not spread."

Reaching down, Callie stopped midway, wondering why she had to prove anything. "What's wrong with being a runner?"

"Oh, nothing if you run for the right purpose and don't beat yourself up in the process. I'll teach you to love your muscles, not just work them."

This subject needed changing. "Care for something to drink?"

Sophie scouted the kitchen for a clock. "It's lunchtime, and I normally wait until five, but hey, since we're celebrating your move, I'll break the rules. A light gin and tonic, please."

Callie halted at the cabinet door to the glassware. "I was thinking iced tea, but I'm sure my mother has the makings of a drink around here." She pulled out two tumblers and found a new bottle of Bombay Sapphire in the freezer and two one-liter bottles of tonic in the back of the refrigerator. *Yay, Beverly.*

Callie had all the time in the world and no place to be, so why not drink in the middle of the day? "I'm surprised you didn't know my parents since you live next door. My mother took your yoga class, I believe."

"Oh, I know your folks."

Gin glug-glugged into the glasses. Callie was disappointed with herself for being caught unawares. "So you know who I am."

"Me and half the island. The daughter of the Middleton mayor. You married some Yankee."

Callie's shoulders relaxed at the generalization. "Yep, that's me."

Merely being the mayor's daughter suited her fine. Thank goodness Beverly hadn't spread Callie's tragedy over Edisto. Another rare tick mark in the positive column. Two in one day was a record.

Callie sat back at the table. "So why haven't you asked me to dish about next door?"

Sophie's short hair shook as her earrings bobbed under her ears. "Not here," she said. "Your house is clean. Outside. Later." Then she hunched over and whispered conspiratorially. "But I definitely want to know the details."

Callie's phone rang. "Well, hello Mother," she mumbled at the caller ID.

Sophie waved. "Tell her hey for me. If she knows I'm here, she might not talk long. Honey, I know how to handle the Beverlys of this world."

"Mother," Callie answered.

"Hello, dear. I wanted to check on you and Jeb. Gracious, what a shock! I barely slept last night. Have they caught the man?"

The lightheartedness of the last hour fell away at the image of Papa Beach's home violated, his life stolen. "It's too soon, Mother, but we're taking precautions."

With no weapon found and no suspect to compare prints against, assuming he was in the system, the perp could most likely elude authorities. Police departments only announced the ones they caught, not the ones that got away . . . more often than the public knew.

"Well, stay in touch with the police, dear. Keep us apprised."

"I will, Mother. Thanks for the gin, by the way."

"Oh, I forgot that was there."

Sure she did, like Callie knew nothing of Beverly's own five-o'clock habit.

"Hello, Mrs. Cantrell," hollered Sophie.

"Who is that?" Beverly asked.

"Sophie Bianchi," Callie replied.

Silence hung on the phone a moment. "Oh, that Bohemian woman," Beverly replied dryly. "Be careful. She's an odd bird. Circus material, in my opinion."

Callie loved her new neighbor even more.

A siren blurped down the street once, then twice, as if trying to part traffic.

Sophie leaped up and ran to the front door.

"What was that?" Beverly asked, breathless in her drama. "Are they going back to Henry's house?"

Little happened on the island to warrant a siren, so maybe a taste of drama was in order. "Let me go check it out, Mother. Probably a traffic stop. The tourists are pretty thick."

"Let me know—"

"Later, Mother." Callie pocketed her phone and hurried to the porch. Sophie stretched over the railing and studied the house fronts along Jungle Road.

"Where did they stop?" Callie held a hand over her eyes, feeling every bit the rubbernecker like those she'd seen yesterday.

"Two places south of mine. That's the Rosewood home." Sophie spun around, mouth open and eyes wide, like a child longing for her turn to perform. "You want to run down there with me?"

Oh God. Every crime came with the pain-in-the-ass snoops who craved a glimpse of blood.

Sophie scrambled down the stairs. "Get your sunglasses!"

Callie snared her glasses and locked up only to find Sophie running back up the steps to grab her wrist.

"Girl," Sophie said, shaking her head. "We've gotta talk about that Fort Knox habit of yours. Come on!"

By the time they reached the Rosewood residence, a dozen people gathered to gape. Callie stayed back under a tree next door, arms crossed, wishing to stay invisible after her exhibition on the beach the day before. However, Sophie dove in, interrogating everyone, flitting in and out of the gathering onlookers like a chipmunk searching for the right nut.

An empty Edisto Beach PD vehicle sat in the drive. A woman's voice drifted from inside the house, distraught but not over-the-top crazy.

Someone in the crowd spoke up. "Anybody else get murdered?"

Callie shook her head at the public's thirst for calamity, then recognizing the ranks she'd fallen into, she took another step back.

A truck slowed, the driver studying the commotion. Sophie went to him. They conversed and then he drove on. She returned to Callie. "What're you doing standing back here?"

"Staying out of the way." Callie glanced around, then whispered, "Find out anything?"

"Yeah, that was Jackson Peters in the truck. He's the handyman around here and was working across the street, and honey, he don't miss a trick. Somebody broke into the house while the Rosewoods shopped in Charleston. Sometime between eleven and one. They barely missed him." She hugged herself. "What if they'd been home? Like Mr. Beechum." Her aqua eyes widened as her voice hitched an octave. "Could've been another murder, you know?"

"The Rosewoods live here year round?" Callie asked.

"Yes," Sophie exclaimed. "Does that mean something?" She gasped. "And both cases have been on our street! What if they're targeting everyone on this road?"

"It was just a question, Sophie."

A dead body one day and a burglary the next. How did anyone *not* overthink this?

Another Edisto blue and white pulled up. Seabrook's long legs stepped out as the door opened. He headed toward the stairs, the locals shouting, calling him by name as if he were a celebrity walking the red carpet at the Oscars. He stopped when he saw Callie and Sophie. Speaking into his radio, he veered in their direction.

"Ladies," he said, then peered at Callie. "Can we talk?"

Sophie winked and returned to the small throng of the rumor machine. Heat warmed Callie's cheeks at the unspoken insinuation.

Seabrook nodded in greeting. "Mind if I run some of this by you?"

Callie straightened, welcoming the overture to express her professional opinion. "What you got?"

"No *body* this time," he said.

"Always good," she replied.

He glanced for eavesdroppers. Callie stepped closer, his sandalwood aftershave striking her nose.

"The burglar stole money kept in a dresser drawer," he said. "Left the jewelry. Sounds like a kid or a tweeker, right?"

She shrugged.

He took his voice even lower. "But then he poured himself a Jack and Coke over ice and had a drink. Barely a ring left on the table."

"Doesn't sound like a kid or a drug addict." She scanned the crowd. "A bragger with something to prove, and he needs an audience to do it."

Seabrook nodded. "Yeah, but what he did next connects him to the Beechum murder."

She focused on him instead of who was listening. "How?"

"This guy deposited a 1903 antique silver dollar on the table. Like he was leaving a tip."

A calling card. A warning went off in her head, the way it used to on a fresh case with all its clues scattered around for the gathering. "One of Papa Beach's coins?" she asked. A 1903 would be one of the Morgan dollars. Worth a hundred or so, per Papa.

"We think so. We'd like you to look at it, if you don't mind."

"Sure. You know where to find me. In the meantime, check out a man named Jackson Peters. He was supposedly working across the street at the time and may have seen something."

Seabrook winked. "Thanks. I'll do that."

"And has anyone called Pauley Beechum?"

"Yeah," he said. "I notified him about his father's death late last night."

"How'd he take it?"

"He seemed distraught, but due to his father's age, wasn't surprised," Seabrook said.

"Was he at home, or did you call him on his cell?"

"Cell," he said, forehead knotting. "Why?"

Seabrook's puzzlement showed he hadn't considered the son in this crime at all. Callie, however, hadn't ruled him out. Family always served as the first, and best, suspects. Pauley's whereabouts needed confirmation. Then she told herself to tone it down. She wasn't lead investigator here. She wasn't any kind of investigator anywhere. "He and Papa weren't close, is all. I'd want to know where he was when Papa died."

"Okay, um, thanks. But what do you think about the coin thing?"

She shook her head. "Don't know, but I'm sure you'll figure it out."

Her head played all the options thus far. She couldn't help it. It'd been over a year since she'd worked a case, but her instincts still kicked in.

Ordinarily, she'd have considered these two crimes unrelated, but the coin changed things. This criminal left his mark. Chances were he would leave it again. This was a personality who'd tasted getting away with murder and wanted to let the island know he enjoyed it.

And unless she was premature in her logic, he enjoyed playing the game with the permanent residents.

He knew these people along with their daily itineraries. He might strike again . . . and take more chances. Getting away with murder empowered some people to raise the bar. And heaven help her, a part of her wished she could be there when it happened.

Chapter 6

AS CALLIE CONTINUED to chat with Officer Seabrook, Sophie stared over her shoulder from the herd of snoopy onlookers in the Rosewood yard. The afternoon blazed with heat, the sea breezes lazier than usual, but the weather didn't deter the curious from the burglary scene.

"What about SLED, the state boys?" Callie asked. "Don't little towns get that sort of assistance? Especially with a murder."

"Those guys came and went like a rain shower," he replied. "They reckon Beechum was a robbery turned homicide by a local kid. A *call-us-if-you-need-us* thing. Guess they're slammed, too."

The tall, soft-spoken man carried a genteel way about him, a quiescence that maintained itself amidst everyone else's agitation. Not the usual beat cop nature. She liked it.

"Seems we have a sophisticated crime spree," Seabrook said. "Without a police chief, we can use the help of a professional." He dipped his chin and regarded her. "You showed up just in time to assist, Detective."

The offer blindsided her. Tempting, yet frightening. That way of life represented the highest peak and lowest valley of her life, and she was afraid of riding that roller coaster again. Still . . .

"I left the badge in Boston," Callie said, the words painful in so many ways.

"Badges are a dime a dozen," he said. "What we lack is experience. I doubt you left your instincts back there."

She diverted the subject. "So your ill-tempered Deputy Raysor is here because you're short of uniforms?"

Seabrook scrunched his face and shook his head. "Colleton County always shares a deputy or two with us. Our old chief got offered a job in North Carolina—bigger beach. I'm the interim honcho for now, leaving us with six uniforms. No replacement yet."

"Budget?" she asked.

His mouth gave her a halfhearted upturn. "Town council tends to think the lure of the beach will offset salary expectations."

She got that. She'd only shopped big city departments out of college for that very reason—salary. "Hope you get the job."

Walking away, he spoke over his shoulder. "Not applying for it."

She watched him stroll away into a crowd that seemed to settle down with his presence. He took two stairs at a time up to the residence.

She'd have smiled at the *dime a dozen* comment if the situation weren't so dire. People came to this secluded piece of the world for solitude, where the community allowed little commercialism, no franchises, and no motels except for the Wyndham at the tip of the island that housed the more urbanite souls. Eighty percent of the housing properties were rentals. The seven hundred long-term residents usually harbored a backstory—pre-Edisto. This skinny stretch of land between ocean and marsh was about living in the moment with the tide. Anyone could walk in your front door or share a drink on your porch.

Unfortunately, now a criminal seemed keen to join in, too. Six cops weren't nearly enough to cope if this guy got weird. However, her doors would stay locked, her Glock and .38 handy, and the Sophies of the island could continue to knock to be let in.

Callie walked the two short lots home, glad for her sunglasses. The three o'clock sun was fierce. Sophie caught up, her beads and bangles rattling like a New Orleans parade. "You leaving?"

"Nothing to see." She could easily bid the woman goodbye. However, something about this *Tinkerbell* breached Callie's steel wall of trust. John had been her last close friend. Besides Stan, of course.

Sophie took her arm. Callie stiffened mildly at the unexpected intimacy.

"Love to know what Mike Seabrook said to you all private-like back there," Sophie said.

Callie exaggerated a Southern drawl. "Sugar, he was just asking about you."

Sophie sucked in. "Really?"

Wow, this woman was too easy to mess with. "No, he asked me if I remembered anything more about the Papa Beach incident, that's all."

"Humph. Seemed more than that to me."

"Not interested, Sophie. He's all yours."

They climbed Callie's porch steps. Sophie rolled her eyes and clicked her tongue at the sign of keys. Callie swung open the door and surveyed the immediate rooms. "Think of it as locking in the sage for safekeeping."

The AC kicked on as they entered the kitchen.

"What's your man-story anyway?" Sophie reached for a napkin from a shell holder in the middle of the kitchen table and wiped away the condensation puddled under her now-warm glass. She grabbed more ice from the fridge, as if the kitchen was her own.

Callie dumped the warm contents of her melted drink down the sink and refilled with water. "No man-story. I used to be married to a great guy. Now he's gone."

"Oh," Sophie said. "Dead or divorced?"

The glass halted inches from her lips, then lowered. "You would ask that? Seriously?" Callie didn't talk about John with strangers. Or anyone, for that matter.

"I could ask your mother," Sophie said, trying to tease.

Callie gulped her water, reminding herself Sophie was riding the crest from the metaphysical energy of the crowd down the street. "If she intended to tell you, you'd already know, wouldn't you?"

Sophie's face softened. "I just sensed something there, Callie."

Callie went to the refrigerator. "You want cheese with that drink? I've got grapes and can slice an apple. Hopefully my paring knife won't slip in your direction."

"Go ahead. Keep to yourself, sweetie, but I'm telling you, it's not good for you."

Callie washed an apple, then rubbed it dry with flourish. She ripped the stem off. "You're naïve as hell, you know that?"

"Maybe, maybe not."

The knife sank into the pulp, banging as it hit the cutting board, splitting the fruit cleanly in two. "Drop the topic, Sophie."

AN HOUR LATER, Sophie left for home two gins looser than when she arrived. A daydreamer, Callie deduced, crimping a blind to watch her neighbor take the steps, but Callie had to admit Sophie had rolled with all of Callie's punches. She tried to guess how children named Zeus and Sprite would turn out under the parental influence of such an ethereal spirit.

Nowhere near the likes of Beverly.

She never wanted to be Beverly to Jeb. Like any teen, he chomped at the bit to be free of oversight, but not like she'd been with *her* mother. He bent over backwards to tend to Callie, being the strong arm on days she found tough to endure. She wanted him to attend college with its social exposure and independence, like any kid his age, and not have to worry about her.

She'd envisioned this time with John, the two of them teary-eyed as they helped Jeb carry his belongings to a dorm room, Bonnie darting around their legs asking a hundred questions.

Callie poured the gin and tonic she denied herself in front of Sophie. A tall one in an iced tea glass, suiting her thirst. She'd abstained long enough. As she headed to the porch on the screened and shaded side of the house, the turntable snared her attention, along with its assorted array of seventies-and sixties-era music. Most of the LPs were her mother's Neil Diamond vinyls. Twenty of them. Placing her drink on the mantle, she stacked the player with three of them, marveling the record changer still worked, not the least surprised her mother hadn't replaced this music on CD.

She blew dust off the needle like Beverly had taught her as a child. She tapped it with her index finger to check the speakers. A smile crossed her face at remembering the routine. She turned the player on. As the arm lifted and the album dropped, she retrieved her gin. At the opening bars of *Crack-lin' Rosie*, she flopped into a deeply cushioned Adirondack chair out on the porch and laid her head back, singing the words softly to herself, waggling her right foot to the beat.

Beverly should have named her Rosie, considering the million times she'd played this song. It hit the music stores a few years before Callie was born. She knew when most of Diamond's songs came out, having listened to her mother prattle on about the genius of the music. Each song sank Callie deeper into the cushion.

At the end of each album, she emerged to refill her glass.

As a jogger passed her home, she remembered she hadn't run. She'd force herself back to that routine in the morning. She wasn't old enough to go soft yet.

She sipped her drink, light-headed.

Callie hadn't come here to solve cases, but the taste of the island's crime spree had whetted her appetite. But she didn't do that anymore. So, what the hell was she *supposed* to do?

A question she hadn't wanted to face.

Her deep exhale barreled out from an imprisoned frustration she couldn't pin a label to, and she was grateful to have no one around to question why she seemed down. Just birdsong and distant murmuring waves. Low tide from the sound of it.

The turntable's arm lifted, whirred, and clicked off. That final click comforted her in an odd way. Silence pervaded the night, her porch, her thoughts. *Just me alone in this place. Just like it'll be in the fall.*

Her unsteady gaze settled on the knickknacks of coral and aqua hanging around the screened porch. Faded yellows and baby blues accented decorative buoys hung on white rope; a miniature sailboat floated on a rattan end table next to coasters made of shells and glued sand.

The first place of her own. Residing the past year in her mother's Middleton shadow had stunk, often yanking her back into an old attitude she thought she'd outgrown. Two weeks after her graduation from the University of South Carolina criminal justice school, she'd moved out of her parents' home and hadn't told them where she was headed until she packed her car. Beverly assumed her dramatic I'm-so-hurt role, her father puffing up all protective of his wife, as if Callie had betrayed them. Maybe she had, but years later, nothing seemed to have changed.

An ice cube slid into her mouth, and she crunched it after sucking the alcohol off.

So why the hell had she run home this time, knowing exactly how the age-old scenario would play out? Was it the logistics of the Southern family? A culture she couldn't escape? Had Beverly trained her as a child to think of home as the ultimate sanctuary, the only proper place to go when life turned to shit? How ironic. She only felt like shit when she came home.

Her ears rang. She would get up and put on another album, but her legs weighed heavy and cumbersome. The instant she used them, the room would spin, and she wasn't sure she'd make it inside, much less aim her mother's precious record player needle on one of her oh-so-priceless albums. Besides, the music still played in her head.

"I'm home, Mom." Abruptly she sat up. She'd never realized how much Jeb sounded like John.

His feet slapped the floor in his flip-flops. Finally, he poked his head out the door. "Mom?"

She held up her empty glass. "Right here, pretty boy."

He stepped out holding an empty gin bottle and regarded her with a mixture of surprise and disappointment. "How long have you been out here?"

"Have no clue. How long you been gone?" she slurred, then winked.

"Ms. Morgan?" Officer Seabrook walked out of the darkness behind Jeb. "Er . . . I came to show you the coin."

"Damn," Callie whispered, and then giggled. "Busted!"

"Geez, Mom." Jeb squatted in front of her. "How many did you have?"

Callie threw her head back and closed her eyes. She held out her arms, still holding the glass. "Here I am, drinking at home. I'm not driving, not wandering the street. Yet"—and she pointed a finger—"I'm judged."

Jeb's face took on a pained, red-hued expression.

Seabrook laid a hand on the boy's shoulder. "I'll come back tomorrow, son."

Jeb flinched and reacted in a raised voice, as if having to save face in front of the tall cop. "Mom, what's the deal? I thought you quit doing this sort of thing."

Callie laid her head back. "No big deal, Jeb. I needed something to ease off to sleep."

Seabrook moved back to the doorway. "I'll call first next time." He left and spoke over his shoulder. "Y'all take care."

Jeb continued to kneel and study his mother. After several heavy seconds, her man-child shook his head and went inside.

Callie listened for his bedroom door to close then slowly stood. Leaning on the wall for balance, she ventured inside, lifted the albums on the spindle until they caught, then restarted the player. As *Cracklin' Rosie* played again, she filled her glass with tap water and chugged the contents with two aspirin, as usual, singing and humming random phrases along with Neil.

Back outside, she collapsed in her chair, sloshing water on her khakis. She tilted her head back and listened, humming.

And when the song was over, she cried.

Chapter 7

DEEP, REVERBERATING jolts of pain pierced Callie's head at the unholy buzz of her alarm. She shut off the noise with a blind sweep of her hand, shoving the clock off the back of the nightstand. *Damn it to hell!*

She hated hangover sludge in her veins. It would take a full day of heavy hydration to resettle her system. Digging her head into her pillow, she mashed the cool percale against her flushed cheek, while her alcohol-logged mind fought a tug-of-war with her conscience about whether to drag her butt out of a perfect-temperature bed.

The overhead fan whirred. A truck rolled by like a freight train. The odor of cooked eggs floated from the kitchen, and her stomach roiled.

Voices drifted under her door.

Flinging the coverlet back, Callie dropped off the high bed, her feet smacking the floor, and she reached for the nightstand at the unexpected room-spin. A stomach lurch reminded her she hadn't eaten dinner, much less breakfast.

She opened a tiny crack in the door. Jeb busied himself in the kitchen dressed and fresh, chatting to a boy roughly his age. The guest had black curly locks that danced about as he spoke. A white tank top accented his deeply tanned muscular build.

Excellent. She smiled. Jeb brought home a friend.

She hadn't exercised in days, and her head hurt, but as much as she wanted to add a day to that neglect, she wouldn't. Back in Middleton, after one of Beverly's marathon cocktail hours, Callie would rise, dress for a run, then sit for a half hour with her head in her hands trying not to ralph into the community garbage can. She'd abstain for three days, return to the track, then get roped into drinks again with her mother.

She didn't have to do that here. And she wished she'd told herself that last night.

Callie threw on her running shorts and standard long-sleeve sports top to cover her arm. After wiping a cold washrag across her face and brushing her teeth, she made for the kitchen.

"Hey, guys," she said, rounding the breakfast bar, almost bumping the guest. "Who's this?"

Jeb put an omelet on a plate. Oatmeal filled two bowls, something foreign dotting the soft beige surface. "Zeus Bianchi," Jeb said, setting a plate and bowl in front of his friend. "Is that a cool name or what? He's starting a fishing guide business."

"Hey," Zeus replied. "Mom told me all about you. A detective, huh? Awesome."

Jeb set the skillet back on the stove. "You want me to fix you some of this, Mom?"

She scrunched her nose, her gut not so eager to engage with food. "I'll pass." She peered over one of the bowls. "I think this is oatmeal, but what's with the weird bits hiding in it?"

Zeus's laugh bounced easy, deceptively confident for his age, as if he owned the air around him but would be happy to share it. "Pumpkin seeds, flax, and goji berries. I promised to try Jeb's breakfast, including the yolk and whatever non-meat item he wanted, if he'd try mine."

"Enjoy the heat," she replied, wondering about the level of spice Jeb hid in those eggs.

"Oh, I can handle the sun," Zeus asked. "I grew up in this heat."

"Mom," Jeb interrupted before she revealed his surprise of jalapenos, onions, and Tabasco. "You all right after yesterday?"

"Of course," she lied.

Zeus leaned on his elbow and wove a large coin from one finger to another, then back again, like a parlor trick.

Callie caught herself watching it, a little disturbed. "What kind of coin is that?"

Zeus ceased the flipping and studied the piece as if for the first time. "Says dollar on it. I found it on the kitchen table next to Mom's orange juice this morning when I got back from fishing. Figured she was baiting me to do the dishes."

Geez. Sophie's house? She reached out. "May I see it?"

The silver dollar read 1921, another Morgan, and, if she was right, one that remained in immaculate shape from its life on Papa Beach's wall. Tingling apprehension sprinted through her. Sophie's open house had welcomed a secret visitor.

"Where's your sister?" Callie asked.

Zeus's brow lifted to the edge of his long curls. "With Mom at yoga, why?"

Thank God no one had been in the house when the visitor entered. However, having Chelsea Morning sandwiched between Sophie's and Papa's crime scenes now gave Callie a vulnerable sense of exposure.

"I'll give you ten bucks for the coin. I'm sort of a collector," she said.

Jeb turned from his kitchen duties, puzzlement on his face.

"Seriously?" Zeus asked. "How much you think it's worth? I might want to keep it."

"Tell you what," Callie said, holding the dollar up between two fingers. "Next time I go into Charleston, I'll get it appraised." She lifted three fingers. "Scout's honor. You can have the money, whether from me or the appraiser. Deal? Least I can do for Jeb's new friend and the son of my new neighbor."

Zeus beamed. "Sure! I'm supposed to be able to trust a detective, right?"

She winked. "When does your mom get home?"

"Nine thirty if she doesn't get to talking too much. Hey, I really appreciate this." Zeus stood and held out his hand. "Great to meet you."

Callie returned the firm shake. "A pleasure, Zeus. Bet that name gets attention."

"Girls love it," he said, grinning.

"Yeah," she laughed. "I suspect so."

"You seem calmer than I expected," Zeus said to her. "Everybody's still talking after seeing you on the beach with a gun."

Callie fought the wince and shrugged. "I only do that to get Jeb to come home for dinner."

"Mom!" Jeb protested, as Zeus chuckled.

"See you guys later. Time to run."

"*Namaste*, Miss Callie."

Outside, she bent her left leg, her foot touching her butt to stretch her thigh. She jogged the three blocks up Cupid Street toward the ocean. The ninety-degree temperature promised a record high by afternoon.

At Beach Access 7, waves licked the pier's posts forty feet out, the salt spray flavoring gusts of wind. The tide was rolling in, but she still had firm sand to run on. After another hamstring stretch, she tucked the silver dollar in her pocket with her house key and toyed with heading toward the Pavilion to catch Sophie. Not wanting to get roped into yoga, however, she took off southwest toward the beach curve that faced St. Helena Sound. Swimming-suited tourists would dribble out over the next couple of hours, but for now, the beach lay wide open except for the occasional loner stretched out on a towel reading or dolphin watchers studying distant breakers with binoculars.

When she'd worn a badge, she contemplated cases as she ran. Pondering clues and replaying interviews helped carry her until she'd achieved second wind. Then she would run forever, often finding new angles to pursue. After losing John, however, she'd abused the routine, pounding herself into the pavement to earn a stress fracture in her right foot. Being grounded the next three months almost drove her crazy.

That's when she learned to appreciate a good drink.

Callie's shoes dug into the sand as she fought for rhythm. Think. Think about the coins. Were they the burglar's target? Weirder things had happened. Papa didn't talk about himself much, unlike Sophie, so the number of people who knew the collection existed would be limited.

Why kill him, though? Unless Papa had recognized the person or caught him in the act. A young, inexperienced hoodlum could freak out, but the shot was too clean—right against the temple. Too steady.

Her feet found the best sandy strip and fought for a pace. Breathe-two-three-four.

Seabrook mentioned torture. Bruising? Broken bones? Did Papa have hidden assets? Maybe the son-of-a-bitch burglar was simply a sadistic bastard. The thought of the latter sickened her. She'd been right next door, for God's sake. She could've made a difference.

But then Jeb could have been left an orphan, too.

Family. They were always a consideration in a murder. The first people detectives interviewed. Papa's wife had predeceased him, leaving only Pauley, who'd rather take a beating than see his dad.

But what if this crime was a message to *her*, the coin turning up to scare *her*? He could be telling her that he knew exactly who she was and where she lived.

Stupid, stupid, stupid. Now she saw everyone as Russian mafia.

Her hand strayed to her pocket, feeling the Morgan dollar. With Sophie's house wide open all the time, no telling who had made himself at home. She'd been lucky, this time.

Callie had no choice but to take the coin to Officer Seabrook. She owed Zeus fifty bucks for misleading him, the approximate value, she guessed. After all, it wasn't his treasure to keep.

Two piers down, she passed a lanky fisherman in cargo shorts and a loose white T-shirt, his cooler and bait bucket beside him. Licking her lips, she distanced herself from the smell of fish and refocused.

Breathe-two-three-four. Breathe-*deep*-two-three-four.

She passed a half dozen loggerhead turtle nests. Each sported orange tape, four stakes, and a note informing beachcombers not to disturb the unhatched babies. Callie remembered walking along the sand with Papa Beach, inspecting whichever turtle nest he agreed to monitor that season. She'd never once witnessed the hatchlings escape to the sea, but she spent little time at the beach during the summer, the most active season for loggerheads, as well as for tenants willing to pay top-shelf rates for vacations. That's when Chelsea Morning earned its keep, and Callie stayed in Middleton. Maybe this year she'd see hatchlings.

She gulped and fought for air. Geez, what on earth forced her to run today?

A half mile later, Callie sucked salt air like it was gelatin, thick and uncooperative with her stride. Her legs moved like stilts fording mud as she sought any sort of rhythm to make the effort less unforgiving.

Her gut lurched. She gulped down bile and slowed her pace. Before she'd left the house, she should have taken a swig of juice, a few bites of oatmeal. What the hell kind of berries did Zeus say? She imagined that coming back up and gulped again.

Callie pushed on in a slow jog.

As she passed joggers, she threw her shoulders back and quit mouth breathing, pretending to be the strong, ritualistic enthusiast. But the second after they nodded in acknowledgement, she sagged, and her ragged panting returned.

No way would she make three miles, much less five. Ten was bucket list level.

Shit, another jogger. She held her head up, chest out, arms pumping.

He approached, sweat indicating he'd already put in a couple miles. She nodded.

"Hey," he said, slowing. "Hold up."

Callie glanced back and slowed to a stop, grateful for the excuse.

"I know you," he said, as he walked toward her. Hell, he wasn't even huffing.

Her guard went up. Wait. The jogger from behind Papa B's house. Mason Somebody.

"Did you catch the kid pilfering your trash?" He towered at least six-foot two.

Her empty stomach twisted. She stooped over, leaning on her knees. "No, no I didn't. Sorry . . . sorry if I sounded harsh."

A sympathetic smile crept across his thin, tanned face, his dark hair whipping around in the stiff breeze. He wore no ring, but his watch was no doubt expensive. "I heard you were hunting the person who shot Henry Beechum," he said in a nondescript mild accent. "Are you in law enforcement?"

Damn this beach and its small town gossip. She shook her head, tried to rise, then changed her mind.

He reached out. "Well, we need a better introduction than that one. Like I said the other day, I rent Water Spout. Been here three months. Not sure when I'll leave." He spread out his arms. "It's paradise out here."

Callie nodded and gulped, waving off the handshake.

"Hey, tell me what really went down at the Beechum place. I heard—"

Callie vomited, jumping to spread her feet apart to avoid her sneakers. Mason high-stepped backward. "Whoa there!"

Instinctively, she twisted away, closer to the water, and upchucked again. Dropping to her knees, she let nature take its course until she could heave no more.

Just what she needed, another reputation piled on top of her madcap gun escapade, discovering a murder, and being the mayor's daughter. Eyes shut, she touched base with her gut, to see if it had paid all its dues for last night.

Mason took his cap off and soaked it in the surf. "Here," he said, placing it on her head. "That ought to make you feel a little better. Sit here a minute. I'll be right back."

Unable to argue, she plopped her butt in the wet sand. Scooping up water, she washed out her mouth, spitting it back into the sea.

Moments later, Mason returned. "Sip on this," he said, offering her a Coke he apparently bummed from a tenant in a nearby rental.

The sugary bubbles fizzed in her mouth, the ice-cool liquid caressing as it went down. "This is so embarrassing," she said, studying the foam left in a wave's ebb. "Thanks."

He sat beside her and snickered.

"You're laughing at me?" she asked.

"No, no," he said, chuckling.

"Yes," she said, his laughter making her smile. "Yes, you are."

Taking the cap off her head, he soaked it again and positioned it back on her limp hair. "I puked one pier over the first week I moved in. Must be a rite of passage or something."

"*Or something* is right." She sipped again slowly.

"I'm Mason Howard," he said. "In case you forgot."

"I'm—"

"Callie Jean Cantrell Morgan," he recited. "The Middleton mayor's daughter who owns Chelsea Morning."

Of course he knew.

He shifted to lean stiff-armed. "You're the celebrity of the week. I'm sure that'll change by the weekend when they find someone else." He touched her sleeve. "Why the long sleeves, by the way? Aren't you hot?"

"Heat has nothing to do with my sleeves," she said hesitantly.

"Then let me ask something more discreet. What brings you to Edisto?"

"I'm just kicking back for the summer." All he needed to know.

"Like me." He grinned, warm and comical.

"What do you do?" she asked.

"I'm a trust fund baby dabbling in real estate. Grandfather made his money in restaurants. Ever heard of Angus Steer Steakhouse?"

She dusted sand from her thighs, trying not to be impressed. "As in *The Great Steak* jingle?"

Surprise raised his brow. "Nice. Not many Southerners have heard of us."

Damn. Those restaurants are only in Canada. "I—" She caught herself before explaining she used to live in Boston, and she and John made several trips across the border for both business and pleasure. "I used to have family in Buffalo, and I remember the commercials. That song sticks in your head."

He brushed his palms together. "Well, enough about me. Feel like standing?"

Heat crept into her cheeks. "I believe so."

"Let me walk you home." He held out his hand, hoisting her up, the gesture of an interested male. His intentions seemed honest enough, but she wasn't ready to take that step. She almost felt guilty about the calls to Stan, but those were long distance, and he'd known John.

"I'm fine," she said. "Besides, I think I want to walk, at least cover the miles I meant to run."

"May I accompany you?" He tried to take her elbow, and she acted like she lost her balance in the sand and sidestepped.

"Only as far as your place," she said, knowing Water Spout's three stories surveyed the beach a mere three piers away.

"Fair enough," he said. "I have a party every Friday night. You may have heard of them. Consider yourself invited."

She took the last swig of her drink, screwed on the cap, and dangled the empty bottle by its neck as they strolled. "A party's not exactly appealing after the mess I just left on the beach. I think I'm giving up gin for life."

He took the empty bottle from her and waved it. "So come have a soft drink. It's not a keg party, Ms. Morgan. Just adults enjoying the end of the week, staring inanely at the ocean—harmless. Feel free to come."

"I'll give it some thought."

"Fine," he said. "But I'm telling you, I think fate keeps throwing us in each other's way."

What a pickup line. It was a small beach and only the second time they'd seen each other. This guy tried way too hard.

Chapter 8

STILL WOBBLY FROM her hangover run, Callie planted a heavy foot on the first of two dozen steps to her porch. Her toe hit the lip of a riser. Several steps up, she went down, slamming her knee on an extruding nail head.

"Son of a stinking bitch!" Her string of curse words rang out nasty enough to embarrass her mother in the next town. She glanced around for listeners as she hobbled up the stairs to the top, let the pain ease, then limped inside. Did she even have a first aid kit? Luckily she was still good with her tetanus shot.

Showered, changed, knee doused in peroxide, she strode into the kitchen for a banana to settle her empty stomach. She lifted the phone to dial Papa Beach for advice on fixing steps . . . and whispered, "Damn," as she hung up, remembering.

What would he tell her to do? He always used *his* tools. Did Daddy even keep tools here?

She grabbed her keys to the storage room on the ground level, under the house. A bright new toolbox sat behind some hurricane boards on a workbench near the window, the name *Cantrell* etched on a brass plate. Callie knew a Beverly gift when she saw one.

The box took both hands to lift, but she managed to haul it out. But no hammer. She couldn't bury nails without a blasted hammer. She pulled out the heaviest tool in the collection, a wrench, and returned out front.

The first swing missed, but the second hit the nail, glancing off oddly. She repeated the ritual, a grunt escaping with the second and third blows.

"Can I help?"

She jerked and spun.

The scruffy, dark-headed man appeared mid-forties, but the wear and tear lines on his sun-weathered skin made his age tricky. His midsection tested the boundaries of a T-shirt. His tool belt hung low and heavy over skinny hips in paint-splotched cargo pants. Sophie's friend from the pickup truck.

"Oh, hey." Callie relaxed, her face flushing. "Trying to fix this board."

The crow's feet around his eyes deepened. "Not with a wrench, you're not. Let me give it a go." He lifted his hammer from its belt loop, motioned her aside, then in one hit sank the nail. He dropped the hammer back in its home. "Right tool for the job is half the battle."

"Well, I don't have a hammer."

His thin lips parted in a homely smile. "I figured. Who'd choose a wrench over a hammer?" He rested an elbow on the railing. "Let me guess. Henry did all your work."

"Pretty much." She smiled, proud to give the old man credit. "Callie Morgan."

"Yep, the mayor's daughter. I'm Jackson Peters." He shook her hand tightly, his calluses rough. "Call me Peters. Tried to get your daddy to hire me a few times, but he stayed dang loyal to Beechum."

She wasn't surprised. "Papa Beach was like family to us."

"A lot of people will miss that old buzzard," he replied.

Her smile dimmed. "I remember him as a rather sweet gentleman."

Peters held his palm out. "Nothing against the guy. Hope they catch his killer real soon. Hate that happened around here." He carefully smoothed his hand over the railing. "Want me to run a sander over these? Slap on a new coat of paint? And I can take care of all your loose steps."

Papa B came without charge, only expecting a weekly dinner or a chat on the porch in return. Peters would have to be paid, but he seemed honest enough. "How much?" she asked.

His gaze traveled up the stairs and back down again. "You buy the paint, and I'll do the rest. Two hundred dollars. An introductory offer to my services. How's that sound?"

Callie nodded as she pondered the offer. "I'll take it on one condition."

Peters didn't falter, accustomed to haggling. "And what would that be, miss?"

"Tell me how you knew so much about the Rosewood burglary. I saw you talking to my neighbor." She nodded toward Sophie's house. "You knew more than the cops did."

Peters scratched at stubble on his jawline. "I'm the island hired hand. If it ain't new construction, I can do it. Not that I can't *do* the new stuff. Just don't have the right license." He reached into his pocket and pulled out a wad of soiled and wrinkled papers from which he teased out a business card. "There you go. Island Handyman."

She took the bent card. His company name, his name, and a phone number. No address, no website, no email. She held it up. "I don't want to take your last card."

"Got more in the truck. Don't really give 'em out much."

"Where's your office?"

He pointed to the late nineties black Chevy pickup with a dented and scratched white aluminum shell on the back. "Office and home. All I need's a phone."

"You live in your truck?"

"Yes'm. Got a bed in the back that would rival anything in your place. But when it's hot, I often nap where I'm working. Everybody's got a porch 'round here with a hammock or chaise lounge. People leave me sandwiches and such, or I grab a bite at Whaley's or McConkey's. There's always the beach. All these places have outdoor showers. And when somebody wants me, they run down my pickup."

Why not? In a community this small, everybody would know a handyman. It wouldn't surprise her if he had more money than half the residents. You couldn't tell the rich from the have-littles on this narrow strip of sand. Shorts, tank tops, bathing suits, and sun dresses accented the tanned and sun-bleached on Edisto. The dress code applied to all.

And he'd dodged her question.

The first bead of sweat ran down her temple. "So how did you know about the Rosewoods?"

"Had a job across the street from them. Mission Accomplished," he said.

She creased her brow. "Congratulations on finishing the job, but you still haven't answered the question."

"The Effington place. Used to be called Seaclusion, but they sold it two years ago. Bass family owns it now. They call it Mission Accomplished. He sold a patent or something."

"Oh," she said, then, "Oooh!" as she busted out laughing. "I'm sorry," she said. "I know that house as Seaclusion. Guess I've been gone a while. Now, what about—"

"Your question." He grinned and scratched his chin again. "They said you were a cop. Not that I mind."

She enjoyed the exchange. Peters seemed like a decent type. "Come on up to the porch out of the sun. Want a water or Coke?"

"Water's fine," he said.

She retrieved the drink from the kitchen. Back outside, she gave a filled glass with ice to the handyman who'd already claimed one of her rattan chairs. She assumed a place on a matching love seat.

He chugged half the glass and rested it on his knee. "I was washing paintbrushes at the faucet off the corner of the house when I heard Ms. Rosewood scream. I ran over. Mr. Rosewood was inside on the phone calling Mike."

"Mike Seabrook at the police department?"

"Yeah. While he was doing that, Ms. Rosewood asked me if I saw any-body go in or out of the house." He drawled as he spoke, deadpan, as if burglaries happened daily on Jungle Road. "I said no, didn't see anyone. Asked if I could help, then went back to my job. Finished cleaning up and got in my truck. That's when Sophie flagged me down." He finished his water and rubbed the cool glass across his brow. "That's about it."

"Anybody else hear her scream?" Callie asked.

Peters thought a second. "Don't really know."

"And you didn't see anyone come or go? No car parked in the drive?"

She studied his hands, his nails. Typical for a contractor. His laid-back nature was pure island, like nothing could upset him except rain on a day he planned to go fishing. If he'd done the deed, would he be dumb enough to keep evidence in his truck? But then, he could secret the coins away anywhere around Edisto. Him shooting Papa didn't feel right, though.

"Miss Morgan, I was inside painting a bathroom. Cars don't draw no attention anyway." He looked down his nose. "Screams sure do, though."

An SUV crunched gravel at the house directly across from Chelsea Morning. Peters leaped up. "Uh-oh. The boss lady's home. Let me get back to work. Gotta install a hot water heater and a garbage disposal before I knock off for the day." He danced down the steps and then turned at the bottom. "Appreciate the job. I'll get with you on a date."

A tiny young blonde came out of the house not smiling, shading her eyes in a search.

"Here I am, ma'am," he yelled as he darted across the street. "Did a quick fix for your neighbor, but I'll get right on that water heater."

Callie watched him act all submissive, bowing before he entered the residence.

Here was a guy who moved around the beach unnoticed, yet under everyone's nose. She'd get to know him better when he fixed her steps, a safe outside job that still allowed her to study him. She'd never heard of Jackson Peters, but then her family never had to use him. She itched to ask where he was the evening Papa died, but that was Seabrook's job.

The corner of her mouth curled at her curiosity reflex. Maybe Papa Beach had reached out from the grave to stir her subconscious—or warn her to watch her back. Either way, she welcomed the nudge. Sorting ideas was proactive, perhaps protective, and it sure beat doing nothing.

She just couldn't see herself as a detective anymore. A female PI might work. That definitely would rock the gossip hotline of Edisto, but PI work seemed so amateur. And just how much PI work would there be in this tiny community anyway?

Sophie's vintage powder blue early nineties model Mercedes convertible slowed into her drive and stopped under the wraparound porch. With the houses on pilings, residents parked under the houses.

Callie grabbed her keys to lock up, threw on sneakers, and jogged the thirty yards to Sophie's. She fast-rapped the intricate floral stained glass window in the front entrance. Before Callie met with Seabrook, she wanted to find out how Papa's coin came to be in Sophie's house.

She'd dance carefully. There wasn't enough sage to purge all the negative of Callie's theory that a stranger entered Sophie's home and deposited the token. At a minimum, Callie hoped the petite yoga instructor would feel the need to use her house key now.

"Hey! I'm so happy to see you!" Sophie squealed and drew Callie inside.

"You act like it's been months." Callie followed Sophie's tight posterior to the kitchen bar, impressed not a single body part jiggled when she moved.

Sophie reached for the refrigerator door, the sole of one foot flat against the inside thigh of the leg she balanced on—tree pose. "I need a drink first," she said, studying her shelves. "Had twenty people at yoga this morning, and the air conditioning went out. Threw open every window and door." She shut the refrigerator, carrot juice at the ready. "The waves make great background noise, but I prefer AC to sweating like a whore on a Miami street corner." She plopped a water bottle in front of Callie without asking. "Told Thad he better get that damn machine fixed before my next lesson."

Callie was mesmerized as Sophie flitted around like a hummingbird on speed. "I thought yoga made you calm and harmonious with the world."

"Honey." Sophie hopped up on a barstool. "We all stress. At this very moment I'm seeking the calm." She closed her eyes, raised her legs in Indian style, and laid palms up on her knees. She shifted her toned butt cheeks until she reached a comfortable place.

Who the hell crossed their legs like that atop a barstool?

"I need to ask you a question, Sophie. Can you do whatever that is you're doing and listen?"

"Uh-hmm."

Callie pulled the Morgan dollar out of her pocket. "Do you recognize this?"

Sophie opened an eye. "Not really."

"Study it again. Zeus found it on your kitchen table this morning."

"Maybe it's his." She shut her eye. "He gets paid all sorts of ways. Cash, check, bartering. Someone gave him one of those orange-stamped two dollar bills one time. The kind Clemson University fans leave wherever they go." Her fingertips came together. "Spends like anything else."

"He says the coin must be yours."

"Well, it's not."

"Sophie—"

She lost her pose and held up a finger. "Don't."

Callie leaned her elbow on the counter. "Don't what?"

Sophie unwound faster than a rattlesnake, her finger now in Callie's face. "Don't get all detective on me and bring those bad vibes into this house. I don't know where that damn coin came from. Nothing is stolen. My house wasn't broken into. Nobody was . . . Nothing happened."

Callie held up the dollar again, positive Sophie lied. "Do you collect these?"

"No."

"Did Papa Beach give you this?"

"No," she said louder.

"Have you had a house guest recently who might—"

Sophie dropped off her stool, snatched the coin from Callie's fingers, ran to the back door, and yanked it open. She wound up and hurled the silver dollar toward the marsh.

Callie bolted toward the rail. "I was taking that to the police! Where'd you throw it?"

"No idea. But now that ugliness is out of my life."

"Damn it, Sophie," Callie said.

"Damn is right," Sophie echoed. "Now I've got to cleanse my house, and I think I'm out of sage."

Chapter 9

CALLIE RESISTED THE urge to throttle the woman. "That coin was evidence."

Sophie raised her chin. "It was negative energy."

"How'd it get in your house? Think. It's important."

"The answer's the same no matter how many times you ask. No idea."

Callie acknowledged the dead end and left, still riled at Sophie's obstinacy. With the dollar gone and Sophie in outer space, Callie needed to tell Seabrook about Sophie's house being violated. Nothing stolen, the evidence in the marsh, but still . . . the burglar had struck again.

She started her car engine and sat outside Chelsea Morning, still angry about losing a vital piece of evidence. She glanced next door at Papa's empty gray house, recalling such a contrast in personality compared to her kooky neighbor on the other side.

Inside the fabric of Papa's place, she'd spent weekends at the kitchen table eating peanut butter cookies. He'd planted sea tales in her head by day, which later morphed into mermaid dreams at night. He'd attended John's funeral.

She'd only been yards away when he died alone, his assassin vanishing just out of her reach. She owed Papa. He'd done more for her than she could ever repay. She had the skills. He'd expect her to use them.

There'd be other clues; she was sure of it. This burglar's propensity to taunt the authorities would be the hallmark that would cause him to slip up. She'd seen it before.

She drove down Jungle Road, uncertain. Her sleuthing had led to her husband's death, so getting involved in a case now put her on edge. Her frenzied investigation after the fire had gotten her nowhere except burned out and broken. Then, when she'd found herself unable to juggle vengeance and tending a child, she'd quit . . . quit to raise John's son safely.

But Jeb wasn't safe with this creep on the loose.

The Edisto Police Station sat on a cramped triangular patch of land containing the station, town hall, fire department, and public works. A free water station filled jugs for those who couldn't stand the salty tap water. A fire truck parked outside, wet from a wash. The whole place sported brick and beige vinyl siding, with a gray tin roof. An ancient oak reached seventy feet up, a canopy almost as wide, surrounded by a three-foot retaining wall.

As she opened the glass front door, air conditioning sucked her in.

Crisp, clean, quiet. Her sneakers squeaked against linoleum. Seabrook, leaning over the largest of three desks, looked up.

The room was barely larger than Callie's living room and kitchen. A laminated Edisto map swallowed up an entire wall. A bulletin board, commendations, and festival posters hung on the other walls along with the town seal and pictures of hand-shaking politicians and council members. Two full-size wall safes, one slate-colored and one black, sat in a vigil behind the desks. Space, technology, and furniture, but not people. Something unbalanced about that budget, in her opinion.

A receptionist greeted her. "What can we do for you?"

"I got this, Marie. This is Callie Morgan, from the Cantrell house." Seabrook walked over. "What brings the big city detective to our beachfront Mayberry?"

"Can we talk?" Callie asked. "And I'd like my Glock back, please."

He held open the small swinging door. She followed him past the only private office, most likely the ex-chief's.

He motioned her to a simple metal chair in front of his spartan desk. A nameplate, but no family photos. No second grader-designed paperweights or crayon pictures. The closest thing to a personal touch was a plastic cup from a real estate agent on the beach, the one who claimed to be the best on the Carolina coast. Bright red with a gold wave, it was stuffed with pens from what appeared to be every commercial interest on Edisto.

"So," he said, sitting. "What's up?"

She still loved his calm. "Several thoughts. Might mean nothing. One is a definite problem. I don't know these people like you do. And I'm not trying to do your job . . ."

He rocked his chair forward, those blue eyes concentrating on her. "You're not pissing in my sandbox, Callie. Just tell me what you think. We gathered fingerprints from Rosewood, but they don't match anything in the systems we can access. And we talked to most of the people around you."

She liked this man. She crossed her sneakers. "Did you talk to Mason Howard? I met him again this morning jogging on the beach."

Seabrook wrinkled his nose. "Briefly, but he doesn't know anything. So, ol' Mason ask you out yet?"

"He invited me to one of his Friday parties. Sounds like they're open invitation though."

The officer reared back and raised a brow. "He's got better radar than most boats in the marina for the new single ladies. His Friday night parties are practically on the town council's calendar." He ran his hand flat and level through the air. "Slick. Nothing rowdy, though, in case you decide to go. Had to remind him to keep his beachfront lights off once, but that's it."

"For the nesting loggerheads." She understood how lights disoriented hatchlings seeking the ocean.

"Yeah," he said. "People are protective about those turtles."

"Well, I have no plans to attend one of Howard's parties, but thanks for the concern."

"No problem." He relaxed his shoulders. "Serve and protect."

Seabrook's assurance felt rather endearing. His normal behavior . . . or her presence?

"I also met Jackson Peters," she said. "He worked on the house across the street during the Rosewood break-in, but he only heard a scream. Saw nothing."

Seabrook pulled a notepad over and lifted a pen from his red cup.

She gave him a mild frown. "Is Peters okay? I mean, he seems unusually knowledgeable about everyone's house, when they're home, what they do."

"Callie, you just described half the residents on Edisto. But I don't have a problem with Peters. I'd have more of an issue with Howard."

"You told me he was harmless."

The phone rang for the first time since she'd arrived.

"I distrust his type," Seabrook said, watching the clerk take the call. "The temporary resident who stays long enough to infiltrate the community, entertain himself with the locals, then leave when he's had his fill of our quaintness."

"Anyway," she said, impatient at straying from her mission. "Peters seems to be in the know around here. Wouldn't hurt to connect with him."

"Talk to Jack Peters. Check. Anything else?"

"Yes," she said. "I came across another coin."

His head came up, a no-nonsense glare. "Not at your place, I hope."

"Um . . . not exactly. Sophie Bianchi's son had one when he came over to see Jeb. I talked him into giving it to me."

"Zeus," he said with a mild chuckle as he jotted on his pad. "I'll talk to him, too. You wouldn't know how many coins were in Henry's collection, would you? The son I called in Florida knew zilch about his daddy."

"Twenty-five," she said. "Six Morgans, nine Peace dollars, four Eisenhowers, and one beautiful Double Eagle. I used to count them as a kid. Papa's wife framed them in 1975. The collection's worth a few thousand, I imagine. Some of them were in pristine shape. Want me to write up a list?"

He scrubbed fingers across his scalp.

Crap. He thinks I'm dictating how to do his job. "Sorry. I simply meant—"

"I almost wish they wouldn't turn up."

"Why?"

"More coins—more break-ins." He sighed. "But go on."

She didn't want to overplay her city detective role, but he seemed amiable to the help. "The dollars could easily appear at the Pavilion, the grocery store, any of the gift shops," she said. "Let business owners know so they'll turn them in to you. They don't have to show up at crime scenes."

Seabrook nodded. "So, what year is your coin? Did you bring it?"

"A 1921, and, no. I don't have it."

"Keeping it safe at home?"

She huffed. "I wish. Sophie threw it in the marsh this morning."

His brow arched. "Why the hell—pardon my French—would she do such a dumbass stunt, not that I should be surprised?" He wrote on his pad again. "That ditzy woman fishes without bait on her hook half the time."

"She called it bad vibes."

He shook his head in what Callie saw as complete understanding of who Sophie was.

However, Callie still wanted to share another burden.

Heavy footfalls sounded behind her. "Look who dropped in," Deputy Raysor boomed. "Playing cop again, doll? Isn't that what they call women *up north?*"

Callie twisted around. "I'm not from up *north.*"

He walked around her and leaned his hefty butt against Seabrook's desk. "But you lived up there longer than down here. Sorta tells me you made a choice."

She peered at Seabrook. "I came to help."

Duty belt squeaking, Raysor leaned closer. "You're bored because you're out of the business. And you sure ain't on our payroll, *doll.*"

She turned and prodded a stiff finger at the flushed-faced, red-headed clown. "Quit calling me *doll*, or I'll say something that'll leave a scar. And I promise not to use words over four letters."

"I got a Master's degree, so use whatever size word you want."

Seabrook pushed up abruptly, his chair noisy across the floor. "Can I see you for a minute, Don? In Hank's office?"

"What's wrong with here?" Raysor asked.

"Just come with me, would you?" Seabrook squeezed around Raysor, who sneered at Callie as he turned.

The ex-chief's office was right in front of her. The men's voices muffled through the thin wooden door they'd pushed almost shut. She tried not to listen, feeling awkward being in the same room with the receptionist who pretended not to take notice, either.

Callie repositioned, embarrassed for Seabrook's need to wield his rank in front of her. He meant well, and she appreciated the semblance of chivalry, but she could take care of herself. Back talking Raysor was refreshing, a throwback to her days of detectives versus uniforms when the banter became sport. She searched for a notepad to leave a message that she would catch up to Mike later. Muffles crystalized into words as the men's voices amplified.

"Keep her out of this," Raysor said.

"She could be of assistance, Don."

"You're too busy admiring her T and A to see she's damaged goods."

Geez, Raysor, you're such a charmer. She'd watch his glances from now on.

"She was a good detective from what I hear," Mike said.

What did he hear? And from whom? She caught herself moving to the front of her chair. The receptionist stirred now. Callie shrugged and mouthed *Wow* when the woman glanced over.

"*Used to be* are the pertinent words," Raysor continued. "She's lost her nerve."

"She's already shown her instincts."

"You used to be a doctor. I don't see you suturing up people."

A doctor?

"That's different," Seabrook said. "Besides, we're shorthanded."

"Not that shorthanded," Raysor said.

"When's the last time you reported to Walterboro instead of here?" Seabrook's voice took on an authoritative slant, different from what Callie had heard up to now. "Technically, I'm your reporting officer on this beach. How about some respect?"

Yes! The nice cop had teeth!

The door opened, and Raysor stormed off. Seabrook returned to his seat. After a long moment, he regained his composure. He retrieved her Glock from a drawer and laid it on the desk.

"Maybe we ought to talk outside the station next time," Callie said. "I'm not usurping your authority, or Deputy Raysor's, but I can't ignore what's happening around me. Another set of eyes won't hurt, and it's not like I'm green." Raysor had stirred up a piece of her old pride.

"What kind of friend would I be to Papa B if I slinked off, resigned that the Edisto Beach police force intimidated me? These three break-ins occurred within a stone's throw of my door. I'm protecting my son." She crossed her arms, then unloosed them. "I've investigated too many murders to count, and that doesn't mean running crime scene tape and holding crowds back. I ran *and* solved cases."

She briefly wondered where the hell that came from. But her pride had been slightly scorched by Raysor blowing her off like spent cigar ash and leaving before she could snuff him out. It was probably time to go.

Seabrook regarded her. "Sure you don't want to jump back in the water? You're a natural," he said. "Town council would leap at the chance to hire you, especially since you live here. They might even make you chief."

The flattering job offer destroyed her sermon. A voice in the back of her mind even told her to consider it. But the thought of such a commitment sent a chill across her shoulders.

"Sorry. I'm not job hunting," she finally said and walked toward the counter. "You know where to find me if you have a question, though. I'll call if I think of anything."

Seabrook's warmth returned to his smile. "I'd still like to pick your brain some evening. We didn't finish talking about Sophie."

Crap. Hadn't Sophie been the reason she came in the first place?

They made their way outside, walking into a wall of clinging heat. Raysor hung in the shade of the oak wiping his red brow with a handkerchief.

Seabrook let her go ahead of him on the sidewalk. "How about we talk later?"

Callie pulled out her phone. "Give me your cell number and—"

"You like barbecue?" he asked, as Raysor walked back into the station.

Lowering her phone, she stammered, "Um, sure."

Seabrook gave her his number. "I'll pick you up at five."

She should've seen that coming.

Seabrook broke a wry grin. "What can it hurt? You gotta eat."

Indeed, what harm could come from sharing a pork sandwich? But a simple social outing could wind up extremely uncomfortable. She'd forgotten how to dance this dance.

So she changed the subject. "That coin wasn't there when Sophie went to yoga or Zeus went fishing, assuming you can trust what both of them said. Someone left it on the table thanks to Sophie leaving her house wide open."

He shook his head. "Yeah, the culprit busted Papa Beach's door, but at Sophie's he could waltz in, make himself a sandwich, catch TV for an hour, then wait for her in the bedroom for a repeat of Papa B's brain scramble. She's not thinking about the kids."

"In her twisted way, she thinks she is. Talk to her," Callie said. "She isn't listening to me."

Seabrook studied her. "Guess that's a no for supper?"

Callie unlocked her car. "We don't have proof of a crime now, thanks to her stupid karma stuff. The guy might escalate, not happy law enforcement didn't give his new appearance due recognition. I can see him angered by that."

The cop tapped on the roof of her car. "I'll go talk to her."

She prattled on. "She has an alarm, but I doubt it's been used in years."

Inserting her key in the ignition, Callie stopped before turning it. Ignoring his dinner offer wasn't fair, or polite. "I know it seems like I'm blowing you off, Mike, but it's complicated. I haven't . . ." She watched a grackle preen his reflective blue-black feathers on a picnic table near the water kiosk. What should she say next?

"No need to explain," he replied.

This wasn't right. "Wait, want to go grab a tea someplace?" she asked, fighting to regroup. Tea was safe.

"We're good, Callie." He shut her door and backed away from the car. "Watch yourself." He turned and left with those long, strong strides.

Her forehead drooped on the steering wheel. What would it have hurt to accept his offer? Shit and double damn. She felt so out of step.

She once knew how to deflect male advances and still leave them smiling. Co-workers, CIs, witnesses, didn't matter. They never felt bruised, and they often came away marching to her beat. After months as a private citizen, it was apparent she'd lost those abilities. *Damaged goods*, according to Raysor. Maybe he wasn't so far off the mark.

She drove her Escape off the gravel lot and headed back home, where she would . . . do what? Paint? Cook? Garden? Write a book?

She raised her head. Wait. Socializing was the lifeblood of Edisto. The people just didn't have to know they were being interviewed. Maybe she could slip back in the game after all.

Just not the dating game.

Chapter 10

CALLIE'S DASHBOARD clock read three p.m. The two miles home from the police station seemed like twenty as she wondered how to interview people without being a cop. Family ranked first as suspects, but Papa's son was supposedly in Florida. Next in her sights would be the Rosewoods. Yes, she'd contact them. Then Jackson Peters, the handyman and first non-victim on the scene.

A drink would be nice, especially in this heat. Just one to relax and organize her thoughts as she designed interview outlines. She was sure she could stop at one. Besides, Jeb would be watching her, judging, when he came home.

Halfway down Jungle Road, she spotted a white BMW in her drive. Her shoulders drooped. What was her mother doing here? Callie was seeing more of Beverly at Edisto than she had back in Middleton. Wasn't the point to be out from under her mother's oversight?

Callie parked on the crushed shells. Sweat trickled between her breasts, her underarms moist from talking too long in the heat with Seabrook, the trip home too short for the car to cool.

She felt she'd lost the right to call him by his first name.

She climbed the stairs to the porch and stopped. "Daddy?"

Lawton Cantrell leaned on his knees as he pushed himself up off the rattan settee. "Callie Scallywag. How's the new house treating you?"

A smile blossomed at his presence. Daddies could sure make things right. "Why didn't you let yourself in? It's a hundred degrees out here."

Callie put a key to the lock, but the door swung open at her touch. Her stomach dropped. She lifted the Glock from her purse. "Daddy, did you go in earlier?"

"Only knocked. I can't go letting myself into someone else's home," he said. "What's wrong?"

"Stay here." She shoved the door fully open with her foot and metered through the doorway, gun in a low ready position. "Jeb? You in here?"

She found no sign of Jeb or an intruder, saving the kitchen for last. No coin on the table. Everything was in its place, the back entrance secure. She lowered her weapon. Jeb must've forgotten to lock up.

No, keep looking.

She searched under beds, in every closet, in the cubby under the stairs, finally the attic, sensing an itch she couldn't scratch.

"Callie? All okay?" Lawton called from the porch.

She hustled down the stairs and back to the front door. "Yes, Daddy. Sorry. I overreacted." However, coming or going, the rule was the house stayed secure. She turned the latch behind her father. If Jeb forgot his key, he'd have to ring the bell. She'd scold him for this mindless stunt. This wasn't like him.

"You're just being careful after what happened to poor old Henry," Lawton said, one-arm hugging her. "Glad to see it."

"What brings you here?" she asked, picking up her wallet and keys from the hall table, dropping them off in her bedroom.

"Your mother," he said, enunciating each word. "She's driving me mad."

What a surprise. "Come in. Sit down."

Her father entered the living room and flopped on the sofa. "Pour me a drink, honey."

She went to the kitchen. "What are you in the mood for?" She disconnected from her wariness and reached for glasses.

"Bourbon," her father replied. "Neat."

Uh, oh, no water. He came with serious purpose.

She studied the gin bottle. Maybe now she'd have the one she promised herself in the car.

Serving Lawton's drink before him on a cork coaster edged with shells, she dragged over her rocker and sat with her gin. "So, what's Mother doing to you now?" She tucked a leg under her, her eyes still hunting for other anomalies around her living room.

"Callie," he said, resting his ankle across a knee. "Pettiness doesn't become you."

What was it about her mother than extracted venom out of Callie like a syringe in a vein? "Sorry, Daddy, but you mentioned her, not me."

He took his first sip and inhaled, a tight grin showing his pleasure. "First, what have they done about Henry's murder?" he asked, as if requesting a progress report from his town council.

"SLED pretty much wrote the deal off as a robbery gone awry," she said. "Then we had that Rosewood burglary yesterday, which doesn't set well with me. They found one of Papa's silver dollars in the place. You remember that collection he had on the wall over his sofa?"

Worry deepened the wrinkles around his eyes. "Ben and Sarah Rosewood. They hurt?"

"No." She *had* been thirsty. Half her drink was already gone. "Just a minor theft."

Her father shook his head in disbelief. "Well, I'm sure they can rely on you to help."

She set her glass on the coffee table. He was here to talk to her, not learn about her relationship with the local PD. "Anyway, what about Mother?"

He placed both feet on the rug and inched forward. "I've decided not to run for mayor again."

Callie smiled at the news. Relieved. Seven terms was plenty. A lifetime. "I'm glad to hear it, but is that what you want?"

He crossed his legs and settled back, as if releasing the news took away the pressure. "I never wanted the seventh term, but Beverly reeled when I mentioned leaving politics. You know how she loves that environment."

"Let *her* run for mayor, then."

Lawton glanced sideways at his daughter. "There's a big heart behind all her bluster, Callie. She believes we can do Middleton a lot of good."

"I think you've done your fair share, Daddy." Callie continued rocking. Oh, how she used to hate those campaign years. Beverly, however, glowed for the chance to design a catchy new slogan for the next election.

Lawton put down the glass, his eyes petitioning. "I just ask that you let her know discreetly, at your convenience, that you think it's time I retired."

Callie leaned back, less eager to take on this task than she was to investigate the break-ins. "Don't you think that's your message to deliver?"

He rolled his eyes. "Scallywag, I have, on more than one occasion. It's like I'm talking to a, um, a . . ."

"Rock? A door? A concrete block wall?"

"Callie."

"So what would you have me say, Captain?"

"Tell her that we need time for us. To travel or spend time with Jeb. We've missed too many years of his life already."

Beverly's comment about never seeing Bonnie in Boston rang loud and clear. "Oh, Daddy, not you, too."

"Don't read more into what I'm saying." He sipped thoughtfully on his bourbon. "I was busy being mayor. Y'all were in Boston with careers. Nobody's fault, but I can change that now."

Beverly *might* listen to her. The woman had gone to great lengths to tie her daughter down in the Lowcountry, so maybe she was ready to be receptive to that same daughter. "Okay. I'll try."

"But mentioning Jeb brings me to my other topic." He readjusted, resting elbows on his knees. "He's worried about you. Quite a bit."

"I'm fine," she said, her gaze on her glass. This had to be the main thrust of his visit. Jeb must've presented a fine case to her father to bring him all the way out here.

"You've had a rough time, hon," he said. "We want you to detox from life."

If Beverly had said those words, Callie would've barked back about making presumptuous decisions for her. Hearing them from Lawton, however, just made her sad.

"That's why we gave you the place," he said, "so you wouldn't suffer any time or financial constraints. You're at the beach with no responsibilities other than Jeb. Kick back."

Callie stopped rocking. "Kick back?"

"And give that boy some assurances that you've settled down and moved on. He's scared to death to leave you alone this fall. And don't you say anything about this to him, either." He mindlessly tapped the bottom of his empty glass. "Screaming for him on the beach with a gun, coming home to find you drinking. He thinks you're worse than in Middleton."

She froze. Jeb had gone to them about her binge on the porch? *Crap.* "What reactions does he mean in Middleton?" What had they thought they'd seen in her?

"Our house is nice, but the walls are thin, Scallywag." He pointed at her glass. "And our liquor tab practically doubled."

A flush heated her face. "Anything else?"

"You forgot events."

Dodged them was more like it.

"And your temper showed itself inappropriately at times."

Beverly did that to a person.

Her father's soft gaze turned serious. "Do you need to see a professional, little girl? You've been fragile since the day you arrived. Nobody wants to think a member of his family has a problem, but—"

Callie jumped up from her seat. "Why does everyone think I'm off balance?"

He nodded. "Off balance. That's a good way to put it. And I should've said something earlier, but I guess it took Jeb coming to me to see you're still hurting. I'm sorry, honey. Guess my fathering skills were out of whack."

She paced the living room, thinking of Raysor's description of her—*damaged goods.* So that's how her father saw her, too. If Jeb was so worried about her, why hadn't he locked the door when he went out? Such a simple measure took off some of the pressure. What was so damn difficult about locking a goddamn door?

"Try just being a mom," he said. "For Jeb."

Just a mom?

A regular mom couldn't begin to imagine the atrocities she'd witnessed. A body diced and tossed into three dumpsters in an alley. Drug addicted mothers leaving naked toddlers for two days in unheated, roach-infested housing. Shot, stabbed, scalded victims. Kidnappings with bad endings. Those experiences had taught her to see the potential danger in any situation and hopefully react accordingly. Regardless of what the average person thought, sometimes lightning *did* strike twice in the same spot. Neither she nor Jeb could afford a repeat of that night in Boston.

When she accepted her shield, she'd given up the right to be *just a mom.*

That was like pretending bad guys no longer existed.

Bad guys loved that.

"I'll try, Daddy," she said, knowing he'd never understand. Because making him understand would destroy his ability to sleep without a gun under his pillow, too.

Lawton's phone rang. He held the phone out to read the small print. "I knew she'd catch up to me." He punched a button and took the call. "Hey, Bev. No, I'm not in my office. I'm in Charleston at a meeting. No, I'm almost done. Thanks, but we're grabbing dinner. Yea, love you, too."

He hung up. Callie raised a brow at how easily he lied to her mother. She'd never seen that before.

Lawton put away his phone and defended himself instantly. "She had no business coming here with me, Callie. You can see that."

"Not saying a word, Daddy." Like she would light that firecracker.

He set his empty glass on the bar. "I want to check in with an old friend here, so I'll pop back before dinner, if that's okay. Give me an hour and a half."

"Suits me, Captain. Six okay? By the way, who's the old friend?"

"Nobody you know. I'll be back in plenty of time. Don't go overboard with supper." Lawton left and drove south on Jungle Road. No telling what financial backer had a house out here. Maybe he needed to break the news to the supporter himself that the next election would proceed without him.

Once her father left, she checked the other two doors, the previously open front door still niggling at her. Then she prepped all the food, covered it with plastic wrap, and was putting on water to boil for shrimp when her phone rang.

"Callie Cantrell there? Oh, sorry, I mean Morgan?" asked a man on the other end.

She turned down the burner a notch. "Who's calling?"

"Hey, this is Pauley. Pauley Beechum. You're a hard lady to find."

"Oh, hey, Pauley. I'm so sorry about your father."

He let out a brief moan. "Yeah, rough way to go. Eerie to boot, but it wasn't like he hadn't lived a full life."

Callie could clearly hear the no-love-lost in his voice. "Well, *I'll* miss him."

"I hear you were over there after it happened?"

She hesitated, not wanting to go into the details of an ongoing investigation, and she didn't know Pauley that well. "Yes. I was there."

"Scary."

"A bit, yes."

He let out a *hmmm*. "The police told me the killer took the silver dollar collection. Is that right?"

"That's right."

"Anything else?"

"Don't know, Pauley. You need to ask the Edisto PD."

"Listen," he said. "Watch the house for me, will you? Don't let the cops steal anything. They'll listen to you and probably lie to me. I'll be making a trip soon to sell the stuff. Old junk can be worth a lot, you know, plus I'll be filing an insurance claim for the coins. Probably worth ten thousand dollars, don't you think? And I'm putting the house up for sale. Good time of year for it."

No reminiscing. No choked up words. No discussion about how the world would be less of a place without his father. Just conversation about *stuff* and *junk*.

"The house is fine, Pauley. Again, sorry about your dad."

"Yeah, well, nice talking to you."

Her phone felt icky as she hung up. She turned and stared out the window at the empty house next door. She reminded herself to call Stan to check on Papa's son and his background. Family sucked sometimes.

Jeb walked in. She returned attention to the pot, stirring Old Bay seasoning into the roiling water. "Okay, my man. Who left the front door unlocked this afternoon?"

Bewilderment covered his face.

"Despite what Zeus or Sophie think, you can't go out and leave the house open," she said.

"I'm sure I locked up."

Lawton knocked on the door, and once Jeb peered past the glass, hurried to let him in.

Callie had boiled an ample supply of shrimp, nuked baked potatoes, and sliced cheese to go with crackers and pickles. A small bowl of coleslaw. She poured her father another bourbon and decided she could handle one more gin with supper.

Jeb silently pointed at her glass. Callie gave him a quick wave, her expression saying all was good.

She watched her two men immensely enjoy each other's company over sports updates and island fishing, the boy's relief apparent in the presence of his grandfather. When Lawton said it was time to go, Callie let Jeb walk him to his car. Jeb came back in with a jaunty step. She smiled. Lawton had played his role well.

Empty glasses and plates stacked, she started cleaning up. Shrimp peelings piled up deep in a salad bowl that Jeb carried as he joined her at the sink. "I *did* lock up," he said, returning to the table pick up the last napkins and utensils.

She shut off the water and turned, drying off with a dishrag. But before she could start in on her son, he began a speech of his own.

"I worry, Mom. The whole time I'm with my new friends, I wonder if you're freaking out. That's how I know I locked up." He snatched up the placemats, cramming them in a drawer. "You and me," he said, pointing at his chest, then at her. "We're backwards in this parenting business. I'm watching you instead of the other way around."

He stopped short of saying he was fed up with the job.

Frowning, she moved toward him. "Young man, you have no idea what I suffer in my efforts to raise you. But regardless, I'm still the parental figure here."

"Could've fooled me," he said, arms crossed. "Here I am trying to make friends in a really cool place, but I have to constantly explain about that deranged stunt on the beach. And what about that cop seeing you drunk?"

She bit the inside of her mouth. Heart aching at what amounted to Jeb's long-brewing frustration, she realized anything she said would sound like an excuse, or a discount of his concerns. So she suffered his rebuke.

"I'm sorry," she finally said. "I'll try to do better."

"Oh, Mom." He pivoted to leave then spun back. "You don't even see what you've turned into. Someone told me you puked on the beach this morning. Then I see you drinking again tonight."

"I didn't overindulge," she said.

He shook his head. "People feel sorry for me. Do you know what that feels like?"

Dish towel wound tight in her grasp, she searched for the right words. What would John think of this?

This wasn't teenage angst or selfishness. Jeb's lecture wasn't about what people thought. It was anger infused with love, Jeb clashing with himself over an inability to define what the hell was wrong so he could heal his family. He had no father. She had no husband. Fixing all that was impossible, and they both still struggled with the reality.

She wiped an already clean counter with the towel. "I said I'm sorry." Rushing to him might only make him refuse her embrace, so she held herself in check. "We'll get past this," she finally said.

"Goddamn it, Mom. It's what you always say."

What else could she say? Those words had supported her for over two years now. What other words were there? She blinked as she studied the towel, struggling for an answer she hadn't used before.

Jeb blew out an exaggerated breath, then retreated to his room. Soon muted words traveled through the door, hopefully a call to her father, *please* not to her mother, and please not to his new friends from the beach.

Robotically she returned to her dishes.

What other option was there than simply rising each day to see if she could weather it better than the day before? Jeb's college, however, would remove him from the tension of watching his mother stuck in some bizarre dimension. School could be his opportunity to cut loose from her and her demons.

She made a new gin and tonic without realizing it. Her fourth in the same number of hours. However, she had eaten, so the effect should be minimal.

Slipping outside to her screened porch, she nestled in the dark, in the same Adirondack chair as the night before. Crap. The record player. This felt like a *Serenade* album night from Neil. Leaving the drink on the wicker table, she hoisted herself up to stand and froze.

A light was on at Papa Beach's house.

Chapter 11

AT THE SIGHT of lights in Papa's house, Callie slipped back into her living room, flipped the switch off to avoid being backlit, and peered under a blind, cell phone in hand. She paused before remembering which speed dial number was Seabrook's. "There's a light on over there," she whispered when he answered, staring out in hopes to glimpse the intruder.

"Moving or stationary?" Seabrook asked.

"Stationary," she said. "I'm headed over there. Wanted someone to know."

"Hell no, you're not," he said. "Give me five minutes. I'll park two doors down on Jungle Shores. Go out your back door and wait for me at the base of your stairs."

So he lived that close. Backup did make her feel easier.

After changing into sneakers, she slipped the Glock holster on her waistband. She made her way outside, down the steps, and crouched in the shrubbery to avoid the streetlights. *What had she been thinking?* God, she knew better than to go over there by herself. She didn't think she'd had that much gin. Soon her phone shimmied, a text saying: *Coming up behind you.*

Seabrook was good for his word. He hugged the shadows and gave two short flashes with a mini-flashlight before joining her. Dark T-shirt and jeans. Deck shoes, she noticed.

"You can see better from my porch," she whispered as he reached her. "But up there, toward the west corner near the street, you'll see a hint of the light. No movement."

"I see it," he said low, then sniffed. "Is that gin?"

"I'm fine. One drink," she lied and held up a key. "I can get us in the back door."

He held up his own key. "We changed the locks."

They crossed the moonlit yard to Papa's house and climbed silently to the landing. Seabrook eased open the screen door and placed an ear to the wooden one. They readied their weapons. He gently opened the door. As he pushed it, he turned on a rail-mounted flashlight on his pistol.

Soft forties music filled the air, a slow big band instrumental. Seabrook eased across the kitchen with Callie on his heels. Her gaze briefly rested on the spot where Papa's body had lain. She quickly refocused as she braced against a shudder.

Someone had wiped up the stain after the coroner released the scene, but the pernicious smell of death lingered, having settled into the fabric of the place. Seabrook and Callie crept on into the living room. He swept right, she left.

A lone lamp shone next to the old recliner, situated in front of the window as if placed to be seen by only Callie. The dated radio serenaded them from its new position on the coffee table, the cord draped across the braided rug from the same outlet as the lamp. The forty-year-old radio seemed centered to entertain the recliner's occupant.

Callie pushed hair out of her eyes and gripped her weapon, holding her breaths quiet.

They detoured down the hallway, entered each of the three tiny bedrooms, the bath, and checked the linen closet.

"All clear." Seabrook holstered his gun, shut off the flashlight, and put it in his jeans pocket. He flipped on the nearest overhead switch. "Well, that's weird as hell."

Callie walked back up the hallway and halted in the lamp-lit den, scanning the placement of every ashtray, picture, book, and coaster.

Seabrook spoke over her shoulder. "What do you see?"

"Hold on." Her eyes skimmed the furniture, knickknacks, all the familiar items she'd known for years.

A dozen or more of Papa's possessions had been rearranged. An ashtray in a new spot. A doily on the sofa instead of the coffee table. Naval histories stacked on an old desk instead of alphabetized in their bookcase. She'd been in the house only a month ago, apart from the murder. Wherever Papa B's wife had positioned something before her passing, Papa felt it should remain. Someone had chosen to alter that.

The wrecked items from the previous break-in were no more. Pictures on the wall leveled, the broken frames picked up and set on an end table like they awaited mending. Furniture righted.

"You have anybody come in here to straighten up?" she asked.

"Nope," Seabrook said. "Tape's still on the front door. Locks changed."

Like tape stopped anybody. Like a key couldn't be copied. Like a locksmith wouldn't saunter right in at the request of someone he trusted to have the proper authority. Or, like the proper authority wouldn't consider having some fun of his own.

"He straightened up, then moved things around, as if to claim this place as his own," she said.

Seabrook scratched his head. "But who?"

Callie scouted the room one more time. "Papa's son is in Florida. Maybe Peters? Any of your people? A greedy real estate agent? Somebody who could enter your office and give a good excuse you'd believe for the key. Or your receptionist."

"Are you always so suspicious of everyone?"

If he only knew. "It can save lives, believe me," she mumbled, scanning harder.

What *was* the damn situation here? Callie reminded herself to call Stan in the morning, to see what he found out about Henry Beechum's past. This extension of the original break-in reeked personal. But personal against Papa, or personal against her? Who else would have seen that light and reacted?

Or did someone love Papa and sneak in to relive his memories?

"Who came to see him when he was alive?" she asked. "A lady friend? Another child, um, person like me?"

Seabrook shook his head. "Nobody I know of. Henry either went out to see somebody or stayed home alone. Thought you'd know that."

But I always came to see him, she thought. *We met in his house because my parents were always in mine.*

"I'll call it in to the county," Seabrook said. "Forensics will wait until tomorrow. If they think I need to stay here until they arrive, I will."

Would it be so selfish to hope he stood vigil? Something threatened to unravel inside her, and she didn't like it. Not over a stupid lamp and old music.

They entered the kitchen, Seabrook punching in a number on his cell.

"Shit," Callie whispered, then, "Shit!" out loud.

Seabrook stiffened and broke the call. "What?"

Two coffee cups sat on the dinette. She touched the back of her hand to the cup nearest her. "Still warm. Check the coffeepot."

Seabrook shook his head as he felt the cold machine. "Coffee smell would've hit us when we walked in."

"Wait." She eyed the cups closer. Oh no. "This one's tea."

Seabrook stared into the second cup. "This isn't tea."

"No, it wouldn't be. We visited Chelsea Morning in the cooler months, because Daddy rented it in the summer. Papa always fixed me hot chocolate." On the kitchen counter, the box of hot chocolate and box of tea bags still remained in place, just as they'd been the day she found Papa's body. Sweet Jesus. This had to be the same guy. And he'd connected the dots about her friendship with her old friend. Her pulse quickened as she stared at the ceramic white mug, the café's logo in black on its side, above the words *The Original Italian Caffè*. "And that cup is mine."

"Maybe you left it here?" he said. "Let's not stretch our imaginations too far."

"No," Callie said, recalling the Cioccolato Caldo she drank in it, the hot chocolate actually reminding her of Papa Beach when she ordered it.

She pressed her back against the refrigerator. *Someone had entered her house.* Had they hidden in a closet? Watched her undress? She slid down the appliance into a crouch. "I brought that cup with me from Boston. John bought it on our ninth wedding anniversary as a memento from Vittoria

Caffe in the North End."

Her chest tightened, pants going shallow. As she opened her eyes, Seabrook stooped in front of her. "Let's slow down and think about this."

She searched his blue eyes. "I found my front door unlocked today. When I got home from talking to you."

Concern etched his features.

"I'd just unpacked that cup. Someone's been in my house," she repeated. "Jeb didn't forget to lock the door. Someone got in. This is all about me."

"No," he said, placing both hands over hers and lowering them from under her chin. "We don't know that. It could be a joke because someone knows you're an ex-cop. Maybe . . ." He hunted the room for ideas.

The aroma of gunpowder came back to her. Papa distorted, broken. The waiting cups for their one-on-one. "Who else besides me would know about tea and hot chocolate," she said, her voice soft, "except someone who'd seen Papa's murder crime scene?"

Seabrook drew back. "You think his murderer put this show on for you?"

"Or a cop," she added, trying to recall the faces of the uniforms. There weren't that many.

"Maybe it's an asshole with a bad sense of humor. Still, change all your locks tomorrow, okay?"

"Don't patronize me," she said. "I'm a pro at watching my back. My biggest flaw is listening to people ordering me to chill, telling me *not* to look over my shoulder so much. That's exactly when they make their move." She jerked away from Seabrook. "Nobody around here would understand—" Blood rushed from her face. She jumped up. "This is a diversion. Jeb!"

She flew outside and ran home, kicking up shells and sand, her Glock drawn, Seabrook's footsteps keeping up behind her.

Goddamn it! The oldest trick in the universe. Distract, then snatch. Or kill.

As she fumbled with her key, she kicked the back door. "Jeb! Answer me! Jeb!"

The door flew open . . . and slammed into an obstacle. "Jeb—"

Her son hobbled about on one leg, frowning. "Mom! You ran the door over my foot!"

"Have you heard anything? Seen an intruder?" she asked.

"No. I've been in my room. What's happened?"

"Don't go outside."

Seabrook waited in the doorway.

Callie pointed at him, shaking her finger with emphasis on each word. "Shut that door. And lock it!"

The cop obeyed as told. Jeb moved toward Seabrook, glancing at him then back at his mother, waiting for someone to explain. In the meantime,

Callie hurried room to room and anchored every opening to Chelsea Morning.

With nothing else to secure, her mouth so dry her tongue stuck to her teeth, she burst back into the kitchen. She opened cabinets, making sure the mug was gone, as if she needed assurance. Her glances darting around her home, she didn't know what else to do. Someone *had* violated her place, and she wondered what else was gone, or what he'd seen. Eyes seemed to peer at her from every corner, shadow, and crevice.

Someone picked her lock. If she did change them, when would she know to change them again? A riding sense of futility filled her chest like indigestion.

"Someone stole a cup from here and planted it at Beechum's house to freak out your mother," Seabrook said.

Jeb sat on a barstool next to a standing Callie. "What the hell, Mom?"

She gingerly touched his face, trembling. His cheek felt stubbly under her shaky palm. "Someone's trying to scare us, Jeb."

Seabrook settled on the back of the sofa. "We'll figure it out."

Jeb turned and tried to speak with authority. "I forgot your name."

"This is Officer Mike Seabrook," Callie said. "From the Edisto Beach Police Department. You probably saw him—"

"Mom, look at me. Are you okay?" Jeb pressed her shoulders to stop her tremors.

Balling up her fingers, she fisted them to her chest. She had to maintain her edge; her unceasing wariness was a necessary vigilance. So that she didn't lose her son. So that her son didn't lose his mother. Crap had caught up to her at a consummate Garden of Eden. Apparently, she couldn't relax anywhere, even at Edisto Beach.

This place was not the almighty solution her parents thought it was. "Listen, Jeb. The season's at its peak. We can sell this place in a snap."

"No," he said, rising to his feet. "Who says any other place would be different? I'm fed up with not being settled. Fed up seeing you like this. Fed up with your . . . *spells.*"

She rubbed the creases between her brows, a headache raging. "Yes, I'm having a spell." Then she pounded the counter. Jeb jerked. Seabrook moved toward her.

"I'm also enraged, and I'm frustrated off the goddamn chart about our lives being slung around." Salty tears reached her lips, and she roughly rubbed them on her sleeve.

Dammit, she was stronger than this. She recognized the alcohol talking and hated herself for allowing it to lower her defenses. Of all times for a crisis. The detective in her ought to be the driving force right now, not some pasty-skinned damsel in distress.

Seabrook fixated on her, analyzing.

She could no longer carry this secret alone. Time for Jeb to hear the truth, for his sake and her sanity. To leave the nest, he needed to appreciate the dangers she'd hidden from him so he'd be more aware. All he knew was his father had died in a fire. Knowing the truth, maybe he'd realize why she'd become who she was . . . and forgive her over time.

Seabrook turned away. "I'll head back to the house and call in."

She touched his arm. "I wish you'd stay." If Jeb hated her for concealing the truth, maybe the gentle cop would help soften the blow and give her credibility in front of her son.

She turned to Jeb. "I'd like you to know why I react to situations like I do. I only want to explain this once."

Seabrook poised on the arm of the sofa. Jeb waited, his stare glued to her. She decided touching him was not wise. When authorities divulged John's true cause of death to her, they tried to hold her hands, touch her shoulder, reach out arms for her to fall into. Those condolences were now branded into her head as forebearers of doom, a far cry from consolation.

"Jeb," she started, chin up, swallowing once for strength. "Your father didn't die in the fire."

His eyes went wide. "What? Wait. I was there with you. The house . . ." and he trailed off. His squinting eyes wary, they belied the denial creeping in. "What're you trying to say?"

However she told it, the truth would be cruel. "True, baby, he was in the house. But your father was shot before the killer set the fire. And they were probably after me."

Now her son's eyes narrowed.

Callie stole a glance at Seabrook. "He died . . ."

Seabrook nodded as if to say, *Stay with it. You're doing fine.*

She turned back to Jeb. "He died from a .22 bullet to the head."

Pain creased Jeb's brow. "So they got Dad instead of you?"

His reply pierced her heart. "Yes, instead of all three of us."

Callie closed her eyes before saying the words she'd thought for two years. The words she slept with, woke to, and ached about each and every day of her life since that October night. "My job got your father killed."

Jeb strode down the hall and slammed his bedroom door.

Seabrook's head bowed. Callie lowered herself to a barstool, watching the hallway, wondering whether to go console her son. She started to rise.

"Don't," Seabrook said. "Let him be. He'll come to terms with it."

But she remained standing. Then, in a moment of decision, she went to the refrigerator and pulled out the gin. She uncapped it, moved to the sink, and upended the bottle. The liquid glugged as it poured down then spit back up, repeating itself. Fixated on the movement, Callie knew she could buy another, but she didn't have to.

That was the point. The decision was hers. Many decisions were hers. She'd just made one with Jeb and another with the lovely blue bottle emptying down the drain.

She would control her life, or this unknown asshole would do it for her.

Seabrook came around the bar. "You did fine by him. He'll realize that soon enough." Moving closer, he gently laid an arm around her, cupping her shoulder, drawing her close.

She closed her eyes. *Oh, God.*

His musky scent from the humid summer night made her yearn to spin around and lean into that towering strength. He could shelter her, and she could let him. But she was tired of feeling sorry for herself. His pity, her guilt. What good would that do her? Or Jeb?

"What bad guys do isn't your fault," Seabrook said, squeezing her again.

It was on my watch, she wanted to say, but the words caught. She lightly tried to pull away. She needed to be more proactive. Make plans.

He retained his hold.

Just one embrace. She imagined the side of her face buried into his chest.

Her powerful need to stand firm was eroding around the edges. A power she'd been losing control over for a long while.

The muscles in his arm flexed, as if reading her thoughts. "You can't control it all, Callie," he said. "I know how shit happens. Believe me, I do." He tried to tuck her against him. "Just let it go," he whispered.

She pushed away. She couldn't afford to be weak. Not now.

"You are in so much pain it's a wonder you haven't collapsed."

Right now she hated all the world had dumped on her, to include people who thought what was best for her. Even now her grief for John swelled unbearably huge in her chest from dealing with Jeb, yet she hated her husband for leaving her alone.

Oh, how she longed for the physical presence of another soul. The touch. But folding into Seabrook's arms would make her feel she needed someone to be strong on her behalf. Then he'd be gone, and she'd be alone again. Maybe downstream there was comfort to be found in a stranger, but not for her, not tonight.

Seabrook waited, trying to read her.

Sniffling, her cheeks still damp, she took the bottle from the sink, moved to the other side of the kitchen, and threw the empty in the trash. "Thanks for being here, but I just want to be by myself now."

"Come on, Callie. Let me stick around. I'm a great listener."

She was embarrassed enough. "No, Mike. This is my millstone, not yours."

"I was a doctor—"

"I know. And the offer's appreciated."

He moved toward the back door. "I'll be outside."

"And I'll be in here."

She locked the door with Seabrook glancing back one more time. He hesitated before descending the stairs.

The house was secure, but she checked it again, testing locks. She had a cop standing guard outside for the night. Maybe she could relax and sink into her thoughts. Loosen her mind.

But how was that supposed to happen when the murderer had mocked her right next door?

Chapter 12

BREATHS REGULAR, Callie's feet beat the sand with a cadence she hadn't felt in a long time. No gin, a good night's sleep, and a day full of promise. Gulls crisscrossed overhead, as if keeping pace. Salt air filled her sinuses, clearing her head.

Bring it on, life.

Bring it on, you low-life, sneaking, contemptible weasel, whoever you are.

Jeb had left for the beach before she woke, but he'd stuck a note behind a mini-conch shell magnet on the refrigerator. *Gone fishing. Love you Mom.* A doodled happy face with eyes crossed ended the note, putting the bounce back in her step. Mother and son were good again. Thank heaven. She'd beat herself up enough without having the love of her life adding to the punches. Telling him the truth had removed a two-ton mass of harbored guilt.

After Seabrook left last night, she'd cried herself dry in her bedroom—a deep release. After all, she had the comforting thought of him camped out in his car at Papa B's house only yards away. Leaving Chelsea Morning for her run, she waved at his car parked in Papa's drive. He waved back. It was . . . a moment.

Crap, she was acting sixteen. She kicked up her speed, fighting to avoid her heels and push off the balls of her feet.

Last evening had scared the crap out of her. The set up designed for her, after entering her home to achieve it. In Boston, she'd received plenty of hate mail and threatening calls. The winks, the coded words as she passed criminals in a courtroom. She'd been impervious then, Kevlar-coated. Never missed a wink of sleep.

In the dawn of a new day, Callie recognized the intrusion at Papa Beach's house as an intimidation stunt aimed to rattle her cage. The why escaped her, and if she were in Boston, she'd have two or three dozen thugs to blame. Edisto made no sense. After her run and a shower, she'd call Stan again and seek a more balanced viewpoint.

You're not a victim unless you allow yourself to be one.

How many times had she given that advice?

Callie squinted from behind her sunglasses. A jogger approached, but with the sun in front of her, she could only make out his dark outline. Something familiar though. He came closer.

Mason Howard.

He changed direction and ran alongside her, matching stride. The sun hat he used to dowse her hung-over head last time was dry and back on his own, his T-shirt a tie-dyed blue from McConkey's diner. "Hey again, Callie Morgan. Hope you don't mind my saying this, but you sure seem better today."

How could she mind? Frankly, how could she not be better? Her run was strong, her headache gone, and she hadn't puked once. "You're such a charmer." She grinned as she picked up her pace. He followed suit. She enjoyed his periodic glances at her chest. Men were men.

"How's the investigation going?" he asked. "Saw you at the police department yesterday. They put you on retainer or something?"

"And who says I was at the police department?"

"Word has it your car was parked there."

She blew out deeper then went back to her count. "And whose word would that be?"

He flashed a goofy grin. "Light gray Escape, five years old." He jogged easy. "No bumper stickers. Nothing hanging on the mirror." A few more steps. "Nothing on the console. Factory condition and completely nondescript. Pure vanilla."

A nervous shiver crept across her back at the spot-on description of her vehicle. She stopped. "You were snooping in my car?"

He took a back step, his expression feigning shock. "No malicious intention, Callie. When I saw it was yours, I chose to leave so you wouldn't think I was stalking you."

She laid fists on her hips. "Why the hell would you search the inside of a parked car? Just what are the limits to your nosiness?"

"Wow," he said. "You even sound like a detective."

"Answer the question," she said.

"Which one?"

"Let's start with why *you* were there?"

"I was asking about the procedures for owning a handgun," he said. "Don't spread that around, please."

Almost laughable. "I'm not the one who's the walking tabloid. Besides, you're Canadian. Thought they didn't do guns."

He let out a *harrumph*. "Some of us aren't as milquetoast as you Americans think."

She stared down *her* nose this time. Massachusetts wasn't keen on gun-toters, so she'd grown accustomed to the police being hands-on in that regard. But in South Carolina, carry permits were as common as camo ball caps. The tourists had freaked about her Glock the other day because they were predominantly visitors, not residents. But Canadians? Even US law enforcement didn't carry weapons across that border.

He continued jogging in place. "I own my grandfather's .45 Webley revolver. He served with the British Commandos during World War II. It's in the house. I don't want that thief grabbing it, and then I get in trouble for possession."

"This state isn't that way." She stretched her hamstring as doubt about his story nudged her. "But I'm impressed you'd check. Good job. Cool weapon. Get yourself a lock box and bolt it onto a shelf in a closet."

She jogged off. He caught up.

"Quit the chatter," Callie said. "I need to do another two miles, and I was in my zone before you interrupted."

"Yes, madam detective," he said. "Oh, about that party Friday. You're still more than welcome."

"Yeah," she said, fighting for rhythm. "I heard about your parties, playboy."

His hand went to his chest. "Was that cynicism? I'm so hurt!"

"Sure you are," she replied. "But you have a good time."

Digging in, she returned to a respectable stride, giving Mason her back.

The man was likeable enough, with his sophisticated, worldly attractiveness, but damn, he was awful sure of himself. His first aid to her hangover yesterday had been touching, but something about Seabrook's description of Water Spout's wealthy tenant told her that a safe arm's length approach made a lot more sense.

HALF AN HOUR later, Callie walked up Jungle Road to a repeat image of a county and two local cruisers parked at Papa Beach's residence. She was hoping they'd be gone by now, but then, this was an extension of the murder investigation. They'd take all the time they needed. Edisto-time ran on its own clock, and fast wasn't part of the mechanism.

She reached the bottom of Papa B's stairs, started to call for Seabrook, and then changed her mind.

Raysor opened the screen door, barking at someone inside. When he spotted her, he stared a second, as if sizing her up for the deed.

"Hey, Deputy Raysor," Callie said. "How's it going? Need me for anything?"

"Now why would I need you?"

"Just being polite. You ought to try it." She pivoted to leave.

"Mighty odd that none of this shit happens until you move here," he said louder. "If you didn't do any of this crap, you know someone who did. Or at least attracted him here. I smell you all over this, doll."

A ripple rolled through her at his words. No telling what Raysor would think if he knew her past, her weaknesses, her history. He'd project to the entire community that she brought mayhem to Edisto, and that did nobody any good.

Seabrook had said last night that shit just happens. Right now, a thick pile of it strutted around with a badge next door, doing everything in his ability to draw out her bad side. Then she recalled how great her day had started and the strength she promised to maintain. She'd sworn to herself that *victim* would not seep into her vocabulary.

"Well, good thing we have a solid police force to take care of such mayhem so the residents of this beach can live in safety," she said. There. Better.

"One day we need to talk," he hollered after her.

She marched home, raising a hand in casual acknowledgement, but internally she was anything but casual. Fighting not to trot faster, she put distance between her and the rotund man and his stupid grudge. He creeped her out, which was so dumb after all the pervs and miscreants she'd tackled in her career, because to look at him could almost draw a smile. Raysor was such a bubba stereotype.

So different from *Mike*.

She hadn't asked if Seabrook was inside, then realized she preferred to shower first before seeing him anyway. Change into better clothes, throw on lip gloss.

Was she primping?

No, she decided, heading up the steps with purpose. Merely personal hygiene and sun block.

The shower slowed her heart rate, but she still felt off-balance. Not literally, of course. Her legs felt fantastic after three miles, her lungs strong. Figuratively, however, she seemed half a bubble off center. She'd become accustomed to keeping her thoughts isolated, emotions protected.

However, now she'd met Sophie, Zeus, Mason Howard, and Mike. And handyman Peters. Raysor. The new interactions challenged her stubborn reclusive tendencies. Once upon a time, she'd adeptly juggled so many personalities. She knew what to say and how to say it, but that was when her core had been solid and confident.

For the year in Middleton, Callie had hidden away, surfing the web, jogging, making weekly calls to Stan for doses of Boston news. A few school events for Jeb. A few appearances for Lawton's fundraisers and ribbon cuttings. She greeted, smiled, and thanked her father's friends and acquaintances for their compliments, condolences, and best wishes. Her wall of isolation remained with nary a crack in the mortar.

She didn't used to need a wall, but these days she loved its protection.

She'd always been more of a weekend visitor on Edisto instead of a resident. Now that she was full-time, life tugged at her to get sucked into this community of assorted beings.

And this morning she'd been cheerful for the first time in many months. Was she outgrowing her time of mourning? Had these people drawn her out? Or had Mike Seabrook been the first person to give her permission to release all her pent up resentment for outliving John? And what did that make Seabrook to her?

She dried off and worked on her hair, her make-up, but nothing outrageous. Nose against the mirror, she waved a mascara wand across her lashes, reared back, and studied the results. Too much?

This was ridiculous. She set down the wand and ceased the effort. She put on beige linen slacks, a turquoise tank, and a loose white long-sleeve gauze shirt. Maybe she'd offer her law enforcement assistance again, but to do so she needed something more than gym shorts to be taken seriously.

While checking the lock on the back door, movement caught her eye. She pulled the drapes back and edged to the right to peer better across the street.

A dozen middle-schoolers canvassed the area between the dirt road and the marsh. She opened the back door and moved to the porch. Across from Sophie's house, a herd of Boy Scouts studied the ground, the water, the brush. Several maneuvered metal detectors, swinging them to and fro. A three-foot A-frame sign posted on the edge of the thin grass read: *Edisto Boy Scout Troop 154 At Your Service. Please Drive Carefully.*

A blond child, gangly and awkward, staggered over weeds to his waist. Callie grinned, recalling Jeb's sprawling legs at that age. Two other kids bumped shoulders. Snickers galore. Their gazes strayed too easily from their duties, the boys intensely interested in something at Sophie's house.

After locking up, she hopped down her front steps and strolled over to Sophie's. Callie knocked, then tried the doorknob. Locked. Hallelujah for newfound common sense.

Sophie yelled from the other side. "Door's open."

Callie jiggled the knob. "No, it's not."

Cursing, Sophie unlocked it. "Who the hell did that?" She scowled, then waved Callie in, dancing back barefooted in black yoga pants, a black tank, and a yellow and white shirt that draped baggy off one shoulder. "Come in, come in. I don't know how *that* happened."

Seabrook's voice sounded from the kitchen. "I told you, Sophie. You've got to keep this place more secure. I did that when I came in. Get used to keeping it that way."

Forceful, irritated. He'd delivered a pretty harsh lecture from the tone in his voice. "Hey," Callie said, rounding the corner.

A grin smothered his face. "Hey yourself. You seem good today."

Sophie tilted her head. "So, what's this? I get my fanny chewed out by Mr. Grump, and all you have to do is walk in and he beams." With one fist on her waist, the other reached out, bangles jingling as she wriggled fingers. "Okay. Spill it."

"Nothing," Callie said, heat rising up her neck.

"Nothing, my ass," Sophie said.

"I told you someone broke into Beechum's place again last night," Seabrook said. "Callie and I were up half the night dealing with the crime scene."

Her impish grin was ripe with imagination. "Oh, really?"

Seabrook frowned. "You aren't taking any of this serious enough, Sophie. A coin was left here. Chances are something was stolen. What's missing?"

Sophie's eyes narrowed. "Nothing. And I already asked you not to talk about such things in here. If someone came in my house, he made a mistake."

Seabrook shared a sarcastic snap of a laugh. "He paid you a coin by mistake?" He dropped his head back, staring at the ceiling, and blew out. "I'll buy a bale of the damn sage for you. Just keep your doors *locked* and search for anything stolen. Don't be so simpleminded."

"You're not flipping my switch, big boy," she said, sashaying to the kitchen. "Anybody want some tea? Carrot juice? The serious stuff?"

Callie moved to the back window. "I came over to see what Troop 154 is doing out back. They're stumbling around like Keystone Kops." She eased the sheers away to see. "They can't seem to—oh."

A teenage beauty languished on a chaise in a beige lace bikini smaller than one of Lawton Cantrell's Christmas hankies. Thick black curls piled atop her head, her skin tanned golden.

"I take it this is Sprite?" Callie asked, glancing at her neighbor.

Sophie sparkled. "That's my baby."

"And the Scouts are supposedly *scouting* for the silver dollar you threw away yesterday," Seabrook said as he joined them at the window. "Hadn't planned it quite this way, but I imagine they'll search as long as she's out there in all her tempting glory."

"Hmph," Callie said. "They've probably tripped over that coin fifty times."

Boots stomped across the front porch, followed by a heavy knock on the door. Raysor let himself in before Sophie could get there. "Easy pickins', this place. What if I'd been an intruder?"

"You are," Sophie said.

Callie gave her a silent *Amen*.

"You could at least wait for me to greet you," Sophie said, the sparkle gone. "Just because it's open doesn't mean you waltz in without invitation."

"But the door was open. Tacit approval."

"That's not how it works." Sophie strode up to the man who had a hundred fifty pounds plus on her. "You still show manners. What if I'd been naked?"

Raysor's mouth fell open as his face reddened.

Sophie smiled wickedly.

"What is it, Don?" Seabrook asked. "Have they finished at the Beechum place?"

"Yeah." Raysor straightened and readjusted his belt. "They can't find anything new. They think the dude used gloves this time."

"He's getting smarter," Seabrook said.

Callie added, "He's never been all that dumb."

Another knock. "Is Miss Morgan in here?" Jackson Peters peered inside from the other side of the threshold.

Sophie flipped her wrist, making circles in the air at Raysor. "See? He knows how to do it."

Callie joined the clustered gathering in the foyer. "Hey, Mr. Peters. You need me?"

"Yes, ma'am," he said. "I can get to your steps tomorrow. And just Peters is fine."

She reached past Raysor. "Appreciate it, Peters. And I'm just Callie."

He shook her hand, nodding sheepishly before backing up. "Well," he said, "I'll leave you people to whatever it is you're doing." He started to leave and stopped. "Oh, Callie, where do you keep your key in case you're not home?"

Raysor stepped in, blocking the contractor's view of Callie. "On her damn key ring, you idiot." He pointed up the road. "We're still processing a crime scene, another breaking and entering, and you ask where an owner's gonna park a spare key for you and everybody else on this beach? Just think about the damage that could happen from some damn key hid under a stupid gnome in a flower bed."

"But she ain't got no gnomes," Peters said straight-faced.

Raysor's ruddy cheeks flashed redder.

Callie moved around the deputy. "I'll be home, Peters. You can start anytime you like. Just don't knock on the door before eight."

Peters tipped his head and scurried down the stairs in the same loping fashion he'd done the day before. He returned to his truck in her drive.

Once Peters was out of earshot, Callie lashed out at Raysor. "Where'd you learn your manners?"

He ignored her to stare after the handyman. "We interviewed that old hippie yet?"

"No." Seabrook flipped pages in his notes. "Plan to, though. He was the first on the scene after the Rosewoods got broken into."

"I'll do it," Raysor said, moving to the porch to watch the truck's retreat.

"Deal with the tourists, Don. I'll handle the questioning on this case, just to be consistent."

The deputy leaned on the porch railing, watching Peters inch onto the road after waiting for a golf cart loaded with five teens to go around. "He could've done every bit of this. He just told us how he gets access to these houses."

Seabrook returned his small memo book into the back pocket of his jeans, still out of uniform from the night before. "The same way every rental agent accesses these homes? We're talking murder, Don. Don't see

Peters as the type. Too familiar a face."

"I agree," Callie said.

"Glad y'all took these dark topics outside," Sophie said, settling on the porch landing.

Raysor took a moment to appreciate her lotus position, then forced his attention back to Callie. "Not sure where you went to police academy, Ms. Detective, but we were taught the obvious was usually the right answer. We need his whereabouts."

Callie hated the deputy's incessant antagonism. "Listen, Raysor . . ."

He sneered, like the master belittling his protégé, and turned away.

"Pay attention to me, Einstein," she said louder.

"Why should I?" Raysor reared back and studied her down his nose. "You're as much a suspect as he is. You had access, and your alibis are weak."

"Where's my motive?" she replied, jaw tight.

Raysor flipped a quick shrug. "What's anybody's motive? Money, attention, vengeance." He pointed at her. "There's something amiss with you, doll. You're connected to all this somehow."

"Stop it, Don," Seabrook said.

"Let me interview *her*," Raysor said. "You're too distracted."

Callie moved up. "Bring it. Interview me. Give me the best you've got."

"Enough," Seabrook said.

"Then I ain't got time for you, doll," Raysor said and headed down the steps. "City people, city cops. Not a lot of sense between their ears, if you ask me. In the meantime, I gotta go solve a crime."

Squinting at the deputy's back, Callie resisted spouting some useless slur.

"Didn't think he'd ever leave," Sophie said. "His disgusting aura just clings to you. At least I can vouch for you when the Rosewoods were broken into, Callie. I got your back, girl."

Callie gave her neighbor a meager smile.

"Good grief, Mother, I can't lay outside like this. It's like a hotel here. Little perverts and no privacy." Sprite brushed past like a breeze, a sarong wrapped around her slim frame, and disappeared down the hall.

Callie tried to chuckle about the pouty child, but Raysor had stolen her humor. At least with Sprite off the porch, chances had increased the Scouts would find the coin. But Raysor's rancor had struck a chord with her. How many people on Edisto thought like he did?

Wait, was this mentality what the burglar had planned?

Suddenly the light on at Papa's house made more sense. Somebody was sucking her into this crime spree, setting up situations that she couldn't predict or ignore. Making everyone suspect her as part of it . . . somehow.

Chapter 13

CALLIE HUNG WITH Seabrook on Sophie's back porch, observing the Boy Scouts huddled in a group studying the ground across the street. Hopefully they'd found the coin, but they could just as likely be watching a crab. Sophie consoled a pouty Sprite in her bedroom, the seventeen-year-old in a huff over her inability to tan in private with so many pimply adolescent boys on the loose.

"Ignore Don," Seabrook said.

Callie leaned her elbows on the railing. "Not easy to do. He has a right to doubt the new person on the block. Especially someone familiar with the crime."

"You're not a suspect."

"I know," she said, not feeling so sure.

She would try to keep her distance, but someone seemed intent on entwining her in all this. Sophie said she could cover her for the Rosewoods, but the burglary occurred before Sophie had come over. Not by much, but still . . .

"It's too easy to blame a simple guy like Peters." Callie straightened. "We could have the burglaries with the coin, then an anomaly, the murder."

"But the coins at the burglaries came from the murder. How do you explain that?"

She frowned. "I can't."

Seabrook scowled and rubbed the back of his neck. "This is four days in a row if you count Beechum's place last night. Who does that?"

Her backside rested against the railing. "Someone confident he won't get caught."

"Burglaries are one thing, but murder's another. Somebody else is going to get hurt, or worse."

She nodded. "Can you call in more people?"

He snared his sunglasses from the top of his head and put them on. "And do what? Set up a sting? Put a guard on each resident? In this place?"

"You can inform the community to keep their doors locked." She appreciated his frustration, but he needed to get out in front of this mess. "Signs, announcements, educate them. Deter the guy. Make Edisto vigilant." It felt good having a partner to brainstorm with. Crime was never a good thing, but fortunately wrestling with it was what she used to do best.

"Did you ever see the movie *Jaws*?" he asked. "This is tourist season.

I'm Brody on Amity Island."

"And remember what happened when Amity Island didn't take Chief Brody seriously?" she asked. "People died."

Seabrook's mouth flat-lined. "Don't say that," he said, unknowingly stealing a line from the movie.

"Put Raysor to work enlightening the public," she said. "Let him be the one everyone yells at." She grinned wryly. "Would serve him right."

"Forget him. He'd be bitter if you fed him cotton candy and tickled him with a feather. I'd be more concerned if he were quiet. Anyway, we have a phone system on the beach. It'll send a text or voice mail to most of the houses. At least all the residents. It was designed for hurricane warnings. We'll send a reminder to lock up with a burglar on the loose." He lifted his shades and peered into her eyes, and Callie sensed a shift.

"You know how you had a key to Beechum's house?" he asked.

"Yeah."

"I assume *he* had a key to yours since he maintained your place."

Which could have been how someone got into her house. Seabrook had connected the dots, and she felt like a fool not having done so first.

He stared harder. "And did you retrieve your key from the real estate office that used to manage your rental of Chelsea Morning?"

Home run, Officer Seabrook. Good for you. She bit the inside of her lip. "No."

"Hmm," he said. "How about you call someone—"

"Nope." She stared past him at her home that might as well be as wide open as Sophie's. "I'd already decided to drive to the hardware store and pick up three locks. I'll change them myself, thank you. Not sure I trust a locksmith around here anymore." She'd pick up a hammer for her toolbox, too.

Seabrook sniffed. "Good thought. At least nobody gets a chance to make a copy. I can do it for you."

Callie *had* changed a lock before. They came with simple directions. Seabrook would fall over knowing she could pick one, too. "No, you're exhausted. Go get some sleep. I'm good."

"Fine, then I'm headed home. My brain needs shut-eye." He thumbed back at himself. "But still call me if anything happens I need to know about."

She nodded.

"Oh," he added. "Don't stop at the liquor store on the way to buy those locks. I'd rather you call me than hunt another bottle."

Irritation flashed over her. "What?" She poured a whole bottle down the drain. She could stop whenever she liked.

"Never said the word drunk," he said. "But drinking alone is foolish. At least do it with me."

Two Boy Scouts ran over with smiles bigger than a circus clown, one holding up something muddy. "Officer Seabrook!" the taller boy yelled. "We found it! It wasn't as far in the marsh as we thought."

"Good job," Callie said, descending the stairs behind the cop.

Mike held the coin on its edges, between his forefinger and thumb. "1921," he said. "Just like you said, Callie. Thanks, boys. That's it. What do I need to do for you in return?"

"We need a letter to saying we helped solve a crime. This'll count toward a community badge big time," the boy said. "Maybe even an award." The smaller youngster nodded with exaggeration, excitement all over his face.

Seabrook played his role well, as if contemplating the seriousness of the request. "Fair enough. Give me a couple of days, and you'll have the best letter of commendation you've ever seen."

"Yes, sir!" they said in unison, then bolted like fueled lightning to the huddled group eagerly waiting for an update.

A woman's yell stifled the chuckles and chatter. Callie donned her shades and scanned across the yards of several houses. The voice shouted again.

A heavyset middle-aged woman in khaki Bermudas fast-walked between trots along Jungle Road toward the police cars at Papa B's place. "Help! Help!" she cried, her arms out to the side, sagging underarms swaying. "Help! Police!"

Seabrook scrambled toward the road, Callie on his heels. Boy Scouts rushed around the pylons holding up the residence, as if entitled to participate in any action now.

"Over here, Mrs. Hanson," Seabrook shouted.

"Mike," the woman cried, watching for cars before she bounded in a cumbersome gallop across the road. "Oh, Mike!"

He reached her and drew her away from the edge of potential traffic. She gulped, trying to catch her wind. "How could this happen?"

"What happened?" he asked.

Callie touched the woman's shoulder. "Shhh, calm down and collect yourself. Is anyone hurt? Do we need an ambulance?"

The woman shook her head. "No, no." She swallowed down tears. "Somebody's been in my house. *My* house!"

Callie stared at Seabrook. Had the guy performed another trick right under their noses?

"Is anyone there now?" he asked.

She shook her head fast, flustered. "I don't know. I set the alarm while I went to the grocery store. When I came home I put the groceries away, then went on the screened porch to call to my sister." She patted her chest, gathering her wits. "When I came in to get another glass of tea, I found it."

"Found what?" Seabrook asked.

"A glass of wine," she said. "And a big coin. Isn't that what happened at the Rosewoods? They're right across the street from me."

Callie had hoped they could keep the coins a secret, but obviously not. The Rosewoods could have told Hanson after they'd already told Sophie and Heaven-knows-who-else.

Three coins in as many days. Six break-ins total if she counted the two at Papa B's and the one at hers.

They crossed the street with Mrs. Hanson. Sophie reappeared at the commotion, Sprite by her side, still wearing less than Pocahontas.

Leaving Mrs. Hanson outside with Sophie, Callie searched the house with Seabrook, and as expected, found nobody there. They brought Mrs. Hanson inside her kitchen, asking her to replay her actions. A wine glass sat at the kitchen bar beside a 1928 Peace vintage silver dollar.

"I came home, turned off the alarm, and put away the groceries," she said, moving from her kitchen door into the room, opening cabinets in her reenactment. She pretended to pour her tea. Then she exited to the porch with her phone.

"Where were you seated?" Callie asked.

Mrs. Hanson moved to a chaise lounge at the right side of the deck, out of view of the exterior doors and the kitchen.

Callie shadowed her. "How long did you talk to your sister?"

"Oh, not long," she said. "Margaret can talk for hours, but this was one of her shorter conversations. Maybe thirty minutes."

"May I?" Callie asked, taking the woman's phone. She scrolled through the old calls. There it was. "One hour and thirty-five minutes."

Mrs. Hanson nervously covered her mouth and chin. "Gosh, I didn't think we talked that long."

Seabrook stared critically at the woman repeatedly smoothing her clothes. "So, assuming the invader didn't have the alarm code," he said, "he used that ninety-minute window. So what's missing? What did he take?"

"Mike," Callie chided softly.

"I . . . I don't know," Mrs. Hanson said. "The coin made me come find you."

"Well, hunt around while we're here. We'll wait," he said and left the screened porch to go into the house.

Mrs. Hanson, however, remained still, shell-shocked.

Callie took her arm. "Come on," she said. "I'll go with you room to room. Let's start with your jewelry, cash, and the master bedroom."

The woman immediately discovered a sterling silver necklace missing from the top of her dresser. All else appeared in order.

Sophie soothed Mrs. Hanson as Callie pulled Seabrook aside. "He's not taking anything of value. The antique coins are worth more than what's being stolen. A druggie would be sporadic, careless, do more damage. They'd toss the place for loose change and dollars. They damn sure wouldn't sit down and have a drink. Somebody's mooning you here."

Seabrook leaned forward. "Tell me something I don't know, Detective."

She hesitated at this new frustrated, sarcastic side of the man. "I would if I could, Mike."

"I'm so damn tired of this."

Once he took a report from Mrs. Hanson, he asked her to come by the station later to sign the statement. Leaving Sophie to coo over the woman and enjoy the firsthand accounting of an event sure to blanket the beach by dinner, Seabrook departed with a brusqueness Callie felt worth addressing.

"I know you're tired, but what's with you?" she asked as they walked toward his vehicle parked at Papa's. The only cars left in the drive were his and Raysor's cruisers. Her stomach growled, the lower sun indicating it was mid-afternoon, lunch missed a while ago.

"You could have been Deputy Raysor's brother back there the way you spoke to Mrs. Hanson," she said.

Seabrook's jaw worked under the surface. "I know, and I'll apologize this afternoon. We might as well move the police station over here and tell forensics to rent a damn beach house. This creep thinks he owns the street. When a guy walks into an occupied house, he does so knowing he might be discovered. You know how easy a victim she was?"

"Like Papa Beach," Callie said, as they reached the drive. "I know."

He glowered from beside his car. "And he doesn't care."

"May I ask something maybe you hadn't thought about?" she asked.

He didn't answer, but he watched her, waiting.

"The coins may be a new MO for an old crime. How many theft reports did you have before Papa's murder?"

"Not many, most of them sloppy, mostly kids."

"How do we know that one of those burglars didn't cut his teeth on those slipshod jobs, came into possession of the coins, and suddenly decided to get creative in his profession?"

Seabrook scowled.

She didn't give him a chance to say it. "When you're not so agitated, take a moment and revisit your old cases. Just a suggestion, Officer. This person seems familiar with the area."

The local force was trained like any law enforcement; Seabrook should dig in and feel more determined now. Moments like this drove her harder when she'd carried a badge, but Mike seemed befuddled. The Hanson crime seemed to countermine his ability to think.

He got into his car. He lifted a benign hand as he left, much like the first time she saw him drive by her house, and she returned the gesture, somewhat ill at ease with the skill of this police force to catch this guy. But Seabrook also had had no sleep last night, and the case might weigh heavier on the shoulders of an acting chief who didn't want the job. She could see Raysor needling a man in such a state.

Raysor. The redneck deputy seemed awful eager to shift suspicion in her direction. She already wondered if a local had pulled these jobs. Why not a disgruntled deputy with a bully attitude and the ability to come and go as he pleased without anyone doubting his motive?

CALLIE WENT INSIDE Chelsea Morning, dialed the hardware store, and asked them to hold three heavy-duty exterior locks. She didn't even want them keyed alike. She wanted those locks in the original package, untainted, untouched by anyone but her.

She grabbed her purse and left, leaving a note for Jeb.

Raysor's car remained in Papa B's drive. She'd seen his type in many a Boston bar, a few on the force. People perpetually trying to prove themselves in a bombastic manner.

She held out her fob and unlocked her Escape.

"I could take you into the marsh and dump your body in the water for the sharks," said the voice off to her right.

Callie jumped even as she told herself not to, her instincts shouting to prepare for a defense.

"Bet you're not even armed," he added.

"Don't bet your life on it," she said, recognizing the gravelly tone.

Raysor strode out of the ten-foot tall Indian Hawthorn shrubs that served as a hedge to her drive, and he blocked her from the car with his bulk. She'd never realized how hidden she was in the parking area that ran under her pylon-supported house . . . nor how vulnerable.

Her gaze darted, seeking a witness, an exit, a weapon.

"I left Mrs. Hanson purring with a drink, believing some stupid Yankee teenager probably slipped in and took her necklace."

Callie ignored the possible reference to Jeb. "What if I *had* been armed?"

"Not sure what kind of threat you'd be wedged against the car like that. Let's get something straight here."

She moved away, using Raysor's own warning to better position herself. Measuring his mass and lack of physical fitness, she'd already judged how to use that lard and loose muscle against him. He reeked of pompous swagger, but a hint of threat still clung to the man. As pudgy as he was outside, he harbored a degree of malevolence under that spongy skin.

He reached up, seized the luggage rack atop her Escape, and rocked the car. "It was quiet around here before you got here."

"And?"

He shook the car again. "You may have Mike mesmerized, but I see some burnt-out badge who might be missing the fun, and so now she's orchestrating her own."

Callie's pulse kicked up a notch at the concern she'd had about

Raysor's possible involvement in these crimes. "Then you need glasses."

He closed the gap between them, old coffee scent on him. "Could be you doing all this, you know. Might also be your son, or him and his friend Zeus. We only have that boy's word about the coin in his mama's kitchen, don't we?"

She tried to reach past him for the door handle. "Don't you dare talk about my son."

He blocked her. She tried not to back up as he leaned in her face. "What are you up to? Or who did you piss off enough to follow you down here?"

She certainly wouldn't tell him about the Russians. Petty burglary wasn't their style anyway. Killing Papa Beach would have made sense a year ago, but the Russians already had their blood. Like Stan said. Like she needed to continually remind herself—and believe—or she'd go insane.

"Back away, Raysor."

Fear zinged up her back as he leaned closer instead.

Tired of body odor and coffee, she pointed toward the paunch that hung beneath his vest. "Get out of my space," she said, fighting the shake in her tone. "And don't come on my property again without a legal reason."

He stepped back. "I'm gonna figure you out."

Then like earlier, her own suspicion flared. Did he think he would throw her off his scent? The best defense is a good offense sort of thing?

"Why waste your time with me when you've got a real criminal running loose? Someone who practically owns you and your department?" she said.

A sneer crept up one side of his cheek. "That's so weak, Morgan."

"Think so?" Nervous, with a loss of words, knowing full well how much it would irritate a cop to be touched, she poked him. He was out of line, which gave her the liberty to be the same.

He stared down at his broad middle, as if she did nothing more than brush crumbs off. "That's assault in some circles."

Go on the offensive, Callie. "Bring it then, big man. But who's to say you don't have a couple people under your control, guys you're holding something over, and you're the one taking advantage of this beach?"

Wariness replaced his smugness. "People are right. You *are* crazy."

She'd pushed Raysor's button, and he'd taken his finger off hers. "You know who's a resident and who's a tenant," she said. "You know the residents are the only ones with valuables, and coincidentally are the only ones getting burglarized. You have the know-how to execute Papa Beach. Maybe when one of your cronies got caught in the act of robbing the old man, you took care of business. Only I interrupted your plan."

"Jeee-sus. You're out of your fuckin' mind." Raysor leveled his gaze with hers. "Don't think I'm not watching you. And if I hear of you spewing any more of that fantasy shit, there'll be hell to pay. Are we clear?"

"Back at you, Deputy Raysor," she said, muscles twitching in her legs.

"Right back at you."

He left. She dropped onto the driver's seat and leaned against the headrest.

The redneck nuisance had grown from an arrogant moron to a suspect. Seabrook said to watch the man more carefully when he was quiet. The way Raysor had sneaked up on her seemed to fill the bill.

Chapter 14

TWO HOURS AFTER Raysor all but accosted her, Callie tested the front door lock, then gave the mechanism one last spritz of graphite. There. Slick as black ice. All the extra keys floating around to Chelsea Morning were useless now.

She'd been remiss not rekeying the house sooner. "Jeb? Come get your new keys."

He loped into the hall from his room. "There's more than one?"

She dangled them in front of him. "Front, back, and side."

"What a nuisance," he said, studying the differences.

"Well, I don't want to make it easy for anyone." She wiped smudges off the door with a rag. "Everything lined up for school? Any last minute expenses? Remember what I said."

"If it gets tough financially, I might have to work part-time. No problem." His eyes shifted as if deciding what to add.

Callie straightened. "Something on your mind?"

Jeb peered at the keys again. "Nothing serious." He leaned his backside and palms against the oak credenza.

"Don't put your weight on that, son," she said. "You forget how big you are."

He stood, appearing lost as to where to position himself.

Jeb appeared open to talk, so she seized the opportunity. "I'm sorry about keeping secrets about your dad. At the time, I hadn't the strength to tell you what really happened. Time just seemed to crawl away from me. You adapted, we moved. I just . . ." She tried to tease loose the words.

"That wasn't on my mind, Mom." He nudged her. "But while we're on the subject, I think you did the right thing. Caught me by surprise, is all."

Callie went speechless at this boy's flash of adulthood.

Then he gave her that half-grin of his father's. "I thought about it, even discussed it with some friends. I'd have gone crazy wanting to get even with somebody if you'd told me back then. Didn't you?"

"Oh, son, you have no idea," she said, not caring to share the details of those days.

He hugged her. "I miss him so much sometimes. This just makes him more of a hero."

She squeezed him back. "I know."

After a long moment, she held him back and wiped the corner of her eye. "So, what'd you want to say?"

"You own this house, right?"

"So says the deed."

"Does that mean you'll stay here? I mean, like, for a year or something?"

A question she'd asked herself every day since they'd arrived. Several times a day lately. "Haven't decided. We still have your father's insurance, but I'm not sure how far that will take us. There's not much career potential here. Waiting tables, selling real estate, or helping the lady at the consignment store." She had the offer from Seabrook to step back into uniform, but Jeb didn't need to know that. "It's not your worry," she said. "If I move, there's always your grandparents' place for weekends and holidays. You'll still have a place to go." She reached up and flicked him under the chin. "But you know I won't be far."

"It's just, I mean . . ."

"What, Jeb?" she asked tenderly. "Do you like it here?"

There it was, that half-grin. "A lot, Mom. But I like it more with you here."

Her paranoia dragged them both down at times, but she already saw that living at Edisto Beach had lifted her son's spirits. As much as she hated admitting it, maybe her parents knew the beach house gift would help them readjust.

She wrapped her arms around his skinny body already on its way to a rich tan from his few days on the water with Zeus. "I want what you want," she said. "But if you keep trying to please me, you'll never get on with your life."

"Sounds like what I ought to be telling you, Mom."

She reached high and tousled his blond tresses. She wanted to commit to a year or two for his sake, but so far this beach wasn't loving her much. She could leave and draw this criminal away, assuming she was a target. Jeb could then stay at Chelsea Morning. After all, it was paid for.

But the skuzzball might stick around, and she wouldn't be around to protect her son.

"Tell you what," she said. "I'll reconsider matters on New Year's Eve. How's that?"

"I can do that. I like the idea of coming home here. Assuming I don't have a big party in Charleston."

She gently poked him in the belly. "Good."

His slow nod seemed to tuck the date away. "On New Year's we hold a family meeting. And no drinking for either of us. Deal?"

Some of her smile faded. "Deal." She got the message.

The shiny new keys went in his pocket. "Would it bother you too much if I ate dinner with friends tonight?"

"No, not at all." She raised a brow. "Friends?"

"Yeah," he said, his bare feet smacking the floor on his way back to his room. "Zeus, Sprite, and some friend of hers. Zeus is paying for me since I helped him so much with his fishing business the last two days."

He was growing up and drifting away so fast.

After he left, she went to the kitchen to check the clock, her thoughts mixed about her son on his own and hanging around Sprite with her effect on males. Almost three p.m. Cops and robbers had eaten up the best part of her day.

She filled a glass with ice and poured a tonic with a twist of lime. A crisp summer cooler, she told herself. After a sip, it fell far short of a splash of gin. She even reached for the freezer door to locate the nonexistent bottle.

Deal with it, Callie.

When they'd first relocated to Middleton, her runs took an abrupt shift from fanatical to sporadic when Beverly's afternoon *teas* became her replacement habit. When her mother imbibed, Callie followed suit. Two with her mother and two more in her room once her parents retired around nine. The only way she could sleep, Callie had told herself. The only way to cope with the mother daughter quarrels, widowhood, and concerns about the future.

But she wasn't in Middleton now.

She walked toward the bar glasses behind which Lawton kept his favorite single barrel. Nobody else drank it. It wasn't hers to take, but then her father might appreciate a fresher bottle. He'd never know the difference anyway.

Seabrook said call him before she poured a drink. He'd be dead asleep after last night's vigil, though, so she went to the next best distraction she knew. But her phone rang first, the number vaguely familiar. "Hello?"

"I thought I asked you to watch my house."

"Pauley? What's wrong?"

"The police department called me. Said there was another break-in. You're a cop. Why aren't you guarding my place?"

Whoa, time to set this man straight. "First, I'm not a cop. Second, I'm not in your employ. If you want a guard, hire someone, but don't order me to serve your needs. You don't order me, period."

He ignored her retort. "You went in?"

"Yeah. Why?"

"Did the cops take anything? Did they toss the closets? I don't want them thinking they have a free rein to pocket stuff. Those coins they're finding are mine, you know."

Callie's radar got warm. "Where are you, Pauley?"

"Home. I'd be there, but I'm trying to put together the money to make the trip."

The man was so broke he couldn't afford to put gas in the car and pack up some sandwiches? How far was Kissimmee? Four hundred miles?

"Dad's being cremated tomorrow. I'll pick him up whenever I get there."

Huh? "What about a service?"

"I don't want to bother."

Her heart lurched. "I'll organize it. Who do I contact?"

"It'll cost money, Callie. No can do."

What kind of stone-cold crackhead was this guy? "Please, let me do something for him."

"Up to you, but Dad won't be there. Me either. I consider that sort of ceremonial mumbo-jumbo rather stupid, myself, but if you get off on it, knock yourself out."

She dropped her forehead, resting it on a cabinet. Papa deserved a service. He deserved a celebration of his life. Old pictures snapped through her mind like a slide show: Papa on a vintage ship, in New York on Broadway with his wife, holding up a giant redfish with the help of a friend, boating with his son, a lunatic oblivious to the need for closure.

"Well, I'm not keeping surveillance on the place," she said, though she incessantly peered out her kitchen window for movement in the old place.

"Listen here," he said, his order neutered by the nasal in his voice. "I'm holding you responsible."

"I'm not your rent-a-cop. Quit calling me."

Silence hung on the other end. "Then I'll accuse you of breaking in if stuff goes missing. You had a key. You're a single parent now. You probably need the money."

What a freak. "Don't call me again, and don't you dare come to my house."

She hung up and rang Stan. "What have you found out on Pauley Beechum?" she asked, without the normal jokes between them.

"Love you, too, Chicklet. Why, yes, I'm just fine. Nice of you to ask," he said in a buoyant delivery that served to slow her down.

"Sorry."

"That's better. Now," he said. "I take it something happened."

She relayed the light next door, the coin at Sophie's, the Hanson break-in, and then the incredulous conversation with Pauley. Her eagerness to go after someone escalated as she explained each event.

"I see. Well, I did manage to check your Pauley out. Assault about twenty years ago, but nothing along those lines since. However, he's added insurance fraud to his resume twice. Actually did a little time and paid restitution for it. Something about tornados and false claims."

"He does live in Florida. That it?"

"What else you want?"

"He's demanding, tried to be threatening," she said with a grumble. "I want him arrested for something."

"For a change, I'm glad you're not ranting over a Russian."

Her eyes narrowed, and she wished she could stare the big man down. "Are you not taking me seriously?"

"I am, Morgan. It's just refreshing to see you fired up on the offensive. Long overdue, I say. Long overdue."

And with that she smiled, some tension draining out of her at his backhanded compliment. She let the conversation shift to chatter about the staff in Boston and hung up a half hour later.

With the silence, however, came the memories. She ached at what would become of Papa's accumulated life collected in that house. What a selfish, hedonistic son. No closure, no way for her and others to say goodbye.

Even at eighty, Papa had left too soon. She'd have been tickled to share a cup of cocoa with him right now, in spite of the summer heat. Cocoa had been Papa's way of saying everything would be all right. But now the cocoa reminded her of the two cups a murderer had set up to harass her.

On the offensive, she reminded herself. She liked that. Stan's observations had always been pure gold. She dialed her neighbor as planned before Pauley's interruption. "Hey, Sophie. Got a minute?"

"Why?" Sophie whispered. "What's wrong? Every time I see you there's a crime."

"Thanks a lot. I wanted to ask you some questions and not do it under your roof," Callie said, drawing upon her coaxing skills. "Thought we could meet over tea. A ladylike thing, you know."

Sophie's guffaw echoed over the phone. "*A ladylike thing?* Just call it what it is. A drink. I'll be right there."

The knock sounded minutes later, no doubt curiosity driving the prompt arrival. Callie had two iced teas poured, and she set them at the bar before answering. Sophie came inside, glanced uncertainly at the glasses, and perched on her barstool.

"This is tea," she said after sampling to be sure.

"Yes," Callie said. "I'm off alcohol. Dieting."

Sophie studied her then caught herself. "Okay, I can go with that. So, what are your questions?"

"What was stolen from your house when that guy left you the coin?"

"No—thing," she sang back. "Just like I told Mike. And you're going to mess up your house talking about this."

Callie settled on the next stool and ignored the sage referral. "Something has to be missing. It's the way this guy operates. If he left a coin, he took something. Like the tooth fairy."

"Not in my house," she said.

"I think you're being naive."

Sophie's earrings jingled at the back-and-forth of her head. "Maybe. Maybe not."

Callie stood. "Come on. We're going back to your place to search it."

A knock sounded at the door.

Sophie jumped. "Who's that?" she whispered.

"Well, it's not a burglar," Callie said, moving toward the entryway. As she rounded the corner, Mason Howard waved through the window. Well, this was just great. If this man thought he could now gravitate from the occasional run on the beach to regular visits to her home, he had best think twice.

Today she'd become Ground Zero for the daffy, the disturbed, and the philandering.

"Not sure I recognize you without running shorts," Callie said, inviting the man in.

She wanted to dig more out of Sophie about what had happened at her place, then what she knew about the Rosewoods, Mrs. Hanson, maybe Pauley. Some of that might not be appropriate in front of Mason. But then maybe her two guests could feed off each other.

Mason followed her to the kitchen.

"Care for a glass of tea?" Callie asked, keeping the refreshments virgin.

"No booze," Sophie said, holding up her glass. "*Somebody's* on a diet."

Mason snickered. "Tea's fine. How are you, Sophie?"

"Wonderful, Mason. Ready for Friday night?"

Ample charm shined in that smile. "It's just another gathering."

Sophie leaned in Callie's direction, as if sharing a secret. "A *gathering*, he says. It's quite the event. I've been three times and wouldn't miss it now. Shrimp, fish, all sorts of appetizers. And anything you'd like to drink, handled by real bartenders. One time he flew in fresh halibut, for Pete's sake."

Callie poured his drink and placed it on a cardboard coaster from the stack on the bar. "Maybe Seabrook wasn't so far off base when he called you *playboy*, Mr. Howard."

"She won't call him *Mike*," Sophie cooed. "I think she's afraid to."

Letting loose a sigh of disgust, Callie stared at her neighbor for the remark.

"Mike's all right, I guess," Mason said, hiding behind his glass as he drank.

"Hmm," Sophie said. "Mike will be single the rest of his days. Wouldn't you say so, Mason?"

"I've only heard rumor, my dear." He set down his glass. "Keep in mind, I'm a mere tenant. I get all my gossip at the party, but that seems to be the consensus."

Callie scoffed. "So one goes to this party to either hear gossip or avoid being gossiped about. That the way it works?" Then maybe she *should* go, to study all the players and glean for suspects. Discover the secret feuds that always existed in a small community. Endless possibilities.

Sophie reached her arms out wide. "*Everybody's* gossip around here, honey. It's part of the culture."

"Then what do they say about Seabrook . . . um, Mike?" The question just spilled out.

A wicked grin of recognition crept into Sophie's expression, and she jumped on the opportunity. "He can't date anyone more than three times."

"Twice," Mason said. "And he avoids anyone involved with medicine."

Sophie wrapped an arm around Mason's shoulder and lowered her voice as she peered at Callie. "They say he killed his wife when he was a doctor."

Callie's brow wrinkled. "Wasn't that a movie titled *The Fugitive*? Your gossip isn't even original."

"That's the real word," Mason said.

"He's not kidding," Sophie added.

Surely not. Callie got up to rinse her glass in the sink, watching the water circle the drain. The depth of Seabrook's sincerity last night held new meaning for her if any of this was true. He'd walked in her shoes losing his spouse. She shut off the water. "How would *you* two like being talked about?"

"Hey, I'm the playboy," Mason said.

"I'm the Gypsy," Sophie echoed. "Or the hippie, but I don't find that as exciting." She faced Mason. "Don't you like Gypsy better?"

He nodded innocently. "Bohemian."

Callie turned toward them. "So, what am I called?"

The two guests studied each other, no doubt wondering who could come up with a suitable tag. Sophie shook her head. "I haven't heard anything, really."

"You erred at the word *really*." Callie laughed. "I'm sure the gun on the beach gave me some sort of story."

"You killed some guy in Boston after you arrested him," Mason said in a monotone manner, as if avoiding judgment, watching Callie for a response.

She inhaled, waiting for Sophie's reaction to an accusation she'd never heard spoken aloud from anyone other than enraged Russians. But Sophie sat still, as if she already knew the tale. Mason's body language, however, was one of anticipation. Both seemed intent on Callie's validation of the gossip, one way or another.

Zubov's arrest *could* have brought on his stroke, but she'd never let her mind get wrapped around his demise being her fault. Some days she wished she'd slit his throat, up close and personal. On the weaker days, she selfishly wished him alive, well, and never arrested, because then, John might be, too.

"I can see where people would think I killed him," she finally said, ending the silence.

"And you did something that got your husband killed, too," Sophie said with a meek sounding voice.

Callie went dumbstruck as all the air left the room.

"Goodness," Sophie mumbled. "Maybe I shouldn't have said that."

After a moment, Callie realized she held her breath, and released it. She had to recognize this for what it was, addressing the elephant in the room. She'd moved here to start a new life, and those around Edisto might be nervous about her past. Funny. She'd invited both of these people in to interview them, and they'd dissected her instead.

Callie gave a mild grin at her neighbor's daredevil comment, then pointed. "You're devious, Miss Sophie Bianchi. You said that on purpose. You just had to break that ice."

Sophie still didn't move.

"So I kill people, huh?"

Mason watched intently. Sophie nodded.

"Half-truths sure make for a good rumor mill," she said, smiling. "The more you fight the gossip, the more you stir it up. Hell, tell the good residents of Edisto I shot a hundred criminals while you're at it." She bent over the counter toward them. "Which means the gossip about Seabrook is half-truth, too."

"True. True." Sophie bobbed her head rapidly, obviously happy to reach the end of the conversation.

"Hey," Mason said. "This means I'm only half a playboy." He gave her his glass, declining a refill, and Callie placed it in the sink. "That also means I'm not nearly the risk old Seabrook tried to paint me to be. So, Ms. Callie Morgan. How about going to dinner?"

Eyes wide, Callie repeated the question in her head. The dinner invitation startled her more than the murder accusations.

Sophie clapped. "Oh, yes. Take her out. Where?"

"We'll start small the first time," he said. "Whaley's." He walked around the bar and took Callie's hand. "It's casual. You don't even have to change."

She snapped her hand back and glanced at the clock. "It's four thirty."

Mason peered down at his Rolex, a Cellini platinum. She'd noticed the leather band, because John had hated metal twist bands, too. "Yes, it's four thirty," he said. "Great. We'll beat the dinner crowd."

Of course he had no idea what she meant. She preferred to be home when the world turned orange, as day turned to night. When a dying sun reminded her of a dying husband in a house burning to the ground.

But what had she thought on the way back from the police station? Interview everybody with even the most tenuous connection to Papa Beach, only not let them know it. Mason had jogged by minutes after Papa died, oblivious. Maybe he saw something she could tease from his memory, or thanks to his gossip party-line, draw out snippets that could help.

"I don't want to stay too long," Callie said.

Sophie leaped off the stool and ran to the door. "Y'all have fun!"

"Wait!" Callie yelled. "Aren't you coming?" She glanced back at Mason, who shrugged his eyebrows. "Sophie. Come with us."

"Toodles," Sophie cried, shutting the door.

The room fell silent for an uncomfortably long interlude.

Callie collected her courage. The playboy was an ocean of information about Edisto, and she meant to drain him dry. "Let's do this."

He retrieved her purse and the keys beside it on the credenza. She took them and inserted an arm in the offered crook of his. *Gracious alive, I'm going on a date.*

She glanced up to analyze the sky. Plenty of light left. Sunset wouldn't be for another four hours. Then she saw the car.

A gleaming, British, racing-green Jag. She'd seen them, even impounded a silver one, watched drug dealers and mobsters glide by thumbing their noses at her in them. But ride in one?

Mason held the door, and she eased in, melting against the seat. It had been a long time since she'd enjoyed such an indulgence. She stroked the leather, accepting she was on a mission. And as long as the man didn't allow his million dollar hands to wander, the night actually could prove fruitful.

Chapter 15

IN SPITE OF THE early hour, locals, tourists, and renters jammed Whaley's lot from Neptune to Billow Street and all along Myrtle. The only tables open were tall bistros in the middle of the floor. Half the patrons and all the staff knew Mason.

"Hey, Maple Leaf!"

"Mason, I'm ready to party!"

"What you importing for us this week?"

"I'll be there, dude."

He acknowledged them all, women and men, with a wink and a grin before a chivalrous act of sliding out Callie's chair.

"You're popular," she said.

"Free alcohol and food tends to do that. But I have no family, so why not enjoy life with people wherever I go?"

Especially on the beach where parties carried status. She hadn't eaten at Whaley's in a couple of years. Their shrimp platter could talk Northerners into loving grits, so she ordered the dish to remind her of what she'd missed living in New England. Yankee seafood was so different than Lowcountry cuisine.

"Flounder for me," Mason said to the waitress. "Bring us the boiled peanuts appetizer. Vodka tonic for me and a grape soda for the lady."

Unique choice of drink, but Callie could enjoy something creative since swearing off gin. Voices ran loud. Kids talked the loudest. She'd forgotten the ambience of this place with its dated photographs hung amongst mounted fish. She settled, elbows on the tall table. "So what else have you heard, rumor man?"

"Something about break-ins," Mason replied, scooting his chair closer to be heard. "And that the acting chief of police has a new trainee." He grinned wide. "Some interfering woman from up north."

Her nerves relaxed; she enjoyed being back in commission. "If a rumor's not juicy enough, people feel the need to embellish. Truth is, I'm helping Seabrook since he's short of boots on the ground, but I haven't helped much. He's catching some sleep after we spoke late last night." She sniffed. "And I'm a far cry from a trainee."

Mason crinkled his mouth. "Last night? I'm intrigued."

"Sure you are."

The waitress served their drinks, leaving Mason with a wink.

Callie waited for the girl to leave before she leaned in. "Another break-in at the Beechum place. Seabrook was there all night after leaving my house." She took a swig of her drink. *Chew that one over, Mason.*

Mason cocked his head. "Your house?"

"Yes." She sniffed her drink and took another sip. "Thought this was grape soda." She grabbed the menu. "*Grape vodka, Sprite, and cranberry juice.* Not funny, Mr. Howard. I was trying to abstain."

He pulled the glass away from her. "Don't drink it then."

She retrieved it. "Just one," she said. "Almost reminds me of third grade."

He smiled. "How many break-ins are you up to?"

She removed her own house from the count, embarrassed to have been caught off guard, but she also didn't want the world to consider her vulnerable. The rest of the break-ins were rampant island news anyway. "Three if you count Sophie, plus the murder." She took a moment to enjoy the grape flavor, recalling recess on swings, pumping her legs, pretending her eight-year-old feet walked on clouds.

The waitress brought the appetizer, and Callie dove into the boiled peanuts, complimenting Mason for being Canadian and still enjoying Southern food, and kidding him for having no accent to go with it. Fifteen minutes later, she noticed he'd eaten only a few of the soggy legumes, like a person who hadn't grown up on them. Apparently, he'd ordered them for her. Nice touch. Seabrook *did* warn the man was smooth.

The din of the place amplified as customers crammed into extra chairs around tables, at the bar, squeezing into seats in corners. Callie accepted one more grape soda, which seemed to last a long time until she realized Mason had bought her a third. She learned about the Canadian restaurant business, but he evaded chitchat about himself. He could talk details about the bartender, the fifty-something lady at the bar, and the couple snuggled in the corner, more than the normal transient beachcomber should be able to. He knew more about her than was comfortable.

The conversation always came back to *her*, a couple times catching her unawares as she spoke of Boston and briefly about John. Mason took it all in with a sensitive attentiveness.

She had to admit she'd missed the flirtatious bob and weave and the occasional glance from a man observing her body.

"How well do you know Don Raysor?" she asked, returning to business. Raysor seemed over-the-top disgruntled about her presence, and maybe Mason knew why.

"Stereotypical southern bubba throwing that tub belly around," he said. "Few like him around here."

"He sure doesn't like me."

"You're a woman cop," he said.

"Any secrets on him?" she asked, sipping her drink.

Mason shook his head. "Nobody's told me anything. I think he used to be married, but not sure what happened with that."

"Guess you'll have to work harder on your intel."

Mason knew little about the red-faced man from up the road other than as a member of Colleton County Sheriff's Department. Raysor came from Walterboro, an hour away, distant enough to protect his lifestyle, past, and whatever he did on the side.

"Who's the guy repairing your steps?" Mason asked, adjusting his voice to barroom level. "Sure gets loud in here, doesn't it?"

"Yeah," she yelled. "Jack Peters. He starts in the morning. Ever use him?"

He shrugged. "I'm in someone else's rental, remember? But from what I hear, I don't trust him."

"Seabrook thinks he's safe enough."

Mason grimaced. "I'm not a big *Seabrook* fan, either."

The sour response interrupted the casualness between them. The best course of action would be to give him credence for it. "Well, since you're so into the underground, what's wrong with Peters? And then tell me what irritates you about our acting chief."

He leaned on his hand, two fingers up the side of his cheek, coolly watching her. "Peters is too loose for my taste. These people give him too much liberty, and I don't understand why. He showers and eats in a lot of their homes. Like the community uncle."

Mason's concerns had merit per her personal and professional canons. "Everyone does seem to trust him."

"Too much." Mason swirled his drink.

Then he smiled, and she liked the softened facial lines. No stranger to the sun, his dark brows were bleached a shade lighter, his hair streaked. An outdoorsy individual whose financial means afforded him latitude to enjoy beaches, mountains, wherever he felt the urge to roam. She bet all his travails had a Mother Nature flavor versus urban glass and steel.

She wondered what Stan would make of this guy.

"Mike," Mason started, "isn't a bad guy as a whole, but he's damaged. I see him as a perpetual bachelor after what happened to his wife. Too wounded."

"He didn't really kill his wife, did he?" She'd said it too low to be heard over the noise, but Mason seemed to read her lips.

"No, home invasion," he said. "Murdered while he was at the hospital. In Charleston, I believe."

Her eyes widened at the sharp pain of empathy. How could she have been around Mike and not felt the connection? She understood the deep, empty hole in his life and now the lack of pictures on his desk.

Dragging her glass closer, she cradled it, remembering the guilt at not saving John. Routine had separated her just far enough from him for life to go crazy, just like with Mike . . . er . . . Seabrook.

"Did they catch the killer?" she asked.

"No. And he blamed himself for not being there." He reached across the table and stroked the back of her hand with a finger. "Heard he went almost nuts trying to solve the case. They let him go from his position, or he quit, I don't know, but he became a cop to hunt for the guy. He still has his mission, from what I hear. For obvious reasons, Charleston wouldn't hire him, so he came here."

Seabrook ran toward law enforcement, and she ran away from it, after similar circumstances. "Poor guy. How long ago?"

Mason's smile changed to dismay. "How insanely stupid of me, Callie."

His embarrassment pulled her back to the present. After wiping her damp fingers on a napkin, she placed them in her lap. He didn't have to tell her what he was embarrassed about. "It's okay, Mason."

"I didn't think. You asked about Seabrook, and I answered with no consideration of his privacy or your similar past." He clasped her hand between his damp, warm palms. "My deepest apology."

Clever or sincere? She wasn't sure.

"Well," she said and drew back to recover. She lifted the menu. "You can make up for it with dessert."

"Let me." Taking the menu, he held up a finger to catch the waitress's eye.

"Ticket?" the young girl asked.

He flashed that bright smile, which drew out one from the girl. "Not yet," he said. "Bring us a big slice of your Bananas Foster cheesecake and two forks."

Twenty minutes later, Callie scraped the last smear of caramel rum sauce off the plate. She asked what Mason did in his spare time, apart from jogging, and he diverted to trivia about residents. She tried to enter into a story-swapping routine, and Mason soon laughed at one of her Southern redneck tales, with none of his own.

She was about to try interrogating him again when a noisy brawny guy entered to a dozen "Hey, Fred" greetings. A car pulled into the parking lot and parked with headlights blazing into the front door, causing her to squint. They shut off, but her breath caught. The disappearing sun had turned the day to dusk.

"What's wrong?" Mason asked, searching the place for what had suddenly incapacitated her.

"I have to get home." She jumped from her seat, fingers gliding along the edge of the round table for balance. "I don't stay out after dark." But she wasn't sure how she'd face going home, either. That long approach, turning the corner, praying not to see that glow.

Mason threw some bills on the table and placed her purse on her shoulder. "If you weren't so frightened, I'd kid you about turning into a pumpkin, but you're ten shades of pale, Callie."

"Just get me home."

Outside, the thick salty night air had cooled the evening. Staring at her shoes, she settled in the Jag. Mason came around to the driver's side after retrieving an item from the trunk. "Here," he said, setting a lightweight blanket in her lap.

He touched Classical on his satellite radio, and Brahms floated around the interior. "Think about a bubble bath, candles, white roses. Smell the roses?"

"I shouldn't have come," she mumbled into the cotton pressed against her hot face as the car's tires spit gravel.

As the Jag made its way to Chelsea Morning, the Canadian talked to her, transporting her someplace else full of soft towels and violins. He painted descriptions of flowers on a counter and deep, deep carpet. Chocolate in a bone china bowl. Wine on the edge of the tub. Her brain was scrambled, yet he laid stepping stones before her, guiding her home to safety.

Soon, with instructions on where to place her feet, she recognized her own porch, gave Mason the keys, then relaxed as he lifted the blanket away inside her foyer.

"What time is it?" she asked.

"Nine thirty," he said, folding the blanket.

She blew out long, releasing pressure. "Thanks so very much, Mason."

Pain crossed his face. "Not earned, I'm afraid. I didn't take you seriously about the dark."

"My problem. It was a lovely date nonetheless."

His pleasant smile rested on her. He set the blanket on her credenza, and without any misgivings, leaned over and placed both hands on her cheeks. The kiss was tender, assuring, and quickly done.

"I had a wonderful time," he said. "Sure you won't come to my Friday gathering?"

She nodded toward the door, his eyes following.

He grinned in acknowledgement. "Oh, the evening issue," he said. "I could put a tasteful scarf on your head coming and going. Even carry you to your door, m'lady."

The drinks weighed on her, the kiss still lingering on her lips. The date was sweet, but . . . "I'll let you know. I'm not much of a party girl."

"Hopefully I can entice you to accept before summer's end. Good night, my dear."

She smiled, enjoying the word *dear* for the first time in her life. "Good night."

After securing the door, she leaned against it and exhaled. Gracious, she'd been a fool falling apart like that. But the dinner had been fun.

She flopped on the bed, grinning, anxious to tell Stan she'd finally been wined and dined. Tonight her nightmares just might be sweetened by the evening.

JOLTING OUT OF bed, Callie poised in the middle of her blue braided bedroom rug, her Glock tight in shaky hands. She waited rock-still, listening for the next shot.

Another crack, then another.

"Mom?" Jeb yelled from his bedroom. "What's going on?"

"Get in the closet until I tell you to come out."

"But—"

"Just do it, Jeb!"

Heart pounding, she moved deftly to the front door.

Then she quietly cursed. Peters hammered nails into her porch steps with an effort that belied his laissez-faire appearance.

Her forearm muscles went lax and lowered the weapon she'd snatched from under her pillow. "It's okay. He's a contractor I hired to repair and paint the stairs. Go back to bed."

"Like that's gonna happen," Jeb said, standing in boxers as rumpled as his hair. He peered at the gun. "You sleep with that, don't you?"

"I misread the situation. Don't worry about it."

Crap, I forgot to get the paint for Peters.

Jeb smiled. "You thought someone was laying fire on your porch, didn't you?"

"I was startled, butthead," she said. "This isn't my favorite time of day. Why aren't you fishing?"

"Zeus didn't have a client today, plus we got in around two. You were out of it, Mom. Didn't even move when I peered in to tell you I was home." He blinked a couple times. "How do *you* feel this morning? What did *you* do last night?"

The impromptu date flooded back, and she tried to hold a motherly tone while recalling one of the most fun evenings she'd had since . . . life quit being fun. "I feel fine. Had a great dinner with a new friend, then crashed around eleven. Ate too much. Why?"

The pounding started again.

"I can't stand this," Jeb said, covering his ears. "I'm taking a shower then going next door."

"Zeus might be asleep." She felt silly in her nightgown, the gun limp beside her.

"He might," her son said, scratching in places Callie didn't care to note. "But Sprite does yoga each morning with her mother, so she'll be up."

What was this?

"I saw that," he said.

"What?"

"The oh-no-my-son-is-dating look."

She tried for nonchalance. "Why wouldn't you be dating? Wait. Was last night a date?"

"Didn't start as a date, but it kinda ended up that way." He beamed. "So, yeah."

"Sprite Bianchi?"

"That's her name, Mom."

Callie walked toward the bedroom to put away the Glock, dying to know if they'd kissed. "Yes, and it's an easy name to remember." Not to mention the face, the body, all those curls. She especially wasn't sure about the nubile come-hither bearing of a girl that came with such flamboyance.

Jeb left, laughing. "She's cool, Mom. And she's only one year younger."

The numerical difference wasn't Callie's concern. It was the massive pheromone capacity of the girl. Like mother like daughter.

As the water warmed in the shower, Callie hung her nightgown on the back of her bathroom door. She studied her reflection in the medicine cabinet mirror. What was it about Sophie that made the woman so sexy? Was yoga that much different from running?

She touched the creases beneath her eyes and stretched the skin. Then she lifted her chin, checking elasticity. Head turned left, then right, not happy with the circles under her eyes, she recognized the effects of a mild hangover.

Bam. Bam. Bam. Peters was relentless on the end of that hammer.

Jeb's query about what she'd done last night told her he worried about her drinking again. She'd give him less opportunity to worry about that from this point forward. Last night would have been the first of her no-more-drinking plan, except for Mason. Grape soda. Slick date drink, that's for sure. But she could have sent back the drink and abstained, so she couldn't exactly blame the man. She'd just have to start again.

A warmth spread over her, down into her. She'd gone out, socially. The jaunt was meant to be a plan to retrieve information, but still, a date.

She held an arm under the water. Satisfied, she stepped under the hot spray. The stream ran into her hair, soaking it. As rivulets ran across her breasts and belly, she replayed the kiss. Roses, he'd said. She sniffed her shampoo, the too-sweet strawberry scent short-circuiting her imaginary foreplay.

The ride home in a convertible. Brahms playing.

She smoothed body wash across her chest then down to her navel.

His smooth voice relaxing her, in hindsight, tempting her. The wonderful way he'd painted a scene with smells to whisk away her fears. His reassuring guide up the stairs. The look they exchanged in the entryway.

She sudsed her sides, rising up and down her ribs, again and again. She moved to her hips, pretending the hands weren't hers.

That kiss rejuvenated a want that seemed to bloom deep inside her, seeking its way to the surface. His lips had been so gentle, but he could have almost taken her from just the simple, sweet manner in which he cradled her face.

She jumped when her phone rang from the bedroom.

Bam. Bam. Bam. The contractor went at it again.

"Jeb?" she hollered. "Can you get my phone in the bedroom?"

Nothing.

She shut off the water and dried herself, briefly wondering if she was desperate.

John had died two years ago, and Bonnie's crib death had struck them both so deeply they hadn't been intimate for most of the year following. She remembered all the overtime she and John would put in at work to forget and escape. The walls they'd built, as if they couldn't let love sabotage them again.

They'd distanced themselves from each other long before the fire.

And she'd hated him for it. She'd hated herself for letting him.

She snatched up the phone. Stan had left a voice mail.

"Ring me back, Chicklet. A Deputy Raysor called twice about you. Ranting that you're interfering with an investigation and trying to seduce their lead badge. I just listened. Refused to go into detail about you. When I said you needed to be wined and dined, I didn't mean for you to go jump the first guy you met. Again, call me."

She dropped her bare butt on the bed. That son-of-a-bitch Raysor. Her experience dealing with investigations exceeded all of the Edisto Beach uniforms put together, including the illustrious, pompous, loaned-out deputy she read as little more than a security guard.

Finger over the redial button, she changed her mind and hung up. She glanced at the phone's clock. Nine a.m. Crap. She needed to get to the hardware store for paint.

Catching her nudity in the mirror, she stopped. Selfish pleasure with Mason had distracted her from the dangerous reality that somebody still watched her. Somebody who could've sat at Whaley's drinking a beer for all she knew.

This morning started her fifth day at Edisto. A crime every single day since she'd arrived. But wasn't danger an aphrodisiac? Had that been her flaw last night? Cops knew it. Criminals knew it. What else could explain her slip with Mason?

Please God, give this place a day devoid of burglaries and tragedy. For her, for Seabrook, for the natives like Sophie who hadn't grasped the gravity of the crimes. Let the badges find a breakthrough and everyone else enjoy normalcy.

Allow her to think about an ordinary future for a change.

A dab of make-up later, she put on khaki shorts, sandals, tank, and long sleeves.

"Ms. Morgan? Callie?" Peters hollered at the front door. "I didn't see the paint."

"Coming!" she yelled, grabbing her purse.

Peters gave her a crooked grin as she answered. "About to start sanding. Got all the steps taken care of."

"On my way to get the paint now, Peters. Be back in an hour. That okay?"

"Sure," he said, plugging in his extension cord.

The hardware store was only four miles up the highway. On the way back, she'd maybe stop at the gift shop next to the pizza take-out. Surely they would have rose-scented bath salts in stock.

Chapter 16

HOW MANY COLORS of peachy beige were there? Callie perused the selections in the Edisto Lowcountry Hardware store. Beverly once ranted when redecorating Lawton's office about how paint swatches were lighter than they appeared on the wall. But this paint was renovating outdoor steps and railings. Even if it went on darker, wouldn't the sun bleach it in, like, three months' time?

"Can I help you?" asked a young man around twenty-five, a striking oriental tattoo peeking out from under his shirt sleeve.

"I can't remember the color of my porch and stairs," she said.

He gave a smirk that only the young could pull off so cute. "On the beach? Which house?"

"Chelsea Morning," she replied.

"Oh, three rows back." He reached across her and flipped swatches. "This one, or—" He extracted another one a row higher. "This one."

Callie closed her gaping mouth and took the swatches. "How did you do that?"

"Ma'am, I was born out here. So, are you Lawton Cantrell's daughter?"

Her short laugh caused a chubby middle-aged gent with beefy neck and calves to glance over further down the aisle. He raised a coy brow at her.

Shifting to give him her shoulder and no opportunity, she held the colors higher, as if studying them in the light. "Yeah, I am."

The kid cut a glance at the other gentleman and spoke lower. "You found Beechum and ran screaming down the beach. You're famous."

Her humor melted into the scuffed linoleum floor. "Since you know me, you might as well pick out the shade. Which one?"

"Neither will match exactly, but either one's close." He pointed down the aisle. "Do you want paint and primer in one or latex acrylic?"

Callie studied the wall of uniform cans. "I don't know."

He grinned. "The green cans are on sale. Just get those. Let me know how many gallons, and I'll mix it for you."

She had no clue how much paint she needed. "Give me however many it'll take to cover my front steps."

The kid grabbed four cans as if they weighed no more than her cell phone, then hustled back for four more. Sinewy muscles bulging, he lifted them to the counter and got busy setting his color machine. Callie threw a couple brushes in the pile, and twenty minutes later she was rolling a cart to her car with her eight cans of Delta Sand. Seabrook's police cruiser sat parked next to her Escape, its brake lights just going off.

She slowed. Mason's revelation about the cop's past had cast Seabrook in a new light and probably not as Mason intended. Just as she didn't discuss her past to everyone, neither would Seabrook. Not about something so fragile.

What alienated those two men? Neither missed an opportunity to debase the other.

A young uniform hopped out of the patrol car. Short and all elbows, he caught Callie's stare and tipped his head in recognition. "Can I help you?"

"Why are you here?" she asked, surprised not to see Seabrook.

Crap, that didn't sound right.

"Bug spray," he said, brows meeting in curiosity. "You?"

Callie nodded to the cart. "Paint. I'm Callie Morgan, by the way. I expected to see Officer Seabrook get out. He's been driving this car." Then she felt stupid. They probably shared vehicles. A police force this small probably couldn't afford many cars. "I haven't seen him since . . . anyway, how do you do? And you are—"

"Officer Francis Dickens." He shook her hand almost as if she'd deplaned from a foreign embassy. "Nice to finally put a face with a name," he said. "The boss is working a special, so I have his car."

After-hours specials way out here? In cities, cops accepted private hires with malls, businesses, sporting events, for extra cash. Southern law enforcement wasn't a lucrative profession.

"Where would you guys pick up specials? The Wyndham?" she asked.

"Oh, no, ma'am. Not what I meant. He's sleuthing. Said not to disturb him unless it's dire." He ticked his chin to the left. "Bad time for all this, with tourist season and us being down a man."

In Charleston, obsessed about his deceased wife? Or on Edisto, studying the murder and its subsequent burglaries? Asking the deputy, however, would force him to say he couldn't say, and she didn't want to put him in that position.

"Well," she said, unlocking her car. "I'll stay out of your way. Good luck keeping everybody in line. Got to go paint a porch."

As she turned her car back toward the ocean, she pictured Seabrook pursuing some clue, interviewing neighbors. That's what she'd do.

She turned in her driveway and shut off the ignition. *Damn.* She forgot the bath salts. Probably for the best anyway. If and when she decided to release herself into the sensual longings of a man, the terms *playboy* and *gathering* didn't need to be part of the package. She'd never had a one-night stand in her life, and she could have strayed into that one way too easily.

Callie gathered her purse, knowing nobody would fill John's size twelves, though. The shoes of a man who stored sweaty basketball Nikes so long in his car that Jeb demanded they pick up his friends in Callie's SUV. John's Jeep still sat in her parents' garage, having been salvaged from the street that horrible night, parked there to allow her to back out of the garage and pull back in later. Lawton promised to have the vehicle tuned up before Jeb used it for college.

Jeb would drive that six-year-old black Wrangler until it coughed its last mile.

Peters greeted her as she got out. "Just in time, Callie." He lifted cans from the back of her car and set them on the crushed shell drive. "They mixing more paint, or is this it?"

"Um, of course they are. How many do you need?"

"Two or three more for the front. That wood drinks paint like the desert soaks up a rain. Didn't ask if you wanted the back steps done." He paused in stop-sign fashion. "I'm not, repeat, not trying to take advantage of you. Got nothing on my schedule for a couple days, is all, but not like I couldn't use a day or two off. I just need to know. No pressure."

She hadn't thought about the back. Counting the supplies, the two hundred dollar project was fast turning into a thousand dollar deal.

Callie crossed her arms. "Tell me how many gallons for the front and the back, and I'll pay you triple the labor I already promised since there's a side porch involved, too."

"You're a sport, Callie. A fine sport. You got me for three more days."

She returned to the car, recalling their first meeting and the explained ritual the natives used in hiring Jack Peters. "Guess that means I'm supposed to feed you, huh?"

"Oh, any kind of sandwich is fine, ma'am."

Lawton had taught her better than that. "When's the last time someone cooked you a medium rare steak on the grill with a huge baked potato?"

His eyes lit up like she'd proposed with a two carat diamond. "You'd get no complaint outta me. And your steps'll beat anything on this block."

"Good," she said, putting her sunglasses back on. "I'll be back in another hour. I'm looking forward to Chelsea Morning in her new outfit. Let's see just how great you talents are."

CALLIE PUT THE steaks in a marinade and scrubbed potatoes, slathering butter on the skins. She wrapped them in foil and left them in the oven set on a timer. Cooking comfort food for two men felt nice. Peters probably hadn't tasted steak in months, living out of his truck like he did.

Then she returned the overdue voice mail call to Stan.

"Okay, Stan," she said when he answered, "what's the deal with Raysor?"

"What took you so long, Morgan?" he exclaimed without a greeting.

"I had to pick up paint for the contractor to refinish my porches, then steaks for a cookout this afternoon." How fantastic it felt to sound domestic. Somewhere in the universe, karma was letting her skip a day of crisis.

"Two days ago, I had to settle your ass down, Chicklet. I don't mind telling you that I hung up damn worried. You sound good today. Anyway, I get this call from a deputy telling me you were seducing officers and undermining investigations. Told the guy he had the wrong person, but he described you down pat." He drank something.

"Quit slurping." Callie could picture the FBI mug given to him when the department worked a task force with the Boston Field Office. The cup was dark blue and hid the rings of the old coffee he never quite cleaned out before each refill. "The local acting chief wants my help," she said. "You spoke with Raysor, the guy with all the bluster. He's the one I don't trust."

"So they solved the case?"

"Cases," she said. "And no."

"Multiple murders?" His voice crescendoed, hitting that question mark hard.

"One murder and robbery. Then a couple more two-bit burglaries. Not sure what to call the other break-ins."

He got quiet. "Any of this crap scare you?"

Of course it did. But last night's date and Peters' comfortable congeniality had kept her from peering incessantly over her shoulder for adversaries for one day. She hoped Stan wasn't about to ruin the reprieve. But hearing him did make her feel ashamed about lowering her defenses.

"Somebody has a flashy MO, Stan. They don't really break in. They wait until it's easy to enter the house, and, get this, they leave a silver dollar from a collection missing from the murder."

At mention of her stolen mug in Papa Beach's house, Stan started barking orders. "Change your damn locks," he said.

"I did, Stan."

"Before or after the mug was stolen?"

"After."

"Well, why the hell didn't you change them before?"

"Stan," she said, the muscles in her back knotting. "I've tightened up around here. Don't treat me like a child."

"Don't like you being alone in all this."

"I can handle—"

"Yeah, yeah, yeah, I know you're very capable and all that shit. But . . . anyway, be careful."

"So what did Raysor say?"

Nothing Stan said surprised her, nothing she hadn't already heard. The deputy had tattled, like it mattered. Then as if reading her mind, Stan asked, "Would that idiot deputy plant the cup to scare you? He seems a bit over the top. Is that typical of Southern law down there?"

"I declare, are you profiling, Captain Waltham?"

"Heh, heh, heh. You and that damn accent." Paper wrinkled from what she guessed was a stick of cinnamon gum. "Got to admit you sound better this time, Chicklet. Don't take no guff off that guy."

"No problem. It's always nice to hear from you, Stan, even when you're grumpy. I take it you found nothing on Henry Beechum?"

"Other than a military record? No."

She was glad to hear it. "Nice talking to you, Boss."

"Give me a better reason to call you sometime, Morgan."

"I'll try. Tell Misty hello for me."

Silence.

"Stan?"

"We split, Chicklet."

Oh, damn! She couldn't imagine this man single or without Misty. Though his job was a chronic mistress, he never forgot his wife's birthday, their anniversary. He'd been so proud taking her to Ireland several years ago. "Oh, I'm so sorry. What happened?"

"Long time coming."

"Oh, I can't believe that. You two seemed good." She craved to give the big bear a hug, stroke his back, then bring him a coffee so he could vent to someone who wouldn't judge. She hated the thousand miles between them right now.

"Don't worry about me, or her. It's congenial and all that, but if I need a shoulder, I know who to call."

"I owe you at least that much. Again, I'm sorry."

"Yeah, well, take care."

CALLIE CONTINUED mulling over Stan and his split from his wife as she diced tomatoes and ripped lettuce. The innocence of the day had vanished with the news from Boston. Jeb watched the steaks outside.

Peters poked his head in the door. "Smelling mighty good. When do I clean up?"

"Now, if you want medium rare," she said.

He turned to go outside.

"No, no, come inside," she said, dropping her knife and grabbing a kitchen towel. "Follow me. You can use Jeb's bathroom. Help yourself to whatever you need in there."

Peters didn't argue and closed the door behind him with thanks. He soon emerged rosy-cheeked, his hair washed, towel dried, and combed with a part. He smelled like mouthwash and way too much toothpaste. Callie made a note to find the toothbrush he used, in case he didn't have his own.

Jeb brought in the steaks just as Callie put drinks on the table. Peters held out her seat, and Callie smiled, catching Jeb's eye as if to say *See? That's how you do it for a lady.*

Everyone sat.

Peters asked Jeb for the sour cream. "You headed to college this year, son, or you still in high school?"

"College of Charleston this fall," Jeb said, passing the man the salt and pepper as well. "Business, I think, but they make you take stupid general education courses your first year or two. Still not sure what I want to do." He passed the butter. "Do you like your work?"

"Jeb," Callie cautioned.

"It's okay," Peters said. "I like my job well enough. Lets me be independent. Didn't get a chance to go to school. Might not be living in a truck if I had. Could be a lot worse, though." He took a bite of steak. "Hmm, umm, umm. I could get used to eating like this."

"You work for yourself," Jeb said. "So does everyone else out here. My friend Zeus makes good money with his fishing business. I like that."

"What do you define as good money?" Peters pointed his fork at the boy. "I live off scraps from tables of those who did take advantage of opportunity, son. School may seem like a drag, but trust me, it pays."

Callie felt it was time to change subjects. "How're the steps going, Peters?"

"I think you'll like them. Don't go out the front door until tomorrow, though. I hung yellow tape across the top and the bottom. The amount of paint'll be cutting it close with that darn dry wood. Guess it's been a while since Beechum painted them, huh?"

Callie wanly smiled. "Don't know, but you're taking care of them now, and we appreciate it."

Peters shoveled lettuce in his mouth, chewed with exaggeration, and swallowed. "Son?" he said to Jeb. "You've got a jewel of a mom here. Listen to her when she talks to you, you hear?"

Jeb hesitated before simply saying, "Yes, sir, I will."

"Sir," Peters repeated. "That's what I'm talking about. Can't remember when a kid called me *sir.*"

Peters' accent was pure Lowcountry, as was his humor. He appreciated manners and treated Callie with respect. She couldn't see him in the negative light Mason cast or as the suspect Raysor described. Peters wouldn't have lasted this long doing what he did if a single homeowner had sensed the least hint of wrongdoing. Callie wouldn't have asked him to dinner if she saw anything criminal in his ways.

Raysor was oversensitive about the man, his crime-fighting gusto too zealous for her taste. He'd probably never see another murder in his career, so maybe this was sport for him, means for a promotion, or a story to be told at the bar.

Callie caught herself swirling her glass, forgetting it was just water. Jeb finished up the last of his potato. She pushed half of hers on his plate, and he dove into it, adding more butter to her conservative one pat.

Soon, only the aroma of the steak remained with Peters all but licking the plate. Yep, Lawton Cantrell had taught her well. Treat a man with respect, and he'll respect you right back. Too bad Beverly fell short of fathoming the lesson.

Moments later, Peters excused himself and thanked them for dinner. Callie put Jeb on the dishes and retired to the back porch, grateful the sun had already set on the marsh. She punched speed dial on her cell phone; she owed someone a promise.

"Daddy? It's me. I'm calling Mother like you asked."

"Great. Let me get her."

"Wait a minute before you do that," she said. The sun gone behind the water, soft ripples flowed in colors more reserved for a fall forest. She was so happy to be safely at home at this time of day.

"Can you talk to Jeb for me?" she asked. "I'm sensing mild reservations about college. Could be cold feet, or some dumb notion stuck in his head by new friends, but maybe you can instill in him the importance of that degree. Call him maybe? Or better yet, drop by and take him to dinner. Do something before this mild aversion bloats into something he acts on."

Her father gave a mild grunt. "We can't have that now, can we? Saturday night?"

"It's not urgent, Daddy."

"No, no. I'm trying to ease into this retirement mentality. And I meant it when I said I wanted to spend more time with Jeb. Pick him up at five?"

"You're my idol. Now put Mother on the phone so I can get you retired."

Her body tensed when Beverly's voice came closer in the background, chatting the whole way about some early fundraiser she orchestrated in preparation for the next campaign. Lawton said nothing more than, "Talk to your daughter. Be nice to her."

Scuffling as the phone was exchanged. "Callie?"

"Yes, Mother."

"What's wrong?"

"Nothing, but we need to talk. Don't get upset, now."

Beverly gave a ladylike snort. "That's a warning for sure. What is it, dear?"

"It's about Daddy. He's missing Jeb. And I propose something that won't set well with you."

"Oh, it's probably not as bad as you think. I'm a fairly grounded woman."

"Well, how about letting Daddy retire. Let him bow out of politics and enjoy time on his own terms, doing what he wants. Y'all could travel. You could—"

"He doesn't want that," Beverly said, her voice turning cool.

"Talk to him. He might surprise you."

The silence only stiffened Callie's shoulders. More silence. She couldn't stand it. "What, Mother?"

"Is this something you talked him into?"

Oh geez. "Seriously?"

"I'm not happy about this revelation. Don't pry into our lives."

"Maybe it wasn't my idea."

"Sure it was. Your father would've run it by me first," Beverly said.

Callie pushed up from her Adirondack. "Maybe he did, and you weren't listening."

"Oh, I think I'd remember that, dear."

Callie grit her teeth, holding back curses for the woman who'd spawned her. "Daddy has donated his life to public service. Middleton is fine, so let him bow out on a high. Give him a chance to sleep in, go fishing, do nothing. He never gets a day off."

"He has much left to accomplish."

"Damn it, Mother. It's his career, not yours."

Callie could hear the television vaguely in the background playing a Burger King commercial. Dishes clanked, her father pretending to be busy in the kitchen.

Beverly's ire came across in her pause, before saying, "I need to go."

"I'm sure you do." Callie hung up, scowling at the perfect storm that continually brewed between her and her mother, wondering how Beverly would play it out to Lawton.

She jammed the phone into her pocket and mumbled, "Don't think I did you any favors this time, Daddy. But then, you asked."

"Mom?" Jeb shouted.

"What?" Callie hollered back.

The screen door opened. A smiling Sprite glided out as if walking on oil. Callie's mind strayed to thoughts of the girl belly dancing, bending backward, smoothly shaking her assets in her son's face. Jeb followed, smitten from the size of his grin. "We're going out," he said.

"Well, try not to make any babies," she mumbled.

"What, Mom?"

"Try to stay safe," she said louder.

"You always say that. You worry too much." He led his date down the stairs.

"Wait," Callie said. "Who's driving?"

Sprite raised her hand. "I'll be careful with him, Ms. Morgan."

Callie grinned and raised a hand in return. "I'm sure you will, sweetheart."

Chapter 17

CALLIE AWOKE replaying Beverly's accusations about planting retirement into Lawton's head. Give the man some credit. He'd served as mayor of Middleton for twenty-eight years. She shifted her attentions to more pleasing thoughts of newly painted steps.

The house seemed still in slumber. The surf's whisper drifted ever so lightly through her locked window between the random traffic rumbling down Jungle Road. From the quiet, Jeb either slept late or fished with Zeus. She found his bed made and phone gone. Sprite jumped to mind, and Callie searched her memory. Yes, Jeb did come in last night, sometime around one. She scrunched her eyes shut. Was she seriously thinking about having an adult talk with her son about sex?

She dressed, drank a half glass of sweet tea, and headed to the beach for her run. Yesterday contained no crisis, except for the family kind, and for a change the concept of living at Edisto had palatability.

She needed to prioritize who to interview now that she'd handled Mason. Not that she'd handled him that well. He now knew more about her than vice versa. Mrs. Hanson seemed to like her. Maybe she'd start there.

She stared down the beach, the silhouette of Water Spout so obvious. Until Mason returned to Canada, she assumed he'd continue to watch for opportunities to woo her. His rental made for a suitable observation platform for a major section of the beach, especially with a telescope, which she wouldn't be surprised existed the way he magically appeared when she ran.

Not ten minutes into her stride, he caught up with her. "Missed you yesterday," he said. "I didn't go too far with the grape sodas, did I? I'm still sorry about not taking you seriously about . . . you know."

She pulled out her ear buds and tucked them into her shirt. Her opinions about the man swayed one way, then the other. Sophie had told him Callie was on a *diet* from booze, yet he'd slipped her those grape sodas. But the chivalry that followed, to include that delicate, sweet kiss, almost made up for his shenanigan. Frankly, the burden had been on her to not accept a drink.

"No apology necessary," she said. "I'm having the stairs refinished. Repairman showed up early and I'd forgotten the paint. Had to forego the run."

"Ah." He jogged clean and steady, matching her. They paralleled the ebbing water, keeping on the moist part of the beach for ease. "You're still using Peters, right?"

Callie tried to focus on her beat. "Yep."

He rippled a brow. "I enjoyed our date, Ms. Morgan."

"A light kiss, Mr. Howard. Nothing more."

"A kiss is a kiss," he said. "Anyway, let's see what you got." He picked up speed, and she let him take off ahead. Noticing her absence, he soon returned. "Not up to it?"

She put her buds in her ears. "I need to think, not compete. Go ahead."

Instead, he slowed, staying in her blind spot one stride behind her. She almost felt bad not playing along with him, but she needed her thoughts. He'd probably peel off somewhere en route.

As she did in her Boston runs, she dissected the recent crimes in her head.

The amazing thing about this criminal was his appeal for daylight activity. Highly unusual. By day, beach activity and throngs of visitors absorbed the department's attention, but more people could catch the thief in the act. He was street smart. He knew how to blend in. And he had a penchant for Jungle Road. Did he live there?

Was she so sure it was a man? Nothing required strength. No DNA, except maybe on the glasses the thief drank from at Mrs. Hanson's and the Rosewoods'. But such a test was expensive. She couldn't see Edisto Beach or Colleton County forking out money for DNA testing just to define male or female. Boston wouldn't even bother.

Boston. If she were there, she'd have so many cases. Here she could easily fall into an obsession with just one. Not that she even had a case. She could have it if she took Seabrook up on his offer to help the PD, to work for the PD.

She still wished she'd taken him up on his dinner offer. And what was her abhorrence to calling him Mike?

She rounded the curve toward the sound. About three miles. Amazing progress with a clear head.

A family of four huddled around something. She slowed, pensive, hoping it wasn't what she suspected. Tourists often caught sea life and held it, put it in cups, passed it around, studying nature up close, not realizing the damage they did.

Sure enough, a child about six years old held up an eight-inch baby hammerhead shark by the tail. The dad stepped back with a camera. "Smile and hold it up high," he said, the mother and younger sister enthralled at the pose.

Callie slowed to a walk, and still panting heavily, she detoured toward their Kodak moment. "Please don't do that," she told the dad.

The thirty-year-old man eyed her up and down. "It's a damn shark."

"That animal's part of this eco-system, a living creature. That shark probably won't live as it is, but at least give it a chance." She turned to the mother. "If nothing else, don't teach your child to kill. Would you let him suffocate a kitten or a puppy?"

Sheepish, the mother went to her son, and holding his shoulders, directed him toward the water. The child threw the shark back in the surf, not as gently as Callie would have done, but at least it was back in its environment.

"Thank you," Callie said, then promptly turned on her heel to avoid a scene. Time to head toward home.

Twenty yards later, a voice said, "Impressive. Touching, even."

Callie about jumped out of her sneakers. "Oh geez, Mason, I practically forgot about you."

He laughed loud and easy. "Nothing *practically* about it. You did forget. Thought you cops had this super sense about you."

"Out of practice," she said, her heart a tad faster than she liked to admit. She *had* forgotten he was there.

He escorted her back to the sidewalk on Palmetto Boulevard, going past his rental. Conversation danced from sharks to wildlife to what they loved about the beach. Soon Chelsea Morning appeared a block down.

"You didn't have to walk me home," she said, her shirt drenched, hair matted to her sweaty temples. They crossed the road to her house. Peters' truck sat in the drive.

Huge wet splotches saturated the shirt under Mason's arms, and across his chest, down his back. But his odor measured little more than that of warm aftershave. "I don't have to escort you, but in case you haven't heard, there's a killer on the loose. Besides, I want to talk to this guy doing your repair work. See if he's okay."

"He's fine, Mason. And don't touch the new paint." She took his arm and steered him away from the front steps with their yellow caution tape tied around the railings.

Mason smiled. She let him go, awkward at his enjoyment of her touch. "He'd be around back," she said. "What do you think of what's done already?"

Mason felt the smooth rail. "Decent job. Good price? The owners of my place do a helluva job keeping me happy, so I might do a few minor repairs as thanks."

"I guess they do want you happy with what you're paying for *that place.*" Water Spout stood in a rental class all its own with fame and notoriety often accompanying each tenant. She scouted for Peters. "He charges a very reasonable price. But you have to provide dinner."

Peters' tools sprawled random across her back step, the toolbox open, but no sign of recent work.

"Well, another time," she said, a foot on the bottom step. "He must be checking out a different house. I think he juggles several jobs at one time."

Mason leaned over for a kiss, and she held him at bay with a hand to the chest, feeling much more in control in the daylight. "Not this time, Mr. Howard."

"You're going to make us fight over you, huh?" He leaned against her, not yet persuaded to fall back.

"Us?"

"Mike and me."

She outstared him, not falling prey to his ribbing. "I need a shower, and you need to go find another flirt. You want a water before you go?"

"In the shower?"

She mildly shoved him and headed up the steps. "See you later, Mason." She glanced back as she locked the door, and he was gone.

Once in her shower, warm water rolled over her, but she couldn't place herself back into the sensual mood of the previous morning. She dressed, grabbed a banana, and went outside. Peters sanded away at the top steps.

"Where you been?" she asked. "Someone was interested in hiring you."

Peters wiped his forehead with his free hand, the other resting on the sander. "I ran across the street. Got into my toolbox and realized I left a couple things at the water heater job. People just leave my belongings on their porches when I do that, so I was checking the last two places I worked." He ran a leathered palm across the freshly sanded wood. "Okay for you?"

She swallowed the last of her breakfast. "You do wonderful work, Peters. No wonder people use you so much."

He gave her a lopsided grin, lowered protective glasses over his eyes, and resumed sanding, the electric tool rotating under his careful guidance.

She leaned against the railing, enjoying the lukewarm breeze off the marsh, observing a couple walking their Water Spaniel down Jungle Shores' silt-based road. One would think living at an address where the front and back of a house exited on roads would make the noise factor an issue, but the beach was several blocks away, as was the main road. She preferred the peace of a silent marsh to the raucous pounding of the ocean anyway. The two-way drive was just convenience.

The sander droned, but Callie thought she heard someone approaching during its pauses. Sophie soon appeared in cargo pants that molded around her buns just so, and a tank top that accented upper assets Callie suspected were augmented by her ex-husband's pocketbook.

"Zucchini muffins," Sophie exclaimed, lofting a picnic basket in the air. "With flaxseed."

"You must own stock in the flax industry," Callie said, accepting the muffins. She opened an edge of the cover and held it out to Peters, who wasted no time taking the warm treat and forcing himself to take a break. Sophie's tightly-toned hip backed up to sit atop the picnic table.

Callie opened the back door. "Be back in a sec with some tea. Or does anyone want coffee? Water?"

In the kitchen, she pulled out tea glasses per everyone's request and opened the refrigerator. Grabbing the pitcher, she shut the fridge and scanned outside the front window as she passed, forever scouting for anything amiss.

"Oh my gosh," she exclaimed, setting the pitcher on her counter, tea sloshing out, and grabbed her cell phone.

A young adult man held onto a porch post at his house across the street and one address down to the right. His other hand pressed against his head. Re-gripping the post, as if about to lose his bearing, he yelled meekly for help.

She dashed out the front, ripped the yellow tape loose, and leaped down the freshly repaired staircase. At the bottom, as she waited for three cars to pass, she dialed 9-1-1.

As she reached the place, Seabrook came running up from her left, no siren, no lights, no uniform. Not even a cruiser.

"Sit," she said, assisting the injured man to a chaise.

"9-1-1. How may I assist you?"

Callie tossed her cell to Seabrook as he reached her side. He'd know dispatch and get things going quicker.

"What's your name?" she asked, studying the guy's curly brown hair, trying to analyze a wound that didn't seem to have a source. Blood ran from above and behind his ear, a trickle down his neck. At first glance not severe, but head wounds were deceiving and unpredictable.

"Steve . . . Maxwell."

He tried to feel his head, and Callie lightly blocked him. "Don't touch. Medical attention's on its way. What happened?"

"Don't know," he said, shaking his head, then stopping as a wave of dizziness obviously disturbed the effort. "Somebody please get my wife."

Callie stooped in front of him. "Where is she?"

Seabrook, no longer occupied with dispatch, leaned over beside her, radio at the ready. "I'll send a unit to get her. Where?"

"On the beach with our son. He's three. Near entrance eighteen. Both are blond."

"Good," Callie said. "You just worry about you now."

"Guess I'm the next robbery on y'all's list," he said with a wince.

Seabrook lowered his radio. "Come again, sir?"

"I think I must have walked in on the guy." Steve squinted, peering up at the tall officer. "Saw the coin on the table next to a glass. Went closer, then found myself waking up from kissing the floor."

"Stay here," Seabrook told Callie, then he disappeared inside.

"Is this your home?" she asked the man. "You're a resident here?"

He started to nod and remembered not to. "Yes. Watched you move in. Been meaning to come over and welcome you to the street."

Before Seabrook returned, an ambulance pulled up, two EMTs soon reaching Maxwell's side. Callie left them to their business and entered the house. Seabrook sniffed the goblet at the table without touching, a 1972 Eisenhower silver dollar smiling back from a prominent place beside it.

"Mimosa," Seabrook said.

"He drinks whatever's handy," she said. "It's more statement than drinking style." The glass was half empty. He'd enjoyed his drink, taking too much time, apparently, since the owner came home before the intruder could leave.

"No pitcher in the refrigerator, so nothing handy about it," Seabrook said. "He mixed himself one drink after opening a bottle of champagne. The foil's next to the sink, some of the champagne spewed on the counter. I'll ask them later if they opened a bottle before they headed to the beach, but I doubt it. This is the only used glass."

Callie noted the toddler toys, a blanket on the sofa, a sippy cup in the sink. Nothing seemed disturbed. She moved back to the porch, Seabrook behind her. The EMTs escorted Maxwell down the steps, Mrs. Maxwell now shadowing them, the child in her arms. An Edisto unit parked behind the ambulance, the uniform from the hardware store standing nearby as if awaiting instructions, gesturing gawkers to keep driving past.

Seabrook and Callie scanned the activity below, neighbors hovering on the fringes one and two doors down. "You'll have to ask the Maxwells later about what's missing," she said.

Sophie and Peters waited at her place, shielding sun from their eyes, Mason next to them holding Sophie's arm, most likely to hold her back from interfering.

Seabrook noticed the oglers. "You can go back, if you like."

Callie followed his gaze. "I'd rather help than stand around. Makes me feel safer. But that's no reflection on you and your guys. It's just—"

"Proactivity beats waiting. I get that."

She tilted her head toward the uniform guiding traffic. "I'd keep your officer camped out here until the Maxwells return. Put some crime scene tape up."

"I get that too, Ms. Morgan."

She drew back. "What happened to Callie?"

"Just keeping it professional," he said.

It didn't sound that way to her. "You're in jeans, and you show up on foot. Do you live that close, or are you up to something?"

"Just freelancing," he said.

"So I heard. A *special* of some kind?"

"Something like that."

She moved directly into his line of vision to capture his whole attention. "What's sticking in your craw?"

"Craw. We're falling back on our southern roots, are we?"

She followed his gaze, which had settled on the trio across the street. "You know I ate at Whaley's with Mason Howard."

His jaw tightened.

Hers tightened more. "Seriously?"

"Something about that guy makes the hair stand up on the back of my neck," he said. "Told you that before. You need to be careful."

She wasn't believing this conversation. "It was dinner. Very innocent and very none of your business."

His facial muscles moved under the skin.

"I told him like I told you," she said. "I'm not interested." She started down the stairs, then in a second's decision, turned to make an even clearer point. "Get your priorities straight, Officer Seabrook. While you're worried about whom I date, I'm losing sleep over who's skulking around this street, and yes, it's just this street, picking on the residents and shooting your police department the bird as he evades your remarkable prowess."

He dropped his stare to her. "What does that mean?"

She narrowed her eyes. "It means I watch my back and trust damn few people. I'm retreating into my place and barring the doors until you and your force catch this guy. It's obvious my assistance isn't needed, though pray tell show me any progress. And maybe it's time you held a town meeting and let everyone know what's happened . . . and what you intend to do about it."

"We voice mailed and emailed everyone on the beach."

"I didn't get the message," she said.

"Then I suggest you give your email and phone number to the police."

"Makes you wonder who else didn't get it." Her eyes narrowed. "Anyway, check the nanny cam."

His face changed, interested. "What?"

"The Maxwells have a small child. They probably go out and leave him with a sitter. See if there's a cam or two and what rooms they cover. If they can afford this beach house, they can afford cams." She strutted back across the road. At least Mason didn't care if Seabrook showed an interest in her; the playboy considered her a challenge.

Sophie met her first, venturing into the road and walking her back to the group. "What happened?"

"Another break-in," Callie said with clipped words.

"Anyone hurt?" Mason asked.

"Don't think so," she replied. "But it seems our burglar panicked, knocking the homeowner over the head."

Peters stared at the house. "Wait, I thought this guy was just stealing little stuff and having a drink. Just being nosy."

Raysor's words echoed in her head about the contractor being the prime suspect, but Peters appeared genuinely concerned about the injury.

"He's getting bolder," she said, then faced Sophie. "Please lock your doors."

Sophie took her arm. "What else happened?"

"You're making me want to say *move along, people*," Callie replied, not keen on sharing. "Seabrook will take it from here."

"Humph." Sophie's nose lifted in a pout.

"I got work to do anyway," Peters said, stopping at the broken tape on Callie's steps to retie it.

"Don't trust that guy," Mason murmured as Peters left.

"You said that already. Why are you even here? You left to go home," Callie said.

"As a chuckle, I wanted to remind you about the party again, though my event pales in light of all this thievery and violence. However, the invitation still stands, even with you grumpy." He grinned. "I'd be happy to escort you there and back. Hate the idea of you being alone."

Sophie winked and turned away, overplaying the drama of acting invisible.

"Sophie, too," he said. "So nobody can call it a date."

The yoga maven spun around. "Oh, please come, Callie. Please?"

"What is with you two?" Callie exclaimed. "The neighborhood is going to pot, and the party is still on? No, sorry. I'm not in a partying mood."

Mason donned a sad-cow-eyed look. "Hiding at home and shutting down our lives won't cure anything."

Callie maintained her disgust, but Mason's comment resurfaced a thought. The party could host a slew of suspects. It could also occupy people, giving the burglar easy pickings.

He gave her a short nod. "Well, let me be on my way then. I have a ball to prepare for," he said as he slightly stooped at the waist.

Sophie giggled like someone a third her age. "Me, too. You'll still come retrieve me, Mason? I won't rebuff your intentions."

Callie walked away, their dramatics irritating. The crime pattern was becoming blatantly apparent. Full-time residents of the beach. She should lay this out on paper, study the crimes, analyze the similarities and the differences. She was missing a serious connection, but wasn't sure she knew enough about the players to be able to tell. Seabrook would know, and together they might uncover some clue from the facts, but he seemed rather juvenile at the moment.

"Callie," Mason called and fast-walked back to her, Sophie having returned home.

Not again.

"Had a comment I didn't want Sophie to hear," he said. "Peters either."

"And what would that be?" she asked, expecting more plastic endearments.

"Where did Seabrook come from? No car, no uniform."

She found it uncomfortable discussing Seabrook with Mason.

"You noticed, too," he said. "I could tell. He lives across the street from me on Palmetto Boulevard in Windswept. And he wasn't attired for jogging, so what was he up to?"

"I know what you're doing, and thanks for the warning."

"Trust me. I see things."

"Later, Mason."

She went inside. Leaning against the kitchen counter drinking her watered-down tea, Callie decided she'd been premature making friends on this island. These people were too intertwined with each other, making them blind to who might be running this crime spree. And if she got overly involved with them, she'd be just as blind.

No longer would she take hospitality and neighborly attention at face value. The deeper she let anyone into her life, the more she risked. A murderer, a robber, whatever he or they were, she'd let the police catch him before she opened up to beach society.

Everyone at arm's length now.

She called Jeb, identifying his location and estimated arrival. When he came home, they'd have a chat again about whether Edisto's ambience was worth weathering such rampant crime. Boston had had its share of violence. She got that. But she'd run from Russians for too long not to ignore the fact that five houses within sight of her front porch had been violated. She'd be a fool not to think she was somewhere next on the list.

Chapter 18

THE CHAT WITH Jeb did not go well. He blew up when she tightened his leash, requiring a check-in call every hour. But when she'd hinted about Edisto maybe not suiting their short-term needs, he tried to walk away, a reaction fast becoming habit.

"Don't you leave this room until we're done," Callie scolded.

He spun around. "It hasn't been a week, Mom. A damn week, and you're wanting to run away. Thought we had a New Year's agreement."

Her fist had been on her hip so long her hand had fallen asleep. "Murder. Grand theft. Burglary. Aggravated assault in the commission of a felony. Those sound reasonable enough for concern?"

His young biceps bulged as he crossed his arms. "You sound like a cop again."

"What do you expect?"

"And what town *is* completely safe?" he asked. "Recognize this for what it is, Mom. You're running. Running away from"—he waved around his face—". . . from whatever forces keep messing with your head."

She flicked her hand out toward his face, then placed it back on her hip. "I quit the profession for the both of us. But if I can't help solve the crime, I need to avoid it. That's what the smart civilian does. I don't fully trust the local police to solve this. In the meantime, you follow my rules until the final decision is made. And I'll do research on a new security system."

He struck the wall with his palm.

"That's enough," she said.

"My first home since . . . the fire, and you want to take that away."

"You're going to college in two months."

"What, I'm not supposed to have a home to come back to?"

"Of course you are," she said. "You sure this isn't about Sprite?"

"What if it is?"

They faced each other, one breathing hard, the other afraid to.

"I'm a parent, trying to protect her family," she said. "As a civilian, my options are limited."

"Lucky us. The last time you were a cop our lives went to hell," he said deep in a voice she'd never heard.

"How dare you." Her temper flared, but she fought to turn down the heat. He was young, not appreciating the danger. In love? "I'm doing the best I can."

"Mom, face it. You can barely keep your head on straight."

The remark smacked her, and she stepped back as if it had left a mark on her cheek. "Jeb."

His expression flashed a mixture of embarrassment, frustration, and anger before he pivoted to his room, slamming his bedroom door like a thirteen-year-old adolescent. She was tiring of that behavior. He'd been sweeter in Middleton.

She retreated to the kitchen and poured a lowball glass of her father's bourbon, pushing fast to outrun any hesitation. The amber liquid slid down in one gulp. She poured another, feeling justified now, the ice broken. Then she exited to the side porch once she set up three albums on the turntable. Outside she listened to Neil Diamond turned down low so Jeb wouldn't come out and smell what was in her glass.

Three tunes in, the songs weren't doing their job. That's when she poured a refill.

She felt damned no matter what she did, what direction she took, what decision she made. Two more songs, and she started to rise for another refill, then wondered if her father would notice the missing liquor when he arrived to take Jeb to dinner.

She'd just have a new bottle of Maker's Mark waiting when he showed up at five tomorrow. A thank-you for mentoring her son.

"I could kill you again for leaving me, John," she mumbled, then polished off the last two fingers' worth of bourbon.

THREE HANGOVERS in a week meant four days sober. Or that's what Callie tried to rationalize as she fought the cotton in her head the next morning. Ten a.m. per her alarm clock, which, thank goodness, she hadn't set.

Throwing an arm over her face, she chastised herself. She shouldn't have opened the bottle.

She dragged herself to the shower and turned it on, then dropped and sat on the tiled bottom, half dozing, half straining to clear her head, something Jeb said she hadn't the ability to do. Next thing she knew, the water ran cold, and she hadn't washed her hair. By the time she rinsed out the strawberry-scented suds, her wits were sharper and her lips blue.

She had three text messages from Jeb on her phone. One when he left at dawn to work with Zeus and twice again when he checked in. Voice mail had been her intention, but as mad as he was, she'd settle for this, for now.

In the kitchen, he'd left dishes on the counter. She'd find clothes on the floor in his room, too, in a retaliatory gesture—clothes she'd make him pick up later. John wouldn't have tolerated the pout, but then Jeb might not be such a butt if John were here. Or he'd be a different form of butt. Eighteen was not an easy age for an almost-adult about to leave home. She remembered those years under Beverly's roof, then wondered if Jeb felt the same.

Sipping her coffee, she canvassed the windows, studying the steady whiz of cars driving too fast on her street, most with out-of-state tags. Few clouds dotted the intensely blue sky. A real estate agent put a sign in Papa Beach's yard.

What?

For reasons she didn't immediately comprehend, she put on sneakers, locked up, and rushed outside. This was much too soon to sell Papa's house. Wasn't it?

"Hey," Callie called as the agent placed an inch-thick stack of flyers in a plastic box affixed to the sign's edge. Crime scene tape no longer dangled in the breeze. "Isn't this rather fast to list a house in an estate?" She held out her hand. "I'm Callie, by the way, and . . . hey, don't I know you?"

The agent had a smoky chuckle, Callie suspecting a routine of cigarettes and booze. "I have a few years on you, hon, but I handled renters for your dad. Fine man that Lawton Cantrell. Handsome in a Paul Newman way."

Beverly would wring this woman's neck. And Daddy doesn't look anything like Paul Newman.

The tanned bleached blonde wore jewel-toned sandals and a yellow sundress a size too small for a midriff too accustomed to evening cocktails. "I'm Rhonda Benson. And you're Lawton's daughter. I've been to a few of your mother's soirees. Honey, I've known you since you were skateboard age."

Callie recalled the cackling laugh. "Nice to see you again. About the house?"

"Oh, Henry had a life estate, having deeded his home to his son five years ago. You know, to avoid probate and taxes. The son listed it just this morning."

It wasn't Callie's business how Papa Beach took care of his assets, but the whole life-estate deal felt sad. The old Papa she envisioned was too full of life to be planning his end. And she thought she couldn't feel worse today.

"Pauley's in town?" Callie asked.

"Yes," the agent replied. "I haven't seen him today, though. Not that I want to."

So she knew Pauley's charm, or lack thereof, but then anyone who knew Papa understood how completely opposite Pauley was from his father.

"Are you allowed to tell me the plans for the personal belongings still inside?" Callie whispered, anxious for a token remembrance. She should have just slipped into the house and taken a memory to keep. Not like Pauley would want any of it. He couldn't spell sentimental, much less define it.

"No secret there," the agent said. "Pauley's certain that every hatpin and ashtray has antique value since Henry was in his eighties." She waggled her chest and shoulders, assuming a droll, sarcastic voice. "He warned us that he'd file charges if he found anything missing. We suggested he clean out the place first, but oh no. Guy wants this house sold, like by tomorrow."

Callie's dander rose. "Bastard only showed at Christmas, barely slowing down long enough to grab his check."

The made-up agent nodded rapidly. "Sweetheart, you know it, I know it. Everybody out here knows it. Pure A-hole material. He's talking to an auctioneer in Walterboro about selling the contents."

"Auction!" Callie exclaimed. "The house contains vinyl-covered chairs and pressboard end tables. Pauley's better off donating it and taking the tax break."

The real estate lady threw her head back. "Huh. You can't get a refund on what you don't pay. Guy makes his living on eBay. He went on a tirade, fussing at us for being money-mongers and people-users because we charged him our standard commission."

Callie's mouth fell open. "So, if everything doesn't sell?"

"Then he *gives us permission* to call a thrift store, the Baptist church, and the island museum to clear out the place. Of course, that was only after we taught him about tax breaks, which he'd need once he sold the house."

Callie felt almost numb.

Rhonda shoved a few more flyers in the box. "Well, maybe we'll get a better owner out here."

"Damn it," Callie said, irate and down at the same time. How had a man's eighty years come to this? Her bottom lip quivered. An urgency to salvage it all surged through her, then quickly dissolved as she saw she couldn't stash all his belongings in her place. But somebody had to keep . . . something. Who would retain his legacy?

She had so painfully little of John. Not even a sweatshirt left with his scent to take to bed. All she had was his grandfather's watch, luckily kept in a fireproof safe in the closet, three dress shirts sent out to the cleaners, and pictures from his desk at work. The watch would pass on to Jeb once he graduated from college, the shirts were sterilized, and the pictures duplicates.

Callie had nothing other than her wedding ring.

"Your family knew Henry well," the blonde agent said, a silver fingernail tapping the sign. "I saw you around quite often years back."

Callie forced a grin at the memory, then had an idea. "I'm going to ask a favor, and you don't have to do it, but—"

"Spit it out, sugar. You can't trump the crazy-ass stuff I've heard in this job."

"Um, would you mind if I went inside and took a memento? Maybe his Christmas tie I gave him in sixth grade? I'm not talking anything big. Just small tokens to remember Papa, um, Henry by?"

The smile belied her Botox as Rhonda softened. "Come on, hon. I'd be honored to let Lawton's daughter in. Just lock up when you leave. Anybody asks, you're an interested buyer." She hooked her arm in Callie's and leaned her head closer as they approached the steps to the door. "I know we're in the business to sell houses, but poor Henry's body wasn't even cold before Pauley called for an estimate. He's having Henry cremated. No urn, no service, nothing, can you believe that? Dumping the ashes in the ocean. Pointless spending money on dead people, he says."

"What?"

"Yeah, seriously. I mean, damn, who does that? There were enough people here to make for an honorable funeral service."

After unlocking the door, the agent patted Callie on the shoulder. "Don't take too long." She turned and tiptoed down the steps, a hand lifted in the air as if protecting her nails from damage.

"Thanks a bunch," Callie called after her.

The agent wriggled her fingers in goodbye and took great effort folding her unfoldable middle into the low-riding BMW Z-4.

Callie pushed the door open. She inhaled and tentatively took it all in. In another day or two, people would disrupt this aura and remove belongings that meant nothing to them yet had meant everything at one time to Henry and his wife.

A small lump formed in her chest, daring to rise and burst into tears. She'd kill to have something that smelled like John.

She glanced up at the ceiling and took a breath for control. Then her eyes scanned over items, trying not to attach history. If too many mental images slipped into her head, she'd find herself needing a storage unit.

Locating an empty shoebox, she started in the bedroom. She kept a handkerchief smelling of Papa. Moving to the living room, she lifted a pipe and a doily. Three photographs of Papa B: in Korea, with his wife on vacation, on the beach fishing. In the kitchen, she found his favorite coffee mug, an old, scratched spatula they'd used for cookies, and finally, a pair of chipped hen and rooster salt and pepper shakers. He used to cluck from behind the rooster, making it dance toward the hen in Callie's child-sized grasp. She'd laugh at his antics until her belly hurt.

Each item choked her up in a different way. She wandered back around the house again, touching curtains, recalling the old man's scent. Her face now wet, she rubbed her nose across her shirtsleeve and stopped at the front window staring at nothing outside, regretting how time moved, often leaving so little behind.

Movement flitted behind a window in the unoccupied house directly across the street. No vehicles parked in the drive, no towels hung off railings to dry, no blown up sharks and porpoises on the porch. Her family knew the owners; they visited their home in the off season. However, being several rows back from the water, the house wasn't necessarily rented each week, so seeing it vacant wasn't unusual. The For Rent sign confirmed it.

Callie backed away from the window then nudged aside the curtain. For ten minutes she remained there, frozen. There, another movement.

He'd blinked first.

A murderer/burglar could easily stow away in empty rental properties. Hiding in plain sight. He could be from out of town, mingling with beachcombers until he spotted a vacancy. Or he might get to know people locally, to better forecast the houses to use. Regardless, he wasn't a local if he needed a place to stay.

A new theory.

She set down the box and lifted her cell, then stopped. She'd sworn off detective work, telling Mike . . . no, Seabrook . . . to do his own sleuthing. Tough. She'd told Jeb just last night that as a civilian parent, she had to do what she could to keep her family safe. She dialed Seabrook's number. To pass on the information. That's all.

"Hello," he answered.

"I think there's a trespasser across the street," she said, ignoring salutations.

"Which address?"

"13A Jungle Road," she whispered, then checked herself. Nobody could hear her.

"Go on home," he said.

"Aren't you coming . . . wait. How do you know I'm not at home?"

Seabrook hesitated. "Just go back to your place."

Callie waved. Seabrook waved back.

"What are you doing over there?" she asked, then opened the door, squinting from the midday sun.

"Quit trying to attract attention. Go home before you burn me."

She retrieved her box and clumsily tucked it under her arm, set the lock on the door, drew it tight, and returned toward Chelsea Morning, the phone still to her ear. "You surveilling me?"

"No," he said. "I'm keeping watch on the street."

She received her hourly text from Jeb. *Still breathing. Still with Zeus. Why don't you LoJack my butt?* Smart aleck. She'd call her father to discuss attitude when he picked up Jeb for their chat.

She put the phone back to her ear.

"I'm going to catch this bastard," Seabrook said. "Don't tell anybody, please."

"Don't let people know you want to catch the bad guy?"

"No. That I'm staking out the street."

A gung-ho effort. Maybe. But then a mild irritation came over her as she reached her porch. What if Mason's suspicions weren't so far off? What if Seabrook was the one watching residents, waiting for the perfect opportunity, able to justify getting caught by the pure nature of his job? Protecting residents, checking homes, making sure everyone was safe. Much like how she'd doubted Raysor.

But she couldn't quite figure the payoff.

Or was Seabrook that dedicated, doing exactly what he professed, just a little misguided in his tactics? A one-man stakeout with visual on only six or seven houses at best. Four of them already broken into. The effort was long on odds, reeking novice and desperation, in her opinion.

"What were you doing in Beechum's place?" he asked.

"You saw the real estate agent."

"Rhonda Benson," he said.

Callie felt through her pockets for her house key. "She said I could take a memento from the house before they cleared it out."

"Fine. Gotta go." Seabrook hung up before she could.

She set the box on her rattan settee. Where the hell were her keys?

Oh, double damn. Had she set them on the kitchen table? She rummaged the box, thinking maybe they got caught up in the paper towels she used to wrap the salt and pepper shakers. She checked her pockets again. Zilch.

She left the box on her porch and returned to Papa's front stoop. She shook the knob. Of course she'd secured the door tight. She ran around to the back and tried that door. Same story.

Her gaze wandered to Seabrook's clandestine hidey-hole across the street. She eased out her cell.

"What are you doing?" he answered, mildly bothered.

"Locked my keys in Papa's house. Do you have the key on you by any chance?"

"Nope, it's at the station."

No offer to go get it. Either he took this surveillance gig way too seriously, or he still held his childish grudge over her dining with Mason. If it was the latter, this man was forever off her dance card.

"Call Rhonda back," he finally said and hung up.

Callie ran down to the sign in the yard to retrieve Rhonda's number. The agent asked for fifteen minutes. She was showing a house to potential renters a block over.

Thank heaven for front porch shade. Callie leaned against the door, checking the weather on her phone when an old model green hatchback drove up to the house.

Pauley stepped out of the car, wearing knockoff shades probably bought from the rear end of someone's pickup. He tensed as he spotted her. Hair unkempt and draping down to the neck of his T-shirt, Papa's son grinned and moved to block the stairway so she couldn't get by.

"Hey, Callie. Thought I told you not to touch my house."

She started down the stairs.

He matched a step to each of hers, grinning with sour mischief. His thin frame would be no match for Seabrook or Raysor, but he still stood six inches taller and fifty pounds heavier than Callie.

"Pauley. I was just waiting—"

"For the cops?" he said, stopping three steps up to dial his phone. "What're you doing up here? Picking the lock? Detectives know how to do that. That's how they plant evidence and get into places without warrants." He put the phone to his ear. "Yes, I'm at 18A Jungle Road. There's a trespasser here, trying to break in. No, I don't believe I'm in danger. Please send the police as quickly as you can. I don't know what she'll do next."

Chapter 19

CALLIE MOVED DOWN two more of Papa's steps. Pauley climbed two, his grin widening. The son held none of the humor or manners of the father, but something about his wide face and rounded features reminded Callie of the senior Beechum. She'd always felt sorry for Papa living alone, his son never visiting. Maybe that's why Papa had shared so much of his love with her.

She cursed herself about the keys. "Let me pass, Pauley."

"Nope, I'm holding you at bay," he said.

At bay? "Let me by, I said."

"Don't even try it. Hold it right there, or I'll have to pin you down until the authorities arrive."

Callie sized him up. Pauley wasn't a young man, maybe early-fifties. Scrawny. She held onto the railing and came down another riser in the fifteen or so that led to his landing, the wood smooth and sanded from Papa's attentive carpentry. Glancing down, she counted five steps between her and Pauley.

Then she took them fast.

He grabbed her arm as she tried to pass. She welcomed it.

Controlling his fall as he stumbled backwards down the steps in her grasp, she reached bottom and torqued his wrist to put him down. His scream seemed over the top, but she didn't care, because it stopped as soon as his face hit the sandy ground.

A county patrol car pulled into the drive behind Pauley's dated green Mazda. *Great.* It had to be Raysor. The chunky deputy got out, donned his hat, and strode over to them, fisting a hickory billystick with a leather binding. She hadn't seen one of those since Boston's police museum. Why was she not surprised?

Callie tightened her hold as Pauley writhed.

"Arrest her!" Pauley yelled, squirming. "She's trespassing! And she attacked me."

Raysor studied the predicament. "Ms. Morgan, don't make me yank you off him."

She released Pauley and stepped back in case the guy ached for redemption. She didn't want to give Raysor an excuse to dramatize the situation with physical intervention. Somebody would get embarrassed.

"What the hell happened here?" the deputy asked, tapping his leg with the stick.

Raysor should have specified one of them to go first, to avoid competition between the arguing sides, but she let Pauley speak uninterrupted. Her story could counterpunch his more easily that way.

"She was trying to break in," Pauley said, almost wheezing with exasperation. With a taut arm, he pointed to the top of the steps. "Told her before not to mess with my house. She used to watch it for me, but when I suspected she was stealing, I banned her from the premises."

Callie crossed her arms, fighting not to react to the man's lies.

When Raysor just listened, not responding in the positive or negative, Pauley surged onward to fill the void. "She thinks because her father is a mayor and she's a cop, that she can get away with breaking and entering, but I told her I wouldn't stand for it, regardless of her threats."

Callie leaned back, impressed at the detailed fabrication. She'd heard many a story explode with creative prowess when a cop walked up, and Pauley was giving it all he could.

Seabrook appeared out of nowhere from behind Raysor. "I witnessed everything."

Pauley's mouth hung open like a sea bass, opening and shutting, blinking in between. "You weren't here."

"Where the hell did you come from?" Raysor grumbled, his gaze flicking between Callie and Seabrook as he tried to answer his own question.

"I was across the street. Heard and saw it all," he said, his no-nonsense manner commanding the moment. "Mr. Beechum, is your house up for sale?"

"Yes, of course it is."

Raysor's face reddened a bit.

Seabrook turned to Callie. "Ms. Morgan, did you meet a real estate agent at this house right before Mr. Beechum arrived?"

Callie straightened. "Yes, I did." She recognized the deal.

"Did you forget your keys in the house?" he asked.

"Yes, unfortunately. The agent's on her way to retrieve them for me."

Seabrook fixated on Papa's son. "Mr. Beechum, how is that trespassing?"

"Search her," Pauley stammered. "What's in her pockets?"

"No." Seabrook turned to Callie. "Ms. Morgan, do you want to press charges for assault?"

"Oh, I see." Pauley squinted from one cop to another. "It's the blue line, isn't it? You people stick together."

Seabrook raised his brow at Callie. "Do you want to file charges or not?"

"Will you leave me alone, Pauley?" she asked calmly.

"Humph."

"No, I won't file," she said, wanting Pauley to owe her the debt. She also felt the need to compensate him for the coffee cup, chicken shakers, and spatula in the shoebox on her porch. "This is all just a big misunderstanding."

"We good now, Mr. Beechum?" asked Raysor in an attempt to regain control.

Pauley shook his clothes back in place. "I guess."

Raysor walked away, calling in to the station. Seabrook went to sit in the cruiser, apparently not wanting to be seen returning to the empty house.

Callie nodded stiffly at Pauley, giving him a meager benefit of the doubt. Maybe some sense of mourning? "Sorry about your dad."

Pauley stomped up to her face. Seabrook opened his door to get back out, but Callie waved him off. Pauley wouldn't touch her. She'd already put him in the dirt once.

"We'll see if you like somebody breaking into *your* house," Pauley grumbled.

Her blood chilled, her smugness replaced with a cold reality that this guy wouldn't be the first to break in to her place . . . or was he?

At that moment, Pauley morphed from a mouthy simpleton living off scams to a man capable of more if provoked. Street smart, he might hide behind that dumbo persona, making people underestimate him, raising his odds of succeeding with his schemes.

Pauley headed to the back of the house, still grabbing at his shirt. Raysor waved at Seabrook with a finger, indicating he'd be back in a minute, and followed Pauley.

No doubt Pauley coveted money with a passion. He'd done time, not much, but enough to give him social access to more of his ilk. Or was she giving too much credit to a socially-inept, uneducated man? Her quick thinking hadn't been too quick these days.

Callie started to retreat to her own house. *Nope, not quick at all, girl.* Her keys were still inside the Beechum place. She sat on the bottom step, figuring it best to let Rhonda retrieve her keys rather than ask Pauley to let her in. The patrol car waited, Raysor still gone. Seabrook motioned her over.

She wasn't worried what people thought, and Pauley probably watched from behind a curtain now, but she wasn't sure how to read Seabrook. So she went over, curious. At the car door, she leaned down.

"Stay out of his business," Seabrook said.

"What the heck does that mean?" Her words shot out pitchy as she drew back, not appreciating the beat-cop lecture.

"I already pulled him in for questioning, and his nerves are on edge. Probably why he went overboard on you. Give him space. He's lost his dad and had his house burgled. With the burglar running rampant, Pauley thinks everybody wants his inheritance."

"Thanks," Callie said, catching on. "He *is* acting creepy."

"Yeah," Seabrook said. "And you *did* take some of his daddy's stuff."

"Mike—"

The cop shook his head. "I don't care. Just watch the guy."

She whispered to Seabrook, glancing at Raysor coming up to her left, barely out of earshot. "Why'd you come over?"

"Raysor didn't see why you had to put Pauley on the ground."

Rhonda pulled up, got out of her car, and chortled playfully at Callie as she strutted past the patrol car. "Did you leave your keys in the house after I showed it to you?" she said, loud enough for all to hear.

"I sure did, Rhonda. The owner's inside, though. Not happy."

Rhonda wrinkled her nose. "I'll collect your keys. Just stay here."

Raysor got in the car to leave, and Callie backed away to give him room to pull out. She smiled and waved. Seabrook didn't smile back, and she wasn't sure what that meant.

And why the hell had he been hiding in that empty house?

BACK INSIDE CHELSEA Morning, Callie dropped the cardboard box on her kitchen table. She'd returned to secure the lock when Sophie skipped up the front steps dressed conservatively in cargo shorts and a barely off-one-shoulder jersey top, but not without her bangles.

"Like the new color out front," she said. "So what's with the patrol car?"

She wore green contacts today.

Callie smiled. Sophie's impromptu visit was refreshing after the morning's drama. "Just a sec." Callie moved the shoebox to her bedroom. She came back, emptied the coffee maker, and prepared the machine for a fresher brew. "I knew it wouldn't take you long to snoop. First, how was the party?"

Sophie's face lit up. "You *are* curious about Mason's galas. Fabulous!"

"Simple question, Sophie."

The woman gave her a deep study. "You're uptight."

"No, just tired of crap on this street." She leaned on the counter. "Do you realize I have no clue what it's like to live here and not talk to police? I mean each and every day."

"I hear you, girl."

Shut up, Callie. This was not the person to bare one's soul to. Sophie proudly claimed the roles of neighbor and girlfriend; however, the fact Sophie partied with Mason was enough reason to stay mute. One too many drinks, and a Friday night could spread Callie's feelings, background, and flaws across the sea island, to come back at her embellished ten times over.

Would she ever trust somebody again? Not if she saw each new person as a potential threat, and she had no clue how to change that habit after two years of honing the skill.

"Any-way," Sophie drawled, "the party was good. It's always good. This time he brought in these duck canapés and tuna carpaccio with this to-die-for mango chutney." She reached over and touched Callie's arm. "And get this. There was a five-foot salmon pyramid, with the fish shaped like roses. Then later they served these teeny, scrumptious, *warm* chocolate and brandied cherry truffle cakes. Girl! What part of that don't you want to experience?"

Sophie prattled on about the food, the bartender who put drinks in LED lit glasses, and the couples of convenience due to out-of-town spouses. Some band flew in from New Orleans.

"He does that each week?" Callie asked.

"Just about," Sophie replied.

"Why?"

"Who cares? Besides, tell me about Rhonda. What does she say the Beechum house is selling for? I like to know how much equity I own."

Callie's mouth twitched. "You have a hundred percent equity, Sophie. Your ex paid for the place."

Sophie's dangling earrings knocked her shrugging shoulders. "Still like to know what I'm worth. Each time it goes up, I get warm fuzzies."

The coffee maker gurgled and let out a final hiss. "Coffee ready. Want some?" Callie asked.

"Sure. You never answered why the cops were here."

"Pauley saw me on the doorstep and thought I was breaking in. Just a mistake."

Sophie's mouth curved down. "He's always been an odd nut."

Seabrook ought to just post Sophie on guard, give her incentive as the street's unofficial crime patrol. She performed the job anyway. "If you're so nosy, then how come you aren't seeing this thief?"

Sophie pulled a leg up, foot under her, knee resting against the edge of the table, folded in origami fashion. "I've been thinking about that. Haven't seen anybody new or out of place. But then, if this criminal is someone I know, I wouldn't sense anything wrong. Could be Mike, that realtor Rhonda, or even you."

Exactly, Callie thought.

Sophie sipped her coffee. "Can you add some cinnamon to this? And maybe some milk?"

As she walked to the spice shelf, Callie reverted back to suspecting a local resident instead of someone off the grid. Also, Sophie might not possess as keen an eye as she professed. As Callie originally thought, these locals were too caught up in each other's comings and goings to see which one of their own was killing, assaulting, and burglarizing the rest.

"Any of this bother your kids?" Callie asked. "Jeb's not worried enough, in my opinion."

Sophie blew out a breath in mild disgust. "Have you learned nothing from me, because my children sure pay attention. Come on, I know you remember," she said. "It's the defining difference between us, girl."

Callie scoffed. "The whole negativity thing. See no evil, hear no evil, stick your head in the sand and experience no evil. In the meantime, someone comes up and shoots your backside off."

Sophie winked. "Funny. I'll convert you one day."

The hell she would. "How're the boys doing with the fishing business?" Callie asked. "Jeb seems mighty entranced by Zeus's business acumen."

"Good, good. They get along well, don't you think? I love that."

"Um, hmm."

"They could almost be partners. Zeus's daddy bought him the boat, so it's not like Jeb would have to buy into the business or anything. Two friends, earning money, having fun. That's how life's supposed to be. Easygoing and enjoying the people around you."

Callie grabbed the good lead in. "So, is Zeus going back to school in August? I mean, with his job going so well. I don't know how well *well* is, but you know how kids are. They make a few dollars, and they think they don't need the education. The whole Bill Gates story. I hate it when the random young boy gets rich. Throws the rest of the kids off balance thinking that's the norm instead of the lottery pick it really is."

Sophie pursed her lips. "You worried Zeus is a bad influence on Jeb?"

"No, not at all." Callie hadn't meant it to come out that way and thought she'd done a better job of asking the question. Guess her covert tricks weren't so slick anymore. "Jeb is hinting about not going to school, is all."

"And you think this is Zeus's idea?" Sophie wasn't as slow as she let on.

"My son adores yours, and this hesitation about college came from out of the blue, so naturally, my thoughts wandered—"

"To my son instead of your own."

"I'm not blaming anyone, Sophie. I'm just confused."

Her neighbor rose from her seat. "Not being fond of conflict, let me cut this conversation short, so you don't ruin the air in this house any more than it already is."

"Don't be like that, Sophie," Callie said, now feeling bad. "I didn't mean to—"

Sophie waved a finger like a windshield wiper. "You already did. You are crystal clear, neighbor-of-mine. My son is a good and free spirit. He's testing out a business idea. No, I don't know if he's going back to school in the fall, but if he takes time off, the world won't stop. If he quits the job, same deal. Jeb's decision about college is no different. It's his life. Get used to it."

Callie reared back, embarrassed at the sudden turn in the conversation.

"Jeb is a man," Sophie continued, now moving toward the front door. "You have hang-ups about that, mainly because he's the last man in your life. That's sad for you, but it's his life, girl. Not yours. Zeus's only influence on Jeb was pure exposure. Let your son draw his own conclusions. Even if Zeus invited him into the business, what's so wrong with that? Can't Jeb say no, yes, after school, whatever, on his own?"

"Sophie," Callie said, not wanting to lose the woman's fledgling friendship. Plus, Sophie kept her abreast of local affairs. A loose partner of sorts.

"Please, I'm sorry. Come back and sit. I'm sure I have cinnamon in the cupboard."

But Sophie shook her head. "I'll see you another time. Right now, however, I need to pretend you didn't just blame my son for your son's instinctive nature to question his life's choices. And I need to pretend that I'm not pissed as hell that you're so insecure about your family that you have to accuse someone else's to feel good about yourself."

"Wait a damn minute," Callie said, shifting abruptly from sheepish to pissed.

Sophie rapidly descended the stairs. "Nope. This conversation is over." She turned at the bottom for a dramatic pause. "But you're still welcome to come to yoga in the morning. You need it more than ever." Then she fast-walked home, her back stiff and very un-yogaish.

Callie shut the door a bit too loud before she realized Sophie would only be appeased by the noise. She rued her words, chagrined at Sophie's efficient, articulate dismantlement of Callie's questions. She rubbed at her scar, wishing so desperately she had a sounding board to tell her what she could've done differently.

As a detective, decisions once flowed from her spot on right, her logic and deductions so solid that rookies and seasoned officers alike took her word as gospel. A fact, then two, laced with suspicion, glued with dialogue from one party then another. Without much thought, she could sort which pieces completed the puzzle.

She apparently wasn't so savvy anymore. And rude to boot.

But hadn't she told Seabrook she was a loner now?

She caught herself standing before the cabinet, moving bottles aside. She slammed it back shut, recognizing her mindless move to grab a glass and fill it with something other than tea.

Seabrook's open offer to call him before she took a drink floated back. Bet he no longer meant it. Moving to the window, she stared across the street and down, hoping to see his movement in the empty house again. He could have had Raysor drop him off so that he could reenter the house around back.

If he appeared, she'd call him. If he didn't, then screw him. The microwave clock read quarter to four. He had ten minutes.

She jerked back from the window as the back door opened.

Jeb walked in. "Mom? Grandpa still coming? If he's not, I have a date with Sprite."

Callie glanced at the clock. Time had flown by.

Jeb considered her. "What're you doing?"

"Um, thought I saw someone who didn't belong walking the street," she replied.

"How would you know?" He frowned. "You look guilty."

"Nonsense," she said. "Now, what were you saying?"

"Grandpa still coming?" he asked. "If not—"

"Yes, he's coming." Callie yanked his shirt. "Go get ready in case he arrives early. Be thinking where he can take you. And listen to his advice. He's a wise man."

"Boy," Jeb said. "If this isn't a set up, I don't know what is. Wonder what it is you can't discuss that you dumped on him to tell me instead."

"Go!" she said, feeling so damn transparent these days.

A HALF HOUR later, Callie watched television in the living room. In the recliner across the room, Jeb texted on his phone, probably with Sprite, still bitter about Callie's leash on him and his obligation to the guy-to-guy dinner with his grandfather.

Lawton Cantrell would gain the boy's confidence. Callie knew it. He'd get Jeb to analyze himself by guiding the child in the right direction, asking subtle questions, leaving Jeb proud of himself in the end. It had worked so many times on her growing up, sometimes talking her through the latest tiff with her mother. She wouldn't have lasted under that roof without her daddy's gentle patience.

Jeb threw down his smartphone and grabbed the remote off the sofa. "Wish it were football season."

Living in Middleton for a year had endeared him to the sport, in a high school known across the state for its history and trophies. Maybe a football college would attract him more.

She studied him, worried, then returned her gaze to the TV.

Her phone rang, the harsh bell sound ripping the expectant air. "Hello?"

"What're you doing tonight?"

"Mason," she said irritated, "I'm busy."

"You busy later?"

"Not tonight. Seriously, I've got things on my mind."

Jeb heard her and cast a sullen look.

"So, another night then?" Mason asked. "You just said—"

"Not now," she said. "See you later."

As she hung up, Jeb pounded buttons on his controller. "That your boyfriend?"

Ah, part of his problem. "I don't have a boyfriend, Jeb," she said.

"People saw you at Whaley's. Lit up."

She retrieved her phone and, in stride, glanced out to the porch, across to Pauley's place. "That was just dinner." Her dad was late.

"Save it, Mom."

She turned to her son. "Jeb, that evening wasn't—"

The doorbell rang. Callie jerked. When she reached the door, Seabrook waited on the porch in jeans.

She raised her brow. "This is a surprise."

The phone rang, and Seabrook took it from her.

Callie gawked at him. "I don't even know who that is." Time to have a meeting of the minds with the cop. "Jeb's about to go out to dinner. When he leaves, we need to clear the air, Mr. Seabrook. I don't follow what your problem is, but—"

Seabrook stepped into the foyer and closed the door. "Callie, your father's been in an accident. His car left the road somewhere on Highway 165."

Callie felt Jeb's arms encircle her from behind.

Seabrook studied his feet before meeting her pleading gaze. "I'm so sorry. He died instantly."

Chapter 20

CALLIE TURNED AWAY from the receiving line and faced the wall to dab her eyes, the strangling scent of carnations burning her sinuses. Two hundred people waited to console Beverly, Callie, and Jeb, streaming out the funeral home's reception area, into the hall, into the sanctuary fifty yards away where they wove in and out of the pews like a popular Disney attraction. County councilmen, business owners, and assorted government directors stacked up with their spouses on their arms, yet people continued to arrive.

The governor had already come and gone. He left while speaking to the state's junior US senator.

Earlier that afternoon, mentally numb, Callie had groomed Jeb, the child unable to recall how to tie his tie. She'd tried to help Beverly dress, too, only to be told to leave. So with her family tended to, she'd found herself dressed with too much time to spend. She'd wandered out back to her father's workshop, sat down on the concrete floor, and cried for the first time since Seabrook had broken the news in her foyer four nights ago.

Now standing in line, she was bone-weary and wrung out.

Make-up already stained the shoulders and lapels of Jeb's new suit, his pale complexion eliciting hugs and pitiful laments from mothers. An attendant offered all three of them a fresh, cold cup of whatever yellow drink was in the punch bowl. She'd had two cups already and still couldn't identify the taste.

Beverly, adorned in a navy silk suit, the silver blouse accenting her coiffure, held more energy than Callie and Jeb combined. Each mourner revved the widow's spirit, then received a unique word, eye contact, an unwavering smile, their hand grasped by both of Beverly's, one beneath and the other on top. Callie knew her mother'd had a drink, because she'd done so as well, both of them throwing back a gin barely splashed with tonic before entering the fray. Callie saw her choice as alcohol or Valium. Beverly chose both.

Callie had spent two hours with a distraught Jeb the night before, talking to him. He wavered between blaming himself for needing Lawton's attention and blaming Callie for inviting the man to Edisto in the first place. Between his rants, she'd detailed what the funeral director expected and that if Jeb became overwhelmed, he could escape to a certain room reserved for them. Three funerals in three years. Too many for a teen.

Too many for her.

John's funeral had consisted of wall-to-wall law enforcement who understood losing one of their own. They held Callie up for weeks with visits, calls, food, chores, and errands. Some, like Stan, had tended to Jeb's needs with a male shoulder and diversion tactics like a Red Sox game or a movie.

But this. *Jesus.* This was cable television material. She'd seen two re-porters with cameramen already.

She tired of the suits, the perfect manicures, the overwhelming show of politicians and well-heeled businessmen who offered their condolences with one eye scouting who hovered before, behind, or off to the side of them. She had no idea who half these people were.

Her father had appreciated the importance of this type of behavior, but he hadn't operated along those rules. He'd respected the need to glad-hand but had guarded his humanitarian side. Still, this parading, pranc-ing, and posturing sea of people loved him, never quite registering how to function like he had.

Her daddy had been so damn special. He'd sacrificed too many years for these people. He'd sacrificed himself for her. It wasn't Jeb's fault Lawton drove to Edisto. It was hers.

Callie brushed damp eyes and shifted as the balls of her feet throbbed. Beverly, contrary to the other sixtyish women in the room, sported tasteful two-inch narrow heels with a pointed toe.

"How're you doing?" Callie whispered to Jeb as a husband and wife chatted with the power couple behind them. The break offered the grieving family fifteen seconds of peace.

"This sucks so bad!" he whispered through his teeth.

She rubbed his sleeve. "I know, baby. Not much longer. This cere-mony displays respect and gives your grandmother strength."

Jeb scoffed. "She could do this for days, Mom. She's stronger than anybody in this room."

The Middleton police chief made his entrance in full dress regalia. Relief washed over Callie, her knees almost going weak. The image of a cop captured her heart, as if more was right with the world by his presence.

"Excuse me," she said, dipping her head to a middle-aged woman with pin curls dyed auburn to match her dress and enough diamonds on her fingers to fund Middleton's budget for the next two years. Callie moved to the side of the room, the chief in gentle tow. God knows, she ached to spend the rest of the evening in the shadow of a uniform heavy with brass and ribbons.

"Sorry about your daddy," the tall man said, stooping way over to softly speak in Callie's ear.

She bowed her head in return then stared with purpose. "He was a conservative driver. It was five in the afternoon on a Saturday, and he had a light schedule. He told me so. That's why he was coming to see us. He didn't fall asleep at the wheel. He didn't text." She'd already spoken to other law enforcement and said all these things. Just not the chief. He could make investigators dig deeper.

The big man settled back on his heel, as if listening to a speeder's explanation about how he couldn't have been going that fast. "I sent a car to the scene, Ms. Morgan, then I came along forty-five minutes later since the victim, sorry, was our mayor."

"And I thank you for that attention," Callie said. "Daddy deserved it."

He nodded in agreement.

"So what happened other than his car left the road and hit an oak? What made him leave the pavement?" she asked, fighting not to rush the words. She needed answers so badly.

"We're not sure," he replied. "Something took his attention away, and the skid marks indicate he tried to regain control. No contact transfer that we can find. Whether he took a phone call or someone ran him off the road, nobody knows. Not sure we ever will, ma'am."

"I can check his cell phone and most likely rule that out," she said.

Again, the tight, formal smile.

She recognized the cop labeling her as a family member blind to reality, trying to exert her law enforcement connection to gain favor, ignoring what could be a simple driving mistake. Cops grew accustomed to families begging for a better answer for their loved one's death.

But her daddy didn't make such mistakes.

"Mom? Grandma's unhappy you left," Jeb said, appearing at her side.

"I'll be there in a moment." She made firm eye contact with the lawman, afraid to let him go without assurances. "Please take a deeper look, Chief. He was a public figure. You know my background. I appreciate your position. But Daddy didn't *just* stray off the road and hit a tree."

"Accidents happen, Ms. M—"

"Not to me and mine," she said louder than expected.

Jeb nudged her. "Mom."

A dozen people turned.

"Humor me, then," she said, her tone more polite. "Give it another going over. For Daddy."

"Highway Patrol has jurisdiction." His stoic façade barely cracked as his gaze met hers and then softened. "But in light of Mr. Cantrell's position, I'll make the request."

"Thank you." But the promise didn't make her happier, not like she thought it would. She returned to the receiving line where an eightyish woman in a dated blue suit awaited, anxious to speak.

The gloved hand patted Callie's as she stepped back into place. "This must be difficult for you after losing your husband such a short period ago, honey. A fire, wasn't it?"

"Yes, ma'am." Callie marveled at the hunger people had for details of carnage.

"I heard you had a bad time with that."

"Geez," Jeb said under his breath.

Callie tapped the side of his shoe with her own. "Yes, ma'am. I found it quite difficult to have a good time that night."

Jeb grinned to the side.

Beverly grabbed the lady's hand and eased her further along, shooting a short, reproachful glance at Callie. "How are you, Mrs. Ashton? I heard about your lovely roses outdoing themselves this year. You must be proud."

Callie leaned into Jeb. "Sorry, I'm tired."

"That was actually awesome, Mom," he said.

A warmth spread through her, a feeling she thought impossible under the circumstances. That was the first positive remark Jeb had given her in a week.

A girl Jeb's age, accompanied by her father, moved forward. She shyly glanced at Jeb and said, "Sorry about your grandfather."

"Of course, that's another way of handling it, too," Callie whispered, grateful to see Jeb attracted. She eyed the father's watch, wondering if it was too much to ask the funeral director to shut the doors at nine.

Unexpectedly, her eyes moistened, and she fought to push down the lump. She missed her daddy so damn much. This was such a pomp and circumstance, but admission didn't entitle these people to see her cry.

CALLIE ENTERED the family room of her parents' Middleton mini-mansion of forty-five hundred square feet as the hall clock gonged once for half past eleven at night. Beverly stood at the mahogany wet bar, heels off and barefoot. She faced the five-by-seven mirror with exaggerated concentration, as if afraid to glance up and see herself. From the reflection, Callie recognized the makings for a pitcher of martinis.

"Mix that with that fancy French gin, and I'll share it with you," she said as she kicked off her own shoes.

Beverly held up a sixty dollar bottle of Citadelle without glancing back.

"Yes, that one," Callie said, sitting on the leather sofa, avoiding the brown recliner that had been her father's.

Jeb had fallen into bed as soon as they'd arrived back at the Cantrell home. Callie couldn't have slept if she wanted to. The past often overwhelmed her in sleep, driving her frantic with so many memories. Hers and John's wedding day, their academy graduations, late night Saturdays and late morning Sundays that followed. His dislike for eggs and her love of omelettes. The scenes would flash faster and faster until her pulse raced, and she sweated out from under the covers.

She now feared her father's death would escalate the visions and add new chapters to those already in place. Maybe bring on the anxiety attacks again. If she had to stay up and await sunrise peeking past the crape myrtles, she would. Whatever it took to make her drop from exhaustion into a comatose sleep.

Beverly brought over the pitcher, two glasses, and a bottle of green olives. Without asking, she threw three olives and extra juice in a glass, filled it with drink, and gave it to her daughter nesting on the other end of the sofa.

Callie took a sip. "You always make a good drink."

"That's what your father used to say." Then she drank half the glass's contents, studied the remnant, and downed the rest.

Callie now appreciated Jeb's shoes. Was this how he felt watching her? Beverly refilled her glass. "How're you holding up, Mother?"

"Fine." Her mother took in another deep swallow, leaving just enough to cover the olives.

She was taking those drinks fast. "I hope you don't have any obligations tomorrow," Callie said.

Beverly sharply jerked her head toward the bar. "Worried I'll drink it all? You know how to fix another batch. I taught you that much."

Callie winced. The lady's Southern charms were nonexistent tonight. "You indeed educated me on how to find my way around a bar."

"Hmph," Beverly said, pouring her third in a matter of minutes.

Callie's gaze rested on Lawton's recliner. She'd give Beverly the benefit of the doubt tonight. A new widow deserved that much. But she'd rarely seen her mother so blunt, willing to sling ornery so hard. "I asked Chief Warren to review Daddy's accident." Licking off the alcohol, she sucked out the pimento first before consuming the olive. "Daddy was a good driver."

Beverly's slender form deflated into the cushions, showing how much weight she'd lost off a previously size six frame. "Let it be, Callie. It won't bring him back."

Callie sank into her own cushion and her second drink, draining the pitcher. "Don't you want the truth?"

Beverly dragged her gaze from her glass to her daughter as if her eyes weighed thirty pounds each. A white tress of hair strayed from its spray and loosely draped across her vision, but the woman didn't notice. "If he made some dumbass mistake driving, why do I want to know that as his last deed with all he accomplished in life? Let me remember him as perfectly as possible, please." She fished an olive out and ate it, licking fingers afterwards. "You of all people ought to sympathize."

Callie tugged at her necklace. She didn't want to compound her anguish for Lawton with the old grief of John. "Guess we share widowhood now," was all she could say.

"Hmmm." Her mother slid an unfocused stare toward her daughter.

"So we have something in common after all. How wonderful is that?"

Callie's eyes burned, a choke rising. She considered one statement and ruled it too malicious, then another. Shit and damn! She lifted up from the sofa.

She knew how intensely Beverly would suffer. Without a doubt, her mother loved her father completely, unconditionally. Agony would dominate most of her days and all of her nights for months to come. "Mother, I'm going to sit in the courtyard. Tonight you're entitled to be as nasty as you like. But I lost my daddy, too."

Callie silently moved around the woman toward the archway, stroking her mother's shoulder along the way. Beverly shivered.

"The days will get worse before they get better," Callie whispered. "Give yourself time to heal. I get it, trust me, I do." Then she left, the weight of the day mashing each step deeper into the plush cream carpet.

Into the sunroom and outside the French doors, Callie took a seat in a floral-cushioned wrought-iron chair. The view faced a thick copse of pines, blackened silhouettes this time of night, but she knew a foreclosed house half the size of her parents' sat empty just on the other side. In the courtyard, with its decadent horticulture, flagstone, and landscape lighting, she could pretend no bad luck or evil deeds existed. This was where Beverly would hide for a while. Callie didn't blame her.

Callie set her glass on a short table and scrubbed her face with fingertips. This wasn't her home any longer. But Edisto wasn't either. Boston was out of the question, with no chance of affording that cost of living without a job. Boston PD might take her back, but she didn't want to be a cop again. Besides, she'd never leave Jeb a thousand miles away. Maybe he'd come with her? What kind of tuition would that be?

No place felt right.

Daddy, did you give us the house to keep us close or make me put my life back together again?

Moths fluttered around a coach lamp. A mosquito sang in her ear before she brushed it away for it to quickly return. A sweat bead trickled down her temple. It was too hot and irritating out here, even for June.

She reached to collect her glass, but between the dark and the gin, she knocked it off the edge. Thin crystal shattered into slivers and shards and skittered in all directions.

She fell back, lifting bare feet off the flagstone. "Well, shit."

Beverly stuck her head out the door, her shoulder leaning on the frame for balance. "Why don't you go back to Edisto, dear? I don't need a sitter." She started to shut the door.

"Mother!" Callie called just loud enough not to wake neighbors or Jeb.

The door reopened. Beverly repositioned herself against the other half of the French door with her blouse dangling wrinkled and unkempt over her skirt, waiting as if she'd made her move, and it was Callie's turn to draw a card.

"You might need some help," Callie said, struck awkward at her mother's remark. "You stayed with me when John died."

"I seem to recall someone telling us to give her space," Beverly slurred. "Your father and I left two days after the funeral."

The air between them had been thick as pudding then, as Callie recalled. Lawton had known how to temper the tense moments when his daughter's nerves unraveled and Jeb couldn't get out of bed. Her mother, not so much, which stung Callie sharply at the time, because Beverly Cantrell had a full grasp of social etiquette and the proper phrases to say. Just not words meant for a daughter in need.

"Well, I had Jeb. You have no one," Callie said.

Beverly lifted one shoulder, brushing off her daughter's remark. "My friends will harbor me and tend my needs. Tomorrow I'll receive even more food, more cards, calls, and visits." She waved slowly toward the stars, as if beginning a soliloquy. "The Cantrells thrive here. From your great-great-grandfather to your father, four generations of public servants. Mayors, councilmen, state representatives. The legacy means the town holds an obligation to pay its respects for the long term." She lowered her arm. "I'll be anything but alone. You"—she pointed at Callie—"on the other hand, will stand in a corner observing, picking up used hors d'oeuvres napkins and washing *unbroken* drink glasses in an attempt to stay busy and avoid societal well-wishers."

Callie rose up and turned to her mother with an exhausted anger. "You love the attention. I don't."

"Yes, you do," Beverly said, her stocking-covered feet still inside, protected by the marble floor. "Just on your own terms, and most people don't tolerate your terms. Makes for a short list of friends, I'd say. Those who *get* you, as you used to be so fond of saying."

Callie stepped forward. Glass pricked her left foot, under her toes, then another under her right heel, but she walked over to Beverly anyway, not stopping to analyze the damage. "You're a mean drunk, Mother."

"Are there sweet drunks, dear?" She took another sip as if to anchor the question mark.

Callie hated her mother's word play. "Maybe I *should* leave." She edged around the woman and went inside, walked a few feet, and then noticed the trail of dark marks on the beige marble floor of the sunroom.

"Stop. Don't go any further and track blood on my hall carpet. Here," Beverly said. "Take my napkin."

"A real mother would sit me down so she could tend her daughter's cuts." Callie leaned on the stair banister and lifted one foot, then the other, noticing the heel bleeding, but the ball of her foot not showing the tiny piece she still felt embedded.

Beverly pushed off the door and moved with a shaky dignity toward Callie. "Sit down, then, if that's what you need."

"Can you even tell how many feet I have right now? No, thanks."

Her mother halted, swaying slightly. Leaning on the cherry hall table, she softened her expression. "What will we do without your father, Callie?"

Callie studied this lady who'd birthed her, not sure she felt the genetic connection as deeply as she should. Lawton had bridged them. What *would* they do?

"I don't know, Mother."

Beverly shoved off the table and weaved her way back toward the family room. "Well, I meant what I said. Go back to Edisto. Leave Jeb if you wish, but if you stay we'll cause a nuclear holocaust this town doesn't need to read in the *Journal Scene*. I think you follow, dear."

Even in mourning, her mother worried about appearances, but for once, Callie agreed. If she stuck around, she and her mother would only rub each other raw and make for gossip which would only be remembered as the atrocious, uncouth manner in which the Cantrells commemorated their monarch's passing.

Guess she'd go back to Edisto . . . for now.

Chapter 21

AROUND TWO P.M. the next day, Callie drove the long way to Edisto along Highway 61. The old road ran ten miles farther than Highway 165, but she couldn't bring herself to pass the accident's location. She begged Jeb to take the alternate route as well when he returned to the beach in a few days. For now, he could stand guard over Beverly if Callie couldn't and return in John's old car. Lawton never did tune it up.

Driving with a grip at ten and two, she felt more alone and vulnerable than ever. This road ran more traffic than the other, and a driver couldn't be too careful. Four-and five-foot wide oaks climbed seventy-five feet toward the clouds, dripping ten-foot clumps of Spanish moss under a canopy of branches. The highway guided cars from Middleton, past historic Middleton Plantation and Magnolia Gardens, to the West Ashley area of Charleston. Sunlight flickered like a disco ball through the leaves. Emotional exhaustion dragged her into the seat, but this wasn't a highway to drive tired on. Not with the oaks almost atop the asphalt.

Punching the radio search button, Callie dialed for hard rock, any sort of musical racket. Screeching Rolling Stones, Aerosmith, Metallica. Distraction. The radio blared a few decibels short of max, but she could not clear her head or shut down the continual unsettled concern over . . . she wasn't sure what. Everything?

But fact was she had nobody to call for aid anymore.

After Seabrook delivered the news five days ago, she'd thrown clothes in the car and held it together until they reached Middleton around ten p.m. Seabrook's headlights had followed them most of the way.

Jeb had locked himself in his room. Her mother had medicated herself, and Callie had tucked her into bed. Callie had then taken a bottle to her parents' courtyard and slung it across the yard in grief, wanting so damn much to drink it down like an iced Coke on an August evening.

Now, her wheels hummed easy on the pavement.

Callie wasn't sure what Beverly was to her now. Lawton had kept the family civil. And Beverly's first overt action as a widow had been to ship her daughter away. Jeb already served in Lawton's stead. Okay to a point, but Beverly was not dragging Jeb too deeply into her world.

The stark reality of her family's hobbled state had first engulfed her when the funeral director told the three remaining Cantrells where to stand for the receiving line. Beverly and Jeb were all she had left. A family that had shrunk from six to three in two years.

She had no reason to return to Chelsea Morning, yet had nowhere else to go.

Callie smacked the steering wheel. *Stop it!* Her mind wandered in ridiculous directions, with common thoughts twisted into misshapen anxieties. Where was her head?

She caught herself thinking of Seabrook again. She'd thrown up a wall from the moment they'd met. Of all the characters on Edisto, Seabrook could probably relate to her the most. He wanted to sympathize, yet she hadn't let him near enough to express it.

He'd been patient with her running on the beach, gun in her waistband. Hiding from the evening sun. And he'd probably given up on her. Completely alone, she could see herself leaving the television on, going out, and coming home terrified someone had broken in. Or worse, someone hiding in a closet or under the bed.

There had to be a reason for her reluctance to let him close, but she didn't want to think about that now.

Who would be her foundation now? Tears spilled down her face. Her father was gone.

Highway 17 appeared in the distance. Her gaze dropped to the dashboard. *What? Shit!* Her speedometer read ninety. She yanked her foot off the accelerator and slammed weight on the brake. The car fishtailed. Her fingers vise-gripped the steering wheel. Her forearms and biceps knotted rock hard.

The car squealed to a halt ten feet into the crossroad, missing the rear end of a passing Honda by a yard. Her whole body shook as she flipped the transmission into reverse and eased back behind the stop sign.

She searched the rearview mirror for blue lights . . . then gasped at her reflection.

Tears coated flushed cheeks, shiny with red blotches. Eyes wide and red-rimmed, she appeared completely emotional. A cop would have given her the once over and snatched her keys, maybe her license, and hauled her in until somebody could determine her state of mind.

Arms crossed on the steering wheel, Callie rested her forehead on them. Inhale. Exhale. Count it out.

She thought she'd made progress with this shit.

This was regression. And she was driving back to a serial criminal. A murderer. But heaven help her, she preferred the beach and its calamities to the echoes of her mother's mini-mansion.

The hammering in her chest settled back into a lesser degree of somersaulting thump and bump. She didn't expect calm for quite some time to come, but for now she was sane.

Callie checked her mirror again. What the—

A red smear swished across her brow. She licked her fingers and rubbed, licked them and rubbed the spot again, this time recognizing the telltale copper taste. Studying her face, then the rest of her, she was surprised, then wasn't.

Somewhere between Middleton and an almost-disastrous halt at Highway 17, when her brain tore her sensibilities to pieces in a maelstrom of bass drum and steel guitar, she'd clawed at the scar on her arm. Irregular maroon shapes dotted her linen shirtsleeve, the material now ruined with blood. She gingerly pushed the sleeve up to her elbow. Shallow scratched wounds oozed blood in a dozen places.

She didn't even remember digging fingernails into the scar.

A waiting car honked.

Accelerating, her car barely missed a truck veering out of her way. She pulled into the traffic pattern, pulse revved again.

She didn't crave a drink this time. She wanted the whole bottle.

WEAK-KNEED BUT in better control of her car, Callie slowed as Chelsea Morning came into view. A rented white Taurus sat in the driveway.

Parking on the other side of her stairs, up under the house, she tucked her Glock in her jeans waistband and slung her purse over her shoulder. Peters was nowhere around. She sure would appreciate his presence now with a stranger on her property.

One hand on the refurbished outdoor banister, the other reaching behind to her belt, Callie stepped on the bottom riser, staring up, giving time for the visitor to show himself before she committed too far.

"Chicklet!" growled Stan Waltham with a Chuck Norris grin, rising from one of her rattan chairs.

"Stan!"

Callie sprinted up the stairs and tackled the huge man so eagerly that even her tiny frame moved him back a half step. Then she leaned back to take full gander of her old boss.

"How long have you been here?" she asked breathlessly. "How did you know to come to Edisto? How long can you stay?"

"First get me out of this steam bath," he said. "Damn, it's hot!"

She giggled irregularly, excitement ruling. "Of course." Fumbling in her purse, she found her keys, then scratched the doorknob trying to enter. "I can't tell you how happy I am to see you," she said, stopping once to wipe joyful tears away. "Was your flight okay?"

Stan laughed at her childish excitement, but then concern etched his expression, turning down the corners of his mouth. "Flight was fine. They gave me three days off. Everyone sends their best, by the way."

"Tell them thanks. I so miss them."

Callie ignored his expression and let her old friend in. She locked the door, glanced out the oval window, and hauled Stan by the hand to the living room.

She hugged him again, arms barely meeting around the bulk, the squeeze tight enough to draw a grunt from him. Stan pried her off. "Got something cold to drink?"

"It'll have to be a soft drink or water. I just got back in from . . . well, anyway, I can make iced tea if you don't mind waiting a few minutes. Or I might have bourbon."

"Cola's fine, if you got it," he said, sitting on the sofa.

Ice clinked in the glasses. The pure delight of seeing her boss shot her spirits through-the-clouds high, as if God decided to intervene. This was Stan, the man who understood her and remembered what she used to be.

Drinks on coasters, she sat on the sofa, two feet between them, stroking his sleeve briefly once.

His smile fell away. "I'm sorry about your father."

Her smile vanished as well. "Thanks. Got your voice mail, but, you know, we were so scattered for several days. I'm not sure it's sunk in yet. There's just this big hole. Daddy was like, immortal in a Dick Van Dyke kinda way."

His glass seemed so tiny as the big man took a drink and set it back. "Flew in when I could. Your phone must be turned off, so I had to call your mom. She told me you were headed here."

"So you just arrived." Callie leaned over to the end table and retrieved her cell phone. The screen wouldn't even light up. She plugged it in and set it back down. Two dings rang out as texts came in from Jeb. She returned to her seat, still giddy.

Then it hit her that Stan had come alone. "How're you holding up without Misty?"

"I'm fine. We're fine." He took her hand, then with his other, pushed up her sleeve now dried with blood. "What's this?"

She drew back, but he held firm. "Nothing," she said. "Scratched myself without thinking."

"The hell you say." He rose to his feet. "Where's your medicine cabinet?"

"The bathroom," she said, pointing.

Stan returned with the supplies. He laid a towel on his knee and tugged her arm over, causing her to scoot closer. Cotton balls dabbed peroxide on her cuts, teasing the clots away, prepping the small wounds for a bandage. "I remember when this thing was a mess," he said.

"Yeah."

"I remember when you were a mess."

She gave him a half smile. "Yeah, that too."

They sat in silence as he taped the gauze, maybe overdoing it, but she knew the slow actions were his way of leading into something. Stan never was one to leap into what he had to say.

A new text dinged on Callie's phone.

"Your mother?" Stan asked, applying the last piece of tape and lowering her sleeve. "I imagine you two are close these days."

"Jeb," she replied. "I make him keep me posted each hour he's away from me."

His brow raised, giving his old supervisory expression. She'd joke about her being a civilian now, but the time didn't seem right.

She pushed the first aid supplies to the center of the coffee table, her way of changing the subject. "These break-ins bother me." She gestured toward the entryway. "A little over a week ago, someone came in while I was gone. I found the front door unlocked. I *never* leave a door unlocked."

Stan's button-down tropical shirt over khakis and loafers gave him a CEO-on-vacation appearance, especially with the salt and pepper, tightly-groomed hair. He reared back on the sofa, arm draped over the cushion, one ankle over the other knee. The man projected a huge presence, commanding police troops like a two-star general, but those near to him knew his personal side more resembled a gruff linebacker cradling a puppy with a few baby-talk words.

"See the gray house over there?" Callie nodded toward the porch.

He leaned forward and peered outside.

"That's where someone set me up. Put a lamp in the window and a radio on a table. Then in the kitchen they placed a coffee cup John gave me, with hot chocolate in it!"

"So you said. Sounds like pranks, Morgan."

She huffed, irritated, desperate to make him see. "Except for coming in my house and stealing the cup to do it. Then placing it in a house where my friend was murdered. That's more than a prank."

"I know, I know. Just taking it in. Don't get your hackles up."

"Male animals have hackles."

He grunted. "What are hackles anyway?"

"Stan."

Unfolding his legs, he rested elbows on his knees. "What do you shore people do for dinner down here? Is it the same? Crabs and lobster? Can I take you out someplace? And I didn't see a hotel. Do I go further down the road or what? This place is in the middle of nowhere."

"More like shrimp, snapper, tuna, mahi mahi, sea bass, flounder, grouper."

"Hmph, listen to you. A shore native already."

"It's beach, not shore. I told you that. And we aren't going anywhere. I have the fixings for a shrimp dinner right here. You can stay in Jeb's room or upstairs in the guestroom, assuming you don't mind pastels and a twin bed."

"Don't want to put you out," Stan said from his seat as Callie went to the freezer and set two pounds of shrimp on the counter.

Peering around the open refrigerator door, she shook her head at the man. "You're the best thing that could have happened to me at this moment. I'm not letting you out of my sight." She drank in the crisp coldness of the appliance. "Damn, it's good to see you."

The doorbell rang.

"Want me to get that?" Stan asked.

She hesitated, and he noticed. Before she decided whether the local crowd needed to know about Stan, or whether she wanted to start accepting their condolences, he took charge and strolled to the door.

"May I help you?" she heard him say.

"Colleton Deputy Don Raysor."

"Hey, Don. Stan Waltham. Come on in. Nice to finally meet you."

Callie stiffly entered the foyer, noting that the men greeted each other like college buddies. "What do you want, *Don?*"

The ruddy-faced deputy held his cap. "Came to tell you I'm sorry for your loss, Callie. And to see if that rental belonged to who I thought it did." He turned to Stan. "How was the trip, my man?"

"Good, good," Stan said.

Callie sensed a set up, and the fact Stan was involved cut into her gut. "What the hell is this?"

Raysor smirked.

Stan, however, stepped toward Callie and took her arm. "He contacted me about your daddy, Callie."

"Whatever."

He avoided taking sides. "I know, but he at least showed concern."

Bullshit. "He also accused me of interfering with their police work and fraternizing with an officer." Her voice had escalated, and she fought it. The last thing she wanted to do was demonstrate weakness in front of Raysor. "He cornered and threatened me."

Stan peered at Raysor who lightly shrugged.

She surprisingly thought of having to re-sage her house with this sleaze under her roof. For the first time, Chelsea Morning took on a sense of refuge, and she wasn't having that fragile retreat violated.

"Get out," she ordered in a voice once reserved for arrests.

"Fine," Raysor said, backing up, as if innocently accused but too polite to cause a scene.

"Okay, well, thanks for checking on me, Don." Stan took the man to the porch for another handshake then returned inside.

Callie waited beside the hallway credenza, seething.

Betrayed.

She shrugged off Stan's touch once he came back in. The fire in her chest grew, and if she didn't contain it, it would turn cold, then into a full-bore anxiety attack. She counted in her head.

"Chicklet," he said. "Jesus Christ, what's going on with you? You've been scattered since I arrived."

She pivoted back toward the kitchen. Banging and clanging, she set a boiling pot on the stove for the shrimp. Stan watched from the edge of her bar as she began peeling potatoes.

What else, what else? She shoved aside mayonnaise, milk, pickles. She needed groceries. No coleslaw. No corn. Nothing else went with shrimp. Slamming the refrigerator shut, she threw fists on hips, lost what to do next, muscles twitching.

Stan slowly walked in and placed the shrimp back in the freezer. "Come on. I'm taking you out. Wining and dining, remember?"

She turned on him like a provoked dog. "These people don't need to know about you. I don't like them knowing anything about me. And Don doesn't need to be in my business."

Stan waved his arms out. "Fuck 'em! What difference does it make?"

The Stan she knew was smarter than this. "It gives them more targets, Stan! The more they know about me and mine, the more damage they can do. Somebody out there is messing with me, can't you see that? Who says it's not Raysor?"

By now her entire body shivered.

He came over and embraced her, rubbing up and down her back. "Shhh. Settle down. We'll sort this all out. And I'm a big boy, in case you hadn't noticed. Let me decide if I can handle being the talk of the shore."

Callie wanted to correct his *shore* to *beach* again, but instead grit her teeth. Stan rocked with her. For long, slow minutes they let time pass with no noise except the occasional sound of tires on asphalt as tourists drove down Jungle Road and birdsong in the palmettos growing outside her kitchen window.

She ate up the hug, his breath in her hair, and the slow movement of his massive palm on her back as if he offered her water after two parched days in the desert. She couldn't help but drink it in.

Chapter 22

ONCE CALLIE CHANGED into fresh clothes, Stan drove her to seek dinner. Three p.m. She directed him toward the Wyndham, hunkered in her seat, still pondering the tete-a-tete between him and Raysor. The deputy's past behavior didn't jibe with what had happened on her step. Stan, her last bastion of strength, chummy with the man who hated her most on Edisto.

They wound up at Grover's, the most discrete eatery on the beach. Soft jazz played in the background. Few people populated the higher-end golf-resort bar and restaurant, since most tourists preferred the sandwich and pizza places.

Stan crossed the hardwood floor to the bar that bordered the empty dining room, and Callie hung back, not wanting to appear needy for a drink. Stan spoke to the waiter, then came back to escort Callie to a bistro table off in a corner. He held out the tall chair as she hopped up, then he settled into his own. Meal order placed, they sat silent.

The waiter arrived and placed a gin and tonic before her and a Scotch and water in front of Stan. Flashing back to her date with Mason, she hesitated at the thought of yet another man pushing a drink at her. She reached inside herself for a reason not to drink it . . . or a better reason to chug it down. She didn't order a drink on purpose, but once it was there, she justified its existence. Her life was a mess . . . amen.

Then she sat there, not speaking a word, wringing the empty glass.

Stan studied her a second, then waved at the waiter for a refill.

"Go over this entire situation, Morgan. From the day you arrived to the day I got here. The crazies, the straights, the situations, the clues the PD don't take seriously, and your gut. Throw it all on the table. I take it you got no place better to be?"

Callie shook her head. "Nope. I'm unemployed, uprooted to a new place, and have no connections to anybody, no goals, no future whatsoever."

"I get it, Chicklet."

No, he didn't. No damn way he could. His congeniality with Raysor was like John having coffee with one of her perps. The two had no business together.

"Pretend we're in my office. If it takes a couple of drinks to settle your ass down, then fine," he said, then he seemed to change his mind. "Unless you ought not be drinking."

"I can drink," she said, not wanting to lose it now.

Then Stan sat and listened as the gin loosened her up, sometimes inserting a question, but for the most part he gave her the floor. By the end of dinner, they conversed easily, just as they'd done long ago.

Stan wiped the butter on his empty plate of flounder with a last bite of yeast roll. "Hmph. Never thought I'd eat grits." He washed the swallow down with his water, his one drink emptied an hour ago. "On the porch, I told Raysor to take you seriously, by the way. So you wasted all that mad energy."

Callie shoved half of her BLT away and wiped her mouth with a napkin. "He's an ass. He cornered me behind bushes in my drive, talking about dumping my body in the marsh. Still love the guy?"

"He tested you, Morgan, that's all. He thinks you're a lightweight, but neither one of you knows about the other's past." He set his napkin on the table. "At least he called and tried to find out more. You never asked me to check him out."

"He's a cop," she said, hunting for a reason.

"Don't take this wrong."

She snorted a laugh. "I can imagine what *that* means." She waved at the waiter.

"No more drinks," Stan said.

"I'm not on duty, *sir*. And like I said, I have no place to be. Hell, I've got you as my designated driver."

He didn't find her remark humorous, his eyes sad while she ordered her fourth gin. "I thought the old Callie Morgan would eventually come back. Maybe to Boston PD, but more so in terms of personality. But she seems lost somewhere."

"She is lost . . ." Callie trailed off, swirled her glass of half-melted ice, and gazed toward the long windows where a huge wash of sunshine reflected off the landscaped greenery. This was the fatherly side of Stan. The side she liked the least. The side that had often kept her in check back in the day. The fourth gin arrived. She sipped the crisp, unwatered-down freshness of it.

Sophie walked in, an unidentified woman friend with her. She waved, cocked her head at Stan, and started to come over.

Shit. Now what?

Callie gave a tiny shake of her head. Sophie halted, winked, and returned to her dinner partner.

"Let's go, Stan. People are starting to come in." Callie dropped off the tall chair and misstepped.

Touching the small of her back, Stan led her to the exit. "So who don't you want to see me?"

"Everybody," she said. "You're my secret weapon, and they might use you against me. Raysor already tried."

His mouth went askew in a playful manner. "Makes me feel loved, Morgan. So we go back to your place, or you want to show off your beach?"

A small grin creased her mouth. "You got *beach* right. I'm proud of you, Boss."

Callie wasn't about to show the man the main sand, either end of it, and especially not the in between where she'd dashed about armed in her frantic search for Jeb. And the last thing she needed was for Mason to jog up, all curious and eager for details.

So she guided Stan off incorporated Edisto Beach, up Highway 174, to the more secluded Botany Bay. They parked and strolled to the narrow causeway, a three-quarter mile boardwalk to the beach across a vista of marsh and water birds hunting clams and fiddler crabs, fringed by cabbage palmetto, wax myrtles, and oaks.

He scanned the flora. "Different."

"History," she said, avoiding the edge of the walk due to her unsteady gait. "Over three thousand acres protected in its original state. You don't swim here, too dangerous. It's a rustic stretch of water, so no hordes of tourists and kids."

Stan draped an arm over her shoulder. "I like this. Kinda humid, but at least there's a breeze. How do you feel?"

"Drunk."

He encircled her shoulder and shook it a bit. "That's all right. Relax for a change."

She nestled into his hulk of a shape and let him guide her toward the water. "When I'm clearheaded, I can show you more. Daddy brought me out here many times." Her speech broke at the sudden memory. "It's two cotton plantations, owned by the Townsends back before the War."

"Which war?"

She rolled her eyes. "The War of Northern Aggression, silly."

He chuckled. "Oh, *that* war. *The war* means Revolutionary in my parts."

"Well, you people actually controlled this area for a while," she said.

He hugged her. "Well, I'm glad we gave it back."

They reached the sand. Stan took in a deep, belly-bulging inhale. "Very nice, indeed."

She left the protection of his arm, enchanted by the water. En route she wove in and out of the wooden boneyard that displayed skeletons of leafless oak trees reaching up to scratch the sky. As expected, only a few visitors wandered. She kicked off her shoes.

Waves rolled in around her ankles, then receded, taking sand from under her toes. She sidestepped to keep her balance and let it happen again, now a yard farther into the surf. A particularly big wave rushed in and splashed up to her knees. With a wobble, she tried to lift a leg to reposition, but the water impeded her effort. Stan caught her before she fell.

His rolled up khakis showed meaty calves not nearly as tanned as the men around the Lowcountry, his socks and shoes back on the beach. He half-grinned as she checked out his legs. "Five hundred dollar Italian loafers and salt water don't mix," he said.

Callie rolled her shoulders then stretched out her arms to the side, then over her head. "I think John smiled on us just now," she said.

"I know how you must miss him, Chicklet."

She let her arms drop, following the movement to gaze down to the water where tiny shells and sand grains tumbled and flickered in the sun and then rolled swept away. "Yes, I do. But Papa B's murder shifted my reality somewhat." She couldn't take her eyes off the back and forth of the moving beach under the water. "John's turning into my past, Stan." She faced back toward the water's horizon, eyes moist.

Stan patted her back.

"I'm sorry," she said and wiped her eyes. "How are *you?*"

His shrug seemed small and pitiful on such a huge body. "I'm in a small apartment not far from the office. Gives me more time at work."

Callie couldn't imagine losing someone still living. "Aww, Stan."

His shadow of a grin thanked her. "Misty could have taken her career in other directions, but she stayed with me and my job. Guess it bothered her more than I thought. My twelve-hour days at the department didn't help. She says she gave it her all, and I didn't appreciate her sacrifice."

This time Callie wrapped an arm around his waist and leaned against him. He squeezed her close, petting her back.

Callie was first to pull loose. She shook off the relentless melancholy and moved back from the water. "Come, let's sit." She tottered ahead to sit ungraciously on a fallen tree trunk, the hollowed out sand around it showing that others had held the same idea. Feet dug in, legs stiff and straight, she perched on the horizontal three-foot thick tree.

"As far as the other stuff around here, sounds like someone in the community has a vendetta," Stan said, as the tree shivered slightly under his weight. "If you still worked for me, I'd start with gathering history on everyone. Since you have this bad vibe about Raysor, and a hint of one about Seabrook, start with them. Want me to help you with that when I get back?"

She nodded. "Yeah, that's good. Then I need to see what's up on the neighbors who were broken into. What their backgrounds are. I can use Seabrook for that, keeping him close while using him."

"There you go," Stan said. "Who else?"

"The lady you saw at Grover's. Sophie Bianchi. I doubt she's an issue, but I'm not sure about her son or her ex. Then Peters, the contractor. I guess some of the real estate agents." She turned and almost fell off the tree. "Henry Beechum's son is real high on my list, though. Pauley wasn't necessarily in Florida, and frankly, I wouldn't put it past him to kill his daddy for the money. Nobody on Edisto likes him."

They went around and around with supposed motives and insinuations, Callie's spirits uplifted by the mental exercise. Stan had helped her define her focus and feel better about herself. She hoped she'd done the same for him, though she couldn't see how.

Almost nobody left on the sand, a few couples walked toward their cars. The sun settled, its dying light off toward the west, making foamy saltwater wave tips shine yellow and orange with spits of white as they curled over and softly exploded onto the ocean floor. Even with her senses muted from the drinks, Callie's heart picked up its pace. They might have waited around a bit too long.

She gripped a limb crooked at a forty-five degree angle to balance her. "We need to go."

Stan frowned. "Why?"

She headed toward the boardwalk, jittery. "Because . . . it's late."

"But it's not." He faced the sea. "Check out those boats on the horizon. Sure wish I had binoculars. And the light. This is just remarkable, Chicklet. Let yourself bask in the evening. Come." He held out his arm. "Let's talk some more. It'll be good for you."

"No, Stan!"

A glower fell over him. "What the hell is wrong . . ." Then realization showed in his eyes.

The late sun caused the shadows behind Callie to deepen, the ocean roaring. The waves, however, reflected brighter. Flickering. He reached for her at the sudden understanding.

But she bolted and ran for the parking lot.

The boardwalk strung out forever, her footfalls pounding wood, then sand. As she dashed around two older women, she tripped. Touching ground for balance, she righted herself and took off again. She finally made it to Stan's car and yanked. Locked! She spun and searched for a haven. Stan hustled up the walk awkwardly, shoes in hand.

Callie ran to him. "Give me your keys!"

He rummaged his pocket and tossed them to her.

She unlocked the vehicle, crawled into the driver's seat, and cranked up the engine.

"Nope." He opened the door. "You're not driving. Not with all that booze in you, and not in that frame of mind. Move over, Morgan."

She obeyed as he dropped into his seat, put the car in reverse, and headed back. He asked directions once, but otherwise they exchanged no words as Callie stared at the floorboard. Fifteen minutes later, they ran up her fresh painted steps, entered Chelsea Morning, and secured the door.

She headed straight for the hall bath. Leaning over the sink, she wet a cloth and buried her face in it to take in the moisture. Her mouth so dry. Stan should have eased her nerves, set her to right. She thought with him there, she wouldn't—

"You okay?" Stan asked from the other side of the door.

"Yeah," she answered from behind the cloth. "Just a second."

"You gotta get over that shit, Morgan."

Morgan, not Chicklet. His tough love tone. She wrung out the cloth and hung it on a rack. Her ears still hummed, her vision not quite clear, but it was time to face the boss. Her top straightened, she exited the bathroom shaky, pretending she wasn't.

"No doubt I'm staying here tonight." Stan headed into the kitchen. "Go get on the sofa. Where's your coffeepot?"

"The corner of the counter." The overhead fan ran on high. With her shoes kicked off on the floor and a stack of Diamond albums on the turntable, Callie shed the long-sleeve blouse, leaving her in a tank and capris. She pulled the sand dollar blanket off the back of the sofa and drew it around her. Stan soon handed her a mug.

She sniffled and blew across the top. "You remembered how I like it."

He set his on a coaster on the coffee table, sat next to her, and leaned his head back. "Haven't heard that song in ages." He let the Diamond tune play out and another take its place. "Yes. I remember one sugar in your coffee. I also remember what a setting sun used to do to your nerves after the fire. You said you'd moved past that crap, and the doctors."

Of course she'd lied to him, but her words didn't feel like lies, not when she'd said them. Stan always made her step up, expecting her to perform at peak. Trouble was she had no more performances in her.

"You're worse," he said, his voice monotone.

"I just buried my father," she said. "My childhood friend and neighbor was murdered two weeks ago. Doesn't that give me some room to backslide?"

"Maybe." Even his fingers held still. He moved nary a muscle when he doled out discipline, making the person across the desk feel the need to fidget for him. "What does Jeb think?"

She recalled when her father sat where Stan sat now, telling her how worried both he and Jeb were about her. How concerned Jeb had been that first day when they'd arrived. Her son was bitter at her of late and reclusive. To avoid another lie, she shrugged.

"Your mother?" he asked.

"She ordered me to leave Middleton and come here. We've never been on the same wavelength, so what she thinks doesn't matter."

"Nightmares?"

"Sometimes." *All the time.*

He shook his head, reached over, and lifted his cup. "I don't think I'd want you back on the force if you asked, Morgan."

She snapped around. "Why the hell do you think my ass is stuck on this beach? I can't return to that world. No way would I jeopardize Jeb again. That job ripped my heart out."

Yet not that long ago, she told Beverly the opposite. That the job had defined her. As a civilian, she possessed little power to deal with any threat efficiently. That was becoming obvious.

Who was she kidding? She doubted herself more than Raysor, than Jeb, than her own mother. Her flawed judgment of the criminal element had probably caused John's assassination.

If she'd failed so miserably then, what the hell use was she now?

"You've made Jeb your crutch," Stan said.

Heat flushed her cheeks as her temper flared. "Don't you dare." She bit each word, the growl angry. "My son is everything, and he isn't up for discussion."

Stan's tone was level, but his enunciation made his awareness of her screwed up mentality crystal. "Then quit throwing him into the mix, Chicklet. He's not your problem, and you damn well know it."

The use of her softer nickname disarmed her. He still refused to move, but she dug her butt deeper into the cushion, cradling her mug. "Stop. Just stop."

Stan's forehead creased deep. "Don't bullshit me then. You're scrawny, and those bags under your eyes aren't recent. You've lost your edge. And Edisto doesn't agree with you too damn much, if you ask me."

"Who asked you?" Infuriated, she punched his chest, the power tempered by the drinks. "And who the hell do you think you are going all judge and jury on me?"

He encircled her arm with a tightness that shocked her into silence. He forced her to scoot toward him. "Listen to me." He shook her. "Look at me, too, dammit."

The ferocity on his face almost made her cringe. "Stop this!" he bellowed. "The only person who can straighten you out is you. You used to dare me to challenge you, and you took no guff off the worst of us. John loved you for that. Hell, I loved you for it. And another thing." He released her with a small thrust for emphasis. "A murder would have turned you into a hell-raiser not that long ago. None of this waiting and watching, hand-wringing and whining."

"I'm not whining."

"Well, you're damn sure not hounding this local PD to get their shit together like you would have once upon a time. Surely your Papa Beach deserved better than this."

"Shut up, Stan."

He raised his voice again and pointed. "No, I won't shut up. You're cowering, refusing to live." He counted down the fingers. "McDonald, Franks, Stubish, Lancaster, Scottie. Do I need to go on? You ran these people down. Relentlessly, I might add. You caught Leo Zubov, for Christ's sake."

Tears welled. Angry, hot tears coated her cheeks. "And it cost me my husband!" A sob escaped. "We hadn't made up about Bonnie yet."

"Would John hold any of that against you?" he asked, pain in his eyes.

Tears dripped off her chin, and she wiped them on her shoulder.

"Fix this." His frustration ebbed now. "Get your head screwed back on straight. Cops make sacrifices. John was a heavier price than normal to pay, and you didn't deserve that, but you don't roll over and die because of it, either."

She sniffed. "Is Misty your sacrifice?"

"Probably."

"I'm sorry, Stan. Sorry I wasn't there for you. How long has it been?"

"A month. I think it's for good this time."

Her moist eyes filled again. So much pain shared between them.

The big man kissed the top of her head at the sign of her tears and wrapped his massive arms around her tiny body. "Oh, Chicklet, I know, I know. Shhh."

"You're the only one who understands," she cried into his shirt.

He continued to rock her. "I know, but you can't stay stuck like this, honey. It hurts me to see you run over so easily. Please get better." He bent to kiss her head again.

Callie raised her face and let her lips meet him instead.

He drew back. "I don't think so."

"Please, Stan." She leaned in. "Don't turn me away. I can't take losing you, too."

After a pause, he let her lips touch his again. He responded gently at first, testing. Doubting. But when she crushed against him so passionately the third time, he held her in place to kiss her deeply. Her heart pounded against her ribs, sending a pulse throbbing up her neck and down.

It was okay, she told herself. She *should* feel grounded with this man. John respected him. Jeb was in awe of him. Stan was as close to how life used to be as she would ever find. Everything she could ever want in another man.

Callie arched as an intense ache pushed into her groin. She held him tighter.

John was gone. Stan was separated. The house was empty.

Please, give her this one night. She moaned, and she feared he'd break the kiss. If he would only take her to bed. She'd be fierce, assertive, forceful. If only he'd stay the night and help make everything right.

It had been so long since she'd felt alive, and maybe this was how she could start.

Chapter 23

STAN'S FINGERS ROAMED under her tank top, her bra. Disheveled sofa pillows supported Callie as she lay back, the big man's body warm and intense in its heavy power atop her. Unable to hide what was natural, he rolled as he kissed, moving up then back since his height measured so much more than hers. His shirt was unbuttoned, his pants still on. He checked himself, trying not to mash her petite form, trying to avoid her bandaged arm. His breaths wove amidst low groans that revealed how much he fought his urge to take her. Like a storm trying to decide whether to invade the coast.

Callie tried to tug aside the light throw each time he drew back, to give him full access. Frustrated at the attempts, she pushed up to entice Stan to the bedroom. She craved the wide flatness of her bed and crisp sheets on a naked body with ample room to turn and explore. Instead, Stan held her down and kissed deeper.

"The bed," she whispered.

"No," he growled.

"Back up." She broke free. Now unencumbered, she flipped around and nibbled his neck then up to nip his earlobe, wrapping her leg around his waist until she'd maneuvered into his lap, the throw no longer tangled in the mix. She dove to his other side, biting his neck. Dammit, if he didn't lift her shirt off, she was going to rip if off herself. "There's nothing wrong with a need for each other." This was her in charge of her life again, she told herself.

"It's too rash," he said.

She kissed under his ear, then around to his lips. "And this isn't?" she said into his mouth.

He held her back. His tongue licked his lips once as he seemed to be putting them back into their proper place.

Callie avoided his eyes, fearful to see doubt. She snuggled down tight against his chest. Misty had ditched him. Callie was single. Couldn't it be as simple as that?

His hesitant sigh blew across the top of her head.

She loosened his waistband, feeling his gaze on her but not meeting it, then ran her hands down and around, gripping his buttocks.

He jerked to stand and lifted her up, her legs around his waist, her arms clasped tight around his neck. With minimal effort supporting her teacup size, taking huge steps across the floor, Stan entered her bedroom, kicked the door shut behind him, and laid her on the bed.

As he shed his shirt, she shed hers. Her pulse tried to burst from under her skin as she awaited his touch, such that she almost came at his touch when he removed her jeans. Raising her bottom, Callie studied the man's nude chest, his age hidden behind days at the gym with only the slightest bulge around his middle. A bulge that disappeared when he dropped his pants.

While she'd socialized little with Stan, the man was no stranger. For years she reported to him, discussed cases over lunch. Patted each other on the back as cuffs snapped on a perp. He knew her darkest fear, child violence cases, and her major love, mint chocolate anything, just like John had.

As he lowered himself down, he turned her on her side to face him. He kissed and nuzzled her chin and neck, the gentle yet aggressive manner sending flutters into her belly. She melted into the quilt.

His home life made her wonder how he meshed his gruff manner with a wife that seemed anything but. He held a controlled strength Callie admired. Then she went home to John, who read Callie's needs and loved her more than she deserved on some days. John was all she'd ever needed. She still missed him so damn much.

Stan was the link to those halcyon days. But here, in her bed, with John gone, she wanted her old boss as she envisioned in fleeting thoughts during their coffee breaks and staff meetings.

No one was at fault. They tended to each other. The moment matched their needs.

Those big hands roamed across her stomach, covering so much skin with so little effort. She felt so small and malleable under those fingers. This was a man she could be vulnerable with. He could do what he wanted with her now, and she could trust him. How long had it been since she'd trusted someone? How much was Misty still trusting him?

"Chicklit," he half-whispered, a warm palm stopped across her stomach. "I didn't intentionally come down here to—"

"Shhh," she hushed. "You came down to take care of me."

She directed him, and he reached down and teased her warm, moist region, then he crept up and cupped her jaw, those big fingers wrapped from her chin to behind her ear as he kissed her again. She laid her hand on his, so enthralled to have a man cradle her like some sweet, endeared doll.

Like John had. But John wasn't here and never would be again.

But Stan would return to Boston. What the hell was she doing to him? *Don't think about it.*

Her old boss was hard and holding back. She guided his strokes away from her face, to the part of her that wanted him the most, to toss the conflict from her mind. Her heart hammered. She prepared for the first time since John.

She would pick up the pieces afterwards.

Stan's phone rang. She paused, but he didn't.

Someone left a voice mail from the ding.

Callie returned her attention to matters in hand, literally, her strokes almost fierce, taking them both to the edge. Making them forget.

Someone left a text message.

His eyes scoured her. *He wants me.*

Another text.

He bent down to kiss her; she arched up to meet his lips.

Again a text.

He shoved her down, apart, then poised over her.

She held her breath. Is this really what they needed?

His phone rang.

"Stan?"

"Don't, Chicklet."

"It might . . . be important."

"That's what I'm afraid of."

She eased back, breaths still rapid, watching him fight to ignore who might be on the other end of those messages. "Check it, Stan. I'll be right here."

Releasing a deep groan of frustration, he rolled off the bed and fumbled in his clothes for his phone. The device came alive and illuminated Stan's face as he scrolled and read messages in the dark, then tapped buttons to retrieve the voice mails.

Fist on his nude waist, he turned his back to Callie, phone to his ear. "Shit," he whispered, punched buttons again, then apparently replayed the message.

Elbow bent, leaning on her hand, she admired his shadowy silhouette as her pulse slowed. She no longer saw Stan as a boss; the lines had blurred reckless between them. A mild disappointment took root as she waited for what she wouldn't be surprised to hear. Her head back down on the pillow, she wondered whether to go ahead and retrieve her clothes.

Stan disconnected the call and fixated on the opposite wall.

"Misty?" Callie asked softly.

"Yeah."

"It's okay, Stan," she said and chose the right words instead of the ones that would coax him back into her bed. But even as she convinced herself of the logic, tears threatened.

To call at this time of night, Misty missed her husband in her own bed.

Stan reached down and retrieved his clothing, slipping into each piece quietly, as if afraid to stir the air too much.

Callie eased out of bed and around the man to her closet, avoiding skin contact, and retrieved her robe. When she returned, he worked his shirt buttons, clothed except for bare feet. She yearned to play in his hairy chest one more time before he completed his task.

"I shouldn't have started this," she said, lying as cleanly as she could. If Misty hadn't called, Stan would be inside her at this moment. But her friend needed to hear the proper words to take his conscience home.

The bedside clock read almost three a.m. She couldn't have fallen asleep if she tried, and she knew Stan was a whirlpool of confusion . . . and regret. "I think I'll fix coffee and sit on the front porch. It ought to be close to high tide, so the breeze should be lovely. Care to join me?"

Silently, he followed her into the kitchen and then helped her carry the cups outside.

Wind pushed up the stairs and tossed the edge of her robe aside. She tied it tighter as she folded herself into the white settee in the far corner of the porch. Stan took a rocker two feet away.

They sat silent for most of an hour, and Callie almost dozed to the distant lullaby of the waves. She opened her eyes to see Stan's mind at work, his focus on the sago palm growing at the foot of the newly painted stairs.

She sipped the remnants of her cold coffee as if it were still good. "Not that I know her well, I mean, we only met at the occasional barbecue, but she seemed to suit you. Twenty years, right?"

"Twenty-one."

Callie already knew they had no kids. "That's a long time."

"Yeah."

She winked at him. He released a tight grin.

With a chuckle, she tried to lighten the mood. "I'd have screwed your eyes out, you know."

"Hmph." He grinned bigger. "You're not making this easy, are you?"

She sat up straight. "I'm truly sorry, Stan."

"Don't worry about it, Chicklit. Nothing we hadn't both thought about before."

Minutes passed again, each letting that visual rest.

"So what words of advice will you leave me with?" she said. "If you were me, what would you do about whoever's disrupted tranquility here in paradise?"

They rehashed each crime and each victim, each suspect and each investigator. Slowly at first, as if they couldn't remember how to do their jobs anymore. She feared she wouldn't have his advice for a long while once he returned north. Actually, she heard nothing she didn't already know, but Stan needed this swan song to justify his trip. To help put things back to right between them, between him and Misty.

Orange soon tinged the sky behind dark gray, shadowy palmetto trees, spreading into the navy of the night like watercolor seeping across a page.

"Get up, Boss," she said. "The Seacow is open for breakfast by now. How long can you stay?"

He studied his cup. Her core hurt so much at what she read in that simple unspoken reply. "That quick?" She pulled him to his feet, taking the lead for his emotional sake.

They went to the kitchen and rinsed their mugs. "She said if I stayed any longer you would undermine us."

Callie couldn't think of a response to that. She couldn't argue with Misty's logic.

Stan set down the towel. "I'm changing to an earlier flight."

The pain of his sudden departure surprised her. Maybe her energies around Stan hadn't always been so hidden. She briefly wondered if John had ever noticed. "Tomorrow?" she asked.

"Today," he replied.

"Then let's take two cars to breakfast since it's on the way off the beach anyway."

"Yeah," he said.

AN HOUR LATER, Callie sat at the restaurant table as Stan kissed the top of her head, paid the tab, and left. She sipped on another cup of coffee, to adjust to the embarrassment. Then she left and slowly drove to the beach. She wasn't ready to return and see her bed tossed.

It wasn't his fault. She'd let him bruise her soul—a soul that needed bruising, because the pain had awakened her. Made her want again.

Just maybe not Stan.

But it hurt. Like a frostbit limb regaining circulation, nerve endings came alive with pins, needles, pain, and throbbing as they remembered how to function.

Rays glinted harsh on the water as she strolled from pier to pier, finally kicking off her sand-filled shoes. The tide curled its way out, gulls enjoying what each wave left behind on the land.

The shore.

She'd released him for selfish reasons as much as empathetic ones. She needed him to still be on the other end of that phone during the hard times. She'd made a mistake taking him to her bed. If they had consummated their need, she would have regretted it. Stan even more. The salt air rushed into her face and she inhaled it.

How much damage had she done to their friendship?

Two miles down the beach, she turned and retraced her steps. Once she climbed onto a pier, tightroped it out a few yards, and let the splash sprinkle her. What did the world find healing about water that lashed so relentlessly, so loud, so vicious? If she jumped off the barricade, over her head, the waves would bash her against the wood. Over and over. What was calm about that? Yet here she balanced, seeking peace in the midst of turmoil. She didn't see it happening anytime soon.

She had no idea what to do now. She'd even welcome one of Mason's surprise jogs. Sun dawning brightly over the Atlantic, she searched the water's edge as far as she could see but didn't spot him.

So she walked back to her car and drove home.

On her way up the freshly painted steps, she realized she hadn't seen Peters since before the funeral. Sometime today she'd call him, maybe invite him to another dinner. It was the part of his payment he probably appreciated most anyway.

The new lock, still graphite slick, quietly secured her door. Heavy silence blanketed the house. Come winter, with the tourists gone and Jeb entrenched in classes, this would be her every day. Maybe she needed a cat.

Out of habit, she glanced over at Papa Beach's house. Still dark. Even if she believed in spirits, she didn't sense Papa's spirit hanging around the place anymore. Maybe he'd moved on. If Callie asked, Sophie would certainly address that issue.

Nine o'clock. Sophie's yoga class ended about now. She would have spotted Callie jogging if she'd bothered looking. The Pavilion held a long, clear view of the water's edge, both north toward Kiawah and south toward Beaufort. Callie thought maybe she should give the class a go one day.

A yawn broke free, then a bigger one, making her eyes water. She returned to her bedroom, the coolness of her sheets calling for her to recover the sleep she'd missed last night. But as she entered, she gasped and reached for the door frame.

Papa Beach's box of memorabilia sat amidst the rumpled covers, no longer hidden in her closet. The cup had been used to smash the chicken salt and pepper shakers. Its broken handle sat two feet away from the rest of the pieces.

Who knew about the box? How the hell did anyone get in here?

She ran to the phone, half dialing the number for Stan before she hung up.

He'd return if she asked, but Misty would never accept her husband choosing Callie over coming home to mend their marriage. Especially someone who'd been a detective trained to manage danger on her own.

Her shades were drawn. No one could see her room from outside.

Frantically she started with her nightstand, snatching drawers open, hunting for wires, anything that pointed to a camera. She tore apart her lamp, turning over the clock. Then the curtains. Clean. She ran fingers along the dresser mirror, searching.

She ripped apart the busy clusters of blue silk hydrangeas, slinging the leaves and stalks . . . and hit a hard object. She parted the leaves and petals. Floral wire anchored a cam into the arrangement, aimed at her bed.

Without thinking, she snatched it savagely out of the flowers and hurled it against the wall. It cracked, two pieces skittering across her floor, a nick left in the wallboard.

Who the hell had done this?

She screamed at her moment of stupidity. Falling to her knees, she retrieved the main guts of the cam. It was destroyed, but still, she held the lens inches from her face. "You stinking son of a bitch. Come get me, you hear? Do whatever it is you think you need to do, because I'm so ready for you." She slammed it into the floor and stomped the remnants.

Then she rushed to the side porch to check Papa's house. The paper taped in the window displayed a message for her eyes only.

Whore.

"You bastard!" she screamed.

Exhausted, she dropped onto a porch chair. Fighting the scary fear in her head, the mind that once reacted in split-seconds to life-threatening situations, she pondered who to call.

She was sick of this crap. Phone raised, she clicked a picture of the paper. Then another. She scurried into her bedroom and took another, again and again. *Yes.* This was more like it. The camera on the floor. The vase of torn flowers. The damaged wall. *Hell yes.* This was how she wanted to feel. Proactive. Refusing to be victimized. Pulse pounded as she scrolled the pictures. Evidence. *Yes.* The son-of-a-bitch had entered her home and violated her privacy. And she would use it to nail the bastard, or at least instruct Edisto PD how to do this right.

Her hand shook with the phone. In hers and Stan's moment of weakness, a stranger watched. *Christ! Who should she call?*

Raysor's threats removed all sense of trust about him. Seabrook operated oddly these days, as he slipped in and out of empty rentals, his too-calm behavior telling her he wasn't totally trusting her either.

Her finger hovered over 9-1-1. There were other officers. Dickens, maybe?

Think, Callie. For the first time in many months, she regretted relinquishing her badge.

Shit! She hadn't cleared the house. He could still be here.

Like a bottle rocket, she darted back into the house to her bedside table. The Glock 32 she kept under her pillow, the gun she had moved to the nightstand with Stan in her bed, was gone.

Enough. She dialed 9-1-1 as she bolted to the credenza in the entry hall. Yanking open a drawer, she tossed aside a folded tablecloth. Her backup .38 waited untouched. Of course. The cam couldn't see in here.

What about more cams?

First things first. She ran back to peer out the kitchen window.

An intense bang rattled her front door. She jerked around. Then a rapid succession of hits on the glass. A short shadow of a person paced on the other side of the etched window.

"Callie! Callie! Please be home. Unlock the fucking door!"

Callie threw down the phone and drew the gun. She peered outside to see Sophie still clad in her yoga tights, frantic with her fists. When Callie undid the lock, Sophie shoved the door open and slammed it behind her.

"What do I do?" Sophie said, eyes darting. "I don't know what to do!" She ran to a window to peer out toward her house.

Adrenaline exploding, Callie jerked Sophie's wrist. "What is it, Sophie? Slow down and tell me what's wrong."

Slow yourself down, Callie.

Recalling old training, she attempted to settle herself first and deal properly with the crisis. Compartmentalize. Like a crime with multiple casualties.

Sophie rubbed her wrists, wincing, then pointed toward her place. "He's there. He's in there."

"Who?"

"The guy who steals. He's in my house! He came back to get me."

Callie's eyes went wide. He'd moved from Papa's place to hers to Sophie's in one day?

He'd quit being careful.

Or Sophie was part of the plan.

God, she just didn't know anymore.

Chapter 24

THE 9-1-1 OPERATOR scolded Callie vehemently on the other end for being told to wait. She ran into Jeb's bedroom to see out his windows and finally relayed information to the operator, but the crime she called about had to shift from broken trinkets and a hidden cam to a real culprit rummaging around Sophie's home.

"We're in my house next door. Yes, we're safe. I'm armed. The man hasn't left the Bianchi house that I can tell."

"Yes, ma'am. Stay inside your home. I'm sending a unit right now."

Hanging back to the side of the window, Callie watched through a crack between the slatted blinds, still unable to see anyone next door. With the opportunity to catch this guy eminent, her pulse echoed in her ears, louder than her breaths.

Her gaze darted toward Sophie who slipped in to peek out the next window. If she was part of the breaking and entering deals on Jungle Road, she was faking her fear pretty well.

"Back away." Callie moved toward the door. "I'm going over there. Do not stand at the window, hear me? Here." She pushed the phone to Sophie. "Stay with the operator." No way was this guy disappearing while she waited for 9-1-1 to dispatch someone. She had to know who the hell it was.

Her neighbor followed her to the exit. "I'll lock up behind you."

Callie left. No time to marvel at Sophie's new need to lock a door.

Knowing that the kitchen was positioned in the front part of the house, where the burglar, if this was the same guy, would wind up for his drink, Callie slinked outside to the back. Up the stairs. She flattened herself against the white siding, for once grateful Sophie left her windows uncovered so Callie could sneak a glance inside. From the back porch, she could peer through the living room into the kitchen. A straight line view.

She eased to the edge of the window. Paint-stained pants appeared below the open refrigerator door. Throttling her .38 through a backdoor unlocked as always, Callie burst in like a Marine. "Freeze!"

The handyman went stock-still, but the refrigerator door hid his body.

"Peters. What the hell are you doing in here?"

Eyes wide, his eyebrows almost hit his hairline. "Um, getting a drink."

She poised in the living room, her stance instinctively sideways to lessen her exposure. "Back away. I want to see your hands."

Peters backed up one step, palms in the air. The fridge slowly eased shut with a whump.

Relieved to see no weapon, Callie poised on guard, no longer in tune with the handyman's laid-back personality. "Do you work for Sophie?" she asked.

"No."

"So what gives you the right to come in here?" she demanded.

His eyes spread round as saucers. "Your house wasn't open. Hers was."

Good grief, this was too stupid to be happening. She waved her gun arm. "Sit down, Peters. Somebody will want to talk to you."

He sat. "Honest, I would've just gotten water, but I thought about a Coke and checked out what she had. I didn't think she'd mind."

"Just sit."

"Yes'm."

Callie perched on the arm of the sofa, weapon in her lap, still dumbfounded. A siren sounded only a minute later. Seabrook rushed in, Dickens behind him. Peters started to stand, and Callie pointed at him. He sat back down.

But Seabrook glanced at her first. "Really? A weapon?"

"Mike, he entered a private residence without permission. Sophie's in my house terrified." Her respect for him wavered again. Inexperience? The Edisto environment? He needed to take all this more seriously, because someone had shot Papa Beach and hit Maxwell. This was a break-in. What did someone have to do to raise a threat level to anything higher than green around here?

Hell, she had a busted cam on the floor in her own house. And her Papa Beach souvenirs destroyed. *One crime at a time, Callie.*

Seabrook turned to the handyman. "Peters, what do you have to say?"

He shrugged and raised palms in supplication. "I wanted a drink of water, man. Don't know why Ms. Bianchi didn't say hello or something."

Seabrook dropped his chin to his chest in thought.

Callie saw where this was going. If she were Seabrook, she'd have doubts, too, but she'd ream Peters for being so stupid. And Sophie for being so lax. Damn these people being so loose out here. Nobody thought crime could happen to them.

"Go call in," Seabrook ordered Dickens. "I got this."

Callie caught a small grin on the young man's face as he exited.

"Oh," Seabrook added louder. "Have Sophie come here so we can wrap this up."

The officer waved two fingers.

Walking over to Callie, Seabrook spoke down an octave. "This won't stick, you know."

"It could if you wanted it to. He had no business in here. Let Sophie inspect her house for anything amiss. Then check Peters' pockets. But Mike, this man has got to stop making himself at home in peoples' homes."

Crow's feet crinkled in doubt, the lawman shifted his weight toward her. "It's what he's been allowed to do," he almost whispered. "You hire him, you feed him, and let him use the shower. I agree he went too far here, but he might not be guilty of anything other than being thirsty. I'll talk to him."

Harmless or not, one day Peters would upset the wrong person, get accused of theft, or worse, walk into someone's bullet. "That's the problem with small towns," Callie said. "They let personal relationships interfere."

Seabrook closed the space between them. "Maybe Boston taught you to keep it in overdrive, but here we factor in who's who. It's a positive, not a negative. Maybe you don't know how to work a small town."

She leaned in. "Says the man who hangs out in empty houses and thinks the bad guy will walk by and wave."

Seabrook narrowed eyes at her and turned to Peters. "You can't just enter someone's house, Peters. If they aren't home, don't go in. Someone might shoot you. Now empty your pockets on the table."

Callie moved closer, sliding her gun in her pocket. No silver dollar fell out amidst the pocketknife, change, and various wadded bits of Peters' receipts and stubs.

"When did you try the door to my house?" she asked.

"About a half hour ago," Peters said. "I waited until your gentleman friend left."

"Which one?" she asked.

Seabrook eyed Callie. She pretended not to notice.

"That big guy," Peters said. "Never seen him before."

Peters could be telling the truth, or he entered her house, did the damage, planted the cam, and left before she arrived home. The man could practically build a house. Surely he could break in to one with little trace.

"Well, you seem to have a good measure of activities," she told Peters. "What else did you see?"

He seemed confused, his face a blank slate.

"Was there a car you didn't recognize? Did you see anyone else who didn't make sense? At least try to help yourself here. Sometime while you were rattling doors, somebody broke into my place."

Seabrook scowled. Callie glanced over and raised her chin in acknowledgment, but they had to deal with the handyman first before they got into a discussion.

Peters mashed his lips together and scratched his head. "Not that I noticed. Your man was the only odd thing. Sure he didn't do it?"

"He was with me, Peters. Did you see anyone go into Henry Beechum's house?" To put a note in a window, by chance?

He gazed at the ceiling, as if to scavenge through his junkyard of thoughts, then answered, "Uh, no, ma'am."

Sophie halted in her kitchen doorway. "Peters," she cooed, as if soothing a hurt child.

With a gasp, Peters spun around, flustered. "This is all screwed up, Ms. Bianchi." He reached out and spread his things across the table for all to see. "That little pocketknife isn't dangerous," he said to Seabrook. "And I wouldn't hurt you," he said to Sophie. "I'm sorry if I scared you."

"Awww." Sophie rushed over. "I know you wouldn't hurt me. You just caught me unawares, is all. But you need to watch yourself with this robber on the loose. You could run into him."

Callie walked toward her. "You could have saved us all this trouble, Sophie."

Sophie shrugged. "I came in, saw the back of a man in my house and hauled butt to your place."

"I think we're done," Seabrook said. "Soon as you pick up there, you can go, Peters."

"Gotcha, thanks," the man replied. "Hey, Callie, while you're here . . . can I collect my money?"

She frowned at his nonchalance. "I'll put it in my mailbox when I get back."

He jammed his belongings in his pants pockets.

"Peters?" Callie asked. "You're not bothered we suspected you?"

"Not really. I didn't do it," he replied. "Y'all would figure that out. Now what about dinner?"

"Can't." Callie had no desire to let this guy grow accustomed to the inside of her home now. He already admitted he'd tried her door. She motioned for Seabrook to follow her to the back porch. "Can we talk?"

As the glass door closed, Seabrook touched her elbow. "Sorry again about your daddy."

She reflected back to that night Seabrook had broken the news to them. He'd been so calm, so sympathetic, and had followed Jeb and her most of the way to Beverly's place. "Yeah, thanks so much for how you handled it. I asked them to reanalyze the details. Daddy doesn't drive into trees."

Seabrook just listened, much like the Middleton chief had.

"Anyway," she started.

"How'd you injure the arm?"

She pulled it against her body. "Old wound, bad habit."

His words hung up, as if he changed what he had to say. Callie sensed a waffling conflict between cop and doctor, and under other circumstances, would've appreciated the concern.

"Regardless how Sophie's break-in turned out," Seabrook continued, "I'm glad you called us. The guy might not have been Peters."

"Don't you think it's time you held a town meeting?" While Edisto needed its tourists, it also needed to be vigilant and let tenants and residents alike know about the break-ins.

"Already did," he replied. "While you were in Middleton. Had to keep it pretty general, though. Just told people to lock their doors and report anyone unusual. What else we going to tell them?" He seemed to gnaw the inside of his cheek.

"What?" she asked, noticing he held something back.

"Your name came up."

She wasn't surprised. "So?"

"Some think you have the talent to do these burglaries yourself."

Seriously? "And the murder?"

"That too."

She shook her head, raking her scalp with her nails. "Un-friggin' believable."

"Stand in their shoes, Callie. Nothing happened until you arrived. I know that's happenstance, but they—"

"I smell Raysor all over this."

With pursed lips, he shook his head. "Nah, he wasn't even there."

"Still . . ."

"Ignore the rumors," he said. "Nobody that matters suspects you."

Like nobody suspected Peters. Great. She was in such good company. She so wanted to trust Seabrook. He made more sense than anyone else out here. She just couldn't comprehend the law enforcement methods on this beach. "Listen, I'm not some high-strung idiot. And somebody really broke into my place this morning," she said. "For real."

Seabrook's expression turned dark. "Steal anything? Leave a coin?"

She described the box and the destroyed contents. "But I want you to see the rest."

Together they returned to Chelsea Morning. Callie led him toward the spot in her living room that gave her the window view of Papa's house. The light was off. The paper gone. Pauley's car not there. Embarrassingly, she couldn't recall if it had been there before.

"There was a sign . . . crap." Callie hurried back to her bedroom. The box was still on her bed, the items broken and damaged.

"This"—she motioned to the debris—"happened while I was out on the beach."

Seabrook bent over the items. "Junk's all broken."

She yanked his arm and spun him around. "It's not junk. It's Papa's stuff. That matters, don't you think?"

His raised arms in concession. "Okay, calm down."

She picked up the smashed cam pieces and pressed them into his hand. "And this has been watching me in my bedroom."

He turned the broken unit over. "A camera? This the only one?"

"I haven't checked yet. Found it about the time Sophie beat down my door." Why wasn't he more upset?

You liked his calm, remember?

"Wish you hadn't busted it," he said. "I'm surprised you even touched it for fear of messing up prints."

"Sorry I didn't pull out my gloves and fingerprint kit, Mike." But he was right. She'd freaked. Feeling inept, she studied the indentation on the wall where the cam hit.

Seabrook held the pieces up. "Why would someone do this to you and nobody else?"

"If I knew, would I need your help?" she exclaimed, her etiquette filter gone. Then she snatched out her smartphone, punched buttons, and held up the picture of the sign. The screen outlining her porch made the word *whore* illegible.

"What's that say?" he asked, almost as if fearful of asking.

Twisting it around and deeming it worthless, she shook her head. "You people beat all I ever saw."

"Wait. Who are *you people?*" Seabrook asked, his mouth tighter.

"Raysor, Sophie, Pauley, the Edisto PD. You think I'm flawed, or damaged, or, or, whatever." She fingered the gun in her pocket, the only sense of solace she had. No point in putting it away while he was still in the house, either. He might take it away again.

Damn it, nobody seemed to be trying hard enough.

She snatched the cam away from Seabrook and shook it. "This is perverted! This is dangerous! This stands for something far more sinister. Get your act together, acting chief. Do something!"

Seabrook dipped to her level. "I've been as tolerant as anyone can be with you in light of all your . . . demons. I let you keep your precious mementoes. I agree this hidden camera needs our attention, but—"

"You've had a homicide, an assault, and multiple burglaries." Arms now stretched out to each side, she shook with emphasis. "I dealt with that on a daily basis for years, and all you can see are my *demons.* You have demons too, from what I hear, *doctor.*"

The minute she said the words, she regretted them.

"That was mean, but I'm still on your side," he finally said. "Settle down if you want to think clearer. If you were in my shoes, you'd tell your victim the same thing."

Victim? She sucked in air, wanting to believe him. And goodness knows she wanted to settle down.

"I'll let you know if we come up with anything," he added. "What else?"

With nerves stretched thin and too little sleep, quivers traveled across her back and shoulders. "My Glock was stolen."

"Well, damn." Lines deepened across his forehead. He extracted his memo book. "That's definitely not good. Come down and file a report. I'll put out a notice."

That was it? Apparently, the laid-back air of Edisto came with an ability to not express excitement. And the more frustrated she became about it, the crazier she knew she appeared. Her blood began to boil. "Listen to me, Seabrook."

"I've *been* listening," he replied.

"I tell you my gun's gone, and it's a problem." She wished he weren't so tall. "But when I show you broken mementoes, you think I'm nuts. I tell you about a sign in the window, and you don't care. The cam and the gun barely got a rise out of you."

"You're overwrought, Callie," he said. "It's not like that."

"No?" She shifted her wide stance. "Either I'm crazy or not. You believe me or you don't. Because my little *signs* and broken *junk* might be real clues, chief. Or I could have lied about the gun or planted the cam myself. Am I credible or not? Make up your damn mind."

Callie's jaw ached. *Damn him!* It took a murder and a stolen gun to get Seabrook to just raise his brow. And instead of finding a burglar, Raysor wrote traffic tickets like they were Class A felonies. Maybe she'd install her own security cameras and record the proof they needed, because they sure wouldn't deduce anything on their own.

"I'm not drunk, by the way," she said. "Get that out of your head."

"Didn't think you were."

Sure he didn't. She bet he gave her a few good sniffs and analyzed the whites of her eyes before he came to that conclusion.

"Bet you didn't check the nanny cam at the Maxwell place like I suggested, either," she said.

He shook his head.

"Why not?"

"They said they didn't have one."

"And you believed them?" she jeered. "Of course you did." An affluent couple with an only child and no nanny cam. Maybe paranoia ran thicker up north, but these days she'd post a camera on people who kept her toddler.

Seabrook gave Callie a glance she couldn't read. She didn't like it. She didn't like anything anymore.

"Callie?" Sophie appeared at the base of the stairs.

Callie turned. "What, Sophie."

In bare feet, Miss Yoga padded up to them, having slipped in the back door.

"Before I leave, you want me to help you hunt for more cameras?" Seabrook asked low.

"No," Callie said sternly. "I'll take care of myself, like I've already been doing."

He blew out. "Call me if you find anything else."

What would he do about it if she did?

Seabrook turned to leave, halting long enough to say to Sophie, "I'm tired of telling you to lock your doors."

"It was a false alarm, Mike," she said.

He stooped to her height. "It's your pretty little neck, Sophie. This guy's still out there. Don't welcome him."

Sophie shrugged and mumbled, "Peters wasn't a break-in."

He left. Sophie ran to the door, locked it to Callie's surprise, and watched until Seabrook got in his car. Then running back, she drew Callie to the kitchen and seated herself where they first met. "Fix me a drink," she said, her words rushed.

Callie retrieved two glasses and imagined Maker's Mark on her tongue, in her system, soothing nerves that never seemed to stop misfiring. She put one back. She set a bourbon before Sophie. *Maybe once Sophie leaves I'll pour a small one.* God knows she'd earned it.

"What's your problem this time?" Callie asked as Sophie moaned with her first, deep sip.

The pixie woman bent over the table, her arms and shoulders knotted as she coveted the drink. "Someone did steal something."

Callie jumped up. "Now? While Peters was here? I need to get Seabrook—"

"No, no, no," Sophie said, snaring Callie's sleeve. "I'm talking about the last time with the coin. I realized it later and was afraid to say anything. Then time got away from me, and I didn't want Seabrook to get mad at me."

What the heck? Callie scrunched her brow, anxious to hear what moronic piece of withheld information might still require her to call the cop back. "You sure it wasn't Peters today?"

"Positive."

"What was it then?" Callie asked.

"It was my ex's NFL ring. Never told him I kept it," Sophie whispered. "I couldn't after he filed an insurance claim for it."

Callie dropped her head to the counter. Then she lifted up to peer at Sophie. "Surely you're smarter than this. It's a clue, for goodness sake. Like the coin you threw in the marsh. So, tell me where you kept the ring."

"Sunbeam's litter box."

"What?"

"I know, I know," Sophie said rapidly. "It sounds stupid, but it's my way of both hiding it and treating my ex in the manner in which he deserves."

Grabbing a notepad from a drawer, Callie laid her gun on the counter and started taking notes. "Have you scoured that house from top to bottom?"

Sophie stared at the .38. "Yes. Nothing else is gone."

"Okay. Describe that ring. Did you hide it in a baggie, a box?"

"Neither." Sophie pouted with a flash of humor in her eyes. "I let Sunbeam poop all over it. Made me have to use gloves changing the litter, but it was so worth the satisfaction. Damn thing stayed green and nasty."

Callie wrote that down, too, but what gnawed at her already worked-up stomach was how anyone would know to go in a litter box. Not a stranger anyway. She needed to take this to Seabrook . . . later. Now she had to hunt for more cams. And chill herself down a notch.

Sophie drank her bourbon as Callie made notes and relaxed to a slower, forced rhythm.

Little jolts of panic wouldn't let her reach calm, though. Someone had wandered around her house after she'd changed her locks. Possibly hidden and watched as she entertained Stan.

Most likely recorded them in her bed.

A key tried her front lock, fumbling, missing its mark.

Callie retrieved her gun. Sophie squeaked and tucked her legs beneath her, wrapped in a ball, hands over her mouth.

Chapter 25

SOMEONE JIGGLED Chelsea Morning's front door handle, and then per the scraping noise, attempted to work the lock. Callie lifted her .38 from the table. She'd drawn her weapon more in the last two weeks than the last five years.

Sophie sat twisted in a knot at the kitchen table. Callie, however, skulked toward the entryway edgy, hungry, and sleep deprived.

It had been a long damn day.

The person behind the distorted glass image jerked the handle once more then pressed a face against the glass. "Callie? Let me in. My key won't work."

Callie opened the door. "Mother?"

Beverly waltzed in chin up, as if she still owned the place. "Did you change the locks? I hope you made me a key."

"Geez, Mother. Let me know when you're coming, please. I could have shot you."

Beverly's eyes widened at the gun then moved to Callie's bandage. "Oh, dear, have your episodes become that bad?" Her words fell out in a *Bless your heart* manner, a condescending cliché of pity.

A hug would have been nice. Any move of compassion welcomed, but no, her mother's stinging criticism remained true to form.

"Pour your mother a drink, dear." She drew back, squinting. "You're complexion is horrible. Haven't you been sleeping? We gave you this place so you could rest."

Callie rubbed a tired eye. Her irritation festered just under the surface as her mother consumed the room. "We don't have time for a social call, Mother. And I don't have any booze," she lied.

Beverly raised fingers to her neck. "Since when do you keep an empty bar?"

Callie held back a retort. She was spent, with only a fine, thin filter between her manners and a red-hot temper.

The older woman fanned her face. "Tea will have to suffice, I guess. This heat's oppressive." She rounded the corner toward the living room and came up short when she saw Sophie. "Oh, who do we have here?"

But Sophie didn't miss a beat. "Sophie Bianchi, Ms. Cantrell. We've practiced yoga together." She jumped up, inserted herself in the woman's space, and took her hand. "I'm so, so sorry about your husband. My deepest condolences. He is watching down on us, you know. He so wishes to be here with you and Callie."

Leery, Beverly tried to discretely add distance between their bodies, but Sophie only moved closer. "I'll burn a candle for him," she said. "But don't hold onto his spirit too long. He needs to pass over."

Before Callie could moderate these two worlds colliding, Beverly yanked away. "How dare you speak of my deceased husband, you . . . you Bohemian thing."

Callie shoved a glass at her mother. "Here's your tea."

But Beverly continued to glare, and Sophie stood her ground. "If I can help you, let me know," Sophie said, like a nurse to a patient.

Callie intervened and directed Beverly to the side door to the porch, still feeling mildly paranoid about hidden cams. "Let's go sit outside."

"Why?" Beverly said, settling into her cushion. "It's June, for God's sake."

Fine. Coddling the woman might work quicker. "Have your friends been over?"

Beverly seemed glued to studying Sophie, then forced herself to turn and reply. "Why, I've been swamped with my friends. They're helping me weather this difficult time. Since I'm all alone in that house."

"You sent me away, and Jeb stayed behind so you wouldn't *be* alone," Callie said. "But I'm glad to hear you had company." She glanced at the doorway. "Where is Jeb, by the way?"

"At home," she sighed, staring up the ceiling, as if forced to venture out solo.

Callie wished Sophie would read the vibes and leave. Instead, the neighbor propped up on a barstool, leg under her, observing, her fear of the morning's events gone. "What brought you out here, Mother?"

"Can you stay?" Sophie asked. "I'd love to have you in yoga in the morning. You'd feel so much better."

Beverly shifted an arrogant glance at Sophie and returned her attention to her daughter. "I came to pick up something."

"Sure, what is it?" Callie asked.

"My Neil Diamond albums," she said.

"Wh . . . why?"

"They're special to me. That's all."

Surprisingly unnerved, Callie went to the kitchen and rinsed a glass. This could not be happening. Those albums were her musical diary. She knew which covers were bent on their corners, which still had their sleeves, and how the water ring accidentally found its way to the *Love Songs* cover. In Boston, this music had celebrated Callie's promotion to detective, even Jeb's spelling bee ribbon. She'd relied on those songs when John left for a week shortly after Bonnie died, to collect himself. Then after the fire had consumed her collection, she'd paced the confines of an extended stay motel, pulling up a custom radio station on her laptop to play Diamond for twelve hours straight. These songs were her childhood, her freedom to mourn, forget her past, or avoid her future. They'd helped her accept Chelsea Morning as home, welcoming her as part of the house's being.

Callie's mind raced as she returned to the living room, searching for some damn excuse to keep them. She'd never replace the antique sound of that LP player, the texture of its linen speaker cover, or the slight squeak of the top's hinge. Until now she didn't realize how much those details meant to her. But every argument for Callie was equally as justified for her mother.

Fact was, the records had never belonged to Callie. She rubbed her forehead. This was stupid, so stupid. She ought to just give the woman the damn albums. So why was it so challenging not to?

"They're just old music," Beverly said. "I've had those forever, and they make me feel better."

Callie scratched her scarred arm. "Let me buy you a set of CDs to replace them. Or an mp3 player. If you need the albums, I'm sure I can find them on Amazon or eBay."

"Good, then find them for yourself. If you need my credit card, let me know."

Callie shut her eyes again, to hide building tears she could not define the root of. She sniffled and rubbed the corner of her eye. Another hole in her world, that's what this was. First her father and then Stan. She wasn't sure she could stomach another loss, even if it was just music.

Confused at the dizzying onrush of weakness, all she knew was that this package, this player and its twenty LPs, connected her to sanity.

Tears sneaked down her face at the realization that they might be Beverly's sanity, too.

She gripped the counter's edge. What was wrong with her?

No, she was more mature than this. She straightened. Maybe if she relinquished the albums, she'd take her first step toward healing. If she couldn't function without them, she'd go on a mission to replace the vinyls. Hell, Mason would adore the opportunity to find them, even fly them in for her, anything to make her beholden to him.

"Don't make me remind you that they're mine," Beverly said.

Callie's back went rigid as her sympathy dissipated like smoke in a March wind, replaced with the familiar, raw-edged rancor that defined her relationship with Beverly. Callie turned and faced the arrogance seated on her sofa, rabid at the callousness in this woman's soul. Now that Lawton was gone, she could picture her mother deteriorating from annoying to two shades away from malicious.

Beverly pondered her daughter. "Antidepressants might help you. I can put you in touch with a good doctor. Amos Canady has done wonders for your father, and Harriet from my Sunday school class says—"

"I don't need your help," Callie replied, still raw from Seabrook's similar reference to her *demons.*

"Honey, you're a mess. Sure you need help. You're like your father in so many ways."

"Thank God for that!"

Beverly never flinched. "Get those pills. It'll temper you from being so pernicious."

Callie rolled her eyes and sighed deep. "I've had it. Leave, Mother, before I get so damn *pernicious* I throw something."

Unruffled, Beverly crossed her legs. "I'll need that new key first."

Callie bent closer to speak plainer, colder. "Chelsea Morning is my house now, not yours. At first I thought it presumptuous of you to tell me where to live, but we've decided to make it work."

Beverly grinned, and Callie about came undone. "Exactly what I told your father would happen. See? We may be older, but we knew what was best for you. I'll need the key so I can check in on you periodically, to make sure you're on the right course."

A tremble racked Callie's body, then continued in little aftershocks down her arms.

Jeb walked in the back door. He halted and took note. "I don't see blood on the walls—yet."

"Hon-ney," Beverly cooed, arms outstretched as if reunited after months of separation.

Jeb shook his head. "I just saw you two hours ago, Grandma. I told you I'd be coming back to Edisto today."

She beamed. "But I never tire of you walking in." She turned to Callie. "Now, get my key, pull out my albums, and—"

"How about we split them. Ten and ten," Callie said, alarmed at the desperation in her own voice.

"They're mine, dear," Beverly said. "And they aren't safe with all these burglaries."

Callie wiped her face on her sleeve, ready to give in. Her mother raised a brow, as if waiting for Callie to admit she'd stolen cookies from a plate destined for one of Beverly's afternoon teas. And in that moment, Beverly's plan became so clear.

"You'd planned to sneak in and take them." Callie's fuzzy mind mapped out what her mother had schemed, and it sickened Callie. "You would then head home, as if nothing happened," she said with a crack in her voice.

The tiny reaction on Beverly's mouth told it all. "So what? They're nothing to you."

"I would have gone crazy thinking I was robbed." Callie let that comment sink in a second. "How do you even know what those records mean to me? You never just talk *to me* to understand anything *about me.*"

Beverly scowled, her lips pursed, the red lipstick making wrinkles more prominent. "Oh my word, Callie. You're not sixteen. Temper the drama."

Betrayal filled Callie, like she was about to accuse a spouse of cheating when the evidence wasn't clear. But the danger overrode any embarrassment in the words she was about to say. Alarm seized her as to what had been seen or heard on hidden cameras. A hidden cam would have revealed Callie inviting Lawton to come over, when he could be intercepted. When Callie was home, when Jeb was asleep and vulnerable. Surely Beverly wouldn't . . . "Did you ever slip into this house before I changed the locks?"

"What?" Beverly said.

Jeb echoed, "Mom!"

"May I offer everyone some chamomile tea?" Sophie hopped off the barstool. "I can crush some lemon balm in it, *Melissa officinalis*. Soothes tempers, plus it tastes great. Won't take me a sec—"

"No," Beverly said. "It's probably got marijuana in it."

"Grandma!" Jeb exclaimed.

Her heart aching at the thick tension, Callie almost heard her father storming into the room to holler, "Enough!"

Beverly strutted across the den, jerked the desk away from the wall, and yanked the turntable's plug loose. "Enough of this," she said.

Callie shivered at the bastardized use of Lawton's command. "What are you doing?" She tried to sound even-tempered, a farce after all that had been said.

With the cord wrapped around her hand repeatedly until it was contained, Beverly lifted the player and commanded, "Jeb, open the front door."

He scrambled to do her bidding.

"Good boy," she said. "Now, go retrieve my albums."

Fear crossed his face, and he searched for an answer via a long, desperate stare at Callie.

"Jeb? Didn't you hear me?" Beverly said from the porch. She made it down the first dozen steps to the landing.

Jeb studied the back of his grandmother, then swung around. "Mom? What am I supposed to do?"

"Mother," shouted Callie. "Don't put Jeb in this position. I'll give you—"

Thuds and thumps rebounded from the stairs. A crack sounded, a smash. "Umph" and a long moaning "Oooh."

Then silence.

"Oh no, Mother?"

Beverly lay sprawled at the bottom of the steps, face down, the turntable busted in pieces around her.

Chapter 26

JEB DASHED DOWN the stairs and knelt by his grandmother who sprawled belly flat across the shells and gravel. "Grandma, are you okay?" Jeb jerked around. "Mom!"

Callie hurried around the other side of him. "Mother, can you talk? Jeb, get me the phone."

"No," Beverly ordered. She pushed up, then rolled to her bottom.

At least she seemed okay. No blood except for her right palm. "Don't move," Callie said, feeling down the woman's arm, then across her back. "Let a doctor go over you first."

Beverly shrugged Callie away. "I said no. Give me a second to catch my wind."

Callie plopped on the last step three feet away, watching as her mother inspected herself. Hopefully the hole in the side seam of her pants wouldn't be discovered until she got home. Jeb gave his mother the phone and squatted, obviously lost as to what to do.

Sophie flew out of the house, the door slamming behind her. "Here's a wet cloth."

"Did you hit your head?" Callie asked Beverly. "Sophie, there's a medical kit still on my coffee table."

Sophie scampered back up the stairs, the door slamming again.

Beverly dabbed the rag to her face then felt her scalp, touching tenderly. "All right, I think. Nothing hurts."

"Arms seem all right?" Callie had managed too many accidents in her job not to know that adrenaline disguised injuries, and this way she'd make Beverly concentrate on one body part at a time. Eventually, the verdict was Beverly suffered no more than scrapes, bumps, and bruises on her backside and legs, maybe her shoulders. Regardless, she'd be sore for a few days, especially at her age.

"You still need to go to the emergency room," Callie said. "I'll take you."

"No, I most assuredly do not. Hopefully nobody wasted time with 9-1-1."

"No, we didn't, but I'm still not sure we shouldn't. Let me at least bandage those cuts." Callie took the medicine kit from Sophie.

Beverly reached for Jeb, who assisted her up. She slowly unfolded, trying to hide the fact she sensed for damage, then she shuffled a step, appearing able to manage herself. "I seem to recall that Cantrell women tend their own cuts."

Touché, Mother.

Sophie held up the record player's broken arm. "I put the pieces in your back seat, Ms. Cantrell, but I'm pretty sure the player's DOA."

"What?" Beverly turned her head, as if listening from one ear.

Sophie held out the arm. "I mean it's busted to hell."

Beverly's sigh could have blown the trees along Charleston harbor an hour away. "So be it," she finally murmured. Callie spotted the hurt in her face as she turned away, and for the first time in a long while, she felt something for her mother. Beverly had fought to hold onto old comforts in the place of her husband. Callie now felt heartless.

Beverly snatched the arm from Sophie and owned it like a microphone, snapping Callie from her reverie. "I'm going home."

Lips pressed tight, Callie nodded for Jeb to return inside. "Go get them."

With youthful leaps, he ran up the two dozen steps. Gone only a moment, he treaded carefully down again, arms loaded. "Here, Grandma." Carefully, he placed the LPs in the backseat.

"Thank you, sweetheart."

Sophie held out the woman's purse. "You're still welcome to come to yoga. I can show you how to ease those muscles and—"

Beverly spun on her. "I don't need your goddamn yoga, girl. How dense can you be?"

The lot of them fell silent, chastised like children as Beverly strode to her car with nary a limp.

Jeb leaned against Callie. "Mom . . ."

Callie walked toward the car. "Mother, let Jeb or me take you home and help put you to bed. We'll be happy to stay with you."

Beverly looked back from the driver's door. "I'm not ancient and definitely not some old woman needing your pity."

Jeb moved a step forward then checked himself. "We didn't say you were, Grandma."

Beverly wanly smiled. "You're a good boy. Come see your Grandma once in a while, would you?" She eased into her seat and shut the door, then winced wrapping her seatbelt around her.

The BMW cranked up, and it seemed to drive away slower, as if achy itself. The three of them stood stoic, still stunned, as the vehicle disappeared up Jungle Road.

"Should I follow her?" Jeb asked.

"Yes," Callie replied. "Call me when you get there. Need gas?"

"No, ma'am, I'm fine. I'll go get my keys."

As he drove out, Callie plopped on the bottom step again, too exhausted to climb back inside. No sleep, Stan, Peters, Seabrook, hidden cams, and now this. Thank heaven there wasn't more than twenty-four hours in a day.

Sophie joined her. "Wow, your mother's worse than my ex-husband."

"Hmmm," was all Callie could say.

"You okay?" Sophie asked.

"No. And I'm sorry you had to see that." Callie tried to rub the edge of a headache out of her temple.

"Where's that man you were with yesterday?"

Callie moaned. "So not a good time for that question, Sophie."

Sophie reared away. "Okay, okay."

Time ticked by. Then the yoga teacher brushed off her behind and took steps toward her house. "Want me to bring you anything?"

"No, thanks."

"Well, you know where I am." She hesitated to leave. "I do want to thank you. You know, for taking charge when I freaked about Peters being in my house. You were awesome, Callie Jean Morgan."

Callie smiled.

Sophie returned one of her own. "Do try to relax. As spacey as you may think I am, I do worry about you."

"Sophie—" Callie didn't need girl talk right now.

The neighbor zippered her mouth shut with pinched fingers. "See you later. Be happy."

As the sun sank, Callie escaped back inside, spent and mentally comatose. She had no gin to dull her thoughts of regret and missed opportunity. The bourbon was her father's, and for some reason, she wanted the last quarter of that bottle to remain untouched, in remembrance. Too tired to drive to the liquor store, she remained sober by default.

No record player. No music. Yet plenty of noise galloped in her head.

And she still had to search for cams.

A half hour later, she'd combed every nook and cranny in her room, the kitchen, Jeb's room, and the living area. Her eyelids weighed like fishing lead, her feet like anchors. With an iced tea, she retreated with notepad to an Adirondack on the screen porch, in an attempt to regroup and refocus on whom she wanted to interview, and in what order. She read her old notes, but the words blurred. She avoided thinking about Beverly.

About someone maybe running her off a highway, too.

Callie jerked awake and put down the notebook that had tried to slip from her fingers.

Her mother would want little to do with her for at least for a week or two. To think that before today, Callie would have relished that thought, like she had in Boston. Lawton's absence, however, made a difference. He'd expect more of his daughter. Guilt had her gut in knots, but she hadn't pushed her mother down the stairs. She'd simply denied her the albums, which in hindsight seemed dense.

She took a sip of tea. Stan probably walked in Misty's door about now.

A shiver rolled over her at the memory of his hand on her belly. She dropped her own across her front, as if to emulate the warm touch.

Work. Think work. *Use your skills.* Doing nothing was like allowing the situation to worsen.

She glanced up at the window in the Beechum house where the sign had appeared, then disappeared. No light.

That one word: *Whore.* A word to tease her reaction? Pauley came across as a dufus, but would he dare plant cameras? She shivered at how much of her the creep might have seen.

But was it even Pauley? Her cup had been stolen before Pauley returned to Edisto. Or had he been here and not made his presence known?

She ran the cold, dripping glass across her face to wake up. Then she wrote interview questions, asking the various players to describe what they saw or heard and whom they considered guilty. Why they might have been chosen as targets. Geez, she wished she could interview Pauley. No chance of that happening.

She expected no answers of substance from these people. Everyone ignorant or oblivious. It would take someone like her to sift their remarks for clues. But not tonight. She threw down the pen, lifted the tea, then thought about the liquor store barely a mile away.

No, Callie. Besides, the store's closed.

Eyes closed, she designed a mental map. All the victims lived on Jungle Road. All were permanent residents. A fortyish couple, a young family of three, a middle-aged woman. Sophie, Papa, and her. The Rosewoods had lived on Edisto for twenty plus years. Mrs. Hanson the same. The Maxwells two years. Papa for fifty. Sophie three. Callie, not quite two weeks.

Wait. She rubbed her stinging eyes. She could call Rhonda Benson, the real estate agent, and obtain a layout of the area, lot by lot. How many residents had been overlooked? Or rather, who hadn't he burgled *yet?*

Why hadn't she come at it from this angle before? Why hadn't Seabrook?

And why hadn't there been another break-in while she was in Middleton for four days?

She heard a car turn into her drive and park under the house. She recognized his footfalls on the stairs.

"Mom?" Jeb called. "You on the porch?"

How well he knew her. "Yeah."

Jeb gave her a once over as he ventured onto the porch. Pleased, he smiled and sat across from her. "Grandma took a sleeping pill and went to bed. I called that lady from the mayor's office she seems to like and told her about the fall. She'll check on her tomorrow morning. I started to stay, but she acted all embarrassed." He leaned on his knees. "That was just crazy."

"Yes, your grandmother is a breed all her own." Callie smiled at all that was right with her son. "In case I haven't told you lately, I'm so proud of you."

"Let's hope you still think so after I tell you something."

"Great," she whispered, as the back of her head hit the wooden chair. "What else can happen today?"

"You haven't had a drink. That's what happened today, and I can't explain how happy that makes me, Mom. Especially with all that went down around here."

She laughed. He had no idea. "Guess that proves I'm not a drunk, don't you think?"

"Don't ask me a question like that." His seriousness made him sound ten years older.

"Is that all you wanted to tell me? You scared me for a moment."

"No." His elbows bore into his legs as he peered down, then up. "This is."

She laid both arms atop the Adirondack chair's arms and sank into her seat, full attention on her son.

"I postponed college for now."

She jumped upright. "Oh no, Jeb, don't." The entire day's drama, all of it piled together, now seemed mild compared to this. "Please don't do this." Tears streamed down her face unchecked. The day had gone on too long, and her exhaustion consumed her.

Jeb lunged over to sit at her feet and peered up at her eyes. "Mom, stop crying. Remember all you've done for me. You moved. You left your career. You took care of me after Dad died though I saw how much you were hurting." His own eyes moistened. "Now you need somebody. And who else will take care of you better than me?"

She held his blurry face. "But if you don't go to college, I've failed. Your father—"

"Would accept what I'm doing in light of everything." He gave her that Johnish half-smile. "Maybe I'll go next semester. Or a year from now. But you gave me that lecture about civilians needing to take care of their family, avoid danger, secure the home. Go ahead, nod, you know what I'm talking about."

She sniffled, that speech still fresh. As a civilian, she couldn't do much. If anything happened in her house now, all she could do was call 9-1-1 or shoot. Callie stroked her son's shoulder. "How do you feel?"

He raised a brow. "About college? I'm good. I have years ahead of me. Besides, I still haven't decided what courses to take, so maybe this is good in several ways."

With a flat palm, she wiped her face. Lawton had been on his way to talk to Jeb about this very issue. How was she to interpret fate's role in that?

Jeb leaned over and hugged her, and she kissed the side of his head. "I love you, Jeb."

"Love you too, Mom." He straightened. "Don't take this wrong . . ."

"Again? What else is there?"

"You need to take better care of yourself," he said. "Cut the booze, go back to exercise, get some friggin' fresh air, and try to sleep. You look like hell. You're prettier than this."

"Oh." Her cheeks warmed at the compliment. She chuckled, sniffling again. "Yes, sir. I'll try."

"And I think I know what to give you for Christmases and birthdays for a while."

Her dulled head soon caught on at the unspoken reference to Neil Diamond records. "I guess you do," she said. "Listen, it's after eleven. I assume you're going out fishing again early tomorrow?"

"Yes, ma'am. And I assume you'll sleep in."

"Yes, sir. Good night."

His bedroom door shut, and she was left alone with the lingering belief that she'd failed a little as a mother.

The night breezes were warm and getting warmer with June almost gone. Feathered island creatures went to bed at dusk, but she could hear the snickers and clicks of squirrel and foxes. Deer would eventually nose curiously at trash cans finagled open by raccoons, emboldened because their refuge awaited only across the street in the safety of the tall marsh grass.

A slow car made its way up Jungle Road, bar lights dormant on top, and she wondered if it was Seabrook, then doubted the interim chief had to pull night duty.

A rougher wind than usual blew across the porch, and she heard a larger roar from the beach. A front moving in. Sixty percent chance of rain tomorrow per her phone app. She closed her eyes and smelled for it, but no ozone hung in the air. However, that water seemed awful playful, rolling, rolling, then a demolishing whoosh as waves collapsed in on themselves and smacked the sand before falling back. Small one, small one, then there, another crasher.

She hummed in her dozing half-sleep. *Play Me.* John hadn't known Diamond songs, but he loved it when she hummed. Behind closed eyes, she remembered him nuzzling her neck as she did dishes or some other mindless task, to whisper in her ear how her hum stirred him.

She shifted to *Red Red Wine,* well into the second verse before she realized the change. Such a tender song, so conducive to drinking away sad times, to ease the pain of lost good ones. She tried to hum another song, but this one stuck. It made her want to drink. She'd promised Jeb—

Her eyes flew open.

She stopped humming.

But the song continued to play . . . from Papa's house.

Chapter 27

STUNNED, CALLIE listened to Neil Diamond's words floating on the night air from Papa's house next door. Usually one of her favorites, the song made her skin crawl, as if someone delivered a message. *I know you so well.*

Who knew her penchant for this music?

Who was she kidding? She played the songs daily, loud enough to hear two doors down. Plus, Pauley still must be irritated at her from the embarrassment she caused him in front of Raysor and Seabrook. She peered to her right. The green Mazda sat parked in his drive. Had to be Pauley playing one of his pranks. And if he proved to be the one who set up the light, played the radio, stole her cup, and posted signs in his window, she'd do her damnedest to be there and throw the cuffs on him herself.

Quickly she doused her outside light, then the one in the den, and returned to the porch with her cell phone. She set it on video, the lit side held to her chest. Then she changed her seating, hid against the wall, and clicked record.

She almost started humming as the chorus repeated. How dare Pauley get in her head?

A light came on. The music stopped. She coiled wadded up in the chair next to a cabinet that stocked cushions in the winter.

Pauley's face peered out the same window that had flashed the handwritten sign earlier. Nose against the glass, he leaned left, then right. He drew back and disappeared.

She glanced left as a window went up. "Callie Morgan!" he yelled.

She jumped, then reminded herself she was not visible.

"I'm not falling for your tactics!"

She remained silent. Finally the light went out. The evening quieted. She continued to wait, just in case Pauley watched in the dark. Her arms wrapped around her legs, Callie stared into the black night for movement. After five minutes, she turned the video off and folded herself back up.

Palmetto fronds rattled as a gust surged, and a raccoon chattered somewhere across the road. The surf roared in the distance, rowdy. At any other time, she would have appreciated the night noises and their contrast to the tourist white noise of the day.

The inability to move cranked her mind into high gear and increased her frustration. She dug her toes into the cushion, her thigh muscles tensed more from irritation than their statue-still pose. Whoever was screwing with her had done a sufficient enough job such that everybody questioned her mental health. Not totally Callie's fault, yet she couldn't give full credit to the culprit, either. Her life with all its craziness, inserted onto Edisto Beach, had culminated into a perfect storm of drama, crime, and death.

How could she not feel somewhat responsible?

How could Edisto not blame her?

She never believed in being reactionary, always preferring the proactive route, ever ready with a plan. But when she'd turned in her badge, somehow that trait had disappeared, as if the forfeited shield stole her power. Callie Morgan had forged her own trail before the badge and surely could continue after it. What had made her forget that?

The Russians.

As her fingers rubbed the scar, her gut told her there wasn't a Russian connection here. They were ancient history. Besides, they'd have just shot her, knifed her, or put a bag over her head.

She could call Seabrook and hope he would take her seriously about Pauley's harassment of her, but Pauley would blame her and she'd blame him. Tit for tat. Plus, wasn't that all it was? Irritation? What harm did a song do? She sniffed. Hell, her phone video could be interpreted as a souvenir recording of her own harassment of Pauley and her enjoyment of Pauley's reaction.

This is what she got for being too passive, too trusting. Too civilian.

After an hour of contemplation, she came to a conclusion. It was time to deal with this charade on her own damn terms. And she didn't need a badge to do it.

She'd give this deviant idiot no reaction whatsoever. Her inane response to each incident had probably satisfied this creep. He got off on it. Calls to 9-1-1 and the police department, her weapon drawn in public. Each time made her appear crazier. The trained, experienced detective inept without her shield. With her fingernails, she dug long grooves into the chair arms, ending with white-knuckled fists.

Time to fuck him back.

Time to act like nothing mattered.

Time to watch him get sloppy as he fought for her attention and stepped a little more into the light, making himself known.

We'll see how you like that, you bastard.

AT TWO IN THE morning, Callie finally dropped into bed. She woke shortly after dawn, however, her mind not allowing her body to sleep. An hour later, cereal bowl to her left at the kitchen table, she'd found a turntable online. She needed to make this situation with her mother right. Afterwards, Callie intended to focus on her mission, a mission that woke her in more ways than one and wouldn't let her rest regardless of how tired she was.

By nine, on her third cup of coffee, Callie called Beverly. Her mother moaned, some of it legit, but Callie could tell she was walking with her phone. Ice clinked into a glass. A cabinet door opened, then shut. Birds suddenly sang, then abruptly cut off as her mother went outside then came in.

"You in bed or on the sofa?" Callie asked.

"Oh, on the sofa, in my good gown and robe." Beverly sighed.

Callie smiled. Dressed for visitors. "I had a thought, Mother."

"Always good, dear."

Her mother's remarks couldn't faze Callie today. This morning she woke with purpose. "Listen, I found a turntable online that's not much different than yours. I could have it there tomorrow for your albums."

Ice shifted in a glass. "No need. I already spoke to Agnes at Town Hall, and she knows of one. I'm hoping she'll be by this afternoon. I'm so in need of mood music."

Of course Beverly lied, and she never failed to put on a good show. Callie heard all the confirmation she needed and turned around to her computer. She hit send, shipping the turntable to Middleton. "You sound good. But you know that Jeb or I can be there in forty-five minutes if you need us." Callie thought she heard a slurp, and for a second, yearned for a taste of what she knew sloshed in her mother's glass. "Are you drinking this early?"

"Good gracious, no. Not before noon. And I'm dandy. Stiff, sore, banged up, and bruised, but this widow will make it."

Callie hung up, shaking her head at her mother, the phenomenon. First chore done.

She then texted Jeb that she had errands to run. Then she started to leave for Charleston when someone knocked. She listened for Sophie's bangles. Hearing none, she ventured slowly toward the door, her .38 slid out of her purse and in her back pocket, purse set softly on the floor.

Would Chelsea Morning ever be a real beach house? The type someone actually relaxed in?

She gave a start at the man on her porch. In wrinkled khaki shorts, too long and baggy for his short, lanky size, and a faded navy logo T-shirt probably from Papa's wardrobe, Pauley peeked in the glass. When she opened the door, he frowned, hair unkempt and cowlick wild. "This yours?" he demanded.

The LP in his hand waved slowly, like a fan.

She told herself not to react, but her gut flipped at the title. Neil Diamond's *Just for You*, the oldest album in Beverly's collection. Released in 1967 before Callie was even born, when her mother was still a teen. If Beverly inventoried the records and missed this one, she'd skin Callie alive.

And from the antique sales sticker on the corner of the cover, this album indeed was Beverly's.

When had it been stolen from her house?

Callie quickly collected herself. "I don't believe it's mine, Pauley. How would it get in your house? Wait, was that you I heard so late last night? I started to get up, but then it cut off. I was so tired."

He squinted.

"What's the problem?" she asked.

He jerked toward her, like a gang member testing another. "I don't *believe* you. Somehow you got in my house and put this on my dad's record player."

Callie jerked back. "Well, get *over* it. I didn't. Why would I waste my time doing such a thing? Especially with my own album." She shook her head as if unable to grasp what Pauley was saying.

He studied the album cover like she'd seen people do CDs in stores as they decided if the playlist was worth the purchase.

"Anything else, Pauley?" *Keep cool. See what he intends to do with it.*

He waved the album high then swung down, in essence shrugging with it. Callie's eyes followed in fear as she waited for the LP to fly free. Records shattered so easily.

"Wasn't me," he said. "Never saw this before in my life. I was in bed."

"How the heck could that be?" Then she widened her eyes and gave a dramatic inhale. "Did someone break in? You should've called me. No. You should've called 9-1-1."

He held out the album. "For this?"

"You had a trespasser in your house, Pauley! He might've been the one who shot your father, for God's sake."

He blew out once, with sarcasm. "You're more messed up than I heard."

"But the music . . ." Callie noticed nervousness in his eyes.

"I'll just change the locks," he said.

"Good idea." But she was nervous, too. If Pauley wasn't taunting, who had the balls to break in to his place for the satisfaction of alarming her? After taking the album from her living room? The audacity and daring of this guy unnerved her.

The guy could've easily killed Pauley . . . and tried to pin it on her.

How was she supposed to report something like that to the police? It was Pauley's house broken into with nothing done by the culprit but play music. Too far-fetched to believe, that's for sure. Which told her Pauley might still be the likely suspect, and he posed here for show, probably itching to make a buck. Lying through his teeth.

Hell, now she had to change her locks again.

Pauley held out Neil to her. "Here, do you want this?"

Don't get excited, Callie. He's nutty as a Snickers bar. "Um, I might."

He withdrew it. "How much you willing to pay for it?"

"Seriously?"

"Want it or not?"

"Five bucks? It's old."

"Twenty, it's antique."

She huffed. "Hold on one second." She shut the door with its slick lock, grateful for the graphite. She went to her bedroom for her wallet and returned. "If my mother didn't like his music so much, I wouldn't care. Here." She held out the bill and took the record. "It better not be scratched."

Pauley crammed the bill in his pocket. "Ain't your mother I hear playing this music." He turned without a goodbye.

Callie shut the door, flung herself back against it, and hugged the album to her chest. This baby would stay on Edisto.

After she hid the album in her closet, in a zippered suit bag protecting a haute couture outfit worn once to meet a senator, she finally left for Charleston. She needed those nanny cams more than ever now. She had to keep check on the devil she knew next door and the devil who continued to work the island homes. Wouldn't it be grand if he were one and the same?

Fifteen minutes later, as she reached Highway 17, she still mulled over Pauley's lack of concern about an intruder in his house, on top of his aloofness and insensitivity about Papa's murder. The stereotypical sociopath.

But if he had been in Florida as he said, and not been involved in the crimes that preceded his arrival, a devious personality remained on the loose, one whose skills she couldn't help but respect.

Pauley could have killed Papa for the estate and chose to harass Callie for reasons she couldn't fathom. However, she didn't see him being discreet enough to vandalize all the other homes. His return to the island would've been noticed.

She reached the mall. Inside the electronics store, the wall of cams dumbfounded her. Technology was not her forte, but she held an above average knowledge. As many wires as she'd run and surveillance toys she'd used, the cams seemed excessive.

A freckle-faced college kid appeared in his uniform of khakis and blue polo shirt. Five minutes later she held out a credit card, turned down the warranty, and headed out the door.

Two hours after she'd left Edisto, she returned across the marsh to the beach carrying two bags. An hour after that, she'd read the instructions and strategically installed five wireless nanny cams around her house, all Wi-Fi driven with internal DVR and the option to check the footage via her smartphone. Technology could make anyone feel slick.

And she'd found no other cams hidden in her efforts to install her own. Thank heaven. Now she knew how easy it had been for someone to set up the cam in her bedroom. Wireless. Phone apps. *Please don't let my nudity show up online.*

New locks on the doors, again, she now scanned the street for Peters. Callie couldn't afford to put all her money on Pauley as the serial intruder, which meant subtly communicating her new message to all the other players.

She didn't see a hint of him on Jungle Road, so for efficiency's sake, she got in her car and located him two blocks up and three blocks over installing coach lamps at a residence. She stopped on the grass's edge, the engine still running. "Hey, Peters. Did you find your check in my mailbox?"

He grinned and approached the car. "Sure did. Thank you kindly. Sandwich was good, too. Ain't nobody given me a steak since you did, though. How're the steps working for ya'?"

She hesitated, which made his smile dim. "My mother fell down the front steps yesterday," she said. "Near the spot where I cut my knee."

His mouth went agape. "Not sure how that could happen. Is she bad hurt?"

Burglar or not, criticize Peter's hammer, and he was hooked.

Callie shook her head. "She's fine, but could you check the stairs again, just in case?"

"Oh, be glad to." Peters thought a moment. "Tomorrow okay?"

"Sure. How can I thank you?" Callie halted and raised a finger, as if she recalled more overlooked items. "While you're there, think you could install new lights in the storage room, secure a couple shutters, and rig motion sensors outside the two doors? These burglaries have me spooked."

His brows met together. "Motion sensors? Out here? They'll be going off every time a critter steps on your porch."

"Absolutely. I go to bed every night listening for a burglar to the point I can't sleep. At least this way I can sleep until woken up, know what I mean?"

He sucked on his teeth. "Guess I can see that, you without a man and all."

"Yeah, I know," she replied, knowing damn well she had more self-defense skills than any man on this beach. Why didn't she tell herself that two weeks ago, when panic was her trip switch? Why hadn't she installed sensors and cams then?

"There's a gift certificate at Dockside in it for you, too," she said, adding another worm to the hook. "Of course, that's if you can get to those tasks within the next couple of days."

"You beat all, Callie." He grinned wide. "You got me for at least two days, maybe three."

The better she fed him, the longer he'd stay. Easier to watch him. Easier to see him misstep if he was inclined to do so.

"Wish more out here was like you," Peters said as she put the car in drive to leave.

Me, too, Peters. Me, too.

INSTEAD OF HOME, she drove to the Edisto Police Department.

She was feeling her oats today, the only downside being she couldn't share the rush with Stan. Once he mended fences with Misty, and he was released into the wild again, maybe he'd call. God, she hoped so.

"Can I help you?" said the receptionist as Callie entered.

"Callie Morgan, remember? Officer Seabrook asked me to come in about a stolen item."

"Sure," she said, with a professional shyness. "Let me get him for you." The woman punched her phone. "Mike, a Ms. Morgan is here to file a report. Where are you?" She listened. "Sure thing."

Callie creased her brow. "He's not here? I can come back."

"No need," the receptionist said. "He'll be along in a couple minutes."

Seabrook entered the office five minutes later. "Sorry," he said. "I prefer to troll instead of waiting for something to happen."

He ushered her past the swinging door to his desk, his musky scent apparent from his day in the summer humidity. They sat positioned as before. He pulled up a screen on his computer, much like the sympathetic yet effective Seabrook she'd first met on the beach. He typed introductory information about her missing Glock.

"How're you doing?" he asked.

"Good."

"Did I hear something about your mother?" he asked, focused on the screen. "She fell down your steps?"

Sophie had fed the grapevine. "Yes, but she's fine. Sore, but okay."

"Glad to hear it." He typed, tabbed, typed, then tabbed again.

"Where's Raysor?" She glanced around the small station, as if the big man could hide that girth.

"Off today."

"He checked my background, you know."

"Yeah, and I bet you checked on him, too. I also bet both of you were disappointed about what you found."

She smiled. "Yeah." However, she hadn't heard from Stan about Raysor's background. Not like she could call and ask about it now.

"Dammit," he whispered, clicked a few times, then seemed to start over. "Heard you had a guest." He glanced up then went back to his work.

She was no longer surprised at what people said they *heard* anymore. "My former boss came to give his condolences." She kept the answer brief to avoid another sour reaction.

"That was nice of him. Sure he wasn't worried about your . . . um . . ."

"Mental state?" Callie checked her ruffled feathers. "Raysor can surmise what he likes, but Stan and my late husband and I go way back. I'd fly to Boston if Stan lost someone. You know how it is when you work with a person. They're like family."

Seabrook turned his attention from the report. "You could stand a few more pounds on your bones, but you sound good, Callie. In spite of everything." He smiled with what appeared to be sincerity, and it was like a wall melted between them. "You seem to have settled into your life."

"I think I have, Seabrook." She wanted to open up, to call him Mike. He was easy to like, but was he too convenient to trust? She stuck to her plan. Show no worry. Show no concern. "I've decided *you people* out here have the right idea. I'm trying to shift my paradigm."

He chuckled lightly at the reference that had sparked the last argument between them.

"Thanks for being concerned," she said. "You still sound like a doctor sometimes."

He turned back to the computer. "Well, let's get that report filed."

CALLIE LEFT THE station and parked her Escape in the drive after a quick one-bag run to the grocery store. Peters walked around under the house. "You got here fast," she said.

He scratched his head. "You sure you want these motion sensors?"

"Positive."

"Let me see what kind'll work best, then I'll go find them tomorrow."

She climbed the stairs, happy with Peters' eager desire to fulfill her wishes. And if he dared come into her house, her own cams would seal his fate. "What would this beach do without you?" she said.

He laughed. "Fall completely apart, Callie. Piece by piece, it would just collapse into ruin."

She went inside. The cams remained asleep, with no recordings triggered in her absence. Jeb continued with his hourly check-in schedule. He was still with Zeus, meaning Sprite, since most fishermen would be back by now, but he'd be home by dark.

She changed clothes. It was hot, and she wasn't fond of jogging at six in the evening. Too many people on the beach, the sun vicious in a runner's eyes, but run she must. After a small glass of water and half a banana, she made her way in shorts, sneakers, and a long-sleeve, dry weave shirt. Ninety degrees would make her sweat like a plow horse in those sleeves, but she didn't display her scars to the world. These people weren't entitled.

The first mile zapped her enthusiasm sooner than she preferred, probably from all the reasons Seabrook alluded to: little sleep, not eating well, and stress. The tide was high, so her path was also littered with bathers, sand pails, beach towels, and kids, with the occasional dog cutting her off in spite of the summer leash law.

At the end of mile two, she slowed to a mild jog, chastising her de-conditioned state. Her calves would remember this tomorrow, and after another half mile, she slowed to a walk, her body drenched.

Water dowsed her head as a wet floppy hat threw shade on her face. She smiled.

"I'm so glad you decided to walk," Mason said, not nearly as sweaty as she. "I paid my dues this morning, like a sane person. What the hell are you doing out here in the afternoon?"

"I've missed almost a week," she said. "I was bored, and Jeb wasn't home. The sweat is my price to pay."

He started to put an arm around her and changed his mind. "Yuck," he said. "So not attractive right now."

"No charm, huh?" she said.

"Every man has his limits. You finished?"

She readjusted the hat. "I believe so. This run sucked the crap out of me, but I still feel better today than I have in weeks. Maybe that's why I came out here. Like when you get over the flu and overdo it the first day."

"Want a lift back, or will you torture yourself with more penance?" he asked.

Callie wiped off her forehead with a sleeve. "Since that's your place two piers down, I believe I'll let you chariot me home, kind sir."

Callie made Mason cover the Jag's passenger seat with a towel and then leaned back to enjoy the convertible's short drive to her door. "Thanks for saving me with the lift."

"No problem." He pulled to a stop. "You've got company."

The truck was still in her drive. Good, Peters hadn't left.

Mason watched the handyman reach for something in his truck. "What's he doing here?"

"Installing motion sensors outside and repairing a few more items. My mother tripped on the steps he repaired, so he feels beholden to me." There, he knew as well as Peters that she wasn't bowing down to the fear. The more people knew, the better. And Mason chatted up the beach almost as much as Sophie.

Peters jotted on a pocket notepad, jumped into the truck, and took off.

Mason craned his neck as the truck turned the corner down the street. "You shouldn't let him do the work if he botched it up the first time."

She opened her car door, eager to head inside. "Mother most likely tripped herself, Mason. She tried to carry too much."

The sun was making its dive behind the palmettos across the street. So much for the rain forecast, though the breeze still acted up more than usual.

Following her out of the car, Mason walked her up the freshly painted stairs. "I gave you more credit than Sophie. With Peters' habit of entering homes unannounced, how can anyone not consider him a threat?" He shook his head. "It's just not how things are done where I come from."

"He's outside, and my house's locked." She opened the door and turned to him. "You won't ruin my day, Mason. It's the first good one in forever."

He bowed. "My apologies, m'lady."

She grinned at the fake accent. "So, you want water or not?"

His nose crinkled. "I'd love it, but from the pungent aroma of your clothing, it's best if you go take your shower. Somehow, I don't see you letting me watch."

"Another time, then," she said.

"To watch?" he asked, brow raised mischievously.

"To share a drink."

"Ah." He headed down the stairs and halted at the landing, just a step away from where Beverly had fallen. "Don't be alone in your house with Peters," he warned. "This street is attracting a serial criminal, and the victims are your neighbors. He may not be done."

Callie kept smiling until he drove away, the engine noise of that Jag so sweet.

In the bathroom, she peeled off wet clothes and turned on the shower taps. Her reflection made her do a double take. She agreed with Seabrook that she needed to gain a few pounds. She stretched to turn on the shower and allowed the spray a moment to get warm.

As she studied herself again in the medicine cabinet's mirror, she grinned. Now the suspects were in play, short of Raysor. The cameras were in place to catch whoever dared to enter her home. Everyone would construe her behavior as stronger, on the mend. Sophie would sense the difference, too, and label it for the better.

And whoever she missed, the rest would tell. That was the Edisto way.

Callie was not suffering the victim role any longer.

Taking her time in the shower, leaning on the wall, she let the water run down her back, and she basked in her newfound confidence. Instead of last night's scare on the porch stealing her strength, it had flipped her switch.

She shut off the water and stepped onto her plush bath rug with a large sand dollar image in the center. Bent over, she toweled her wet hair with a frenzy. Tossing it over, she combed it back slick and studied herself again. Yep, she was 10-8, in service, and thoroughly wired for duty.

Chapter 28

CALLIE CHEWED ON wheat toast slathered in raspberry jam, her interview notes scattered across the breakfast table. Even after scrambling a couple of eggs for a serious breakfast, her nerves still jittered. Food couldn't hurt; she needed the pounds. She just craved a dash of something stronger in her orange juice.

She'd risen early unable to sleep, her mind awhirl with plans. Running wasn't in them with so much to do. She had hoped to interview the Rosewoods first, but they wouldn't be home until noon, much like the day they were burglarized. Callie had already noted the pattern. The burglar would have, too.

So that meant Sophie first. Callie's head hurt at the thought of how convoluted that conversation would be. Her neighbor greeted every dawn, so when Callie called and asked to come over early, at the top of the hour, Sophie agreed completely alert. The stove clock gave Callie ten more minutes.

Purchased with the cams, her new handheld recorder seemed simple enough. Astounding even. Flash drive capability as well as internal memory. Seventy-hours of recording time on the batteries, but she packed extras in her pocket. Always be prepared. She'd still depend on her notes, fast written and organized in a method honed in Boston, but she didn't want to risk a he-said-she-said situation. She'd transcribe the recordings later and make mp3 copies of the recording, covering all her bases. Callie closed the note-book and thrust three pens into her purse in case one decided not to work. The tools, the interview outlines, hell, just the fact she was doing something productive, cranked up her adrenaline like she hadn't felt in two years.

A badge sure would make all this easier, though. Badges could force a degree of cooperation, but without that shield, asking someone to swear to an oath could shut them up faster than a bear trap. So no oaths. She'd have to finesse. That was okay. She knew how to read people's eyes.

After placing her dishes in the sink, she checked herself in the mirror and headed next door.

"Hey, girl, come on in," Sophie said as Callie arrived on the top step before she had a chance to knock. "So what is this about?"

"Seabrook asked me to interview people who were involved in the break-ins." Sort of the truth.

Sophie tilted her head, blinking fast in her daily choice of brown contacts. "Can we move outside on the porch?"

Callie shrugged. "Sure."

The gypsy woman headed to a picnic table on her porch, earrings jingling. No way Sophie could burgle with that racket.

With the recorder placed between them, they covered the basics of date, time, name, address, and occupation. Then Callie began her interview, maintaining eye contact with Sophie so she wouldn't be distracted by the recorder. "What was stolen?"

"An NFL ring."

Check. "Where was it kept when it was stolen?"

"In Sunbeam's litter box. Not in a bag, either, but in all the nasty stuff. It was crusty."

Sophie was doing great. Callie continued. "Explain what was found in your kitchen."

"He poured himself an orange juice and vodka and left a coin on the table." Sophie dipped her chin with a nod, as if putting a period on the end of her sentence.

"Wait a minute," Callie said. "I thought it was just orange juice."

"No." Sophie shook her head. "A screwdriver. I smelled it when I washed the glass."

They tended a few more questions to settle Sophie into a routine, then Callie asked, "So he left a coin?"

"I guess. You said he did."

Callie reworded. "Did your son Zeus find a coin beside the orange juice?"

"Screwdriver, but he didn't know that, because he didn't wash the glass. I did."

"Sophie! Did Zeus tell you he found a coin next to the drink?"

"Yes. That's what he said, and my boy never lies."

"And what was the date on that coin?"

"1921, though I didn't see it until those Boy Scouts fished it out of the marsh."

No problem. Callie had seen and held it before Sophie pitched the silver dollar to the fishes.

The interview took two hours. Could have taken one, but Sophie had her tangents.

In the end, Callie learned that Sophie knew Papa Beach. He had been her go-to person on things that went wrong with her house, just like the Cantrells had used him. She didn't socialize with the other victims but had seen the Rosewoods at a few events like the Arts and Crafts Market and last year's Governor's Cup, now just a few weeks away. She'd been broken into early in the morning, when everyone knew she would be at yoga.

Callie quickly gathered her papers and recorder. "It's ten till noon. I've got to go."

"How did I do?" Sophie asked.

Callie squeezed her fingers. "Brilliantly. Didn't hurt a bit, did it? Sorry, but I have another appointment."

"With who?" Sophie asked as Callie sprinted toward the door.

"Thanks," Callie said, evasive. "I appreciate it." Sophie might tell the whole street what she was doing. Callie was tired of scooping up clues in this guy's wake. It was time to maneuver in front of him.

She rushed next door, bolstered by the first interview. Ben Rosewood escorted her in. A middle-aged man in beige slacks, and in spite of a casual, loosely hung shirt, he seemed stiff. No Bianchi energy here. "What is this about again?" he asked, skepticism in his eyes.

"I'm helping the police department with interviews about the burglaries." She prayed the couple didn't stir up a fuss. Callie had scheduled these visits back to back. Mrs. Hanson expected her at three. The Maxwells at five thirty.

Sarah Rosewood waited at a beautiful burled maple kitchen table, coffee cup on a woven gold placemat. The whole house gleamed in an aura of tasteful decoration.

"Mike's already been here. You aren't even a cop," Ben said, irritated.

Callie bit back an order for him to take his seat.

"Wait," Sarah inserted with a soft touch. "We'd like to say how truly sorry we are about your father, Callie. We knew him."

The woman had visited the funeral home but said her husband had obligations elsewhere. Callie felt awkward with this overlap of her personal and investigator life.

Ben didn't appear to hold much sympathy, and instead, picked up the phone. "I'm calling Mike. This doesn't feel right."

Callie's pulse quickened. She nodded, as if he had the perfect right to call, while her heart pounded like timpani drums.

Sarah blushed, briefly shutting her eyes at her husband's behavior.

Callie prayed that Seabrook covered her butt. Prior to their weird, unspoken falling out, he *had* asked for her help. Hopefully he remembered.

Ben held out the phone. "He wants to talk to you."

She placed the phone to her ear. "Hello?"

"What the heck are you doing?"

She created a bright-eyed look for the Rosewoods' sake. "That's right. I finally got around to that assistance you asked for. Daddy's funeral set me behind."

"I'm not sure that's appropriate," he replied, but Callie heard enough in his tone to sense flexibility. "You've had too much personal involvement to be objective," he added.

"That's right, Mike. Years of training. I don't mind at all."

The silence gave her pause.

"Get those interviews to me ASAP," he said, resigned. "Tomorrow at the latest. Understood?"

She forced the laugh, hiding the relief. "Sure thing. Appreciate that, Mike. You're sweet."

She delivered the phone back to Ben, and soon he sat stoic across from her at the table, next to his wife, explaining all he knew about the first break-in after Papa Beach's murder. They acted like being burglarized was beneath them. Callie couldn't explain Sarah's odd case of nerves, a subservient manner, as if she'd been warned how to act. But Callie got her answers.

An hour later, Callie left with tight, simple responses to her questions. The burglar had poured himself a lowball glass of bourbon and Coke. He stole sixty dollars from the bedroom. The coin had been a silver dollar dated 1903. They'd met Sophie, knew Papa from a small job he'd done for them when Peters wasn't available, and were familiar with Mrs. Hanson and the Maxwells only via waves across the street. They frequented the golf course at the private club.

So why take a small amount of cash when the home flaunted wealth?

Mrs. Hanson, bless her heart, waited for Callie with the door open, chocolate chip cookies at the ready, the chips still gooey. Callie took one as soon as she set foot inside and moaned at the pleasure. Lunch had come and gone unnoticed, her stomach making itself loudly known.

Mrs. Hanson was a retired teacher, and Mr. Hanson traveled on the road five days a week. Her phone calls to a sister occupied much of her time, a routine any break-in artist would relish. Mrs. Hanson knew Papa Beach well. Though Papa had ten years on the lady, Callie would almost swear there might've been a more social connection than chocolate chip cookies from the melancholy manner in which Mrs. Hanson spoke of her old friend Henry. She even dabbed an eye.

The perp's drink of choice, wine. Mrs. Hanson said the alcohol belonged to her husband, and she never imbibed. Callie hid a smile at the tiny lie. The coin, a 1928 silver dollar. A sterling silver necklace stolen.

Kind older lady. Easy target. Easy enough for a repeat performance.

"I want you to change your routine," Callie told Mrs. Hanson as she packed up. "Lock up more often, and don't tell people I came by."

"Why?" she whispered.

"The bad guy might not like us trying to catch him," Callie whispered back.

With leftover cookies in a plastic bag, Callie backed out with innumerable thank-yous, goodbyes, and promises to be safe before she could escape the poor lady, who without a doubt was lonely with both husband and Papa Beach not around for company. Callie scurried two doors up to the Maxwells with five minutes to spare, scouring the street for eyes.

She waited behind a Hawthorn bush at the bottom of the steps, now concerned she would bring more flack on these people's lives. She flipped through her notes and compartmentalized her ideas. This interview would be different: The robber had harmed his victim. Why the escalation, and what was unique?

Callie pulled out the map from Rhonda Benson, and the breeze caught the corners, fighting her effort. Black marker *X*s identified each burgled resident's lot.

The day was postcard clear and bright. Motivated and feeling rogue, Callie took a second to enjoy the ever-loving-hell out of her mission. Dickens drove by in a patrol car. She waved. He waved back, probably told by Seabrook to watch the street, maybe even scout for her. No problem. They could watch all they liked. They weren't in her head. She was getting in theirs.

Later, she'd discretely interview Seabrook, too.

One detail remained consistent amongst the violated residents. None of them had seen Pauley for months, which lessened the suspicion she had about him, especially for the break-ins prior to his supposed arrival. Mrs. Hanson and Sophie knew of him. The Rosewoods didn't.

But she still didn't fathom why this criminal, whoever he was, would give away coins. Why not steal them from Papa Beach and keep them? And why use the oldest, most valuable coins as calling cards? Apparently money was not a motive. But what was?

"That you, Ms. Morgan?"

Callie glanced up. Steve Maxwell peered down. People could spot like eagles from their upstairs porches. "Yes, it's me. You ready?"

"Sure, come on up."

She climbed the stairs and followed Mr. Maxwell inside. His three-year-old ran room to room, toy to toy, with the energy of ten adults. Alyce Maxwell stood guard, an eye on the child and an ear on Callie and her husband at the kitchen table, multi-tasking as young moms did. The woman was lovely with long blond hair tied up on her head, accenting her cheekbones and jawline.

The trespasser's drink had been a mimosa. Coin was a 1972 Eisenhower. The Maxwells didn't socialize with any of the locals, and their closest friends were ten miles inland. They had met Papa, though. He'd built their mailbox. Callie smiled. Mailboxes had been his specialty.

"So what was stolen, Steve?" she asked. The man had been too injured to answer before.

"A sterling silver mirror from my wife's dresser. The set was a gift from her aunt at a bridal shower."

The little boy darted past them, running his hands along the table, then vanished into a bedroom.

Callie's gaze followed the streak, then she turned to Steve. "Any chance your Flash Gordon loved the pretty mirror and hid it under a bed somewhere?"

"We scoured the house," Alyce said, then disappeared after the child.

Callie jotted a few notes. "Bet she keeps busy."

"You have no idea," Steve said. "She's endless energy. Wears me out watching them both."

Says the twenty-nine-year-old, she thought. The child zipped past again, the mother after him, and Callie's conversation with Seabrook the day of the break-in came back to mind. "Steve, do you have a nanny cam?"

"Um, no. We don't go out much."

Callie's internal lie detector flashed red at the dart of his eyes. She'd just confirmed how inexpensive nanny cams were, how easy to install . . . and hide.

She pushed back her chair and wandered into the family room. "My son's headed to college," she said. "Wish I'd had the conveniences that parents have now. A nanny cam, for instance. Don't even have to wire them; some store internally on their own memory." She walked past the entertainment center, with glances back at Steve. "If I were you, I'd install one somewhere around . . ."

Steve's eyes squinted.

"Here," Callie said, finding a cam peeking over a bookend.

"Good Lord," Alyce said, covering her face. Steve broke eye contact.

Callie appraised them both. "What's the problem? And before you try to create another story, I want you to know that whatever it is, I've seen and heard worse. The point is to catch who injured you, before he does worse to someone else."

They held humiliated poses, throwing glances at each other.

Shaking her head, Callie returned to the table and sat. "Sex tape would be my guess."

Alyce cringed. Steve's gaze fell away. *Bingo.*

Callie's heartbeat raced at an opportunity for bona fide proof of the burglar, but she maintained her calm. "Listen, nobody cares. We want the burglar, your attacker. Let's try to ID somebody on the tape. Is it on a motion sensor?"

Surprisingly, Alyce spoke up first. "Okay, we accidentally recorded me dancing nude for Steve. We forgot it was motion activated and didn't think to turn it off when we came in."

Her husband's head jerked up. "Geez, honey!"

Alyce pointed to Callie. "I don't mind showing it to *her*. I just didn't want that bunch of guys at the police station drooling over it, you know?" She walked over to the table and glanced back quickly at the toddler finally playing on the floor. "Is there some way to cut out just the pertinent part? I almost deleted the whole thing, but couldn't do it. There *is* a guy on there."

Fantastic. This was the first damn piece of concrete evidence that could break this case open. "Can you make me a copy?"

"All of it?" Steve asked.

"If you don't mind."

He walked to his computer housed in a small cabinet in the den's corner and retrieved a flash drive. "We weren't sure how to cut off parts. I worried it would destroy its ability to stand up in court in case somebody, like you, needed it."

She changed her mind about them, impressed at the forethought. She was so excited at evidence that her facial muscles twitched.

She waited for him to pass it to her instead of acting like it was hers to take. This evidence might mean everything. While she, or Seabrook, could get a subpoena, the Maxwells volunteering the evidence would clinch a more cooperative spirit, for now and later, if it indeed went to court.

Steve gave it to her. "Don't let those regular Edisto cops see any of it, you hear? You don't know how this island can be."

Callie gingerly accepted the drive. "I'll do my best. I know exactly how the gossip works around here. You have the original in a safe place?"

"Oh, yes," Alyce said, the sterner of the two. "And the minute you no longer need it, it's going in my fire pit out back."

Fingering the drive, Callie stared at one, then the other. "Before I study it, tell me if you recognized him."

"It's not so obvious. It was a man, though," Alyce said.

Steve just nodded as a ditto to his wife's comments.

Callie asked a couple more questions, more to settle them down and maintain their confidence in her than gather facts. She was still in their house, and they could change their minds. But her guts churned with anticipation.

Fifteen minutes later, she hugged Alyce with reassurance they'd done the right thing. Steve walked her to the porch. "Please don't let me find any of that on YouTube."

Once he went inside, Callie jogged across the street to Chelsea Morning.

Her laptop wouldn't come on. She ran for the adaptor and plugged it in, booting up the machine. She poured a tea, kicked off her shoes, and returned with a notepad. She caught herself rocking in her seat. This was too good, too damn good to be true.

She itched to see who would appear in the video. The Maxwells naturally would have told Seabrook there was no nanny cam if he or Raysor were on the recording. Her thoughts zigzagged. *Hurry up, machine.*

Finally, she plugged in the flash drive and located the file.

Scenes started and stopped, triggered by the sensor. Mrs. Maxwell belly danced nude for an inebriated Mr. Maxwell backed up to the kitchen sink in his boxers. As comical as this would be any other time, Callie couldn't care less now about their kinky home life. Nude, they finally moved off camera.

The picture changed abruptly, the sensor again triggered. A man kept his back and side to the camera, but summer light pouring in the kitchen allowed her to see his beige cargo pants, thick waist, and T-shirt. A ball cap hid his hair color, but the edges showed a man in need of a trim. His movements weren't young, more middle-aged. No noticeable jewelry.

He rummaged items in the refrigerator, withdrew the champagne, seeming to take time to study the label. In no hurry, he popped the cork, poured some in a glass, then found orange juice to top it off. Not the standard mixology steps for a mimosa, but he got the ingredients right. After sipping, the concoction pleasant per the head nod, he set the glass down and left the camera's range. He returned from off camera with something that might be the silver mirror.

Turn toward me.

There! A front-on face shot. Peters!

He dragged out a seat and sat, reached down with considerable effort, removed a shoe, and extracted something crammed all the way down to the toe. Callie felt eighty percent sure the man now held the coin. She became a hundred percent confident when he set it on the table and adjusted it to suit him.

Dang it. At Sophie's, Callie had told Seabrook to make Peters empty his pockets. She had never considered having him take off his shoes.

An acute rush of relief fell over her, but then so did regret. She hated Peters screwing up this way. The man was not a nasty guy. Yet here he was, proof positive, in at least one case, that he was the silver dollar thief. He wore no mask and made no attempt at disguise. *Damn it, Peters.* He was either overly confident or plain stupid.

But she couldn't envision him killing Papa Beach.

Peters exited. The picture went dark. Callie sat back and waited through the intermission. The picture popped back up as Mr. Maxwell triggered the cam when he entered the kitchen, pausing, puzzled by the champagne foil on the counter, and opened the refrigerator. A portion of a man entered stage left, a bigger man, in a polo shirt, again in a ball cap but a different shade, the face mostly hidden by the appliance door. After he grabbed the champagne bottle from Steve's grasp, the intruder hit him in the head with it. Steve dropped to the floor. The intruder stooped over, even more hidden, then straightened, his back to the camera. Light briefly appeared at the top of the screen, flashing a sunburst at the camera as the attacker left the house, his victim motionless on the linoleum.

Callie replayed the recording a dozen times, each time seeking a new fact, noting the time stamps. Clothing, body language. She wrote notes, each replay focused on another aspect of the scene. *Damn it all to hell!* No definitive image whatsoever on the second guy, but she at least noted a ring on hands that weren't as big as the first invader.

Two different people.

Replay. Again, again. She worked on her interview statements, prepping them for Seabrook, then went back and replayed the scenes, hoping the break had heightened her observation abilities.

Her phone rang, the caller ID indicating Seabrook. He could cool his heels. An hour wasn't nearly enough time to dissect the recording and put her interviews in proper order. The call went to voice mail, but he immediately called again.

"Hello," Callie answered, her gaze stuck on the screen, eyes unblinking, this time watching the floor for shoe recognition. The second intruder wore deck shoes versus Peters' sneakers.

"Where are you?" Seabrook asked. No salutation, no lead in.

Callie stopped the recording. "Why?"

"Not the best answer," he said with a severity she didn't like.

"I'm at home, with evidence from the Maxwell house that'll make your day. What's wrong?"

"Don't leave the house. An officer ought to pull in your drive any second."

Her blood turned to ice water. Was there another murder? She jumped up, her heart almost erupting. "Is Jeb all right?"

"This has nothing to do with Jeb."

She rushed to the door where Dickens already held his post. "Stay inside, ma'am."

Seabrook's cruiser crunched shells in her drive. He stared up from behind his windshield at her, both with phones hugged to their ears. He hung up first, excited, and headed up her steps.

She watched, trying to discern his mood, and met him at the top riser. "What—"

"Go back inside," he said, his mouth flat and serious. "Raysor's been shot in the back during a traffic stop. With your missing gun. Now do as I say."

Chapter 29

SEABROOK ESCORTED Callie back into Chelsea Morning, hand at the small of her back. She recognized the subtle gesture as mannerly, yet close enough to react and grab her if she bolted. Dickens stood at parade rest as if he guarded the barrier between Heaven and Hell. *Un-friggin' believable.* Seabrook seriously suspected her, when she was the most powerful tool in his box to hunt this guy.

"Why the backup officer, Officer Seabrook?"

He didn't respond.

She was fed up with his passive, irritating, almost pouting ways. She reported her Glock stolen, dammit. He shouldn't be surprised it was used.

Once in the kitchen, he pulled out a chair. "Have a seat."

Screw him. She crossed her arms, not pleased with the sudden scrutiny. "After you."

He didn't, so she backed up to her kitchen counter. "How's Don? Was he wearing his vest?" Her alibi's validity depended on the exact time Raysor was shot. She should have taken her missing gun more seriously. Seabrook as well. And she should have installed security sooner.

"His vest took all three bullets," Seabrook said. "He's in the hospital with a broken rib and possible internal damage."

Callie closed her eyes. "Thank God." Then she opened them. Seabrook watched her intently. All bullets hitting center, as if the shooter knew about the vest. Her butting heads with Raysor. Who wouldn't suspect her?

"Where were you about an hour ago?" Seabrook asked, memo book open.

"So this just happened?"

His tone hardened. "Answer my question."

"You'd get better cooperation if you asked a question properly." Defiant, she tapped into her experience as she pondered who the hell might have shot Raysor. Pauley and Peters remained her top two candidates. She was dying to speak to both of them now, but she wasn't ruling out anyone. Maybe Raysor was the good guy in all this after all, getting too close to the truth.

Callie recrossed her arms. "Where were *you* an hour ago, just so we're even here?"

"On another call at a rental," he said. "Seventy-year-old woman fell in her hot tub."

"And I was here," she said, "going over the Maxwell interview and evidence you need to see."

"Anybody with you?"

"No," Callie said. "But—"

"What time will the Maxwells say you left their house?"

"Quarter to seven." She slapped her notes on the table, then laid the recorder beside them. "I noted it in my interview."

"That cuts it awful close."

"My car hasn't been cranked today. I've been here on this street, talking to the victims." She felt moisture building on her palms, her respiration building though she was innocent. Who had really tried to kill Raysor with her gun? If they would shoot Raysor, they'd shoot anyone touching this case. "Tell me what happened."

Seabrook showed no emotion. "Raysor pulled over a speed violator," he said. "He stopped the car on the side of Highway 174 in front of the turnoff to the Serpentarium when someone in a nearby vehicle saw him get popped three times. Raysor's bulk blocked the driver's view. Once Don went down, the driver lost his head. He couldn't recall his own name."

"Probably realized how easily one of the bullets could have been his." But evidence carried more weight than an eye witness. "How do you know it was my gun?"

"The casings were .357 Sig Sauer, used in a Glock by law enforcement types. Don't see that in the possession of too many civilians."

True, but that still didn't confirm her weapon. "I didn't shoot him. If I had, he'd be dead. Someone's setting me up."

"Unless you wanted to scare him, or get even."

"That's your guess, Acting Police Chief? No wonder you don't want the job full-time." She pushed off the counter. "Seriously, his distaste for me becomes my motive for shooting him? Like he had no other enemies."

"Add it up, Callie."

She pointed at him, careful not to touch him. When she was on duty, an aimed finger at her chest always set her off. "No, you add it up. Raysor's rude to coworkers, victims, and suspects, an equal opportunity ass with a long history. Maybe he discovered something we didn't and pissed somebody off. Or he orchestrated a scam, tossing his ample weight and authority around, holding threats over people's heads to make them work for him." Her face tightened in a tense, low anger. "What the hell do I have to gain from shooting Raysor?"

Seabrook's brows shrugged, head tipping to the side. "Assuming you aren't the burglar, assailant, or murderer? Nothing. But don't think people around here haven't suspected you, the new unknown resident with a questionable past."

Son of a bitch. "Again, you protect who you know and blame those you don't. While you're trusting all these people you know, someone out there laughs at how you're barking at shadows."

He didn't raise his voice, but his demeanor stiffened more, accepting her challenge. "You're a cheap firecracker, unreliable with the potential to pop off at any moment. If you still possessed your old cop sense, you'd recognize why you're a person of interest."

Forensics had found no prints in Papa's place, no prints on her broken mementoes from Papa's house. There'd be no prints on the spent brass except hers, since the shooter had no need to load it. "Talk to Pauley," she said, groping for a comeback. "Ask where he's been for the last hour. I still say he had the most motive to kill Papa Beach, so why not Raysor?"

Seabrook frowned questionably. "He doesn't even know Raysor, Callie."

"Why does he need to know him? He only wanted to make a point with my gun."

The chance these crimes were connected flashed neon in her mind. Just like with her gun, all the facts weren't necessarily clues to the crimes. Some seemed too convenient, too attached to her, too opportune. And when details seemed too obvious, maybe they weren't clues. They were distractions for the likes of Mike Seabrook and Don Raysor.

And Pauley's hatred for her seemed way too over the top.

"Please, just ask Pauley those few questions." She held out her hands. "And feel free to dust me for gun residue. Dust my car. Go get my hamper and test those clothes, too."

She wished she'd installed the motion sensors before now. They would have shown the time she came in her house. "Wait!" she said and snapped her fingers. "I recorded myself on my cams. And once I show you proof that I was here when someone shot Raysor, *please* watch Maxwell's cam recording while I've got you. They do have a nanny cam. Quit screwing around with me. We've got to arrest Peters before he disappears."

Seabrook leaned toward her, finally attentive. "Just show me the recording."

"Come over here." She ran to her laptop. "Tell me what you see."

"A young couple getting it on," he said, after a long minute of sitting in front of the screen.

"Keep watching," she said from behind him.

He groaned seconds later as Peters mixed his mimosa. "I hate this. Does it show him hitting Maxwell?"

"Keep watching," Callie repeated.

The mystery man appeared. "Wait, who's that?" Seabrook asked.

"I have no idea. Not enough of clear view to identify. However, we definitely know Peters is the thief. I could get him to confess to every one of the other burglaries."

"Callie?" came a familiar voice from the door.

Both of them turned. Dickens held Peters back in the entryway. "I need to know how much you want to spend on those motion sensors," the handyman said. "The hardware store has three different kinds."

SEABROOK CONFIRMED Callie's cam evidence that she had been home when Raysor was shot. But he still told her to not leave Edisto. Hearing such an order from an officer's mouth other than her own gave her a new perspective on being a civilian.

After an hour sitting idle, unable to study the recording since Seabrook confiscated it as evidence, Callie put in a call to the station, craving an update, halfway expecting Seabrook to blow her off.

"How's it going?" she asked, stunned when the receptionist patched her to Seabrook.

Peters' exclamations of dismay echoed in the background, his frantic yelling completely out of the character she'd come to know. "I did not hurt anybody. I did not shoot anybody. You people know me." Over and over, as if he were afraid that being quiet would be his undoing.

Seabrook had banned her involvement with Peters' arrest. A wise decision, she had to admit. Plus, it was dusk, and with a shooter loose, she preferred to be indoors, blinds drawn to the fiery sunset across the marsh that she found way too visible from her back window. She'd already called Jeb to come home.

"Well?" she asked. "Have you learned anything?" As she spoke, she studied Pauley's house from her kitchen window. She should have installed a sensor pointing toward his place.

"Not sure I ought to be talking to you," Seabrook said.

Pauley drove up in his drive. She jerked back from view. "Don't tell anybody, then. Pick my brain, please. I might be able to help. What did he say?"

"He confessed to the break-ins."

Damn. She'd caught the man flat-footed in Sophie's house. Peters might've been hunting a drink, but most likely he'd found her neighbor's house too easy to pass up for a second effort with her doors unlocked. "How the hell did he find Sophie's NFL ring in the litterbox?" she asked.

"Kicked the litterbox in his hunt for a souvenir," he said. "She probably discovered it missing in cleaning up the mess."

Then she had to ask the obvious, not sure she wanted to hear the answer. "What about Papa Beach?"

"He swears he didn't kill Henry Beechum. Nor did he assault Maxwell."

Callie retrieved the map from her back pocket and snared a new notepad from a drawer. Seabrook had confiscated her recorder and notes.

"We need to nail down Pauley's activities for every day since this mess started, too, you know."

"One guy at a time, Callie. By the way, Peters lawyered up."

She pushed away the map and let her eyes rest on the trees turning into shadows outside her window. "And he's still rambling on like that?" She turned on more lights in the room.

"He's not that bright, Callie. The attorney's meeting us in Walterboro since we don't have jail cells here. We're heading over there now."

"He hated Papa Beach," she said. "That's why he broke into residents' homes. All the guy did was thumb his nose at people who hadn't given him their business. He was enjoying their conveniences and stealing tokens. Almost harmless, if you think about it."

"How do you figure that?"

"It came to me after talking to Mrs. Hanson. Then I confirmed it with the Maxwells." She reread her scribbled notes jotted around the Xs on her map. "Peters only broke into houses where Papa Beach did work. Papa didn't do the jobs for payment, so his reach was no more than the people on his street. Anything else was too much bother because of his age and having to haul heavy tools. He wouldn't deal with the rental houses either, since the real estate management companies kept their own contractors. I think Papa's death triggered Peter's crime spree, unless he killed Papa to get rid of his competition." But that still didn't ring true. "I can't believe that, though."

"Okay, that makes sense," Seabrook said.

"Papa cost Peters some business. It's that simple. If the break-ins weren't felonies, they'd be comical. Did he say anything about the coins?"

"Yeah," Seabrook said, "but not sure how much truth is in it. Said he found the collection in a trash pile on Jungle Shores Road. Says he's never been in Beechum's house."

"Who throws away coins? And where's the rest of the collection? His truck?"

"Yes. Give or take a few he spent. He knew enough not to throw too many of them around, apparently." He spoke to someone in the background. "Callie, I've got to go."

"Wait, what did he say about my place?" she asked.

"You were a good guy, Callie. He liked you."

She mildly smiled at the irony. "Because with Papa dead, I hired him to do work for me." And fed him a steak.

She'd been right suspecting that the crimes on Edisto involved two criminals. Her smile gave way to the disturbing image of another man roaming the beach with no qualms about inflicting harm and no worries about getting caught.

"Do you think the nanny cam footage helps him against the assault charge?" she asked.

"Depends on the spin a defense attorney puts on it. They'll probably throw it all at him and see what sticks. There's still the possibility of an accomplice. Time stamps might sort all that out, plus the second guy doesn't quite physically fit Peters."

"Well," she said. "We can take Raysor off the list."

"Never had him on it."

She still harbored distrust for Raysor and a light, residual concern about Seabrook. He was too quick to doubt her, too slow to believe her, and too similar to Raysor in having the opportunity to run a burglary ring from behind his badge.

But she hated feeling that way. Somebody other than Peters was guilty, and the not knowing was making her suspect the world.

"I'm eager to see if things settle down," Seabrook said. "Even if Peters had a partner, removing half the team might be enough to dismantle it." He hesitated a moment. "Call me if you feel the need to . . . if you need any-thing."

Callie hung up, pleased at getting Seabrook to talk to her. He no longer kept her at arm's length. Good for him. Her attitude about him, however, held him at a comfortable distance. She was quite convinced his so-called street surveillance was no more than a study of her, a suspicion. She was the new person on the block and not one of the regulars, the folks he was so proud of making excuses for . . . like Peters.

She hoped Seabrook was right about one thing, though. Hopefully the crime spree was handicapped with Peters out of commission. But if Peters admired Callie and didn't target her with flickering lamps, window notes, and broken chicken figurines, then who did? What had she done to rate such attention?

Regardless what Jeb wanted, Chelsea Morning might go up for sale sooner than New Year's Day. No one had bothered them for the year they'd lived in Middleton. Even the Russians had stopped their threats in Boston.

This harassment had started in Edisto.

Jeb arrived home around nine thirty, showered, and planted himself on the sofa with a remote. By the time Callie came out in her nightgown and robe, he was engrossed in an online game.

"Jeb," she said.

"Shhh," he said, glued to the screen. "In a minute. I unlocked the se-cret level."

His innocence moved her to wait. They weren't going anywhere to-night. So she moved to the enclosed screened porch to wind down, to let the surf's distant, lazy churning soothe her to the point she could nod off. It felt later than ten. So much was happening.

Callie shook her head to nobody there. And why would he need a part-ner? He was a loner by nature with the expertise to enter homes without assistance. Peters didn't seem the murderous type, especially now that she'd gotten to know him.

Now that she'd gotten to know him. Hell, she sounded like Seabrook.

A light came on at Pauley's place, and he glanced out one window, then another. He was as paranoid as she was. Or he was watching for her, calculating his next move.

The Maxwells probably slept poorly, worried about their video. Callie wanted to knock on their door and tell them Peters was in custody, but doing so might make them lower their defenses. An invisible partner waiting in the wings would love that.

"I see you," yelled her neighbor. "Sitting over there in the dark. Probably waiting for me to go to sleep so you can sneak in."

The man was daft. "Pauley, I don't care about your house. I simply want to enjoy mine."

"Then why are you surveying me?"

It's surveilling, stupid. "I'm seated on my porch. It happens to face your house."

"You have other porches."

"Leave me alone, Pauley."

"I'll be watching you. Come in here, and I might shoot."

He'd shoot his own foot off first. She wrapped her robe around her. Pauley seemed somewhat of a chump, endowed with the gray matter of a duck. Yet he possessed a shifty enough edge to worry her. While her detective senses had dulled of late, she still gave them a smidge of credit, and right now they told her not to lose her guard around him.

Or maybe her alert status was stuck on red. She just didn't know anymore.

Finally Callie went to clean the kitchen before she headed to bed. In the phone call, Seabrook said they planned to charge Peters, topping the pile with home invasion on Papa Beach, a more egregious crime than burglary, but not nearly as grievous as murder. A heavy load. She tried to cast aside the sympathy she felt for him.

Sun-kissed from his day in the sun, Jeb put his own dishes in the sink and joined her on the porch. "Who were you talking to?"

"Our stupid neighbor. Still paranoid about people stealing his stuff."

"He's not dangerous, is he?"

Callie wasn't so sure. "I think he's all right, but steer clear of him."

"Then I'm going to bed," he said. "Today's job on the boat wore me out."

She was exhausted, too. The inside cams posed vigilant. Maybe she would sleep better tonight, but she wanted Jeb to sleep easier, too. "They arrested Peters today."

He froze. "Don't tell me."

She nodded.

The boy's eyes widened, the whites a contrast to his tan. "*He's* the one who broke into the houses? The same man who ate dinner with us and told *me* how to live *my* life?"

"Appears so."

"He's a murderer?" Jeb exclaimed, his voice rising an octave.

Callie shrugged. "He admits to the burglaries, but not the murder or the attack on Steve Maxwell. But they're booking him with all of it, nonetheless."

"I'll be damned."

"Jeb."

"Eighteen, Mom."

"But I'm still your mother." *And your protector.* "You going out early with Zeus tomorrow?"

"No client," he said. "We're sleeping in. Good night."

"Night, sweetheart," she said.

John would be disturbed at his son's choice of charter fishing over college. But he'd be proud of how Jeb stepped up for her—maturing faster than she could ever imagine. Life never traveled the way she expected anymore.

Pauley yelled something, muffled by the closed windows and locked doors.

"He talking to us?" Jeb asked over his shoulder.

Callie shook her head and shut off the living room light. "Who knows? Just give him a wide berth, okay? There's something not right about him."

Pauley was probably saying the same about her.

Chapter 30

"MOM!"

A toddling Jeb scurried under a table, Callie chasing him much like the scene at the Maxwells'. He peered out, giggled, and vanished like a fairy. Straightening, she scanned the kitchen, the living room, under her bed.

"Mom!"

The little scamp had developed supernatural powers, disappearing yet calling out to tease. Why did his voice sound so old?

Bang. Bang. "Mom, wake up. Get out here!"

Callie jolted upright. She slung off the covers, grabbed her .38 from the nightstand, and yanked the door open. "What's wrong?"

Jeb moved shirtless and barefoot in basketball shorts to the kitchen bar and pointed at the breakfast table. Callie slid on her robe.

Out of habit, she stepped noiselessly on the balls of her feet. Entering the bright yellow room, her nightgown barely moved around her legs as she glided in stealth mode, almost expecting the silver dollar and glass of bourbon on the table to jump up and bite.

Jeb approached her side.

"Don't touch it," she ordered, moving closer. A 1977 Eisenhower piece. Not from Papa's collection. A copycat crime? Or had the murderer taken another stash of Papa's coins she didn't know about? Her fingers kneaded the seam of her gown.

"What do we do?" her son asked.

Good question. "First, stay out of this room. Check the doors and windows to see where he came in. Look for anything missing. He always takes a souvenir." She glanced at the microwave clock. Eight a.m. No question she had to report this, but for the moment she wanted to wrap her mind around what had happened. Her investigative techniques were more experienced than the collective police force, and her analysis could make a huge difference in how this case, her case, might be solved.

She fought to wrap her mind around what the burglar would choose of hers, or Jeb's. The trespasser took money from the Rosewoods, a necklace from Mrs. Hanson. The NFL ring from Sophie and the mirror from the Maxwells. Before the cops arrived, Callie would like to be able to tell them what tokens had disappeared from Chelsea Morning.

She inhaled deeply. Peters was in jail, so this had to be an accomplice. Hopefully her nanny cams would ID him. The best way to manage this situation was to remain calm, think methodically.

Difficult to do when someone walked through locks like a ghost.

She rewrapped her robe around her, and pissed off, she tied it snug enough to bite into her waist. Touching her personal items ran a close second to touching her, as if stripped in public. But what boiled her blood was the fact someone relaxed over a drink in her house as she and Jeb slept only feet away. But that's all right. She had the son-of-a-bitch on her cams.

She moved toward Cam One's hiding spot on a book shelf. *Wait. What?* Gone. She rushed to Cam Two, in a pile of greenery around a candle. Also gone. Cams Three and Four, likewise missing. A deep-rooted chill shook her shoulders. How did he know?

One camera left. Cam Five, the one installed in her entertainment center with the best wide angle view of the living room, kitchen, her bedroom entrance, and two of three exits, remained in place. She studied it closer, pushing down her fear. It appeared bent, cracked, and broken, as if squeezed with a wrench . . . with a foreign cam installed beside it.

When had she last checked them? Yesterday, before bed. Good God, he not only breezed past the locks, but he'd installed his own eyes as well as enjoyed his drink. The bastard had hovered only feet from her bedroom.

He must have secreted a camera days before in order to know where she'd planted hers. Or he was just that damn good to thoroughly search and defeat her devices. In spite of her fear, she respected such abilities.

But if he was serious about harming her, why hadn't he done so? That thought alone kept her from freaking out at the moment. He definitely had held the advantage. All he had to do was simply open a door.

Recalling her stupid knee-jerk reaction to throw the once hidden bedroom cam against the wall, she grabbed a CD case and wedged it in front of the lens. Son-of-a-bitch's view was blocked now and fingerprints preserved, not that she expected this guy to have left any.

What had he watched? How much of her life did he know? Scurrying back into her bedroom, her pulse pounding, she prayed three things weren't touched. Surely he hadn't had the nerve to come into her bedroom as she slept, but she knew no limits yet to this guy's behavior. She yanked open her dresser drawer. Bonnie's blanket rested in its tissue paper. She turned. The family picture of all four of them at the beach remained on her nightstand. In the closet, her Neil Diamond album still hid behind her suit.

In her doorway, she held onto the frame, thinking. Then she knew. The cup from Papa Beach's house, the one John had bought her in Boston, the one the culprit had already stolen once and left at Papa's for her to find filled with hot chocolate.

Callie dashed to the kitchen and searched the cabinet over the dishwasher. The cup was gone. She scanned the room, devouring details, hoping to identify his mistakes. Angry impatience tested her resolve to visualize each detail methodically.

"Nothing's missing in my room," Jeb said, returning to her side, standing closer than usual. "Why didn't I hear anything?" The hint of panic in his voice told Callie the danger registered clearly with him.

"Check the doors and windows?" she asked him again as her gaze roamed for more signs of the guy's presence, to distract herself from her own surge of hysteria wedged in her chest. As she steadied her voice, she worried if the intruder had audio abilities as well as visual.

Jeb rolled his eyes, pain on his face. "Damn it, no, I'll check them now." His breaths accelerated as he scratched his neck, his thoughts seeming to scatter.

But she gently took his hand away from its scratching and stilled it. "Stay calm." She nodded toward the entertainment center, to the odd-angled CD case. "We had eyes on us. May still have, if he hid another cam."

"Wha . . ."

"Shhh."

He nodded.

"Good," she said. "I'm going to get dressed, and then I'll call the police. You can change, too. Nonchalantly, okay?"

Jeb nodded again and went toward his room. She lifted her phone from her dresser, carrying it in the closet to grab pants and a shirt. She refused to behave as anyone watching would expect her to, like a crazed, emotional woman.

Before she could lift the jeans off their hanger, someone knocked on the front door with ridiculous incessant repetition. Not Sophie. Too loud. Naked, she clutched her robe back around her and hid the phone in her pocket, to hold her weapon ready.

The knocks turned into heavy-repeated blows, followed by a shout. "Callie Morgan, get your ass out here!"

The voice was Pauley's. "I don't have time for you," she said, voice raised to be heard through the glass.

"Did you turn over my garbage cans?"

She blew out with irritation and lowered the .38. "No. Go away," she yelled.

"No," he hollered back. "You come out here."

She ignored him and turned toward the living room. But she didn't make it to the end of the hall before outside traffic noises suddenly sounded too unexpectedly clear. She whirled, taking aim.

Pauley filled the doorway. "Whoa! Is that how you answer the fuckin' door?"

Callie held her bearing. No question how the burglar had entered now. She was damn sure she double-checked that lock when she went to bed. A brand new lock not two days old.

Not so much fear as an antsy uncertainty skipped across her shoulders and made her step closer, almost too eager to draw down on this man. "I'll warn you one time, Pauley, I'm in no mood to fool with you. Get off my property."

Hearing footsteps climbing the stairs behind Pauley, she tensed, now nervous about brandishing a gun. Lord, don't let it be one of Seabrook's cops.

Mason's head appeared, then the rest of him as he reached Callie's irritated neighbor.

Pauley turned, and Callie hid the weapon in her robe pocket. "Both of y'all, please go."

Mason glanced around with uncertainty. "I just came by to ask you to come with me on a run."

"Not today, Mason." Not wanting the crime scene violated, Callie moved to the porch, herding the others before her. "Y'all need to go."

A scowl swept across Mason's face. "What's wrong?"

Jeb came out to the threshold, frowning. "Mom? Oh, I thought the cops had arrived. You called them, right?"

As she reached for her son, Callie caught Pauley's gaze roaming over her. She tightened her robe, the urge to throw him down her front steps overwhelming.

Mason noted the moment of lust and shoved the man. "Get the hell away from her."

Pauley stumbled back, fright in his face as he windmilled to keep from diving down the stairs backwards. With a last minute save on the banister, he righted himself. "Stupid son of a bitch." He spun and punched Mason in the gut.

Then he laughed and shifted his attention to Callie. "What you gonna do about that, Miss Detective? All half-dressed and off your game. I just nailed your boyfriend."

Mason had doubled over with the light punch, but Callie recognized Pauley's feeble attempt at violence for what it was, a counter statement for the embarrassing afternoon when she'd put his nose in the dirt. However, his lazy lifestyle prohibited anything physical from being lethal. She stepped out of their way, instinctively holding an arm in front of Jeb.

Jerking upright, Mason snatched Pauley by the shirt, set him up properly, and plowed his fist into the man's jaw, propelling Pauley backwards. He stumbled and brushed past Callie into the house. After dancing for purchase on the rumpled entry rug, he went down on his backside, a whiplash motion smacking his head on the floor.

Mason followed inside, ready to snatch his adversary up off the floor and test his mettle again.

"Don't," Callie said. "The two of you—out!"

Pauley's angry finger shook back at her. "I've been assaulted in your house. I'm suing." He rose to his feet with a stagger. "And I'm not leaving.

The police will hear my side on this, right where it happened."

Jeb stepped between him and Callie. "Speaking of cops, where are they, Mom? They can deal with both this guy and the break-in. Maybe he's the burglar come back to see how we reacted."

"Wait a second. I haven't been in your house." Pauley stepped in Jeb's face. The boy braced himself, his posture daring the shorter, older man to try something.

Mason's forehead creased with puzzlement. "Did the intruder come here last night?"

"Yeah," Jeb said, his stare still on Pauley. "While we were sleeping."

"Did you see anything?"

All Callie saw was intent to destroy her confidence and sense of well-being. Raysor was in the hospital, Seabrook busy. Some green cop would only strut and not know what the hell he was doing with all this.

"I saw Peters drive away just a little while ago," Mason said.

Wait. What? She snapped around. "Peters was here?"

Mason shrugged. "He pulled out of your drive."

Instinct held back her response. Peters couldn't have done this, not unless they'd released him on bail or he'd escaped. In either case, Seabrook owed her a call. Unless something happened to Seabrook, too. Or, as lame as it sounded, the cops were involved.

Who the hell was she supposed to trust? She ran her hands over her forehead, stunned and confused, nothing ringing right about this break-in.

Mason pushed a piece of hair out of Callie's face, then reached around and nudged the front door closed.

Jeb scowled at the tender gesture. Callie's posture went rigid at the sudden confinement.

"How did you not hear anything?" Mason asked. "Have you called 9-1-1?"

Nothing made sense. "They arrested Peters for the burglaries last night, Mason. He confessed."

Mason raised his brow in a brief micro-expression of concern . . . and Callie saw it. She juggled her own split-second of doubt . . . then she remembered the Eisenhower coin left on her table, a silver dollar not from Papa Beach's collection, and her thoughts began to gel.

Pauley spoke up. "Told you it wasn't me. You've been in my house, but I never came into yours."

"Shut up, Pauley." Callie's personal alarm shot up tenfold, but this wimp wasn't the man to fear.

Jack Peters had resented residents who'd used Papa Beach, Edisto natives who inadvertently had shirked the handyman. But what had Seabrook told her last night? *You were a good guy, Callie. He liked you.* Even if Peters were loose . . .

Mason touched her shoulder. "Callie? Want me to stay until the authorities arrive?"

She fought the flinch, but her gut feeling gave her away. Mason was lying through his handsome, whitened teeth. She had no time to figure out why. Muscles tightened down her arms and up her legs, instinct telling her to prepare. She eased her hand into her robe pocket.

Mason reached around into her pocket, too, his clean intervention muscling the .38 away. "I don't think so," he said as another weapon found its way under her neck. He waved Callie's piece with a whiff of bravado and then hid it in his pocket.

She recognized a suppressor . . . on what appeared to be her Glock. *He modified my gun!*

Her chest tightened. What other lies constituted the illustrious Mason Howard? Assuming that was his name.

"Wait a minute." Pauley moved hesitantly toward the back door. "I ain't a part of this."

Mason's stare stopped him in place.

Callie froze stock-still, but Pauley's mouth quivered as terror caused him to stutter and ramble. "This don't make sense, man. I mean, not that I—not that you—"

"Shut up." Mason shifted Callie around, gun still to her neck, to better watch Pauley, his pinched expression flashing annoyance with the man. Jeb stiffened at his bedroom doorway. Callie ran logistics, scenarios, and maneuvers, but none of them could outrun Mason's bullet.

"You should've called the cops," Pauley mumbled.

"Yes, when you pounded on my door," she said.

"Such a low-grade life form," Mason said. "So slow and blue collar."

Pauley lost his hang-dog pout and glowered at the insult. Then he inched toward Jeb. "No need for guns, man. Your beef is with this bitch, not me."

"Stay away from my son, Pauley." Callie shifted, even constrained in Mason's grasp, furious at her neighbor's cowardly effort to use Jeb as protection. Unable to intercede, she locked eyes with her son in an attempt to get him to fall back into his room. He made a slight move to follow suit.

"Unh unh. Stand right there," Mason said.

He had all three of them before him. Callie's heart galloped at how quickly they could be dropped. There was only one reason to use a suppressor. No witnesses.

"What the fuck is going on?" Pauley tried to cling to Jeb, who shoved the man aside. Pauley tripped then quickstepped back in place, as if magnetized to the boy. He clung to Jeb's arm, and the boy shrugged him off again.

Shifting her stance ever so slightly, Callie judged the distance, Mason's bulk, the angles, and the odds of overcoming her former jogging partner. Her heart thumped triple time. Nobody knew anything was amiss in Chelsea Morning, and it was all on her to cope with the situation.

"Call Seabrook," Mason said. "Phone's in your pocket. Whether he answers or it goes to voice mail, this is what you're going to say. You can no longer deal with the shit on this beach, so you and Jeb are going to your mother's until all is clear on Edisto. You wish to be alone. No more, no less. Sound distraught, but not hysterical. Otherwise, I drop your kid where he stands."

Pauley let loose of Jeb and whimpered. "I'm not involved, man."

Mason ignored him. To Callie, he asked, "Do you understand?"

She quashed a serious urge to backtalk. "Yes."

His stare still on Callie, Mason swung a stiff arm around. Three rounds pierced Pauley's chest in smooth succession.

Callie jumped at the muffled thuds of the rounds cutting Pauley's torso and into the wall, inches from her son. Jeb screamed and fell back into his room. Pauley slumped to the floor with an anguished gawk of disbelief. Instant death.

Callie rushed forward. "Jeb!" Had a bullet strayed? Hadn't she seen all three hit center mass? Was she sure?

Mason's arm slung her back. "Tell her you're fine, Jeb." A cynical expression on his face, he added, "I wouldn't have missed, Callie. You know how easy it is to hit at this range."

Jeb peered around the doorframe. "I'm . . . I'm okay, Mom."

"See?" Mason said.

Robe crunched in her fingers, she sensed the presence of a hit man who'd fabricated a hell of a charade to get next to her. But why? Why the cam? Why all the pranks and scares with the music, lights, the stolen cup? As fervently as she'd pushed the Russians from her mind, even as long as they'd ignored her, nobody would hire a hit man for her but them. But this was not their way. She tried to sort the chaos in her head and snag some logic. Her on-duty skills to compartmentalize were rusty.

"Make the call," Mason repeated.

He made her hold out the phone as she dialed. With the device on speaker, her heart fell when the call went to voice mail. She recited the message as directed. Then Mason lifted the phone to ensure the call had disconnected. He pocketed it and then asked for Jeb's. He waved mother and son before him, toward the kitchen, and as they reached the bar he yanked the landline cord out of the wall.

The unspoken plan was elementary. Mason had already made it appear as though Callie'd shot Raysor, not knowing she'd been cleared by the cams. Or maybe he did, and now she would appear to have shot Pauley with the same gun. No gun residue, but—

Mason jerked her over, forcing her back tight against his chest, between his arms. Mashing her hand between the both of his, his finger on the trigger, he shot two rounds out the back window toward the marsh. Glass shattered across her desk and back stoop.

Jeb ducked, covering his head, but Callie remained rigid, grasping the intention. No mistaking gun residue now. And bullets into the marsh wouldn't be noticed by tourists headed the opposite way to the surf.

Mason lowered the weapon, hugged her tighter, and whispered, "Details, sweetheart. I think you know what I mean."

She did. And God help her, the cams she'd planted to prove the facts were gone. Nobody knew, or would know, a damn thing, unless she figured something out.

"Jeb?" Mason called.

"What?" Jeb spat back. The boy's young lean body trembled, his fists opening, closing. A large quaking shiver racked him once, tearing into Callie's soul.

"Put a shirt and shoes on, son," Mason said, not in a mean way, but like a favorite uncle would coax a ten-year-old. "You're coming with me."

Callie gasped, then wished she hadn't.

The boy's desperate eyes searched for her guidance, but all she could do was say, "Don't fight him, sweetie."

Inserting the endearment was a miniscule effort to lessen the blow, but if she never saw Jeb again, at least that tiny token of love would be remembered between them. Her quiet restraint would hopefully help him perceive that temper only meant death.

But right now she couldn't think about that. Apparently time was on her side, or they'd both be dead. Mason would take Jeb, goddamn him, but the playboy had to hold some purpose for Callie. For the life of her, she couldn't see what, but she'd fight to take advantage of every second she had.

"Why not just take me?" she asked. "And what have I done to you? We never met before I moved to Edisto, and . . . I thought we were friends, Mason."

"We are friends." Mason pointed toward Pauley's crumpled body. "He and I are not. Big difference." He waved the weapon toward the entertainment center. "Uncover my cam, please."

She removed the CD cover. As she returned it to its place in her library, she tried to ignore the mild shake in her movements. Peters may have entered all the other homes, but no doubting Mason had been her own personal intruder. The reason, however, escaped her, that unknown more unnerving than the actual break-in.

Jeb reappeared clothed.

Mason's happy-go-lucky expression moved from Callie to Jeb. "We're going out the back."

"Mason." Callie choked out the name, moving two steps toward them. "Don't take him. I don't know what you want. I'll do whatever it is, just leave my son out of your plans."

Slick and oh-so-smooth, Mason's smile spread easy across his face, as if to ask her again for a date at Whaley's. "Thanks for asking. I *do* need you to do something."

Jeb flashed a blistering frown. "Don't do it, Mom."

Mason tousled the boy's hair, and Jeb ducked out of reach. "But you don't know what I'm asking, son." He turned to Callie. "Put on your party clothes, my dear. It's Friday, remember? I expect you early, say, around 5:30 so you can help set up. Have Sophie drive since you won't need a ride home."

Callie's eyes widened, completely caught unawares. "This is about your party?"

A deeper, devious grin melted into place. "Oh, Callie. This is about so much more than a party."

Chapter 31

AS HE ESCORTED Jeb firmly toward the back door, Mason spoke over his shoulder to Callie. "Don't leave the house except to retrieve Sophie." He glanced toward the cam. "Trust me, I'll know. You found one of my babies. There are others."

His words gut-kicked her. Had he seen Jeb's comings and goings? Her session with Stan in the living room, in the bedroom? God, he could've snatched Jeb at any time. No wonder he knew when she ran.

Or was it a bluff?

"I already took care of your dad. Arrive with your happy face, or I'll kill Jeb and the illustrious *Beverly*, too. Primp. Make me proud." He winked. "Let me see a dress on you for a change."

Callie swayed and clutched the porch railing at the mention of her father. Tears blurred her vision as she watched Jeb. His expression ripped at her sanity. This was too much. Too, too much. "I don't understand, Mason," she pleaded. "Please, explain it to me." She couldn't let them drive away.

"Just do as I say. Stay indoors and keep Pauley company. I'll see you at 5:30. Any earlier or later, and . . . you know. I have friends all over Edisto. Even Sophie would tell me where you went." He yanked Jeb's arm. "Say goodbye to your mother."

Jeb's face reflected wet with angry tears, but Callie registered the tenderness in spite of the fright in his eyes. "I love you, Jeb." She choked as the two men descended the stairs, her stolen gun nudged against Jeb's kidney.

"I know. I love you, too." His forehead creased in agony as he defiantly glanced back. "This isn't your fault, Mom. Remember that."

She held the banister, knees almost buckling as they walked away. How could any of this not be her fault? She had ignored her instinct to keep Mason at bay. The reason for his behavior totally escaped her, which left her powerless. He hadn't expected Peters to be locked up, that much was clear. Maybe he'd planned to kill Pauley all along and frame her with his murder. But why? Who the hell was Mason, and what was his motive?

What the fuck was she missing?

Her heart's crazed beat blocked all else. Lips parched, her gulps of air grew more hitched and ragged as Jeb's car crunched gravel and shells out of the drive. The Jeep cruised up Jungle Shores then turned left, Jeb at the wheel, Callie branding the vision on her brain.

Her nails dug splinters from the freshly painted wood. Bonnie's death had torn her soul to shreds. John's drove her borderline psychotic. Lawton's crushed her sense of family. Losing Jeb would . . . She rushed back into the house and shut the door, tears dripping off her chin.

Callie drew up short. Pauley's cold eyes stared from a body that had ceased oozing blood.

Suddenly the room was a vacuum.

Spinning around, she bolted for the outdoors, needing fresh air, only to halt. Mason warned her to stay inside. Controlled. Captive in her own home. Without her child.

She dropped to her knees. Her heart battered against her sternum. No . . . time for . . . anxiety attacks. This wasn't . . . about her. But her airways clinched tighter, suffocating, ignoring her duty as a mother. She counted, like she had the seconds to spare, but her brain didn't register. Black crept in around the edges of her vision.

No, no, no. Jeb needed her.

Blackness took over as she dropped to the floor.

BIRD TWITTER WOKE her, her cheek resting on her blue braided rug. Past the legs of the dining room table, she saw Pauley propped against the wall outside Jeb's bedroom, and like the crack of a .38 shot, she remembered.

The dead man's odor permeated her home, a reminder of her murdered Papa Beach. Fresh, acrid death. She sat up, the robe twisted around her legs. To her left, the cable box across the room read ten thirty.

Seven hours until the scheduled meet. Jeb. Her fear couldn't compare to his, which she refused to imagine. He was naive enough to hope, and she prayed he would, but in her experience as a cop, ultimatums went sour more times than not. Bad guys lied, pure and simple. They made promises they never intended to keep. Her hands twisted material and became entangled in her gown as she saw no alternative but to do as she was told, knowing she walked into a noose. The only question was what would happen to her and Jeb before Mason pulled the lever . . . assuming Mason hadn't dealt with Jeb already.

Deep in her belly, a ferocity built. Saliva spilled as she tasted the carnal urge to scream. But instead, she remembered the cam she'd been told to uncover, and those she probably hadn't found yet. She had to believe Jeb was locked up somewhere, still alive, his captor watching for her to make wrong moves. She came to her feet.

Somehow she had to make this right.

Think this through.

Corral that useless emotion and channel it. *Think, Callie, think.* She hadn't expected Mason to be involved. What spurred him? Why now?

She suspected that Peters' low-key arrest last night, done without fanfare and without public awareness, had unexpectedly exacerbated today's events and caught Mason unawares. Mason had frequently made his distaste for Peters evident. Just yesterday, the playboy had sat in his Jag, warning her about the man about to install her motion sensors.

She sniffed and wiped her face. Maybe she had forced Mason's move by expediting the outdoor security installation on her home, unknowingly doing it on a Thursday, the eve of one of his parties. But what the hell did the party have to do with anything? He'd have so many witnesses.

Dragging herself to her bedroom, she shut the door and did a cursory search for another cam. Finding none, she climbed onto her bed and tucked into a fetal position, forcing her analytical mind to work. She had hours to ponder options . . . hours to go nuts. By holding Jeb, Mason knew she wouldn't go to Seabrook or any other authority. He was right. She was in this by herself.

Her forced, scripted phone call to Seabrook would only stall the cop from coming by, maybe a day at best. By then, people would comment about seeing her at the party. He'd question Sophie first, then get worried at the contrast between Callie's phone call and her actions, maybe get irate that she'd misled him, possibly for the opportunity of a date with Mason. By then, Mason would have performed whatever deed was in his plan. The call to Seabrook was a short term fix, because by dawn the next day, she predicted Mason, Jeb, and she would all be gone, in one fashion or another.

Mason had the financial means to hire anyone and bribe the rest. Even if his resume was a complete fabrication, no question he harbored deep pockets. Jeb could be whisked away by hired cohorts, no longer even on the island. Or in the trunk of a car, trussed in a closet, or taken out to sea.

Good God, this was agony!

Images of Jeb tried to block her ability to think clearly. She struggled past those visions, over the disabling fear that Jeb was already too gone to save.

Seabrook had never liked Mason. Mason's direction for her to leave a message with Seabrook told her the cop wasn't in on it. But she still couldn't afford to call him for assistance. Until she figured out Jeb's location, she would comply with her instructions. One slip, and Jeb would be gone. She was shrewd enough to know Mason planned to kill him anyway. Her, too. This was all about timing . . . and recognizing a split-second opportunity.

As a detective, she never related to those desperate people who took matters into their own hands, leaving cops out of the equation. Now she did. She needed complete control of the situation. The local PD had little experience with big crime, and the State Law Enforcement Division would take over the reins and cut her out. The more people involved, the more mistakes would be made. And they'd ban her from participation.

There was no stereotypical phone call or random note from a secluded kidnapper here. Mason would party out in the open at Water Spout with the beach crowd that loved his generous hospitality. And he had already delivered his ransom orally, in person. Mason could feign ignorance to everything.

Thinking of Pauley's lifeless form, she swallowed hard. Rigor would set in soon and almost be complete by the time she went to the party. She had no proof Mason shot Pauley, especially using her gun. Everything she said against Mason could be easily explained away or covered up.

But none of that mattered if she lost Jeb.

Her stomach wrenched, and an imaginary fist squeezed her heart. If she couldn't keep that thought suppressed, she'd never hold it together. She needed proof of life, which wouldn't happen unless she went to that party and played this without the badges.

She slid from the bed, instinctively putting the coverlet and pillows neatly in place. One p.m. If she didn't contact Sophie soon, she might come knocking in all her bangled glory, if for no other reason than to coax Callie again to go to this goddamn party.

As if preparing for company, Callie went to the linen closet and pulled out a quilt and a blanket, ever hunting for another cam. With a toss, she used the blanket to cover Pauley, the quilt to disguise the shape of the body, neither one tucked or smoothed. Just laundry piled on the floor.

Damn Mason for giving her so much time.

She should have listened to Seabrook from the start.

She'd go to Sophie's and leave Chelsea Morning dark and unoccupied in keeping with her voice mail to Seabrook. Callie turned on the shower, her robe dropped to the floor, and as the water warmed, she wrote a note, carefully wording the day. A last declaration. Facts, no emotion. She signed it slowly, without flourish, an ominous veil of no return settling over her. Folding the paper, she laid it on her bed for Seabrook to find.

Then she stepped into the shower. As warm water flowed over her, she shifted positions and recalled with a wave of nausea that at one time she'd fondled erotic thoughts of Jeb's kidnapper sharing her bath.

SHORTLY AFTER THREE, Callie paused on Sophie's porch and adjusted her long earrings. With her hands stretched open then fisted, she inhaled for composure, pained that Mason's instructions involved her carefree neighbor.

Sophie answered with a song on her lips that abruptly ceased. "Callie! I was getting ready to come over and—" She inhaled with drama. "Oh my, look at you. What's up?"

Callie stared down at her cream-colored gauze dress, with gold and aqua embroidery crawling down the side and around the hem that brushed mid-calf. A belt cinched the dress taut to accent her figure, and the bodice dipped between her breasts with four gold chains drawing the eye to her cleavage. Beaded turquoise earrings hung low enough to tease her shoulders. A wide, wrapping multi-colored scarf traveled around her back and draped over each arm, her attempt to cover the burn scar.

"Is it too much?" she asked. "You are going to Mason's event, aren't you? Sorry I didn't call first, but I was afraid I'd change my mind."

Sophie beckoned Callie inside, the ex-cop's gold strappy sandals taking a slight skid on the carpet. Callie had worn them once before, on holiday with John. Actually, the entire outfit had been mostly John's choosing. Never had she hoped to wear it again, but this evening she chose to channel John's presence to save their son.

"Honey." Sophie glided in a circle around Callie. "You are so pretty!" Clasped hands to her chin, Sophie sang in singsong, "You're going to the party." Her sculpted brows waggled up and down. "And getting laid, I take it."

Callie forced down the bile. "This dress okay?"

The squints and head tilts told her Sophie pondered adjustment. "Good base, honey, but we need to deepen the make-up and poof your do. The jewelry works, but don't you ever paint your nails?"

Just what Callie had expected. "I don't have much make-up. Don't own any nail polish, and what's wrong with my hair?" She touched it, as if concerned. "Do we have enough time to fix this? Mason said be there at 5:30 and asked if you'd be nice enough to bring me. He said you'd be more than willing to drive."

With a jump, Sophie squealed. "He's getting you there before dusk, and I'm the pumpkin coach to your ball. This is fabulous! Yes, yes. This'll be fun!"

The squeal pierced Callie's head, and she smiled for show. "You have all this sex appeal, and I . . . I don't . . ." *Don't know what the hell I'm doing!*

"Throw off those shoes and park it on my sofa, girl." Sophie scurried into her bedroom, shouting back. "I have a nail color that'll make those gold sandals glitter decadent. And shadow to give you that come-hither-and-I'll-do-you-right-now appeal. Oh, and I love that you didn't wear a slip under that dress. Nicey dicey, honey."

Callie sat and wrapped an arm across her midsection. A tremulous chill coursed through her body as she fought to put her actions into perspective. Costuming. That's all this was. Dressing for the show. Going undercover.

At four thirty, Callie blew and waved her fingers to dry the polish and hide the shake as Sophie touched up her toes.

Over the past hour, Callie's worry for Jeb would rise to red-hot levels of anxiety, then she'd push it down, reminding herself of why she was doing this. It repulsed her that she performed such frivolous behaviors while Jeb was probably freaked out of his mind.

She rued moving to Edisto. Her father's decision to deed the house . . . She shoved his visage aside. She didn't know why Mason had killed Lawton, but no doubt it connected to her presence, her actions, her inactions, and her ignorance.

Meanwhile, the Gypsy dabbed, painted, and stroked eight different products on Callie's face, at one point smoothing her wrinkled forehead. "Chill. It'll be fun."

At five, Callie rested on the sofa, trying to hold down a Coke as Sophie primped herself in the bedroom, humming and flitting about as if *she* had the date.

Callie stumbled to the kitchen at one point, gulping air to hold down her drink. She washed the glass and hunted for a drying cloth. As she opened drawers in the foreign kitchen, she paused at the one near the stove. In a split second, she pilfered a paring knife, hiding the small weapon in her strappy gold bag. A bag too tiny for a gun and, hopefully, too innocent to warrant suspicion.

"Taa daa!" Sophie spun into the room, a bandana skirt tight and low on her hips but flared and flouncy around her legs. One large bandana tied across her breasts in halter style, secured behind her neck and waist. A dozen tiny sterling silver bracelets complemented huge circle earrings. Long silver chains hung to her naval, some with red glass beads. The lashes were new, contacts a different blue, and her curls kicked up like a Tinker Bell fairy.

"You put me to shame, Sophie," Callie said. The clock read five fifteen. *We need to go!*

Sophie took Callie's arm and escorted her to the door. "I am so thrilled," the neighbor said, scrunching her shoulders. "Everyone will be just too jealous of us."

At the door, however, Sophie took Callie's arms and faced her with concern. "I know I push and prod, Callie, and I may be a bit of a busy gnat, but I have worried so much about you. Are you sure this is what you want?" She licked her finger and touched Callie's brow. "Tell me the truth."

"Sophie." Callie inhaled deeply. "I don't think I've ever wanted anything more in my life."

Chapter 32

AT 5:32 P.M. CALLIE'S bracelets, loaned by Sophie, clanked as she reached for the doorbell beside Water Spout's huge eight-foot tall double doors. White-coated people carried items in and out of a catering van in the circular drive. How late would Mason consider two minutes?

Both doors swung in, Mason poised in the middle, an unlit cigar in his fingers. "Ladies! You're the first to arrive. Welcome, welcome."

Sophie ran in and hugged him. "I'm so excited you asked me to escort your date. The two of you seem so cute together, Mason." She twirled and held out her hand, expecting a kiss on it.

His lips brushed across her fingers. "So delicious. As is my spread tonight. Come in and see what the caterer has on his menu. He might just let you sample, Sophie."

In a flurry of color, she took off inside, knowing her way.

Mason glanced up at the sky. "Plenty of daylight left. You should feel comfortable about that." He held out his arm. Callie strolled in without taking it, but he wrenched her back by the wrist.

"Let me refresh your memory, sweetheart." He shut the doors and pushed her ahead of him, maintaining a hold feigned as taking her elbow. He nodded to two of the catering assistants in passing and exited out a side door to a monstrous wrapped, covered porch that faced the gray Atlantic Ocean. Gunmetal-colored clouds dipped down to the water on the horizon, hinting of the rain expected the day before.

He lightly released her and said calmly, "He's out there somewhere."

She hung her head, crestfallen at his confirmation that Jeb was adrift on the water in God knows what type of boat, with God knows who. Assuming Mason even told the truth, which disturbed her more. She still saw no markers from which to judge the man or determine her potential action.

Cocked against a post, he clipped his cigar. "Then play the part. You're my date. You're extremely happy to be at my side. You're dignified yet smitten. Some of the residents have concerns after so much has happened on your street, coincidentally from the day you moved in. Rumors galore. Tonight we replace it with new gossip of our own making, a tale that will make the others pale in comparison." He lit the cigar, puffed it rapidly, then pulled in a longer draw, the end now glowing orange. The sweet smoke quickly whipped away in the growing breeze.

He was milking every emotional angle of this affair. Assuming he was a hit man, he'd probably been told to enjoy himself—to a certain degree. Or maybe he really was a Canadian restaurateur, with a twisted mind and sick fetishes who'd taken a liking to her and decided to set a game into play. Callie's mind raced now that this scenario was in play, trying to deduce, seeking her bearings, but all she had was thin air and no clues.

"I'll help Sophie," Callie said, itching to search the house for signs of her son, for a camera feed from her house, maybe for a feed to Jeb.

Mason moved to a settee and patted the cushion. "I hire people to tend my needs and then pair them with the Sophies of this world." He waved his cigar toward the water. "Sit."

As if he owned the upscale rental, he spoke about the three-level house being custom designed by some Charleston architect, combining contemporary design features with Spanish influence. The house flaunted a concrete, not shell and gravel, driveway with parking for ten cars; soaring ceilings, multiple arches, floor to ceiling windows, and a four-door sliding access to the deck enhanced the spaciousness. The huge wall of glass offered an immense view of St. Helena Sound from the great room. All anyone would see from the road was parked cars. Action faced the water. Action Seabrook would never see from Windswept, his home right across the street.

After a night in Walterboro with Peters, Seabrook had probably gone home and crashed. He ought to be up by now, shaking his head at yet another extravagant fete by Mason Howard. Seabrook probably had retrieved her voice mail, too, her change of heart niggling at him a bit.

He would worry about her well-being. He might try to call, then unable to get her, drive by her dark, unlit house. Her car would be in the drive, but he'd easily assume they'd taken Jeb's. Nothing appearing amiss. Just a woman who couldn't control her emotions.

And as badly as she wanted him to read the shallowness of her voice mail and hunt for her, call Sophie, contact Beverly, she just as badly hoped he didn't.

If he got creative enough to drop by and question Mason before Callie learned of Jeb's whereabouts, her son was dead. Mason could deny any accusations she made, point to her paranoid behavior, and ultimately blame her for Pauley's death. Maybe even Papa Beach's as well. Seabrook had seen her take Pauley down and brandish a weapon in public; he knew her skills. Nobody pictured Mason in that sort of light, but everyone would suspect her.

But what was worse, in all the time lost in proving she was innocent, nobody would hunt for Jeb until the confusion settled and it was too late, if they searched at all. He was a teenager who ran off. Nobody had seen him kidnapped.

Even Sophie would testify that Callie had painted herself up for the Friday night gala. Who did that and left a body in her home? Insanity at its finest. Or a complete disregard for the law. The ex-detective irrationally taking matters into her own hands. Not too far from the truth.

She'd been suckered into Mason's world and set up to fall. God, he was slick. He was also fucked up, sold-my-soul-to-the-devil crazy, and she was the only person who knew.

"What time does the party start?" she asked.

"Seven, but the eager ones are here by six thirty." Mason draped an arm around her shoulders. "Jeb's fine. Enjoy the moment. The caterer promised some grand hors d'oeuvres tonight the likes that Edisto's never seen."

Minutes dragged. Sophie brought them drinks with a giggle, then disappeared inside. Callie waited until Mason turned to blow smoke away, and she reached over to pour the liquor in the shrubbery.

He caught her arm. "How rude to waste my liquor. It's top shelf gin, bought for you. Drink it."

She downed the drink, his hand guiding her, barely giving her a breath. Like a morphine shot, it radiated throughout her system to warm her limbs and remove a fraction of her fear. She prayed it wasn't drugged.

She wished it didn't taste so good.

Voices sounded in the house. She turned, ever hopeful to capitalize on a chance. Two men appeared. "Mason!"

He stood. "Glad you could make it again."

One of the guys peered around Mason to Callie. "Who do we have here? An import?"

"Oh no," Mason said and swept his drink toward his date. "Callie, step over here and meet some of my guests. Gentlemen, this is Callista Jean Morgan, ex-Boston detective and newest permanent resident of Edisto Beach." He tipped his head. "Come on, sweetheart. Don't be shy."

She made her way to his side, under the auspices of his possessive embrace. For that, she earned the first kiss of the night.

The gentlemen chuckled. "Detective," exclaimed one of the men. "I'm Edisto PD. Dickens spoke of you."

She greeted him with a nod. "Nice to meet you."

"Boy, Boston has some sweet detectives," said the other. "I work at the fire department, by the way."

She nodded. Mason blatantly had the beach wrapped around his finger. Even if she pulled these guys aside to help her, she'd have to undo her reputation to diminish Mason's. A move difficult to accomplish with the players laced with booze and beholden for free, expensive food.

Hell, how was this going to work?

With people arriving, they moved inside. Mason introduced Callie to everyone as his love of the moment. She met town councilwomen, Wyndham executives, several attorneys, and a slew of local businesspeople.

"When did you make your move on this devil, Callie?" asked a flamboyant real estate agent whose name Callie had seen on three dozen signs along the beach.

"I wooed *her*, actually." Mason ran a finger along the nape of Callie's neck. She tried to smile at him as expected. But as she turned her head up, Mason planted his mouth on hers. She resisted. He backed away and whispered, "With tongue, Callie."

His hand behind her head, he kissed her again, his tongue thrusting deep, owning her. She couldn't swallow. Her stomach lurched in disgust, but she needed to hold strong. Then with a swift wrap around her waist, he bellied up against her. Horrified, she froze, but his fingertips embedded suddenly in her derriere, reminding her to reciprocate. She envisioned where this evening would end and almost vomited.

"Damn, Mason," yelled a rotund resident from across the room. "That made me horny all the way over here!"

The room clapped, and a few catcalls bounced off the twenty-foot walls.

Callie drew back and feigned a coy reaction. Women, however, raised brows and frowned around the room.

This escapade was not about sex, but Mason still enjoyed the charade. Who the hell was he, or who did he represent? If she were still on the job, she'd mentally rifle her Rolodex of arrests hunting for a disgruntled perp. But this was tiny Edisto. And she hadn't been a cop for over two years.

Psychopath, mob, mafia, any of a dozen ethnic and terrorist groups flashed in her mind. Any of those would have made more sense, if she'd been in Boston.

Or . . . could he be a political enemy of Lawton?

What was his weakness? He was a murderer. Slick. He couldn't afford not to kill her.

No doubt about it . . . she'd just have to kill him first.

Her eyes darted back to the water that served as backdrop to the house. Night had fallen, and surprisingly, her concern for Jeb had overwhelmed her fear of dusk.

No lights shined on the horizon. But the boat holding Jeb hostage could float dark, or be so far out, north or south along the coast, that he was out of view. Or there wasn't a boat at all. She really needed to search the house.

"Bathroom break, Mason."

He shoved another drink at her. The third. Each more potent than the one before. "Drink this before you go."

She chugged it down and returned the glass, like a mental patient required to take her meds.

"Now I can spare you a minute," he replied, then turned to a new guest carrying a plate loaded with prosciutto-wrapped figs, endive boats of crabmeat, and sea bass wraps. As the food passed by her, she held her breath against the smells that suddenly disagreed with her.

The bathroom in the hallway was occupied. She ran down the hall to another door. Locked. Then further, until she found herself in the master suite. After securing the master bath door behind her, she stooped over the commode, rammed fingers down her throat, and vomited every drop of gin she could muster.

She had to keep sober, or the night was for naught.

After washing her mouth, she turned and rested her forehead against the cool marble wall. Nausea subsided, she snatched open drawers and searched the cabinets for anything to use against the man. With the place being a rental and a cleaning service at Mason's disposal, the cabinets were bare. She pulled out the last. Shaving supplies. She stole the manicure scissors and buried them into the backside of her woven belt. One weapon in her purse, another on her. Too much time was passing. She could feel herself becoming desperate.

She exited into the bedroom, a colorful composite of harsh reds and golds and bold lines of black, with an ornate folk art tapestry of horses on the high wall at the head of the bed. Very masculine with an exotic flavor. Gold braid and tassels.

Hearing nobody coming, she turned back the deep, plush red comforter and searched under the mattress then the pillows for a weapon. He'd stolen two of her guns and probably hoarded a couple of his own. Anyone armed kept a gun near the bed. But she found nothing.

"Callie?"

Mason's voice came from down the hall at the other bathroom door. He probably thought she'd locked herself in.

She smoothed the rumpled comforter. Then she peered in his mirror to put the proper expression on her face.

"What are you doing in here?" he asked in the doorway.

She rubbed her lips together and closed her lipstick tube. "Someone else was in the bathroom. I came back here to use yours."

He strode over, lifted her purse, and extracted the knife as if sure of its existence. "Guess the kitchen's off limits for you." Passing the purse to her, he palmed the knife and escorted her back to the party. Leaning over, he whispered, "You're too cool, my dear. Who puts on lipstick while wondering if her son is alive? I assume you found no weapons?"

With that jolt of reality, she slowed. He grinned, excellent at reading her. Was she too aloof? Not scared enough? How the hell was she supposed to act?

They reentered the throng in the living room, winding amongst Edisto's finest who'd taken over this home. Two waiters could barely keep up with the refills. Mason passed the knife to one of them and took Callie to the porch where at least twenty people draped in the dark across banisters, railings, and chairs, the food and drink having lightened everyone's spirits.

Her nerves hummed just under the skin. She fought the urge to scratch the scar on her arm.

"Drink," Mason said, with another full glass.

She took a sip, then under his piercing stare, drank a third of the contents. His face softened, then as he carried on a conversation about politics, she snagged three hors d'oeuvres from a waiter who glided by. She wolfed them down before Mason could notice, to soak up the booze.

Anything for Jeb.

TWO IN THE MORNING. With most of the guests gone, Mason rounded up the inebriated stragglers and had one of his hired assistants take them home. As he aided one guest down the stairs along with a dramatic dose of thanks for attending the event, Sophie scooted over to Callie in the foyer. "Mike called. Asked why you weren't answering your phone. I told him I didn't know. Was that okay?"

Seabrook was double-checking his message, wanting to make a connection even if she had returned to Middleton. But Callie still couldn't afford for him to interfere. Not yet.

"That was fine, Sophie. There's no need for him to come here and make a scene. I'm with Mason. What about that can't Mike understand?"

"Oh, honey, I get it. Wish I had your problem, though." She rolled her eyes, then cupped Callie's chin. "I knew your life would turn around. I'm so happy for you."

Goddammit, get this woman out of here!

Mason returned, a slight hesitation in his step when he saw the two women engrossed in chat. "Now, Sophie, are you in the proper shape to drive home?"

"Oh, Mason. I nursed one drink all night. My body is my temple, as I tell my yoga students. Your party was divine, by the way."

His charm shined from behind his flawless smile. "I'm glad to hear it. I'll see to Callie's return, if you don't mind."

"Don't mind at all." She fumbled through her clutch and retrieved keys. "Oh, I snitched a few of the canapés." She held up a napkin-wrapped snack. "Well, you kids have fun. Call me tomorrow, Callie." Then she twittered in song the whole way out.

The door shut as if sealing a tomb.

Mason strolled past her to the vast sweep of windows facing the water.

Callie followed, holding her posture strong, her voice steady, while her heartbeat fought to tear out of her chest at what had to be a pivotal moment. "I've performed at your party and become the latest rumor."

"Well played, too," he said, staring out to sea.

"Where's Jeb?"

"In due time," he said, his back to her. "The party isn't quite over."

"Of course it's not," she said, shoulders slumped.

He turned and approached her, at the same time waving for her to meet him halfway, still able to show warmth in his eyes. Any normal woman would melt under that gaze. His long tanned body, alluring with those runner's thighs, flat abs, and dark hair to get lost in. Add the money, and what woman wouldn't see packaged perfection.

But perfection never proved perfect.

"I need proof of life," she said. "If he's dead, then I might as well be, too."

He brushed her cheek, letting his touch fall along her neck, his thumb moving her scarf to caress her collarbone. "Callie, such drama."

She stepped back against the wall. A row of light switches dug into her back, and a few toggled up under her painful reaction to push off them. A set of sconces came on to her left. The porch lit up.

Mason smiled as if empathetic. Then he reached around her and shut off the porch lights. "Can't have the police knocking on my door telling me to keep it dark for those damn turtles, now, can we?" He dimmed the living room lights to a dramatic low, the cloudless night making it seem darker still.

Oh, damn.

His hand stayed behind her, his thumb rubbing up and down her waist.

Would it matter if she let him have her? If it saved Jeb . . . even if Jeb was dead already and she was left alone, it was just a physical act. The man could not possess her mind. In the grand scheme of life, what damn difference did it make?

Unless he was perverted, kinky, sick. Still, for Jeb . . .

His hand regained its position on her collarbone and rubbed. A finger crawled under her necklaces. Like a snake, the scarf seemed to glide from around her on its own, and soon his other hand rested on the opposite side of her neck, operating in tandem.

In a swoop, he shoved the thin straps of her dress bodice off her shoulders. Her arms crossed to cover her bared breasts, her fingers searching for edges of the material to help her recover as icy fear conflicted with her bravado.

Mason let her replace the straps.

This was a game. To her it could be leverage. Assuming she could keep the dreaded sense of foreboding from overwhelming her focus.

"Proof of life, Mason," she reminded him. Even in the immense living room with its floor to ceiling glass and echo, claustrophobia smothered her as he leered only two feet away.

He hissed in a tone he'd never used with her before. "If he's alive, then show me you wish him to remain so."

Her ear picked up on the wording. She didn't discern why, but like a current coming into the line, she felt something familiar spark. "This is a vendetta, not sex. What do you think I did? What did I do?"

"Soon enough. Over our post-coital cigarette, hmm?" His gaze trailed over her, lingering on places. "I could forcefully take you."

"You'd come away scarred."

He brushed her arm. "Like you?"

"Worse."

Mason scoffed. His patience intact.

"I must see my son. He's everything to me," she said. "Maybe you don't fully comprehend the meaning of family."

Darkness flew across his face, wild, a stark contrast to the man's normal demeanor.

Shit, what had she said?

He looked away, then snapped back to stare at her, as if correcting himself. She could see him wrestling with what to say next. Heaven help her, she needed to know what button she'd pushed, because therein lay his weakness . . . and her strength.

Chapter 33

MASON PAUSED off-balance in the wake of her remark. He hesitated, clenching his jaw, then released it as if catching himself.

Fueled by this challenge of discovery, where each word and glance could drop a hint, Callie sought to maintain the conversation and bait him. At least until she could put the pieces together.

"So, you *do* know something about family," she said. "Does that upset you for some reason?"

This ladies' man was a cliché she'd identified the moment she'd met him. His manners enticed people, but he ran shallow quickly. She didn't want to think about how many women had fallen for his suave comportment in hopes of enjoying that red master suite in reward. The lush gold carpet. The opulent red bed. The ornate mixture of colors in the folk art tapestry: the black horses with yellow saddles and red reins. Not standard rental decor. Those were his things he'd added to reinforce his macho, virile environment.

Oh my gosh.

She pushed down a reaction. She expected the danger of rape or the chance of murder, but suddenly she almost audibly heard a clue fall into place.

A sneer lifted the ends of his lips, as if energized by her change, and he wrapped his arms around her. "Oh, Callie, nothing upsets me. You're all I need right now." He shifted and squeezed her tighter, as if making a point. "I assure you I'm quite good. New experiences for you, maybe. Some rather unique, but exhilarating. I promise." He reached down and stroked her damaged forearm. "No scars at all."

A lightning jolt of terror shot from head to toe. In Boston she'd seen the results of fetishes and the stomach-churning methods of sadomasochism. Strangulation taken too far by one particular member of the Russian family.

"Afterwards, I may let you walk away. Maybe even with your son," he said, seating her on the sofa.

Liar. "Mason, please. I . . . I need water." She croaked the words, as if parched and afraid, kneading the cushion to stay focused.

He released her and stepped to the kitchen from the huge living area, continually cutting his eyes at her. No words, just watching. He returned and set a napkin and a drink on the coffee table. "Alcohol makes the experience sweeter."

As he sat to join her, she replied, "*Spasibo*" in Russian.

"*Pozhalujsta*," he said. "You're welcome." His pause melted into a grin. "Very good, Callie."

Her paranoia about Russian mobsters had not been paranoia. The long-time stalker she'd imagined, no, sensed in spite of naysayers had just wooed her instead of shooting her in the back of the head.

He wasn't simply someone's hit man.

As her heart pummeled her ribs, she feared he'd notice the heavy beats with her half-exposed chest. Her head sent klaxon messages to run, but instead, she sipped the drink, both feet square on the floor. "So, which bastard relation to Leo Zubov are you?"

"Georgy," he said, allowing a slice of his accent to show. "Nephew."

"I see." She nodded calmly, while her insides whirled in an uproar. "The family must put a lot of trust in you." Glancing around the living room, she looked toward the kitchen, across remnants of the evening's gala scattered across counters and tables. "Especially to invest so much money into you, this house, the parties, the Jag . . . this vendetta."

She rested her gaze on him and held it. Waiting.

With enough police work over time, cops amass experience. They talk to people, and if they luck out and land a great field training officer, they learn to read nuances. If she focused on Jeb, Mason would win. She had to keep the focus on her, to buy time. If she kept him mentally distracted, she might tap his impatience, and hopefully he'd make a mistake.

A small window, but therein lay her edge.

"The family," he said and spat.

"They never sanctioned you, did they?" she said. "Do they even know you're here?"

Mason snatched her wrist, sending her glass flying. "I do what I want." *Damn! He was a lone wolf.*

There weren't any henchmen. No accomplices. No contract on her. *Shit!* Jeb was probably somewhere in the fucking house. She fought the urge to jump up and run room to room.

He was Russian and hated her. But without the family behind him, what drove him this friggin' hard?

"But you rented this house months ago," she said, channeling control with every shred of effort she could muster. Her eyes couldn't help but dart around the place. Jeb might be within earshot. She yearned to scream his name.

While Mason held her wrist, his other hand ran up and down her arm, rougher this time, in and out from under her bodice, sending shivers. He grinned seeing the goose bumps. "When you moved to Middleton, I came south. I followed you once to your beloved Papa Beach's house. I liked

Edisto with its beaches. A working vacation. And it was close enough to you." His strokes turned into a clench on her other wrist, and he shook her once. "You thrilled me moving here. And the fun began! Like an omen."

She winced at his tight hold. "I threw you by planning to install motion sensors, didn't I?"

"Yes. No more picking your new locks, though I welcomed the challenge each time. Would have been a shame breaking out a window. The cheap locks that agent put on the Beechum house were worthless, with Pauley too stupid to change them. But no matter," he said, his accent slipping between words. "I tired of the game. I've been picking locks since I was ten."

Her fingers grew numb. "Papa Beach was not a game."

He clenched stronger.

"You killed my uncle. Yes, I killed your Papa Beach." He glared. "It hurts deep inside when people whom you care about are taken away. You needed to feel the same pain."

"You took the coins to feign a burglary."

"And your stupid Peters found them in the trash where I threw them." Mason sneered. "He played his own game after that. I just took advantage."

She fisted and tried to pull free. He held firm. "You overpowered Steve Maxwell to stack charges against Peters," she said, "so he'd get charged with Papa's death."

"Stupid handyman should have stuck to building mailboxes."

Yes. He should have. "You bastard. You ran my father into a tree!"

"The goal was both your parents, but alas." He released her and widened his hands. "He gave me such an opportunity on that road. All those trees."

"Why now? Why not in Boston, or even Middleton? Why wait two years?"

He smiled. "I wanted you to feel like your world had returned to normal. So I could ruin it once again."

She'd been wise all along to watch over her shoulder for Russians. Her police skills *hadn't* left her. "You won. Congratulations. Now drive away, Mason. You've made your point. Take your Jag and disappear. There's no evidence against you." She'd go to jail for Pauley's murder sooner than lose Jeb. "It's my word against yours, and nobody—"

He shot to his feet and yanked her up against his chest. "You fail to truly see the man who stands before you."

His creepy stare sent a chill writhing up her spine, but she had to continue this demented game. "So tell me about him, *Georgy.*"

"I'd rather show you." A wry smile crept across his face, but he gave her the barest brush of a kiss. "Tomorrow I'll brag to my family that not only did I kill your husband, but I fucked his wife, the woman responsible for the death of Leo Zubov."

Ringing filled Callie's ears, intensifying. A shadow blocked all light as her husband's assassin slammed his mouth on hers and grew hard against her belly.

Emotion exploded in her head with memories of the second story collapsing, sparks and flames shooting into a night sky. Shrapnel ripping her arm. Jeb screaming.

Mason pushed her off balance and fell harshly atop her onto the sofa. As he weighed her down he raised her skirt, groping her outer thigh enough to bruise. His fingers crawled to her inner thigh, squeezing.

John. In how many ways have I let us down?

Mason repeatedly grabbed at her flesh under her dress, mashing, kneading.

She reached, prying, searching to snare a digit to disable his hold. Unable to grasp one, she shoved at him. His weight only pressed heavier, whooshing air out of her lungs. With a spasmodic jerk, her eyes flew open as he harshly fondled her pubic area. But she couldn't roll out from under him. One arm lay wedged under her, and he pinned the other back. She mashed her eyes shut again when Mason bit her neck.

Jeb healed after the fire because of you. He's a grown man because of you. Don't give up your life when he needs you most.

Mason's crushing vise on her breasts snatched her back to attention. She couldn't fight against his strength, so she said the first thing that came into her head. "You're a sick, twisted, pathetic misfit that your family cast aside."

The ardor faded, his stare a cross between hurt and disdain. "I don't need family sanction," he fired back. "I'm showing *them* how to get their damn balls back."

He rearranged his clothes and went to the bar. Callie lay breathless, grateful to inhale deeply.

He lifted a bottle of Scotch. The bottle neck clanked on a glass as he poured. "Damn soft traditionalists. I showed them in Boston, and I will show them here. Then minds will be changed." He swung his arm. "An entire family disposed of, except for the old woman." He took a drink. "And I might just conclude with her, in her husband's bed. She's doable."

Callie's head spun at the image of her mother's rape. She pushed upright against the arm of the sofa. The cavalry wasn't coming, and her comments would drive the evening. Or so she hoped. She had to hope. "You've proved your point, Mason. It's about respect."

"Don't insult me, Callie. I'm no fool, and we've got all night to play." He downed the Scotch. "Bad for business, they said." The glass landed heavy on the bar. "Bullshit. It sends a message to kill a cop—to kill his family. It delivers a warning!"

His eyes weren't glazed, but they showed the drink. He ambled back toward her, empowered.

As she leaned back, he dropped to the sofa and chucked her under the chin with a knuckle. "Taking your husband, burning your house, all of it sent you packing, Callista Jean Morgan." His countenance darkened. "But the family didn't agree. They will approve this time, though. With your family gone, I can step into a respectable role with mine."

She desperately glanced at the windows, praying for an observer, a beachcomber. But the view lent itself strictly seaward. "Let me see my son, Mason. I'll do what you want, just let me see Jeb." Callie undid her belt, slipping it through her hand as it snaked to the floor in an enticing promise. "Then do what you will."

Frustrated, he pulled her to her feet. Taking her by the wrist, they walked down the hall to the locked bedroom door between the hall bath and his master suite. Breath held, she restrained herself from plowing past Mason to open the door herself.

Jeb lay on the bed, eyes closed.

"Jeb." Callie rushed to his side. It took everything within her to freeze long enough to watch his chest for movement. *Thank heaven, he's breathing.* She opened his eyelids, felt his forehead. Drugged. She felt his body, doing a cursory check for injury.

"So you've seen him." Mason grabbed her away and tugged her back through the doorway.

As they returned down the hall, she fought to peer over her shoulder to catch another glimpse of her beautiful child, but they rounded the corner.

Back in the living room, Mason steered her toward the sofa, shoulders back, stiff with determination. Seeing Jeb alive had energized her, rejuvenating purpose in her. The manicure scissors now palmed from her belt, her thumb rubbed against the metal. She inhaled, primed.

He turned to face her, impatience in his jerk of her arm. But with a thrust and upward swing, she aimed for Mason's jugular. The scissors ripped skin long and deep before sinking off the mark into his jaw, instead jarring to a stop against bone.

Mason staggered back. The embedded tiny weapon reflected light off its grips.

His fingers stiffened at the touch of the steel in his face. Then he yanked the scissors free and tossed them across the room. "You bitch!" Blood drooled down his neck, wicking into his clothes.

He punched her in the face before she could react.

She crumpled to the floor. Blood streamed from her nose. Fighting to concentrate, she steadied herself against a desk and pulled up.

When his hand came away from his wound filled with blood, he growled. "I've changed my mind. First I kill your brat. Then I finish you." He walked back toward the bedroom.

Callie ran after him and leaped. Her heel connected with his outer thigh above the knee. As she went down, Mason's leg buckled, and the momentum carried him into the wall.

Callie scrambled up and scanned the room for a weapon. The kitchen's bar and all its cutlery was thirty feet away. Too far.

Still, she spun to run in that direction, to draw Mason away from Jeb's room. He tripped her. As she struggled to rise again, he grappled for a higher control of her left leg. She fought reflexes and let him draw her closer, then lashed out with a grunt and kicked his wounded jaw with her right foot. His guttural scream rebounded off the ceiling. She pedaled out of reach, her sandal slick with his blood. She scrambled to her feet and headed again for the kitchen, her only chance for a weapon.

But instead of following, Mason staggered back to the rolltop desk and shoved up the top.

Her gaze met his. She had no doubt what was hidden in that desk, and bullets traveled faster than she could. So she turned and bolted toward him just as he grabbed the weapon. In her tackle, the Glock flew loose.

Callie held tight to his body, using claws and elbows. With a downward drive, Mason's elbow whacked her temple. Stunned, she sank hard on a knee, head spinning.

Mason stood, chest heaving, his once ecru shirt bright red. He scanned for the gun and spied it under the coffee table. "Let's wake up your baby boy," he said, panting between words, his enunciation blunted by the wound. "Your son's earned the joy of seeing his mother splattered across the wall." He moved his mouth, experimenting with the damage done. "I'd wanted it the other way around, but this"—he lightly touched his face—"changes things."

The man's body arched, hit from behind by a blur. As Mason fell to the floor, Jeb collapsed in a heap on the mauve and gold rug behind his captor, who fell face down with a smack. Mason slid and bumped into the coffee table, scattering glasses, bottles, and used cocktail napkins across the parquet floor.

The boy moaned, spent, unable to stand and attack again. "Mom . . ."

Mason rolled over and rose up to his knees. "Good final effort, kid."

Her breaths heaving, Callie recognized that Mason could choose Jeb or her for his next offensive move. And he focused too long on her son.

Mason leaned over to retrieve the gun as she grabbed a half-empty beer bottle on an end table. With a swing fueled by two years of frustration, she rose up and smashed the bottle across his head. Glass busted, the butt end of the bottle propelled against the window, beer remnants spraying. The momentum took her to her knees, still gripping the bottle's neck.

A roar erupted from the man as he cradled his head. Crimson ran from his scalp, the fresher red mixing with the darker on his ripped face. Primal Russian slurs poured from his mouth, spraying pink spit.

Mason spun and dove for her.

Callie braced her arm and thrust upward as the man's momentum drove the keen edges of the jagged bottle into his windpipe.

He whipped an arm around her in a constrictor-like embrace as he fell. His fingers dug into her back while his other hand instinctively clawed at his throat. They rolled in a twisted, slick mixture of bodies and blood, him furious . . . her fighting in a frenzy to escape.

Callie ferociously thrust her weight behind the bottle.

His lock on her turned into a seizure, and she rolled herself off him. She scurried crab-like out of reach, praying for his death.

The gurgles and groans morphed into sucking noises. The Russian's eyes bulged as he desperately groped to reconnect some sort of conduit between his lungs and air.

Callie poised rigid, backed against a chintz armchair, panting as Mason's blood slung and pumped across the floor, up and down the sofa. And she eagerly, hungrily watched him die.

A shadow flitted across the dark back of the house, gravitating in starts and stops to the glass doors. Callie retrieved the Glock and with a shaky hand, raised it, taking aim.

Gun drawn, Seabrook appeared in the doorway, his sights set on her.

Callie let the weapon drop beside her foot. Then she stumbled around Mason and the sofa to Jeb, propped against the wall. Her son's view of Mason was obstructed by furniture, but still, she inserted herself between him and the horror, like she'd always done. Like she'd continue to do.

Seabrook stepped in, glanced at the dead man for a long moment, then scanned the mess. "Oh, Callie."

Jeb now slumped in her lap, Callie looked up, covered in blood and beer. "You missed a damn fine party, Mike."

Chapter 34

CALLIE TURNED THE final screw to the front right motion sensor and started down her ladder. A police cruiser stopped in her drive, and Seabrook stepped out. "Wait a sec." He hurried over and grabbed the ladder. "You're still installing those sensors, huh?"

"Just humor me."

His tan had only grown darker as the days grew hotter, a natural in the Carolina sun. Every day since the infamous party, he'd checked on her. She loved it. He towered a foot above her, but he didn't make her feel petite. The friendship was reaching a comfortable stage. She dropped the screwdriver in Lawton's toolbox. "Last one, thank goodness."

He folded the ladder. "Why isn't Jeb doing this?"

Callie wiped sweat off her forehead with a sleeve. "Sprite's been smothering him of late. He's enjoying the attention, and for once, I can take him going out." She closed the ground level storage room and locked it. "Come on up to the porch and get out of this heat."

The Fourth of July weekend had tourists in clustered batches on foot, golf carts, and bikes, as well as in the grocery store, gas station, and every restaurant, so leaving the house was a lesson in patience. Callie stayed home as much as possible by eating Jeb's catch of the day or letting him make the grocery run.

She hurried inside and returned with two iced teas to join Seabrook on the settee. She could enjoy simplicity like this.

"Sensors might be overkill if there are no more Russians."

Callie shook her head. "No more Russians. Stan checked. He actually delivered the notice of Mason's . . . um, Georgy's, death. Apparently, Mason had been on the outs with his family for a long time. Seems he was an embarrassment for them." She sipped her tea and stared over the railing to a golf cart of teen girls rolling too fast up Jungle Road.

Seabrook went to the railing and motioned at them. "Slow it down!"

The girls slowed maybe more than they had to, giggling, taking back glances at the police officer.

The traffic interruption was a welcome diversion from talk about Russians. She still sensed eyes on her. She still studied her rearview mirror, though she knew better. But some days she'd forget. "Heard from Raysor lately?" she asked.

"He's at the cranky stage," Seabrook said.

Callie laughed. "And that's different from the norm how?"

"Don will be Don. He'll be out another three weeks, it seems. Then it might be another week or two before they put him back over here, but he'll show up before summer's over."

Good. She had visited the man in the hospital, both of them awkward in the moment. He'd tried to apologize to her without saying it, and she'd done the same. They talked about everything but Mason, but they now shared the scare of almost dying at his hand.

Seabrook brushed sand off her leg. "So, how are *you* doing?"

"I'm all right, Doctor Mike." Her grin was fleeting. "Not sure what to do next. I mean, Jeb's not going to college. Mother's holding her own in Middleton, actually filling in for Daddy's mayoral seat until next year when elections are held, but I can't leave her. At least not now. So I'm living at Edisto Beach for a while."

He finished his tea. "Glad to hear it. Maybe . . ."

A white BMW pulled into Callie's drive.

"Speak of the devil," Callie mumbled as Beverly exited the car.

The rattan creaked as Seabrook pushed up. "Break's over."

Beverly's shades lifted up toward the porch as the cop peered down. "Yoo hoo, is Callie up there? Have Jeb come unload these boxes for me."

"I'll do it," Seabrook said, coming down the stairs. "Afternoon, Mrs. Cantrell. You look good today."

The woman grinned. "Aren't you the charmer, all tall, tanned, and handsome in that uniform. Yes, that would be nice." Her smile disappeared. "Everything's all right, isn't it?"

"Oh, yes, ma'am. Just a social call." He leaned in the car and hoisted a heavy box on his shoulder. "This it?"

"Yes, Mike, is it?" she asked, holding her arm crooked to support her white Gucci shoulder bag matching her bejeweled white sandals, white slacks, and navy tunic. "Just place it inside."

Seabrook clomped up the stairs as Callie met him, brow knotted. "How many boxes are there?"

"Only two," he said low. "At least she's not moving in."

Callie let some of the tension leave her shoulders. "Whew, thank goodness for that." She trotted to the drive. "Mother, how are you? And what's all this?"

"One of my ideas, dear." She waved the air like a fan. "Can we go inside? It's sweltering out here."

"Sure, come on in. I was about to call you, and—"

"Is this a party? I'm coming over," shouted Sophie from her porch. "I have muffins!"

Beverly rolled her eyes as she reached the top step. "That woman. Who invited her?"

Who invited you? Callie thought, but she and Beverly had been on speaking terms since Mason's party. No cat claws in three weeks. They hadn't been civil to each other for that long since she'd lived in Boston and avoided her mother's calls for months . . . as Beverly had avoided hers.

Seabrook set the second box on the dining room table. At his knowing glance, Callie walked him to the door. "Thanks. Sorry for the interruption."

"I'll catch you later," he said. "Thanks for the tea. Hey, Sophie."

Callie's neighbor skipped up the steps, muffins on a plate with a dish towel thrown over them. "Hey yourself, Mr. Hot Stuff."

He scoffed at the back of her as she flitted across the threshold, then he put on his sunglasses and left.

When Callie returned inside, Sophie and Beverly both dallied in her kitchen, lightly arguing over who would fix the drinks and acting like each of them knew better where the glasses were.

The real estate agency had been told by Edisto PD that Pauley died, but Seabrook refused to release the details. Papa's house sat empty now, unthreatened for quite some time to come with no heirs left and probate taking over.

Callie's house had been sanitized of Pauley's visit, nobody knowing about the body other than Jeb, Callie, and Seabrook, because that's how Callie had wanted it. She wished Chelsea Morning to retain as much positive energy as possible, as Sophie would say. Once news got around about Mason's death, and after much prodding and begging from Sophie, Callie let her sage the house. It did make the place feel fresher.

"I already have a glass, so don't fix me anything." Callie turned to Sophie. "Thanks for the muffins." Then she leaned on the sink facing across the bar at her mother. "What's with the boxes?"

"Not in front of the neighbor," Beverly said, as if Sophie wasn't seated right next to her on a barstool.

"Hey," Sophie said. "I was critical to Callie's rescue, you know. Mike called me, and I told him where she was. Good thing, too."

How conveniently Sophie forgot. She'd covered for Callie at Mason's, diverting Seabrook. Now she was the heroine.

"You took her to that party to start with," Beverly said. "I don't hear you bragging about putting her in harm's way."

Callie lifted a warm muffin and broke it in half, a lemony scent rising. "Not the way it happened, Mother."

Instead of taking issue with the attitude, however, Sophie stroked Beverly's arm. "I admire you, Beverly. You supported your husband, in spite of his deeds, for the sake of Middleton. And now you're stepping into his shoes. You're a strong, strong woman."

Beverly glanced at Callie and then returned her interest to the muffin she now crumbled on her plate.

"What deeds?" Callie asked. Lawton had the ethics of Gandhi and the Pope rolled into one. Her father would have tolerated Beverly, not the other way around.

Standing by him how? Politically, tolerating his workaholic tendencies?

Beverly wouldn't take her stare off the poppy seeds separated from the muffin. So Callie started in on Sophie. "Something I don't know about?"

Sophie jumped down off her stool. "Ooh, got to run. Sprite might be home any second."

"She's with Jeb, Sophie."

"Oh." Sophie's fingers tangled, playing with her rings. "I mean, I need to fix dinner for when she gets home. Later." She scampered to the hall and let herself out.

Callie tapped the bar. "Nobody but us now, Mother. Spill it."

"No point, dear."

"Yes, there is. He was my father, and I deserve to know. As a politician, and a very public person, somebody most assuredly knows his secrets. Would you like me to learn whatever this stupid little issue is from a stranger? On Facebook? You know Jeb would find it there."

Her mother seemed frail as she made eye contact with her. "Lawton didn't do Facebook."

Callie laughed. "I figured that, but that won't stop somebody else from slinging dirt about him. What did he do? Hold out on his taxes? Do favors for friends? What does any of that even matter?"

"It's what we both did," she said. "I'd wanted to explain it one day. With that Bohemian woman gone, maybe—"

"Maybe what?"

Callie had told herself in the days after Mason's party that she could weather anything now, though she had her moments, especially at night. Stan still hadn't called, but it was probably too soon to expect that aspect of her life to return to normal.

But between her husband's life insurance, and now her generous inheritance from Lawton, along with partial ownership in his car dealership holdings, Callie could sit unemployed for quite some time to come. She was on her way back up from bottom.

"It's not like Daddy had an affair," Callie said, the words sounding so dirty spoken in the same sentence as her father.

Beverly glanced at her daughter. "I never held it against him."

"What?" Callie juggled a hundred questions in her head. Some she didn't want to ask, like, *What did you do to drive him away? Was she young?* But most of all, *Who was she?*

Her daddy was a striking man, turning many a woman's head. Beverly was inarguably no easy person to live with. Callie knew that better than anyone. But a real affair? And Beverly didn't gouge the woman's eyes? Or hire someone to take her out?

"I don't have to be a detective to see there's more to this than just an affair, Mother." She reached across the bar and touched the older woman's hand, noting the veins in them more than ever before.

Her mother's lanky frame seemed more stooped. "He wasn't the only one who had an affair."

"Say what?" Callie rounded the bar. She had to sit at that revelation. Her parents were adults, she reminded herself. They could do what they wished. So why was her gut doing somersaults? And how the hell did she explain to Jeb that his conservative grandparents had an open marriage?

"I'd been engaged to someone before your father," her mother finally said.

"That's not an affair."

"It is when you keep seeing him later."

Callie sat back. "Oh."

With a wistful gaze at Callie, Beverly seemed desperate for her daughter to understand, then let it dissipate and investigated crumbs on her plate.

A sudden fear flipped Callie's stomach. "Is Daddy still . . . my daddy?"

Beverly stroked her daughter's scarred arm. "Of course he is, honey."

Thank you, God. "So Daddy got even?"

"No, no. Nothing like that. He met someone at The Governor's Cup one year, when you were a teenager. I stayed in Middleton working on the next campaign. He'd asked me to relax for a change, spend time with him without political obligations, but I was too driven. So driven," she repeated in a whisper. "You'd asked to spend the evening with Papa Beach, so Lawton went alone and . . . met someone."

So, while Callie had made peanut butter cookies with Papa, role playing with chicken salt and pepper shakers, her father had *got it on* down the street. Disappointing, but reality often was. However, even with all this enlightenment, her mother seemed to be holding back. "What am I missing here?" Callie asked.

"I saw Jeremy for twenty years. He died of cancer at forty-five. By then, your father was seeing Sarah Rosewood. We allowed each other's sporadic trysts. It kept us alive in a way and made us realize what we loved about each other. I lost my friend early, is all. And it wasn't right for me to ask Lawton to stop seeing his."

Sarah Rosewood! "Damn," was all Callie could say. This was so messed up, but then it wasn't. Not the way Beverly explained it.

And now Callie understood where Lawton had gone the afternoon he came alone to see her, not letting his wife know where he was. And Sarah Rosewood's heartfelt sorrow after Lawton's funeral made more sense now, as did Ben Rosewood's adversarial position when Callie entered their house.

Of course, Sophie would be aware of one affair and not the other. Jeremy was before her time. Callie saw a mother-son meal in the not-so-distant future. She didn't want him hearing a bastardized version of this *love* story from Sophie, or worse, Sprite. It was important to keep Jeb's respect for his grandparents intact. They represented so much more than trysts.

"So what are the boxes?" Callie asked again, trying to lighten the mood.

"I'm returning the albums and the player you sent to me," Beverly said.

"What?" Callie asked.

Beverly slid off her stool and spun Callie's around to face her. "Honey, I loved your father. Loved him dearly. His presence lingers in Middleton still. Once I got those albums home, I realized how disrespectful that was."

Tears welled in her mother's aging eyes.

"You learned to love Neil Diamond with Jeremy," Callie said softly. "Those songs were your memories of him." Much like her own memories, each song placing her in a special moment, with a special person, taking her back to her youth, to her time with John.

Oh, how she knew the feeling that swelled with certain refrains, the strings, the sensitive lyrics that drove loving pain straight into your heart.

Now Beverly wiped away tears on Callie's cheeks. "Middleton is Lawton's memory, hon, and I owe him to preserve it as such. Chelsea Morning is where I escaped to recall my old days with Jeremy." She led Callie to the boxes. "Please, keep these here."

Callie nodded. And she wished Jeb were present to hear Beverly's words. Callie wasn't sure she could explain this situation as eloquently as her mother.

"So, when I need to come listen, just find me a seat, bring me a gin, and pretend I'm not here." She stroked her daughter's face again. "Can you do that for me?"

Callie threw her arms around Beverly and nodded into the woman's padded, perfumed shoulder. Her mother accepted her embrace and stroked her head.

So much made sense now. Yes, this was the least Callie could do for her mother. After all, they weren't that much different once she thought about it.

SEVEN P.M. BEVERLY gone. Jeb not home yet. Callie donned her running shoes but didn't run. Instead, she strolled to the beach, in no hurry, with no mission, but nowhere near Water Spout. This time of day, most tourists had consumed their fill of sand and surf. Aqua, navy, and gold seahorse towels hung at one house, and ones with crabs, dolphins, and sharks draped over the railings of another. Inner tubes and boogie boards thrown on porches, wet T-shirts laid out to dry. The air hung thick with salty humidity, and gulls screamed at each other in competition for findings on the beach. A gentle wind brought the tide in.

There was something settling about being here without a deadline, unlike all these renters who had to return home on Saturday. A family ate outside at Snow Crab, a rental owned by Michigan snowbirds. Children played in their bathing suits, the adults holding glasses most likely alcohol filled. Callie waved. They returned the greeting. Another family would arrive eager on Sunday to replace them, begin their vacation, and briefly forget their jobs and school, car pools, and PTA meetings. They lived a dream for a week, while she could live hers until she chose not to.

She was grateful now. No, she was insanely blessed.

She needed to digest the Lawton and Beverly story. Maybe that's why she'd been an only child. Would she and John have done something as odd, as distanced as they'd become after Bonnie's death?

Yes, these thoughts would take some time.

Detective work still called her name, though. This whole ordeal with Mason and Peters had proven that. And if she lived at this retreat too long, she'd be unable to return to the job once her skills rusted. She hadn't solved that dilemma yet.

She reached Palmetto Boulevard and crossed, dodging traffic more carefully than she had that first day when Jeb disappeared—when she'd introduced herself to Edisto Beach as that crazy woman with a gun. These new renters had no idea who she was, though. Only the residents did, but what could they say about her now? They'd been sucked in by Mason. But she'd cleaned up their precious community, ridding them of the man. Who knew how gossip would shake that out?

On the sand, she shed her shoes and sauntered along the water which ran about two hours from high tide. A half mile down, she smoothed out a half-built sand castle in front of an unhatched loggerhead nest so that the hatchlings wouldn't be blocked from the water if they ventured out tonight. She sat a few feet away. Being on the Eastern Seaboard, a sunset over the water was out of the question, but the horizon was still beautiful as blues changed to greens, with whitecaps and foam accenting each hue.

"Hey," said a male voice. "Saw you walking on Palmetto. Didn't expect to see you out here this time of day."

Seabrook threw a towel on the sand beside her. His uniform gone, the shorts and T-shirt became him. Worn sneakers and no socks suited him, too. As the wind gusted, his blond hair swirled and danced around his eyes.

His visual analysis of her felt more doctor than cop or potential beau. "It's almost sundown," he said. "How're you doing with that?"

Callie threw her head back, inhaled salt air down to her navel, and held it. Letting it loose, she said, "I think I'm good. But thanks for asking. If I freak, you'll know what to do."

Smoothing the corners of his towel, he studied the sand. "I'm still so sorry, Callie. I stayed a step behind you in all this crap." He grimaced mildly, yet Callie still found him charming. "You left that message for me," he said, "yet I didn't put two and two together and arrive until two the next morning to help. What you did . . . what you had to do."

She'd kick herself about John for a long time to come, but Seabrook now had a double dose of these feelings. His dead wife, and now her. "I couldn't have you there, Mike. Not before I found Jeb. You know that. But I get what you're saying. I really do."

They stared out to sea, leaning back on their hands.

"Seems we're back where we started, huh?" he finally said.

"Just don't throw me in the back of your squad car."

He chuckled. "Agreed. But how'd you like to go to dinner with me?"

She smiled. Clouds reflected the sun going down behind them on the other side of the island. Oranges and pinks showed off in a final wash of color as eight pelicans glided by in a synchronized line.

She turned. "Before I decide, why were you hiding in that house across from Papa Beach's place? If you say watching for other burglaries, the answer's no for dinner. That's just so lame, Mike."

"Watching you," he said. "And that wasn't the only day. I had enough sense to know that someone had set his sights on upsetting you." His feet dug into the sand. "I knew you had the talent to catch this guy, but you were off balance, distracted, and vulnerable. And with you holding me at arm's length, it was the only tactic I could think of without parking in front of your house. Just wish I'd spotted Mason and solved this mess earlier."

Suddenly the scent of a close man teased her on the breeze. "I, um, don't know what to say," she said. "Thank you."

He dared to lay his arm across her shoulder.

She let him, and after a moment, leaned into him. "Yes," she said. "I'll go to dinner."

"Will you come work for Edisto PD?" he added.

She sniffed. "No, not ready for any of that yet."

One step at a time.

The pastels eased into blacks and grays. Callie sat quietly, slightly nervous about being outside, and allowed it to wash over her, as if waiting to turn to stone for staring into the eyes of dusk. But she won over the evening.

No counting, no deep breaths, no heartbeats throbbing into her ears. Just a safe, silent ride into the night.

She could do one step at a time for a long time. Hopefully one night she'd see turtles hatch and think of Papa Beach being proud of her. And she could listen to Neil Diamond any time she wanted and simply enjoy singing the words.

One step at a time.

The End

Acknowledgements

This story propelled me in a direction I never wanted, but proved to be a catalyst I needed.

My editor, Pat Van Wie, pushed me into a new series giving me three parameters: a female cop, an intriguing setting in South Carolina, and family drama. With those sparse guidelines, I wrangled with what I first felt an impossible task and then created a story, then a series, that excited me and opened my creativity toward new horizons. Like having another child, I don't have less love for my firstborn Carolina Slade but instead learned I harbored more than enough love for my second born, too. Welcome to the world, Callie Jean Morgan. Thanks, Pat, for pushing me.

Of course this book would mean so much less without its setting, the illustrious paradise of Edisto Beach. What has turned into my home away from home, took on new dimension as Callie began to wander the beach in my mind in search of herself. My love for the area has greatly deepened, its beauty and personality embedded in my soul. What a grand opportunity now to be able to slip away to the beach "for research" several times a year (and write it off my taxes).

Thanks to the Edisto Police Department for their understanding of my sleight of hand in this story in regards to their duties, staff, and performance. Chief Bill Coffey, I owe you lunch and a cup of coffee, and we can laugh over the details.

Deni, you are an inspiration. Thanks for allowing me the literary license to insert snippets of your spirit in these pages. When you moved to Edisto, you changed lives more than your own, my friend, and I hope they appreciate your influence.

I could not write without the keen, critical, stern, and caring eyes of Sid, Barrie, Sharon, Margaret, Mike, and the members of the Writing Well. You understand how much I've grown more than anyone.

Thanks to Gary for our evenings overlooking the lake. Between our sips of bourbon and your lessons on smoking a good cigar, you listened as I read, vented, spun, and scribbled to bring this new idea to fruition. You're my rock, my light, and the most patient man on the planet.

And I still love you, Neil Diamond, and have since I was fourteen years old.

About the Author

C. Hope Clark holds a fascination with the mystery genre and is author of The Carolina Slade Mystery Series as well as the Edisto Beach Series, both set in her home state of South Carolina. In her previous federal life, she performed administrative investigations and married the agent she met on a bribery investigation. She enjoys nothing more than editing her books on the back porch with him, overlooking the lake with bourbons in hand. She can be found either on the banks of Lake Murray or Edisto Beach with one or two dachshunds in her lap. Hope is also editor of the award-winning FundsforWriters.com. Find out more about her at chopeclark.com

Made in the USA
Middletown, DE
04 January 2017